MW00365438

POP
KIDS

Published by
Black Candy Publishing
www.blackcandypublishing.com

4096 Piedmont Ave #722
Oakland, CA 94611

Design
Anthony Smyrski, Smyrski Creative

Printing
The Prolific Group

Library of Congress Catalog Card Number: 2012954417
ISBN: 978-0-9859572-0-9 (paperback)
ISBN: 978-0-9859572-1-6 (hardcover)
ISBN: 978-0-9859572-2-3 (electronic)

Distributed worldwide by
Black Candy Publishing

POP KIDS

BY DAVEY HAVOK

This book is dedicated to Michael and Jonna. Thank you for your endless support and strength. Without you I'd be talking to myself even more.

Prologue

"It's all Screenames now." I have a very difficult time remembering what we used to call each other before this all began, before I became a Filmgreat, but here in this silent, warming glow, I have time and cause to reflect.

I somehow manage to fondly recall that Stella was Sarah. I just turned down a birthday surprise from her that most guys in my class would trade their entire wardrobes for. During junior year, as she was being dropped off after lunch by college-aged guys in luxury cars, I would watch her with hopeless longing. Now I have given her so much more than they ever could. And she deserves it. *She deserves me.* She's hot, ambitious, knows a good thing when she sees it, and will stop at nothing to get it.

As I think of Holly, knowing who she was, and what was supposed to happen when I opened The Pink Door, I can't remember her old name. It's fine. I shouldn't bother. Thinking about her right now just heightens the screaming in my head.

"I Kissed a girl and..."

"Fuck you Katy," I whisper then cough. The smoke is soothing. But there's more of it than I'm used to.

Stepping back into the alley past the dumpsters, I pinch a weightless piece of ash from the crackling night, and safely admire my work, clicking. My fingers are slick. My hands smell like butane. *I should really get out of here.* I inspect the inscription on my Zippo—one of my many gifts from Bickle, my generous guardian whose bumblebee sweater is now speckled with awful little hard-to-get out bloodstains. It's a shame about that sweater—Shane's sweater. *Weird. His name is Shane. I used to call him that.* Even now, hundreds of scenes later, I can remember naming my protective friend. He so badly wanted a Screename. Leo, Star, and Donny on the other hand, they've all kept their old names. *That's weird too.* They've all remained the same this whole time. I didn't.

I changed. I flourished and became the leading man in all of this, the shockingly well-dressed teenaged emcee of our grand private affairs in this tired town, the glorious director of it all. I became Scorsese."...Score. It's Score for short."

Pausing before I flee, I kneel back down. When I re-introduce myself to the timid grey Manx, whose curiosity has finally drawn him close enough to be scratched behind the ear, he cringes, reminding me that I too disliked the name. Feeling that "Score" sounded too much like the name of someone who should be selling speed in Nevada, I briefly fought against it, but our Screenames stick when they're right for us. Score was the right one for me. I've come to respond to nothing else.

"My name is Score," I confidently proclaim. "And today is my birthday."Though my birthday technically ended a few hours ago, I accept that this cleaning is the true celebration. I am sad that after what happened tonight, the Filmgreats will never again congregate in the same way, but the fire comforts me. As the mess that has been slowly building up around us beautifully burns high into this dark October morning, the warm sound of the flames melts the rich, icy, screaming croon of Old Blue Eyes.

"It's fine."

Looking at me like there's something terribly wrong, the Manx meows, then darts back into the alley.

"Everything's fine."

SUM

MER

The air conditioning in Zach's bedroom is broken. It smells like PE in here. And I'm sweating—which I hate. It's August, and our NorCal valley has been enjoying a modern, shredded-ozone-summer that is commanding both my perspiration and the controversy that's growing in the kitchen. This whole town revolves around grapes, and Zach's parents own most of them. As he and I lay on the thinly carpeted floor between two electric fans, his folks are discussing how this heat wave is going to affect the upcoming harvest. Sue wants Willy to come with her on her next Parisian shopping trip. Willy is insisting that he needs to stay nearby to deal with the late summer crop. It's all very riveting.

Staring at the poster of Joey Ramone tacked above Zach's head, I can hear his Mom's voice ooze between the distorted fuzz of "Personality Crisis." Even with Sue's argument flowing in the background, the grit in the singer's voice sounds perfect coming through the high-end speakers. The Prozens are one of a few rich families in this town, and Zach and his little brother all the better for it: they can basically have whatever they want (though they rarely ask for much beyond phones, computers, video games, surfboards, skateboards, and the occasional car). I'm stuck with middle-class parents, but I at least get to enjoy the benefits of the farmer's wealth by proxy.

Still lying on my back, I text. Sue, compromising, suggests that her husband skip his next camping trip to come to San Francisco with her for the weekend. Willy concedes before bringing up the town's most recent church fire—it's the second of the summer and most people seem to be in quite the tiff over it. With more curiosity than concern, he explains, "They don't know if it was arson or just some freak incident with candles and dried flowers."

"I read that it was flowers," she says, and then returns to matters of shopping. Her voice reminds me of my counselor's whale song CD's

"God damn it." Using his remote, Zach replays the trashy anthem, as his mom begins speaking French. "If only it were the seventies. We missed all the good shows."

"I know man, or the nineties."

"Or the eighties."

"Yeah. And what if we were in England? Think of what we could have seen then," I say. "But you know what city they say is like London, right? San Francisco!" Reading the text that just came in from Sarah, I sit up to beg for relief from the boredom, "Wanna roll out the ol' CC in neutral and drive us to a party tonight?"

"I can't." He stands to unplug his laptop. "Dad re-hid the keys."

Propped against the flyer-covered wall, stretched beside his unmade bed, he taps on his keyboard, sweating. Despite the heat, Zach has been wearing long sleeves to avoid furthering his Cadillac's confinement. During the last week of junior year he got caught sneaking out with Jamie, Drew, and Michelle to see what The Twins' parents deemed to be a "satanic rock band," based on their demonic name, "Vampire Weekend." Zach didn't care about the show, but Jamie wanted to go. He took the opportunity both to put in some work with her and get a tattoo. Using his flawless fake ID, he had a big bearded guy at Blackheart SF drill 'LAMF' into his skin. The following afternoon, his father suffered a displeased call from The Twins' dad and took Zach's car away. Zach and I agree that his punishment comes more from Willy having been forced to listen to the zealous ranting of Mr. Todd than from Zach having cut school to drive the unregistered Caddy. Still, he now wears his GI Jacket at all times to conceal the fresh wound. Willy thinks tattoos are "seedy," and Zach doesn't want to risk having to walk to school this year.

"This is awful. When are you supposed to get it back again?" I tap my touch-screen, frustrated over having lost my favorite driver.

I've yet to get my license, as I prefer to be chauffeured.

"Not until school starts ... man, I've looked for those fucking keys everywhere. He must have taken them to work."

I suggest a hot wire.

Considering the possibility, Zach stops clicking the keyboard. "What's going on, again?"

"Dub Step party at Minna Gallery. Those DJs that the girls know can get us in."

He rolls his eyes.

I should have told him it was a proto-punk night.

Normally, Zach would take any opportunity to get out of town. We all would. Even with the city being hours away and a gallon of gas being the price of a McQueen tie, we'll do whatever it takes to escape, because nothing ever happens in our tiny little town. Ever. Temporary absences, provided by shows and parties in the city, give us the will to not hang ourselves on grape vines. It's never enough though.

Strategically, I use his longstanding crush as bait. "But I think Jamie has the jeep, so if you don't want to go I can probably squeeze in the back..."

I stare at him. Even the prospect of hanging with Jamie hasn't persuaded Zach to break into his own car. He isn't going to drive us and, what's worse, he doesn't want me to leave him. My iPhone buzzes with another text from Sarah. Zach steps over me and grabs a drink from the mini fridge.

"Dude, Dustin found a way into that old hotel. It sounds like it might be the perfect place to do the party. We should go check it out." Looking down, he grins, knowing how badly I've wanted to find a room for my Premieres.

"Okay," I say. "But first, I'm going over to Barbara Johnson's." I snatch the bottle of San Pellegrino from his hand as his fridge purges its precious mist. "She's out being a hippie again, and I've just been asked to come entertain her daughter."

"I still can't believe that's happening for you man. It's really cool."

I grab my splintering REAL deck from the wall by his back door. Dustin gave me the board pre-thrashed. "Well, I've had to wait in line, but it's been well worth the wait."

Sweating from the skate across town, I stand on Sarah's porch. I could just walk right in. But I won't. I can't forget my manners. I bandana my brow, and gently knock.

"Commmme innnn!"

I ease into the cool shadows of the living room.

Leaning my skate against wall I close the door, blocking out the natural light that the heavy eastern blinds couldn't intercept. As I linger in the glow of the giant flat-screen, the TV blares the news that matters, and Sarah types. Sitting on her mom's oversized burgundy faux-suede couch, in her hot-pink boy briefs and sheer, white, loose-fitting tank top, she looks like an American Apparel ad. Usually, she doesn't go bra-less, but here in the heat and the privacy of her living room her fantastic go-getters are getting time to breath. I glance between areola outlines and the small mirror in the entryway. And the TV yammers. And Sarah types.

With her pink Hello Kitty Mac illuminating her downcast baby blues my freshman-year fantasy listlessly dangles her foot, full of cotton balls, in front of a whirring fan. The tangy scent of pink lacquer comforts me—as does her ability to match her toenails to her underwear.

Tapping her keyboard, and without looking up, she greets me, "Hey Mike!"

Clicking my Zippo from within my jeans, I turn to the screen. The guy on E! is making fun of the daughter of an old Hollywood great for having driven her Bentley across a private Malibu beach and into the Pacific. When the cops pull her out of the car she's wasted. And in her underwear.

"What'cha watching?" I ask.

"Did you see this?" Sarah flicks her wrist toward the TV, as if it were a sparkling vampire mosquito. "That poor thing. I don't see why he needs to be so vicious about it!" Her glistening nails return to tap at the keys.

"Please. Look at her. She totally deserves it."

"NO, she doesn't." Looking up, sounding personally offended, Sarah defends the socialite's character. "And she looked totally hot even when they pulled her from the wreck all soaking wet. See!"

The shot of the post-crash blonde being escorted from the car flashes back onto the screen. She does look good—sort of like a Calvin Klein billboard.

"You're right," I concede. "Her father must be beaming."

Silently, Sarah finalizes what seems like a page of typing before snapping shut the Mac.

"Why don't you bring that cute, sweaty, self-satisfied ass over here?"

She called my ass sweaty. I desperately want to freshen up, but can't bring myself to ask to use the bathroom. Hoping to pat myself down with a dishrag within the privacy of the kitchen, I say, "It's pretty hot. Should I grab some fruit pops?"

"Just get over here, Mike." Her magnetic sex electrifies the room.

Obediently, I plop down next to her. I blot my brow with toe-cotton. The E! host's face is eclipsed by two delectable, all-natural treats. From beneath her sheer tank top they challenge me, face-to-face, as Sarah straddles me.

She looks down. Her dark wavy hair hides us from the media and within the safety of our solitude, I watch my hands slide up her soft, lotiony thighs. My fingertips touch the elastic perimeter of boy briefs. I look back up. Sarah shifts her hips, purposefully grazing my lips with her right nipple, and something deep within the darkness of my black denim stirs.

"Oh, dear Michael, what's that?" She unbuttons my Ksubis.

Since we haven't even kissed, I might have been a bit embarrassed by my immediate readiness. If she wasn't so pleased by what springs from my jeans.

In a matter of seconds, she pulls my pants down to the ground, her panties to the side, and my eager Producer up inside her.

She's a good girl.

Her palms push down on my chest, and her blossoming perspiration increases the marvelous transparency of her top.

Sarah is such a good girl.

Lounging alone in nothing but the slowly drying traces of our fluid scene, I'm watching TMZ. The captivating piece on LiLo ends. A commercial for depression meds comes on. I clean off a bit of leftover joy with some cotton balls, slip on my black jeans, black summer shirt, and black Chucks, then head into the kitchen to get the pink lemonade fruit pop I've been craving for the past forty minutes. Discarding the plastic wrapper in the recycling bin, I slink down the hallway to enter Hello Kitty's lair.

With my icy treat in hand, I walk over pink carpet, and past piles of Tarina Tarantino jewelry scattered across the pink dressers. In the pink mirror, next to the Ameripop Girl posters tacked to the pink wall above the pink bed, I pause to inspect myself before breaching the cleansing happening in Sarah's bathroom—also pink.

"OH MY! What ARE you doing in here?" she demands with the drama of a Silver Age starlet. I peek my head into the shower.

"I thought I could help."

"Sure you can sexy!" Immediately physically excited, I'm about to take off my pants when she says, "Hand me that razor on the sink."

Moz, she is so hot and so comfortable with me basking in her steamy nakedness that it's almost making me uncomfortable. Pecking off a piece of my pop, I hand her the fortunate pink and white blade.

She sets it on the plaster shell-shaped soap dish jutting from the pink tiles next to my shoulder, tilts her head back, and rinses her long dark hair. Hoping that she'll ask me to shave her, I discreetly push aside the plastic kitty curtain to get a better view of her arched back, long neck, and wet boobs. She pushes the water from her face, opens her ice blue eyes, reclaims the razor that has mysteriously ended up back in my hand, and stares. I feel like I'm in a Girls Gone Wild commercial, that the possibilities are endless, until in a gentle "Why are you still here?" sort of way, she asks, "So, what's up?"

Shaken, I remember that I did actually come in here to tell her something. "I'm not gonna go with you girls tonight. Zach's being weird and won't steal his car, so I'm just gonna stay and hang with him. You know, he gets lonely without me."

"So do I." She pouts. "It's not going to be the same without you, sexy."

This sentiment is momentary. She will sincerely miss me, up until about the time that she's finished drying her hair. I know this. *It's fine.* I'm not complaining. At least I was her first for today. *Probably.*

Plus, I've got a hotel to sneak into and a dream party to realize.

"Yeah I know," I say, lingering in the steam. "But I promised him that I'd stay. I'll probably still be around when you get home though."

"I'll write you when I'm on my way back." She motions for my fruit pop. It almost perfectly matches the tiles.

As she sucks the pink ice beneath the steamy cascade, her inaudible hum rises. This hum is a primal, witchy sort of sex power. Sarah can turn it up and down but never off. Right now, she has it cranked up high. It feels like a private jet has landed in front of me.

"Since you're not coming maybe I'll ask Becca to come." I say a little prayer to Morrissey that she keeps her promise to text. She slides the gooey stick from her mouth. "You still have to meet her Mike. She's SO adorable."

"Yeah, totally." Enjoying the view, I hang with the shower curtain.

Sarah slides the pop back in her mouth for a final ostentatious suck before becoming bored with the treat and dropping it. It dissolves in a pinkening stream on the shower floor, as she lathers her summer-tanned legs.

"Mike, get out of here. I've gotta shave."

One of the few good things about having to live here is that most everything is close to everything else. I can get anywhere by board. Unfortunately, the foothill that leads to my house is too steep to skate.

After cruising to the bottom of my street, I pop up my deck and start tromping uphill. This is my favorite time to walk home, not simply because sundown minimizes the tanning threat, but because the cats are out. I most enjoy running into Iman—a beautiful green-eyed Burmese who lives with our downhill neighbors. Her owners call her "Blackie," but this bland moniker embarrasses her, so I've renamed her. When she weaves around her wooden mailbox post I stop to say hello then, snapping twigs beneath my feet, finish my off-road climb.

From the bottom of our driveway, I can see Gina through the dusk's reflection of our empty street, stirring her pot of marinara. Her spacious kitchen is one of the "many benefits" of having moved out of Brooklyn, though this vast Californian cooking arena does nothing to assuage my feelings of displacement. I was only thirteen, yet well accustomed to the many perks of city living, when Uncle Cosmo offered my dad the opportunity to help run one of his boutique wineries.

Frank was always talking about how fun it would be to farm, to suffer "dirty nails and sunburn instead of pigeons and paper cuts," and how nice it would be "to get the kids out of the city." Gina, too, frequently voiced other such unimaginable rural-sympathizing fantasies. So when the offer came for farm livin', we packed away all modern comforts and over came the Massis. The move was complete culture shock for my brother and me.

Throughout the entire first month of living here Joey would inexplicably burst into tears, sometimes cryptically uttering nonsense like "1 Oak," "avenue," "IF," "butter," and, "Barneys" in between sobs. Eventually, the fits did stop. And not long after, he ended his misery entirely. I miss him terribly, but I've managed to cope. I've got a few great friends, one desktop, two laptops, and a high-speed wireless connection that helps me get through.

When I walk into our house the smell of Gina's cooking hits me and I thank Moz for giving me a mother who cooks so well in a town deprived of delivery.

"Mmmmm Mm!" I reflexively hum, inhaling oregano on my way from my bedroom to the shower. Leaving her simmering pot, Gina follows me.

"Are you staying for dinner tonight?" she asks, standing outside of the bathroom.

Folding my damp shirt, I twist on the hot water and call through the closed door. "You didn't put the meatballs in the sauce did you Mom?"

"I did that once Michael! Once! You've only been a vegetarian for a month. It's not gonna kill you to be in the same room with a meatball."

I've actually been vegetarian for a year. Practically. And in a sausage and peppers family like the Massis, I cannot be too careful. Being Italian involves facing many monstrous traditions—from carnivorous holiday meals to the even bloodier Sunday morning mass.

I was raised Catholic. My parents were raised Catholic. However, years of education and a coup within our old Catholic church encouraged my folks to stray from the path of the religiously insane. Back when I was a tempting young lad forced into altar servitude, the mother superior of our parish discovered that Father O'Holland was touching little boys during his time off from embezzling thousands of dollars. When the mother superior brought this to the attention of the bishop, he told her that he'd take care of the offender. This he did by allowing the molester-priest to carry on with his private boy-love party in return for giving the bishop all of the stolen donations and occasional Oral Joy. In the end, this meant that I didn't have to go to church anymore. If there is a god, he clearly sucks. Yet for some reason, I still have to say grace.

Like a prayer, Gina recites some archaic *First Testament* wisdom regarding the animals' servile place on earth. I explain that were I to consume even meat juices I'd surely throw up.

"Oh, and could you not put the parm in the sauce tonight?" I step into the inch of searing water rippling at the bottom of the tub. "I'm trying to eat vegan."

"Just this morning you were asking me where you could order cannoli online!"

"I'm getting in the shower now."

"We're Italian." Walking away, she shouts, "We eat cheese!"

Squirting a large shimmery orange glob of soap onto my black loofah, I start soaping away the smell of sex. To my dismay, I'm only able to swap the cotton candy scented memories of Sarah with the fresh fragrance of creamsicle body wash for mere minutes before Gina pokes her head through door. A dagger of cold air cuts through the plastic curtain.

"Dinner is almost ready. You've been in there for almost an hour!"

"I'll be out in ten!"

"I found your lighter in your jeans while I was doing the wash again," she scolds, "I don't see why you carry that thing around all the time!"

Fearing that she might smell Sarah going down the drain, I promise, for the million and one-th time, "I don't smoke Mom."

"You'd better not."

"I abhor it."

"Are you staying out again tonight?"

"Yeah," I say, happy to be off the tired topic. "XBOX party."

"Once school starts, less video games. I'm sure Zach's parents are plenty happy living with their own two sons. They don't need you moving in." Shutting the door, she finally allows me to deep condition in peace.

In my room, with 'Portishead' typed into Last FM, I'm buttoning up a crisp, black Top Man dress shirt. Eddie, my Havana Brown, jumps atop my desk to inspect the moth that's flown in from Frank's herb garden. Drawn to my Tube Top floor lamp, it softly thuds against my window. Eddie's fascinated with moths. I like them too. I have a few.

"Hey girl, how's this look? Should I go more casual?"

Zach's face startles Eddie, as it buzzes my phone to life. I grab it from the charger.

"Dude. Where are you?" he asks.

I read the name of the song on the radio. Eddie returns to batting the glass.

"I'm home." I begin pacing to my brothers room. "I'm gonna eat then come down."

"Awesome! Bring leftovers," he demands. "How were the activities?"

"Fabulous, but we'll discuss later." I lower my voice, inhaling Gina's sauce as the lights of the Audi Q7 sweep the front hallway. "Mom's got spaghetti on the table."

The front door clicks. There are footsteps. Frank greets my cat. "Hey, Chocolate Chip!"

"I've gotta go man, Dad's home and insulting Eddie, I'll see you soon."

Hanging up, I swipe a Massive Attack CD from Joey's collection, toss it into my room, and arrive at the table just as I'm called for the third time.

....

"Hey, Dad." Nervously, I *ting* my butter knife against my empty glass. I'm slightly paranoid that my folks might sense my glowing post-coital state, though I've become quite good at allowing them to see only what I want them to. Trying to mask my feelings, I sit with Frank, feeling that my overwhelming despair must be obvious.

"Hey Mike." He tips his business hat. "What's happening?"

"Nothing. Just starving." *Ting. Ting ting.*

Gina fills a serving dish with pounds of pasta. *Ting ting.* Frank can tell that I'm squirming. *He knows what's consuming me. It's madness.*

Knowingly, he smiles. "Is there something wrong Mike?"

I can take it no longer.

"Dad..." I point with my utensil. "You know that it's not only rude to eat at the table with a hat on, but that it's even ruder to embarrass your entire family by wearing *that* hat under any circumstances."

Gina places the beautiful steaming bowl next to the basket of warm bread and sits down at the table.

Frank, having gotten the confession that he wanted, jovially offers me his straw hat. "Well Mike, someone's gotta wear the crown. It's either you or me son."

Politely declining the kingdom, I bat the woven atrocity away from my freshly styled hair. Returning the ugly accessory to its unnatural position, he takes my hand, then Gina's, and we all bow our heads to thank Moz for our food.

By the time I've reached the flats and begun weaving between the yellow dashes that divide Vine Street, it's just past ten o'clock. The tiny bit of town traffic has dwindled to nothing. With leftovers slung over my back in last year's pink brown and cream plaid Jansport, I skate unseen, cutting in and out of the white halos cast by the streetlights. My board starts to rumble when half a block ahead I see a white light. It's floating above the sidewalk. Alone, waiting for me in front of the empty WAMU building, sitting on the chipped curb, Zach is texting. His home-bleached hair can't decide which direction to dive. It's like a depressed sea anemone.

"Hey man, can you order some conditioner on the Amex? I'm running out and I think it would do us both some good." Rolling up to the curb, I drop my bag and extract the soggy chewed up fruit pop stick from his teeth. I toss the wood into the nearby trashcan. A ping resounds in the emptiness.

"Dude. You've got to be kidding me." Dejected, he looks up from Words With Friends. "A tie?"

"What?" I ask, before realizing he's probably just worried for the safety of my outfit.

I can't blame him. The possibility of getting it dirty during our exploration crossed my mind, but when I decided to look sharp I resolved to be extremely careful.

"Oh. Never mind." Chuckling with a strange look of realization, he points. "I thought you might be freaking over fucking up your clothes in there, but I recognize *that* now."

"You recognize McQueen?" I'm shocked that my friend is versed in high British design. He always makes fun of me for dedicating an hour a night to Perez's fashion blog. I loosen my knot.

"What? I'm talking about that tie. It's part of the costume from that play you were in right? Is that skull painted on with Wite-Out?"

Standing over him, I smooth my silky accessory. It *is* Wite-Out, but it's not a costume. "*Crimes of the Heart*," I remind him. "How good was I in that?"

My portrayal of Barnette Lloyd got a great review in the Valley View High newspaper. The writer said my southern accent was "completely believable"—an accolade that will pale compared to the press I'm going to get after I star in this year's musical. Sitting down on the curb, picturing what I'll wear in the photo shoot for the school paper's local celebrity piece, I unzip my backpack and pull out the leftovers.

"I still think that you're a little over dressed man." Like a wild ravenous herbivore starved for tomato sauce, Zach snatches the warm Ziploc bag from my hands.

I recognize we're not spending a night out dancing at an SF art Gallery with the girls but The Palace was once a nice hotel. Handing him a plastic fork, I explain, "My attire is donned out of respect to its history." Then with an only slightly exaggerated tinge of offense, I tighten my half-Windsor. "And this was Joey's tie."

Zach gives a carb-muffled apology and, in a spatter of marinara, indiscernibly compliments my beloved older brother—who has left me here to brave this town alone. *It's fine.* He's in a better place now. Joseph fled Valley View with a 5.0 GPA, although he was a well-rounded individual as dedicated to his training as he was to school. If he wasn't on a crying jag, studying, online shopping, social networking, or teaching me the ways of the civilized world, he was training. He was my inspiration, my mentor, and my closest friend until, just before his graduation, he left me. He left us all … and ran away to join the circus.

Swallowing, Zach grins and asks, "When do we get to go visit him again?"

Last summer we spent a whole week in Vegas with Joey.

"Welcome to the Jungle" is playing as we take the elevator down from our comped suite to stand on the perimeter of the gaming tables where we meet our driver. He shows us to our Escalade. We drink chilled Pellegrino, while explaining that we don't go to College, as he drives us far off the glowing Strip.

When we pull behind the club, Guy is waiting to sneak us through the back door. He tells us he could get in a lot of trouble for letting in two sixteen-year-olds, but he loves Joey.

Everyone does.

Sitting in the VIP with our hearts pounding up against interchanging pairs of perfectly wrapped cinnamon-scented silicone bags Zach and I learn truths: most of these girls aren't strippers at all; they're hairdressers. And watching your friend disappear under two naked beauticians can be profoundly spiritual.

"I'm sure the hairdressers miss us. Maybe we should go back again next summer ... right after graduation. Before Hollywood is constantly demanding my presence."

"Man, that would be awesome. I so can't wait to get out of here."

Neither can I. We have just over two weeks of summer left and though I'm dreading it, knowing that it will be the beginning of my last days in this town makes me look forward to getting senior year started and over with. I will be applying for escape by way of colleges in LA, OC, Santa Barbara, and *maybe* San Francisco. I'm not that interested in Northern California schools. Cities up here don't offer as many possibilities for a glamorous lifestyle but in the end, it doesn't matter where I am, as long as I'm somewhere else and doing something fabulous.

"One more year man," I declare, eyeing the soon-to-be sauce stains on Zach's olive coat. "Then we're gone."

The Palace was abandoned in the forties and has been awaiting our inhabitance ever since. Tonight, the towering hotel of both former and future excellence is playing coy. Walking toward it, I can see that it's not going let us penetrate its internal wonders without some coercion. I ask Zach how he plans on getting us through the thick layers of protective planks bolted across the front door.

"Don't worry man. We're not going in that way."

He leads us around the side of the building. Across from "Crystal Eyes"—the marginalized incense and tarot reading room—we march to the sidewalk alongside the looming hotel. Inspecting the seemingly impervious structure, I start to fear Zach's plan of entry. There are no windows. No doors. Just ivy covered walls. Clicking my Zippo, I look up toward the second story at the dark outline of a fire escape that looks to be about 10,000 feet above us and begin to question my decision to stay in town. *Click, click.* In a situation like this, the simple cold feel and sharp sound of my lighter can comfort me. *Click, click.* There doesn't necessarily need to be more—a smoking hot girl with an unlit cigarette, a need for a flame. Not always. *Click, click.*

"Check it out." Brushing away dead leaves, Zach reveals a monument hidden in an alcove on the ground.

I read the engraved inscription in awe. "To the ladies of the night that plied their trade upon this site?"

"Yeah. When the hotel opened, this was the spot where all the hookers would hang. I guess they'd turn tricks in the hotel."

"Wow, I already love this place."

A monster truck cop car wrapped in Walmart logos rumbles by on the distant cross street, spewing exhaust into the night.

Though slightly apprehensive, I'm committed to getting into The Palace. I was starting to have misgivings about the breaking and entering, the possibility of ghosts, spiders, and rats, and the risk of ruining my shirt. But this little concrete tribute makes me feel like we're about to enter a sacred place, like we're being watched over by hooker angels. I look back up toward the shadowy vines reaching off the walls and clinging to the skeletal ironworks.

"You don't think I'm going up there do you? I mean, maybe you've confused me with my brother? I'm not that circusy ... maybe if you go up first—"

"Mike," Zach insists in a voice inappropriately loud for illegal moments such as these, "...Settle."

Grabbing two waxy handfuls of foliage, he pulls toward us. An old plank of plywood separates us from the wall to create a gaping ivy-laced mouth. The secret entry to our glorious future moans. A gush of air chills my face. It smells like a trunk filled with vintage Smiths tees. I look into the void. I'm totally impressed.

"I can't believe you didn't say abracadabra before you did that."

Dropping the crushed leaves, Zach reaches into his jacket and hands me a Mini-Mag. I hand it back. He shows me how to turn it on then re-opens the dirty green mouth.

Like a snazzy uncertain suicide on a ledge, I inch my way into the new shadows.

"You're gonna have to hold it a little wider man. I don't want to get leaf stains."

We're in. The mouth door womps shut behind us. It's dark—and it's creepy. I breathe in the cool, antique air. I can taste the ghosts. Creating our own silent rave, Zach and I dance our frantic lights across the walls to inspect the room and make sure that no specters have materialized to welcome us. I see none. The lounge in which the valley's finest travelers once relaxed, read, and retained the service of prostitutes is now empty. There are no socialites. No solicitors. No ghosts. Just barren hardwood floors and cracked plaster walls adjoining in a low archway that leads to the rest of rooms on the ground floor. Just wiring from a chandelier, long ago removed, spidering out of a hole in the ceiling. Just dust. Just us.

"This is totally killer!" Zach shines his light in my face.

"Yeah, and totally creepy." I double check for poltergeists. "I hope it's not haunted."

Zach grins and bolts. As I chase after him, the likely prescient Dead Boys logo that's scrawled in Sharpie across the back of his jacket does nothing to comfort me.

"Nooooo," I cry. "No running! It's too dark! These stairs don't have any railings, man!"

With Zach cackling like The Blair Witch and my heart beating in my head, I'm certain that we're going to die. He disappears over the last stair then somewhere down the musty hallway his footfalls abruptly halt. When I catch up to him, we stand together, panting in the door-less, chipped frame. I unbutton my stifling top button.

The glow of the streetlights assists our Mini-Mags in their illumination of Room 217—four walls, a bathroom, and a walk-in closet. Its ubiquitous peeling floral wallpaper is covered with battle cries, band logos, and bad art. In hot pink, 'Comfortably Numb!' has been sprayed large enough to unify two walls with its proclamation of detachment. The barren wooden floor is littered with beer bottles, lighters, empty Doritos bags, Zig-Zag boxes, and Coke cans cum-ash-trays. Although it's empty, it's claustrophobic. And it smells like a head shop.

"This must be it. This is where those surfers used to hang out." Zach illuminates the ratty sleeping bag stuffed in a corner. "They must have slept in here."

I'm amazed. Even if it weren't totally disgusting, I'd never sleep in this room. It's too creepy.

"What's their deal again?" Smelling stale weed, I wonder about the type of people who would purposefully crash anywhere that neither provides running water nor room service.

"I guess some of them lived here years ago but they're all on the coast now." Zach stomps a can. "Dustin met them surfing. When he told them that he goes to Valley View, they told them about this place. I think he wants to touch the one named Star. She's the one with the house. She's, like, a woman. They're all in their twenties..."

I can relate. I lost my virginity to an older woman. When I was twelve, Lizzy, my twenty-year-old babysitter moved from Essex to attend NYU and prove to me that boys aren't always stronger than girls. In our wrestling match she pinned me down, kissed me, unbuttoned her blouse, and did it to me on my parent's Eames corner couch to the sounds of the Smiths. It was a beautifully surreal experience that has forever changed me. Since that night, I've only listened to UK bands.

"Fabulous," I say, challenging Zach with a beam of light. "But are there supposed to be bigger rooms somewhere? I don't think these empty cupboards are sufficient for our party needs my friend."

"I know. I just wanted to find their old room." His hair turns blue in my Mini-Mag's light as he squints, remembering why it is we've been tempting ghosts, risking life, limb, arrest and outfits. "It's downstairs. Follow me."

Illuminating our steps, we descend through the aged parlor and down to the basement. Zach steps out of the deep stairwell. He grasps the ornate Deco handles of the doubles doors in front of us. They gasp as they part, and our blue Mags shine into a vast empty space. To the right, at the far end of the expansive floor, a semicircle of six shallow gilded steps gradually climb to meet a stage framed with heavy crimson velvet curtains. In a world before Top Chef this must have been some sort of high-class supper club. We cross the ballroom, past the tiers where servers once doted on fancy diners, slightly bouncing from the creaking coils beneath the giving boards.

Onstage, I shine my flashlight toward the treacherous catwalks. My lighter's bright chirp sings to me from the rafters. *Click, click. Click, click.* A dangling sandbag begins to descend. A pulley squeaks. I watch the curtains unfold. They meet, sway, and then part. And I turn to run upstage, into the open arms of the beautiful white wall. It's huge. I glide my palm across its cool, smooth, bare surface. I caress it. Then clap the invasive dust from my hands. Aside from needing a cleaning, this is perfect. This is all perfect.

"Zach!" Speed-pacing downstage, I point back at the wonderful canvas, as he releases his tattered rope. "This is it! We could totally do The Premiere's down here. We could use that wall for the screen."

I have my brother to thank for this idea. Before Joey ran away to join Cirque, he flew to LA. Down there, he worked for a party promoter. Before meeting him, I'd never known that throwing parties could be a profession. When I'd visit, Joey would take me to all sorts of fabulous events. One was a party at the Hollywood Forever Cemetery, wherein hundreds of highly fashionable, very attractive kids come and lay blankets on the grass to watch films with the dead stars. There I saw *The Hunger* projected onto a glowing mausoleum while surrounded by hot girls who looked like hairdressers, well-dressed guys who looked like hairdressers, and Jayne Mansfield resting but a few feet behind me. Though everyone was smoking and had bottles of red wine, I forgave these horrid imperfections in light of the greater good time. One girl, who drank straight from a mini bottle of champagne, had a white kitten with her. She let me hold Mochi through the Peter Murphy scene. I don't remember the girl's name, but I still miss them both.

"Mike." Zach, pacing up through the unsettled dust, shines his blue light against the wall. "The kid was right. This place will totally rule. It's fucking dark down here, but I suppose that's ideal. ... I'll run some lights. We'll need a generator. You can get the old midnight-movie projector right?"

"I can get it." I pet our wall screen.

"We're doing this! Seriously." He palms a dirty Mento into his mouth. "Let's go back to my place and discuss over some San P."

"Fabulous!" Dusting my hands on his jacket, dizzied by the prospect of finally taking my first step toward party salvation, I say, "Dibs on Dustin's shower."

I can't sleep. I've been trying for hours. Typically, only school forces me out of bed before the rest of the world has had lunch. Today, I whimper and slide out of Dustin's slippery purple sheets as the sun starts to rise. The kid is still on the coast and Zach's fast asleep in his own room. He can pass out with a full mind, but whenever I have a moment of genius that needs realization it likes to lie within me until I convince it to put out. And since I've yet to fully seduce our blushing party scheme, I'm already dressed, mobile, and risking a tan at this godly hour. My outfit needs an iron, my shades need some Windex, and I need tea.

With Primal Scream guiding me on my iPod, I shuffle the few blinding blocks from the Prozens' to our one and only coffee-nerd cafe, Higher Grounds. Its witty play-on-words name depresses me. Tripping up a small flight of concrete steps, I catch myself on the iron fence that wraps around the patio and then float through the glass door. Two of the four walls of this place are ceiling to floor windows. The checkered tiles glare at me as I cross them. When I raise my squint, I'm sure that I've drifted into another town. I gasp in mocha air.

Standing over me, a platinum blonde green-eyed it-girl is glowing in the blinding sunbeams and asking to take my order. She's wearing a remixed *Strangeways* tee. She looks like she escaped from a Paper magazine editorial. Glancing up, I wonder if she's wearing heels before realizing that I'm crumpled up on the high counter. I'd like to blame lack of sleep for crippling me at this inopportune moment, but I know why I've collapsed. It pains me to look at her. She has the face of a star.

"You okay?" she asks, bemused. Pressed to my cheek, the cold black granite awakens my tongue.

"Tea. Please!" Weakly raising a ten-dollar bill, I moan, "Just. Need some Sencha. ..." Sparing her a bow, I stand and muster the shiniest pre-noon grin that I can. "And a vegan scone."

"Bags or a loose leaf?"

I try to just say "loose," but instead blurt out, "Who are you?"

Suddenly discovering a girl like this working at one of our few not-so-hot spots is a huge threat to the overwhelming banality of small-town ennui.

Seemingly pleased, smiling a half-smile, she hands me my change and very plainly asks, "Who are you, Michael?"

I run my hand through my morning mop, trying to recover from her unexpected recognition. I can feel my hair growing. It tingles.

"I haven't decided..."

Looking past me, dismissing me, she asks, "Can I help you ma'am?"

Dodging the silver-haired woodsy woman behind me, I casually rake my fingers over the juice cooler, swipe some ice, and retreat to the girls' room. As scalding water rushes from the faucet, I pocket my aviators and dab my eyes with a melting cube. *New Girl is wearing a Smiths shirt.* I smooth my tie in the steam. *I think I saw side-boob.* I slip my tie back under my collar, fix my hair, and smile.

"Michael. Organic green!"

I check my teeth then dash down the hall. Slowing my rush, I stroll to the bar.

"How do you know my name?"

"I saw you leaving auditions last month. And ever since I moved here Sarah and The Twins have been telling me how much I'd love you."

This is the girl I've been hearing about, Becca. She's the one Rick cast opposite me in the fall musical. Finally matching her cool, I ask, "So, do you love me?"

"I haven't decided." She hands me a hot bowl-sized black porcelain mug, turns to the La Marzocco, and begins dolloping foam.

"How was last night?" I ask, waiting for my pastry. I'm hoping that her phone number will be written on its bag. I bet her penmanship is superb. "You went to SF with Sarah and them right?"

"Nah, we just got dinner." She shrugs. "I was going to go but she wasn't sure when she was coming back. I figured that if I stayed out too late I'd end up laid out across the counter this morning." Lifting up on her toes she announces, "*Cappuccino, extra foam for Celeste!*" Then pulls some money from the till and hands it to me.

"What's this?"

"We're out of scones. Sorry."

....

Sitting on toasty black vinyl, with my back absorbing the glare of the window-wall, I text with Hector. He's agreed to let us borrow his generator. I'm telling him to drop it at Zach's as Sarah's voice bursts over the Adele single.

"Hayyyyy beautiful!"

Looking up from my iPhone, I'm about to respond when Becca comes out from behind the counter. The hot brunette smooches the beautiful blonde as if they were two longtime friends meeting at their favorite café on Rue Saint-Honore. They hug, giggle about something, then the vixen in the Smiths shirt skips back to re-make *Celleste's* unacceptable drink—there's too much foam. *Tiking* her way between tables, Sarah sits down at the chair across from me, crosses her great legs, and smiles.

"Hey sexy, what's shakin'?" Her shades match her pink and black-lace Betsey pumps. Her sleeveless black dress looks like it's been slept in. She hasn't been home yet.

"How was the party?" I ask.

"Amazing!" Squeezing my thigh, she begins naming people that I don't know. "Zoe was there, she's so nice, and her friend Kevin totally wants to paint me. And The Cobra Snake came up and got a picture of me and Donovan..."

As she recounts her electro evening, I wonder how she can still look this hot. She's last night's shining casualty. She's a perfect mess.

Silently envying her talent, I sip my tea. She gushes, "His set was SO amazing!"

"Whose?"

"Donny's!" Sarah takes my mug and continues to ramble on about the "amazing party" hosted by her "amazing" DJ friend.

Standing in the corner of the elevated DJ booth, with a vague sense of loss and hope, I watch Leo Di fade down the treble, lean across the turntables, and tongue-kiss Sarah. The red disco lights pulse. As he backs away to the boards, she grabs his McQueen tie, and pulls him in for more. When the handsome celebrity feels her up, Sarah asks...

"Hey, what are you doing here anyway?" She sips my tea. "Why are you up so early?"

"Couldn't sleep." I look up from her cleavage, into deeply tinted lenses. And having not forgotten her promise, add, "I'm surprised that you're back already, I mean, I guess I didn't get your text—"

A treat clinks down in front of me.

Pointing at the desert plate, I ask Becca, "Is this for me?"

"Well yeah. For both of you." She glances across my booth.

Sarah has begun tapping on her phone.

Smiling, Becca turns back to me. "You just looked so disappointed when I told you we were out of those scones... "

"Thanks!" I tear off a large corner of the banana bread. "I usually try to eat vegan but—"

"Well, you're in luck. There's nothing in there. I promise. I made it myself." Confidently, she stands. "I brought some to see if the owner wants to carry them."

Chewing a moist chunk, I am dazzled by the stunning cruelty-free baker. I'm glad Sarah's not paying attention. I doubt she'd care. But I wouldn't want her to cut me off. We've only done it six times. Swallowing, I gush, "You made this? It's delish. So you're vegan?"

"Yeah. You too?"

"I aspire. ... It's so hard to find nice shoes ... though treats are my main weakness. I get really treaty. ... But if someone were baking me stuff like this all the time it would be way easier to maintain my compassionate diet," I proclaim. "...I've never met a vegan girl who's not a hippie!" Becca clearly isn't the type to smoke weed, take shrooms, eschew waxing, or avoid a three-step shampooing—her jeans fit *and* I recognize the designer.

Clacking her phone onto the shiny black table, Sarah objects. "What about me?"

"What about you?" I ask.

"I'm vegan." She snatches the remaining half of the tasty slice. "Except for fish."

As I suppress my sudden suicidal urges, Becca offers, "You want some to take home Sarah? I've got more in the back."

"Oh, no thanks, Babe." She plates the remaining speck. "Calories. But could I get a white mocha?"

"Soy?"

I remove my face from my hand to see if the gracious vegan is sharing my pain. She is unfazed. So poised. So runway.

"Oh, yeah. Sure." Covering her mouth Sarah swallows. "Or whatever."

As Becca walks away, I watch the Cheap Mondays skull smile above her perky butt. A flicked crumb hits my shirt. "Hey!"

I check for stains as Sarah asks, "You're working tonight, right Mike?"

"Oh. Yeah. I am." I had forgotten until now. "I'm gonna be washed up." "Well you should probably take a nap." Her sex-hummed stage voice

turns the head of the businessman paying at the register. "Cuz I'm going to come visit. And I don't want you tired."

Chapter 6

Tired.

I couldn't nap. Lying atop my comforter, I was thinking about the party; obsessing over lighting, furnishing, outfits, and my need to open with the perfect film.

If we do this right, The Premieres could be huge. They could change everything. I could be bigger than the party kid from Australia. I could be signing a contract with MTV before I get my mid-term report card.

Now the clicking of the 10:15 projection sounds like a lullaby.

In the flickering shadows of Booth Six, bolted to the concrete in front of the window, there's an old pair of ragged red theatre chairs. Tonight, they feel like a California King mattress stuffed with purring kittens.

Sunken into crushed foam and broken springs, I slowly blink at the packed theatre below. I yawn. Breathing in the faint smell of popcorn, I sleep—lulled by the *tsk tsk tsk* of the spinning reels—until the foreign sound of rapidly approaching heels interrupts the projector's cadence.

Tik,tik,tik. Tik,tik,tik.

Sarah stalks across the harsh grey floor. She descends. She straddles me. My chair and I squeak as her black cotton skirt slides up to reveal hot pink Hello Kitty panties. I'm delighted. Grazed by the eerie projection light, she traps my legs together with her knees and I desperately fumble to unbutton her sleek short-sleeve school-girl top. Her long untamable hair is tangling the way, but luckily my humming brunette is in no mood for delicacy. Undoing her blouse, she sends a loose button flying. It clatters in the corner as she tosses the top, slips off her pink diamond-grid bra, and forces my face into her warm boobs. I suckle, suffocating on flesh and the scent of cotton candy. The tang of perfume tingles my lips. I'm at peace. *Moz, I'm ready. You may take me now.*

"*Michael, there is a light that never goes out.*" *I walk into the spotlight.*

Grabbing a handful of my perfectly styled hair, pulling me from my deserved fate, Sarah thrusts my head back. I suck in the air as she slides her wet mouth up my throat, pressing down hard enough to choke me. Her spit leaves a cooling trail down my neck. Sealing my lips with her own, she steals my breath. Her tongue feeds me a sweet wad of chewed up gum. It's watermelon.

I can't wait to tell Zach.

I turn, spit out the Bubblicious, stand, and push my gracious guest against the window. The thick glass thuds. Sarah grins, and I attack the pounding pulse above the pink acrylic beads at her collarbone. Digging her fingers into my ribs, she groans. Our audience laughs and I spin her to face them.

The theatre gives Sarah's full frontal a standing ovation. I grant them a regal wave.

The projector *tsk tsk tsks.*

Firmly, I wrap my right arm around her boobs and, sucking her jaw line, slowly press my free fingers down the front of her panties—one centimeter, one inch, two—then Sarah breaks my hold. Dropping to her knees, she tears down my jeans and consumes my Producer. It's fabulous, except that she's no longer obscuring my view. I glance up from her topless skillful licking to the block-buster comedy. A naked, ebullient trans-sexual is the last image I see before my eyes squeeze shut with joy. As I overfill her mouth, another burst of laughter rises from the house. I can't blame them. This part is pretty funny.

Swallowing, Sarah wipes her mouth on the hem of my shirt then stands. She watches me, as I check it for stains. It's moist, but unharmed.

Stepping out of my Ksubis, I slip off my tee, fold my clothes, and then hoist her onto the stainless steel build-up table. Braving the chill of it, she wraps her legs around my waist. A stack of trailers crashes to the floor. Their metallic ringing lingers as we do it, the patent leather of Sarah's pumps chafing the back of my thighs. Expertly, I bring her to the peak of ecstasy, at least twice (I'm pretty sure), before reaching my own second monumental climax. I explode a shockingly tiny amount of joy onto her thighs and then crumple onto the cold floor. I land atop the abused blouse. Sarah pulls it out from under me. After wiping herself down, she balls it up and tosses it toward the trash. It lands in a clump below the ribbon of tape snaking from the steel bin.

Resting my head on my arms, I watch her dress. She pulls her panties over her hips. *Her ass is cinematic.* She pulls up her skirt. Toned calves. *She must do Zumba.*

Tsk,tsk,tsk.

Tik, tik, tik. Tik, tik, tik.

Sarah heels over to the scattered reels and frees my brother's vintage Unknown Pleasures shirt from the pile. She puts it on. I'm horrified. Sliding her wavy hair out the back of its perfectly relaxed neck, she struts to the door. She turns, smiles, blows me a kiss, and then *tiks* down to the lobby.

She didn't say a word the whole time.

Nor did I.

With her having so generously given me wonderful OJ before letting me do it to her on a freezing metal table for ten minutes without hesitancy, I feel that it would have been rude to complain about the tee. I may like her even more than I thought.

After locating and discarding the carelessly spat gum, I stack the reels, break down the film, then run downstairs. The moviegoers have all gone. The door to my manager's office is locked and the one remaining Concession Creep is smoking out front beneath the Marquee. He's locking up tonight. This is good. *Sequoia wouldn't notice if I walked out of here with the safe.* I shove my hand in my pocket. Clicking, I quickly pace over amoebic coke stains on the matted red carpet and back up to Booth Six. *I won't get caught.* I pull the forgotten projector out from under the cabinet. I stash it in my old Jansport. *No one will ever notice.* The Panasonic hasn't been touched since the owner cancelled midnight movies. Stealthily, I sneak down the stairs, out through the back door, and into the empty lot. I desperately hope that no one sees me. I'm going to look ridiculous skating home in just jeans and a backpack.

It's fine. Click, click. I'll get the shirt back. And the night is still warm. *Click, click.*

Everything's fine.

Sleeping soundly with the projector stuffed into my old Sponge Bob sleeping bag, safely hidden in the back corner of my closet, I wake up with a sharp pain in my chest. Eddie kneads down toward my stomach. She purrs. Her rough wet tongue licks my face, and despite the forgivable clawing, I feel fantastic.

Flopping my arm across my red Prima sheets, I grab my phone. 2:12 pm. I unplug the charger, say good morning to the poster of Moz that's tacked to my ceiling, and dial.

Sarah doesn't answer.

I shuffle to the kitchen to grab a San P. from the fridge. A fresh, locally baked low-fat cranberry scone from Cherie Cherie is waiting for me in the breadbox. I glance over the Daily Chronicle. Another church burned down. The Future Farmers of America is holding a livestock competition for 'largest poultry.' City folk are spending millions to buy land for vineyards. Our county is now the number seven marijuana-producing county in CA.

Typical.

I flip to the entertainment section: wine tasting, acoustic night at the wine bar, and the same movies that have been playing at work all summer—most of which are 3-D kid flicks. An Aveda day spa will finally be opening, but not before I'm long gone. If anything exciting is ever going to happen in this town before then, I'm going to have to be the one that makes it happen.

I text Sarah *"Meet for Mochas?"* then walk to the bathroom to begin my morning ritual.

With "Deep Hit of Morning Sun" playing on repeat through my iPod dock, I brush my teeth, shower, shampoo, blow dry, dress, and style. An hour later I look absolutely fabulous. On my way out the front door, with my backpack slung over my shoulder, I check my texts. Sarah hasn't written back.

It's fine.

....

To my relief, Zach's air conditioner is finally fixed. His floor fans now serve as racks for wrinkled inside-out rock shirts. Hiding from the last rays of sunset, we lay stretched out on his unmade bed, propped against posters, each tapping away on laptops. We peruse porn, study celebrity sites, and search for new music while shopping.

I type in 'Joy Division' on last FM. When I first swiped their shirt from my brother's drawer I didn't know that it was a band shirt. It didn't matter. The design was fabulous. When Joey told me that Joy Division also made fabulous music, I downloaded a few songs. They were great. It was no surprise; my brother has always had impeccable taste. And the band *was* British.

I drop ten faux fur Chinchilla throws into my basket and a song called "Blue Monday" comes on. I like it. I add forty CK almost-down pillows to my order and a song by some band called Depeche Mode comes on. I like that too. I search for inflatable mattresses to the euphonious sounds of The Smiths and check my texts. Zach snaps shut his Mac.

"Jamie told me that she thinks Becca's into you."

"Really?" I look up from my mochas message. "She said that?"

He walks over to the mound of clothes at the base of Hector's Honda Generator, pulls his duct tape wallet from a pair of shredded jeans, and tosses it to me. His floor looks like the place where denim goes to die.

"Yeah. She came over with Sarah. Sarah asked me what we did last night. She said that you looked like you hadn't slept when she ran into you at The Grounds. I guess that didn't bum her out too much though! Booth fucking Six!" With a nodding grin, he gives me two thumbs up.

I thud my head back against The Gun Club. "I can't believe I went out looking like that. I just figured I wouldn't see anyone there that early!"

I need to start leaving extra outfits here. I'm sure Zach has a bunch of empty drawers. He's obviously not using them.

"Dude, last night you did it with Sarah in front of a sold-out theatre and I just told you that Becca's into you." He sits down on his virtually unused Marshall. The guitar cab has 'FAIL!' spray-painted in white stencil across the screen. It's just his band's logo, but I feel like the amp is speaking to me. I'm irresponsible. I should have at least given more thought to my hair when I was in the girls' room.

"I knew it. I knew I was a mess. I knew they could tell. Becca kept looking at me! I almost told them that I'd been up all night planning a party. But it's not like we can just start talking about it! It's *far* from legal. You didn't tell Sarah did you? What did Becca say? That I looked like a homeless vampire?"

I should have told her about the party. I should have told them both. They'd have been beyond impressed.

Becca said, "I'm totally fucking hot and I was way into Mike before I realized that he needs to settle." He grins, pops a Mento from the nubby roll that he found with his wallet, and proudly chews. Zach may not understand the importance of looking good, but he does understand the importance of good lookin' out. My dear friend with the loud hair speaks with the calm voice of reason. He grounds me. He is the rock to my roll.

"Okay, yeah. You're right, man. I should see if she's on Is Anyone Up?!" I type Becca into the site's search engine. A topless, tattooed brunette from Buffalo comes up. Her boobs are fake, nothing like Becca's. "No luck." I type 'wwtdd.com' into the browser. "Did you know she's vegan?"

"Did *you* know that *I'm* going out with Jamie tonight? I said that the four of us should do something. Sarah said that she had shit to do, but Jamie and I are gonna go get YoGoGo!"

"That's fine, I have to get to work anyway." I check my phone again.

"Hey." Standing over me, he throws a candy at my chest. "*I* am going out with JAMIE!"

The pink mint bonks off my sternum. It falls onto my keyboard and switches my open window.

Pop Kids | 41

"Oh, right man. That's fabulous! Get her back here and put on "Girl You'll Be a Woman Soon." I heard her tell Sarah, "OMG it *so* makes me want to fuck." You know, it's her *Pulp Fiction* Uma obsession thing."

"No way. Download it. Now." He insists, then notices the details of my Bloomingdales cart. "Dude, get rid of the sunglasses."

Zach is totally generous with all of his friends, and even more so with his best friend Michael Massi. Unfortunately, Willy Prozen starts to notice if his AMEX bill goes over a few thousand bucks.

"C'mon man they're so sweet and only five hun—"

"I just ordered you that million dollar Keihl's shit. If Dad cuts me off, we're fucked for The Premieres. Here, these are sweeter." He assaults me with the remaining mints.

"Owe, Owe. Okay, Okay." Miraculously, I catch one pink projectile and absently drop it into my pocket before getting rid of this season's aviators. "I deleted the shades."

Scoffing at my heartbreak, Zach picks a candy off a pillow and thuds back down on the edge of his firm mattress. Chewing, smacking his mouth, he reopens his computer and we both get back to business. Once we've managed to pull ourselves away from Titty City and finished shopping, I return his credit card, wish him luck with Jamie, and leave through his private backdoor.

From the top of his two shallow steps, I can see the chrome of his wrongly imprisoned Cadillac shining through the spotless garage windows. I go to it. With my hands in my jacket pockets, I peer through the glass. *If only you were free, I wouldn't have to skate to work. I wouldn't even have to be here at all.* Turning back toward the driveway I sigh then rediscover my Mento. I inspect it for lint, blow on it, and pop it into my mouth. I chew three times. It's deelish. I spit it into the dense green hedge that surrounds the Prozens' house. Occasionally I crave over-processed high-caloric treats, but can't stomach the artificial color and flavoring. Refined sugar turns straight into fat. In the end I prefer healthier treating.

I pause to watch a thick string of saliva oozing after the candy wad, trailing off a slimed leaf. It's unnaturally pink. It reminds of Sarah. Smacking, I swallow the last bits of sweet saliva left in my mouth. I sigh. *I wish I had another one.* Ignoring the irrational impulse to salvage the dirty candy, I clack down my board and push off toward the 8-plex, clicking my lighter most of the way.

At work, before I set up the reels I call Sarah. I dial her again at the end of the night in the empty lot behind the theatre. After the first ring, I hear the same message that's been mocking me all day—*I'm a free bitch, baby.*

This is too much. I want to smash my phone against the trashcan on the edge of the sidewalk.

I have to clean.

Chapter 3

As the days creep through the summer heat, the dream of the first Premiere consumes my every thought, while a phone full of unreturned messages competes for my attention.

Yesterday I didn't text Sarah at all. I imagined seeing Becca at the last showing of the blockbuster rom-com at work. When I came home I found a similar looking blonde on PornoTube. I was hoping to run into the gorgeous vegan at her morning shift today but it's already mid-afternoon. Becca has surely left The Grounds. And I have no texts.

The sun shines through our towering windows while I sit with Gina. She reviews humdrum headlines of the local paper: medical marijuana campaigns, bike to work day, another church has burned down.

"It's too bad that the drug dealers weren't in the fire," I lament, chewing. Without looking up Gina shakes her head.

"It is a terrible shame isn't it? That little church was so nice."

I ask if we have any lime.

After finishing my Pellegrino with a twist, rinsing my glass, and cleaning my old Sponge Bob plate, I shower to the sound of "Deep Hit of Morning Sun." I brush my teeth for two Sonicare cycles, pull up my jeans, and then pad shirtless to Joey's room to pick out a piece from his overflowing dresser of treasure. I unfold and refold the words 'FRANKIE SAYS RELAX.' I slip on a black tee that says 'Love and Rockets.' I turn in the mirror. I google the name on my phone. I miss my Unknown Pleasures shirt. I'm not sure that losing the vintage piece to post coital casualties was really worth the rewards. I can't find a replacement on eBay and haven't seen the hot thief who stole mine since she left me on the floor of Booth Six. I think I may have been used for my wardrobe. But it's hard to say.

....

"Oh, no. Not yet," I admit, squirting sunscreen into my palms. "I think her phone is off. She always forgets to charge it or pay the bill. She's always losing it too. Or breaking it. But it's fine, once the party—"

"That totally sucks," Zach shakes his head. "Sarah's so hot man. It would be a major bum-out if you didn't get to do it to her again."

As he blunt stalls on the far coping, I remain seated on my lawn chair beneath the umbrella on the garage side of the deck.

"Yes, I'm aware of that, thank you," I yell over the clacking of wood and metal on PVC. "Speaking of activities, you never told me how it went with Jamie."

Zach purposefully aborts his air and lands planted in front of me, holding his board.

"Mike that stupid song totally worked. I totally did it with her."

"Fabulous! I told you it was a good idea!" There's conflict in my friend's blue eyes. "What? ..." Rubbing white lotion into my cheeks, I ask, "What's wrong? Did you set a speed record? Did it suck?"

The iPod dock shuffles back to the 1960s.

"No, no I was a hero. And it was killer." Zach stutters, looking beyond the roof of his house. Beneath the voices of the Beach Boys we can hear the sound of designer footsteps coming up the driveway. "Her ass is like another planet."

He's not telling me something. I don't like it. On the day of Zach's date, I read a tweet from Hector—something about drinking with Jamie while working on her dad's gazebo. I figured the Coronas would only help Zach's cause.

"What? ..." I pry. "Was she drunk? She didn't throw up did she? I don't think I'd even accept OJ after that—" I prefer the term 'Oral Joy' to 'blow job.' It makes more sense.

The Twins stride onto the flat bottom of the ramp. Becca is with them. Even in jeans and a torn, sleeveless, grey Shattered Faith tee shirt, the beach beauty looks like she's on her way to Parisian fashion week. Without removing their shades, the blonde trinity looks up toward our perch. Michelle speaks first.

"Hey guys, we're walking to get iced coffees. You wanna come?"

I carefully climb down the ladder to offer the girls some San P.

"I would but I'm waiting for Dustin. ..." Zach says. "Jamie said she might stop over too."

"She tells us that you're quite the dancer." Michelle almost smiles.

"What? ..." I ask. "You danced? Like in *Pulp Fiction*?" Singing 'Zach, you'll be a woman soon' I gleefully take the opportunity to do a slow motion twist. My rubber soles slide atop the baking plywood.

"I hate you guys." Blushing, Zach sighs and turns up "Wouldn't It Be Nice."

He really has nothing to be ashamed of. If the new girl in the purple pants were offering activities as a reward, I'd do a single man re-enactment of "All the Single Ladies" and post it.

"Oh come on," Michelle consoles him. "We heard you were a GREAT dancer. That's nothing to be embarrassed of." Zach grins at the implication. "Sarah says the same about you too Mike."

Seemingly, Sarah has been talking to everyone but me.

"Does she?" I ask, and then take a long sip off my chilled, vocal-relaxing Pellegrino. "Well the girl knows good moves when she sees them. I'd be happy teach you ladies a few of them if you're up for it." I rest my eyes on Becca's cheap aviators. Hoping to have inspired a raised eyebrow or a blush. All I see is a distorted reflection of myself.

"Thanks Mike." Drew sounds less appreciative than she should. "I'm sure we'd all love to take you up on that, but our pretend boyfriends are about to meet us at The Grounds. They're from San Francisco. Jesse—"

"Jason," Michelle corrects her sister. "Yours is Jason. And I thought they lived with those kids in Santa Rosa."

She tugs on the delicate golden crucifix around her neck.

"Whatever," Drew says, "My hot boy has a great aunt or something that lives over on Corvina. They're gonna stay there tonight. They're in a psych surf-rock band that's about to get signed. They have, like, ten million hits on YouTube."

Tramping down the transition of the ramp, Zach stops inches away from The Twins.

"Jesse and his great aunt are in a surf band?" He smirks.

I turn to the quiet platinum blonde. "So, is your pretend boyfriend coming too Becca?

"Nah, I don't pretend, How 'bout you?"

"What?"

Climbing out from a second story window of their house, Zach's little brother takes a picture of us, yells "hey chicks" then jumps down about twelve feet into a large hedge.

"My pretend boyfriend just got here."

Speeding over, Dustin's long, straight, light brown locks flow around his navy blue headband.

"Isn't that right Dustin dear?" Lovingly putting my arm around his shoulders, I pull a leaf from his hair.

"Huh?" He looks to his big brother.

"You're Mike's boyfriend."

"Oh, I know!" Immediately playing along, and posturing like a fifteen-year-old queen from Venice Beach circa 1977, the kid stakes claim on me. "Back the fuck off my man, bitches!" he demands, challenging Becca before abruptly dropping the act and introducing himself. "Hey, I'm Dustin." He smiles and nods toward me. "You can borrow him, I don't mind. You just can't keep him. And you have to let me take pictures when you guys fuck." Then, producing a pair of mirrored aviators from the pocket of his plaid short sleeve, he puts them on, grins, and says, "Nice shades."

I hate his hair but love his attitude. Dustin is always on fast-forward, turned up to ten, amped like a four-year-old who's been given the key to the candy store. People think he's coked out, but I know that he's actually just really stoked.

"I don't think I can borrow him, but thank you Dustin." Charmed, Becca shockingly declines his generous offer before turning to me. "Isn't Sarah your girlfriend?"

"Oh. No, we're friends but she doesn't really..." Secretly clicking my lighter, I stammer. "We don't ... I don't have a girlfriend. She's not my girlfriend. But she's fabulous."

With a fleeting low giggle, Becca releases a full smile that kills me even more than my momentary, uncharacteristic lack of eloquence.

"Oh, okay. Yeah. She's awesome." Taking a picture of her, of us,

Dustin dissolves the upsetting conversation, as he frantically begins a report of his recent surfing sessions.

"You guys have gotta come out to the coast with me. Seriously. It's so killer. Last night after hot tubbing Star gave me the most intense fucking massage. She says I have great tone. And check out what Leo gave me." He slides a new Flip cam from his Levis and starts filming Becca. "And they said that Band FAIL! can play on their deck!" Zach and Alvin have a band. It's called Band FAIL! There are only two members, they rarely rehearse and only have half a song written. But the clip has 1.2 million views on YouTube.

"Kickass!" Zach high fives his brother.

"Keep an eye on those hippies," I warn, "They might spike your Pellegrino."

Texting, Drew gives my solid advice a *phhh* and, direct to camera, Becca further cautions.

"Careful of those sharks out there too," before her phone begins buzzing.

Turning, playing with her hair, she paces away from the ramp. "Hey! Are you back? ... We're at Zach's. ... Yeah, he is..."

I admire her side-boob and the skull detail sewn into the denim above her very round butt as she wanders toward the garage to inspect the imprisoned Caddy. Leaving her bra-less, I envision matching lavender panties with matching lavender toenails. Zach asks his brother if he's going to do it with the healing-handed surfer.

"Fucking, I don't know man." Tossing his hair, taking off his shades, Dustin reveals his hopeful hazel eyes. "That'd be rad but, dudes, she's like a woman. It'd be fucking wild right?"

When Becca returns to the ramp, Dustin recommences filming. She seems totally comfortable on camera. *I bet she reads wonderfully on screen.*

"Hey, Sarah's back. They're almost there. You guys ready to go?"

I check my phone. *Sarah's here. She's calling Becca and she hasn't texted me.*

As The Twins walk down the driveway, the vegan lingers. Dustin grabs the skate from his brother's hand, points to his chest, and reminds her 'Dustin,' before demanding, "Watch this baby!" Punishing the ramp, defying gravity, he vocally approves of his own tricks, mid-air. "Sick! Whatttt? No Way! He's so handsome—"

"Are you gonna come with us Mike?" Becca asks.

I don't want her to leave. But I can't follow her. Sarah is waiting for her. And I can't just show up to The Grounds uninvited after she's ignored my last fourteen texts. I'd seem desperate.

"Oh, I would but I've gotta work soon." Tomorrow is relatively soon.

"You work at the theatre right?"

"Yeah."

"That's pretty cool. I'd love to check out the projection room some night." She innocently insinuates, "I've always wanted to see one," which completely rattles me.

I have no idea whether or not she knows—whether she's asking to see the projection room or to *see the projection room*. I wonder if The Twins told Becca of my proclivity for sex on the job. Praying to Moz that she's asking *to see the projection room* I suppress the agitation caused by my inability to read her.

"I'd be more than happy to show you." *A black moth flutters past her white hair.* "Come by anytime. Just ask for me."

"Okay." Sweetly agreeing with a half smile, she pinches the throttle of the motorcycle screened across my tee. "Nice shirt by the way."

Stunned by her praise of Love and Rockets, wondering if the multilayered woman of mystery was, perhaps, born in England, I watch her catch up with The Twins, and then I quickly scurry back up the ramp. I hop over to the roof of the garage. Texting, the three blondes march down the white driveway, step onto the black asphalt of the Prozens' fancy neighborhood, and head toward The Grounds. No one but Zach notices me waving.

Chapter 9

"Tell me, *Miguelito*!"

As I try to convince him to help us transport our supplies, Hector is demanding that I reveal the sensitive details of our illegal party. I don't want it to end before it begins due to a security breach. This, however, poses a problem since we need his El Camino to get all the stuff over to The Palace.

"Could you just please come and get us?" I ask.

David's distant voice echoes, "Tell us *Culito*!"

I hear gunshots over the phone.

"Please? C'mon Hector. Pretty please with corpse paint on top."

Zach is going to the coast with Dustin tomorrow night and with school poised to open fire on our freedom, we absolutely must set up before he leaves.

"You really need us to come right now, *Guapo*? Tonight?"

"Yes, tonight. Now. Please?"

Without bothering to remove the phone from his face, Hector begins a frantic Spanish dialogue. It sounds heated. He and David are speaking so rapidly that all I can make out is the word 'father' over the sound of automatic weapons.

"Okay. I'm gonna come get you guys, but it's gotta be fast, okay? My parents are on the way back from visiting my uncle and we're supposed to be having alone time. I'm not leaving my man on Rambo night. We'll squish. And if you need to, David says you can sit your tiny little *culo* on his lap, which is fine with me as long as you give me road head."

I love The Boys. They're always a joy to be around, and I have deep respect for their unflagging upbeat demeanors. I can't even begin to imagine what it must take for two semi-out-of-the-closet Mexican kids to stay as positive as they do. Nor can I imagine spending a day in their steel-toes. Since they were in junior high, Hector and David have worked construction with their fathers. Construction. There's no way that I'd ever be able to survive the sun and sweat involved in such physical labor, even if I were able to take part in their invigorating lunch breaks. As they are very willing to prove, The Boys have learned how to perfect every man-task from building sturdy foundations to giving secret on-site fellatio while their thick-skinned fathers are out fetching their grandmothers' tamales. They are both very talented. They even give lessons.

"Fabulous, we'll be quick," I promise. "You two won't be without Sly for long."

....

Once the bed of his purple, rainbow-flecked seventies muscle car is over-stacked with Bloomingdale boxes and Band FAIL!'s old PA, Hector squeals out of the Prozens' driveway. Zach is hanging out of the passenger window, using the wind to further un-style his hair. I'm sitting my Ksubis on the creased chinos of the buzz-cut boy with the perfectly manicured side-burns. Snatching the iPod from his strong hands, I quickly find some Moz to replace the abysmal voice that's blasting through the stereo. The Boys love black metal. I find the music terribly unpleasant. Hector runs the stop sign at the end of the Prozens' fancy neighborhood. I reach over, lay on the horn, switch the Immortal to *Viva Hate*, and then direct him to the psychic shack on the forgotten side of town.

"Here? Crystal Eyes?" He pulls up to the curb in front of the empty store. Jumping out, Zach and David quickly begin unloading.

"Yep, this is it." I explain, wandering toward the dark alley in search of the grey Manx I saw scamper away as we parked. "Promise not tell, but the old owner of this place said that if I delivered all this stuff by midnight she'd make us all personalized anointed hemp necklaces. With our power stones woven into them." I turn back and smile. "Surprise!"

"*Dios mio* Michael, I hate you." Setting a box of inflatable couches on the sidewalk, Hector overplays his exasperation. "That's fine, don't tell me. I don't wanna know. I don't even want to come to your stupid movie party." He smirks, and David laughs.

"You'd better be having a Russell Crowe marathon!"

They must have put the pieces of the puzzle together back at Zach's, when I directed them to load the projector.

"You guys can't tell anyone!" I insist. Even in the dim streetlights, their car sparkles like a glitter-dipped grape lollipop. "I really want it to be a surprise, plus it's not totally legal, or totally ready and—"

"Oh settle down, *Guapo*, I'm not gonna tell anyone. I swear." Dropping an Amazon box atop Zach's mini-fridge, Hector runs a comb through his tight, slick hair. "We'd just better get some good seats. ... You projecting this shit in the alley or something?"

"You know I'd offer nothing less than VIP treatment to you two." Pitching in with the unloading, I take the last pillow from David's hand then relieve them of their duties. "Thanks you guys, you're the best. We'll take it from here."

Standing in the middle of the street, I hug the extra-large pillow, breathing in sour smoke of the El Camino's burnt rubber as The Boys speed back to their alone time.

....

"Okay." Underground, sitting on a milk crate, amidst boxes, pumps, pillows, chords and cables, huffing from having gone up and down the stairs far too many times, I shine my Mini-Mag over our wonderfully cluttered stage. "I think that's it."

Zach plugs a woven white length of wire into a power strip.

"What about that?" His blue light illuminates the heavy, drab duffle bag that I left on the ballroom floor. "What's in there anyway? It sounded like you stuffed a hundred bottles of San P. in that thing. You did notice that we had ten cases already, right?" He lights the boxes stacked around the fridge.

"Don't you worry about my bag of tricks my friend." Walking down the steps, I grab my clinking sack of treasure. "I'll handle the entryway while you're setting up. Oh, and close the curtain. The reveal will be more striking that way."

Zach laughs, "Okay, cool." and powers up the generator.

With a gentle whir, the first rays of Xmas lights crawl across the floor. We both smile in the glow. Zach gives himself two thumbs up.

....

In the center of the dark dance floor, I unpack the prayer candles. Songs about pinheads, jet boys, jet girls, getting it on, and banging gongs boom behind the curtain, while I meticulously arrange a path from the upstairs lounge to the edge of the stage. After many ups and down, with a trail of flames behind me, I kneel and light the final white pillar before standing to admire the shadow cast across the crimson velvet. I fix its hair then turn to bask in The Path of Prayers—the glowing shelter deepens the darkness, quavering at the edge of its reach. The music shuffles. I can't wait for my guests to see this. *They'll love it. It's heavenly.* A rocker wails about a love removal machine and I shine a Mini-Mag into a sinister-looking corner of the grand ballroom, just to make sure that hell hasn't crept up into our plans. I've yet to see proof of God but I've seen enough movies to know a potential portal to an evil dimension when I see one. *It's fine. There's nothing.*

Slipping through the curtain's part, I'm about to reveal my flickering installation when I'm halted. Onstage, Zach, inflating purple plastic in all his tall messy-haired skinniness, is being dwarfed by the giant, godlike image of Ewan McGregor. *Velvet Goldmine* is not choppily playing on his laptop nor flickering through a noisy midnight showing in the 8-plex, but regally radiating from the wall screen of our private theatre. *He did it.*

Sensing my awe, my partner stands from his couch-pump to smile in the eerie glow. He looks sci-fi. The projection covers him in cool electrifying light as Morrissey sings of international playboys. And I feel like I'm in a movie.

"Pretty good right?"

I high-step over to pin his arms to his side. Lion-hugging him I pronounce, "This is it. We're in the movies man! We're taking Hollywood next!"

"Okay Martin Scorsese, yeah." Laughing, he says, "But if you wanna hear the movie you're gonna have to let me go."

"All right Mr. Lynch." I flatter back, freeing him and smoothing my found Depeche Mode tee. "I did appreciate my entry music but, yes, please, do show me whatcha got."

Wet from the birth of our new names and trembling with excitement, I'm further amazed as Moz silences to give voice to actors playing seventies rockers.

"See. ..." Lynch attempts to teach me soundboard physics, flicking back and forth between the film and the iPod connection. "We can play music too."

The dialogue of the eye-lined men in the glitter film blares through the PA and I reach through the livening air. Grabbing Zach's face, I smooch his rocket science mouth. Scowling like Eddie, he wipes off my affection with the back of his hand.

"C'mon, man. Settle." He laughs. "Go upstairs and make sure you can't hear any of this from outside so I don't have to hear you freaking about getting caught. Then we'll finish making this place killer."

When I reach the lounge, the bass from below is barely audible. Pushing through the leafy mouth of the hotel, I step outside to make sure that we'll remain unfound. Silence comforts me. I rush back down to the basement to see Zach tacking down the final string of lights.

A few feet downstage from the wall screen, my partner has wrapped a rectangular halo around our clandestine cathouse. In its center, we shove together the king sized self-inflating mattresses, cover them with faux fur pillows and throws, then encircle the beds with our translucent inflatable couches—their purple and greens providing a needed modern flair to the classic vibe of the hotel.

Everything looks perfect. Leaning against the giant wall screen covered in projection, Zach and I inspect our theatre, delighting in our décor. *This is fabulous.*

"I think we did it," I cautiously announce and turn to my partner. Through the decades of floating dust, I mirror his giddy expression, feeling like I'm about to take the lead in a great performance.

"Fuck yeah we did!" he confirms. We both begin running like recess.

Taking our first synchronized dive into Heaven, we land with a soft thud and, enfolded in the luxury of faux chinchilla, surrounded by Xmas decorations and big candy, Lynch and I begin to fantasize.

"Once we get this going..." Looking up at the third run of the glammy DVD, I insist, "You and I will by laying here, cuddled up with Sarah and Jamie ... and Becca—"

"And Drew, Michelle ... Fuck! And some Sweater Girls..."

"Yes! Watching the finest films ... in between activities." The shadow of two raised thumbs obscure the pick-ups of an electric guitar. "We'll be heroes Mr. Lynch."

"Mr. Scorsese, It's gonna fuckin' rule."

Chapter 10

While Zach's partying on the coast, I'm at my desk. Refreshed from an afternoon shower, smelling like an ice cream parlor, I'm working diligently on my first invitation. I type 'Simple Minds' into Last FM then google image *The Breakfast Club."* We've all seen the Hughes' classic a million times, but it never grows old. My guests will love it and, thus, love their host. It will perfectly open The Premieres. Skipping past all songs lacking an immediately discernable English accent, I photoshop with precision. I extract the cluttered quote from the top of the original movie poster, changing 'they only met once, but it changed their lives forever' to 'SCORE AND LYNCH PROUDLY PRESENT: THE PREMIERE PARTY.' I paint the super-text a screaming red then, below the movie's title where Hughes and A&M once had their credit, I type the details:

> *This Sunday, Aug 8, you are invited to an exclusive and clandestine screening of the Breakfast Club, presented by Michael Scorsese and Zach Lynch. Snacks will be provided, but feel free to bring your own treats. All attending must meet exactly 2 hours after sundown in the old WAMU parking lot. If you are driving, we politely ask that you park at least two blocks away. Please be advised that this is a private screening. Do not share this invite with anyone. RSVP to me. Please trash this after you have received it.*

I send the invite to my partner for his approval. Instantaneously, my phone rings. As I pick up, I notice that I have an unread text from Sarah. *Finally.*

"What? Were you looking at porn?" I ask. "That was quick."

Eddie hops onto my desk, stretches, and steps toward the keyboard.

"Yeah. Everyone's out getting fish tacos. I'm waiting for this chick who's heavily into Band FAIL!, particularly the singer." Zach's the singer. "I found this nasty shit that I've never seen before—"

"What is it? Sounding?" I pull my purring Havana down to my lap.

"Ugh, no. So, it's this whatever-normal-porn, right? Some buffo is fucking this tattooed chick with giant jammers, doggie style, then all of a sudden she turns around and he starts kissing her!"

"On the mouth?"

"Yep. Totally ruined my boner."

"That's disgusting." I can hear the twisted porno playing on his iPad.

"Totally. But, man, Mike. That flyer is killer. Good call on *Breakfast Club.* Who are we inviting?"

"Sarah, Jamie, Hector, David, The Twins ... Dustin obviously—."

"What about Becca? She clearly wants to eat your skinny jeans."

"My dear partner, are you implying that I might be the type of gentleman to court two women at the same time?" I google 'Becca Rose.' "Sarah just text me before you called, probably professing her undying love." I find a black and white photo of the blonde standing in long black tee shirt on a dark Venice beach. She's sleeveless, braless, bottomless, and expressionless. I drag it next to the other pictures of girls, celebrities, and suits in my Wish List folder. "I can't just invite some mysterious, smitten, internet model to a private event that will be attended by my paramour." I pull a pic of Becca posing on a Vespa. She is so hot. *I totally want to invite her.*

"Sarah won't care. She'd probably be stoked if Becca came. They're all BFF now."

"We barely know her Zach. Our party isn't exactly legal you know? What if her dad's a cop?"

"Invite her. You said she wanted to see the projection room."

Staring at a shot of her topless, laying boob-down on black

sheets that match her smeared smoky eyes, I sigh. "I'll invite her when we know each other better, *after* she's experienced the mind-blowing wonders of Booth Six."

"Okay..." he laughs, "hopefully you'll be less rattled by her once you've banged her on the build-up tables. Speaking of ... I've gotta find something to bring my boner back before this chick gets here. ... Oh wait, what's with meeting in the parking lot two hours after sundown?"

"I figure it's better that we're not lurking right in front of the hotel."

"Yeah, but why two hours after sundown? Why not something a little more vague?"

"Mystique, my friend. Mystique."

"Of course. Okay, well I'll be back Sunday morning. I'll meet you in the lot an hour and thirty two minutes after sundown, just so I'm not late."

"Fabulous. See ya then Lynch."

"See ya then Score."

Chapter 11

"This cow's not getting any deader!!"

Frank is calling me to dinner. Anxiously, I check my message from Sarah. It says,

"Hi :)".

That's it. It's but two letters away from exclusively inspiring emoticon nausea and yet I'm still tempted to respond. But I don't know what I'm supposed to say to "hi" plus a stupid smiley face.

Throwing the offending phone against my silk-screened pillowcase, I ignore the text, return to my laptop, and send out the invitations. I wish I could invite Becca. She's not the type of girl who'd use an emoticon in her first rudely delayed post-coital text. She had a Smiths shirt on. People who wear Smiths shirts don't use emoticons. She would have hand written me amorous poetry exalting my potency. Or even called. I pick up my phone. As I'm dialing Sarah, Frank yells, "GET OFF THE COMPUTER AND GET IN HERE!"

I let it ring once, hang up, then join him and Gina at the table.

....

Focusing on my plate, ignoring Frank's hat and his monstrous display of devouring bocci-sized murder-balls, I consume about eight square inches of Gina's beautiful eggplant parm before putting on my iPod. Quickly, I do the dishes then rush back to my Mac. As I had hoped, the responses to the invite are already in. And everyone is excited. The thread begins with Jamie:

"*OMG! I LOVE the 80s!!! I'm so there! I can't wait!*"

David adds: "*Mr. Scorsese and Mr. Lynch, thank you for the invitation. My man and I would love to attend. —John Travolta.*"

Hector follows his BF's lead: "*Yes! We'll be there arm and arm. He's keeping his burns but I finally shaved that beard from Dawson's Creek! —Tom Cruise.*"

And, with the continued good spirited mockery of their hosts' Screenames, so comes confirmations from the Olson twins, Tony Alva, and a retracted acceptance from Jamie. Mia Morris will be taking her place on the red carpet come opening night. I don't think Jamie accepts that there's a difference between Uma Thurman, the actress, and her character in *Pulp Fiction*. I once tried to explain the relation of Miley Cyrus and Hannah Montana to her but she just wasn't having it.

Slightly distressed that Sarah has yet to respond, I point out to Dustin that though he thinks he's Tony Alva he is in actuality Alvin of chipmunk fame. Amidst the following LOLs Volta requests that Alvin sing "Christmas Time Is Here" before the film.

Finally, thirty-six minutes later, at the bottom of a long string of replies, Sarah's response appears. Calling herself Stella she writes: "*Amazing! There is no place I'd rather be. Don't you forget about me! Check your text Mr. Score!*"

With intent to immediately respond to her ':)' message, considering sending back a ';)' I frantically retrieve my phone from the bed. Since sending her first soul revealing passage, the poet has written again: "*Mom's away and she left the vegan treats unguarded.*"

I open the text. A self-shot pic of Stella wearing pink panties, lightly touching a fruit pop to her half-parted lips, pops up on my screen. She's topless. Her panties match the pop. Below the picture she's written, "*Come over! xxooxxoo*".

I power-shower. I power-dress. I power-fix my hair then smile in my brother's mirror before powering my board out from under Eddie.

"Sorry girl. ... Bye Dad, bye Mom," I yell toward the elder Massis' room, "I'm going into town for dessert. I'll be back later."

....

From the flats, I call her.

"Hello, is this Stella?" I ask, skating past the 7-eleven, already enamored with our new name game.

"Maybe ... is this A-lister hot ass party promoter Scorsese?"

"You know it." I can hear her sex hum through the phone.

"Well, I'm not sure if I'm the girl that you're looking for but why don't you come to 452 Reisling and see. The door's unlocked. I'll be in my room reading scripts."

"I'll see you in four minutes."

Pushing onward through the warm dusk I speed toward some of the finest earthly delights my seventeenth year on this planet has yet to offer.

....

Stella's bed is unmade. And pink. Soft pink sheets, a soft pink comforter, and soft pink pillowcases are ruffled into the fluffy pink cloud, in which I now languish, nude, like a CK model in Candyland. Lying on my back amidst scattered copies of US Weekly, I reach down past Brad and Angelina's faces to touch nipples while the iPod shuffles from insipid pop song to insipid pop song. I don't think that Stella owns any full-length records. And though I've yet to hear even one UK single, everything is erotically wonderful until Katy Perry's voice nullifies my moment of OJ bliss. The chorus makes me question if there really is a Moz.

Desperately, I play with Stella's boobs, smelling cotton candy, admiring her skilful oral diligence between glances at the promo photo pinned above the pink dresser. Stella's mouth. Katy Perry. Deep naked cleavage. Blue wig. Luxurious brown hair cascading across my belly. Deep, corseted Ameripop cleavage. Moist sounds of suction. "*I kissed a girl and I liked it.*"

Struggling to ignore the unforgivably annoying song, I reach for a tabloid, hoping to find a picture of Megan Fox to help with my progress. The super-couple on the cover is holding babies.

Fucking Gross. Okay, that's it. I pull Stella up to me. We make out. Furiously. For about four, wet seconds. Then she rolls over and grabs the edge of her pink mattress. On her knees, she arcs her back like a house cat in heat and faces her pink wall. "*Fuck me,*" she says, and buries her head in a pink pillow. A fresh, shiny black Kanji tattoo pops through her all over tan. The bold, slightly scabby symbol on her lower back makes me want to learn Chinese.

Happily, I follow her command, forgetting all about Katy until approximately two minutes later, as I spatter pearly joy across the pink baroque wooden headboard, I realize that the three-minute single is still playing. I'm slightly mortified, but Stella doesn't seem upset by the unexpected brevity of our scene. When I return from her bathroom with a pink hand towel, she's contentedly texting. Something buzzes into her phone. She smiles. And responds.

I guess we're not going to cuddle. Wondering who she's talking to so soon after our soul shaking spiritual collision, I wipe down and walk to the kitchen.

"Hey!" Shoving my sex hair into the cooling fridge, I yell, "You want a Diet Coke?"

"Can you bring me that red wine?" Her voice is dry with texting distraction.

"Uh, would you like me to wheel in the cheese cart too?"

"The wine's fine Babe, thanks*.*"

Gross. Wine is just unacceptable. 'Babe' is too. *It's fine.* I don't want to ruin the post coital merriment. And the alcohol could encourage a second round of activities.

With a wide-mouthed pink ceramic coffee mug halfway filled with Barbara's open bottle of stenchy Navarro, I walk back into the frosted pink room. "Poker Face" is my entry music.

With her back propped against the glistening headboard, wearing only a pair of Victoria's Secret PINK athletic shorts, Stella is carefully erasing something she's penciled into The Breeders copy of US.

"Sorry, I couldn't find any stemmed glasses." I hand her the mug. "Won't your mom freak when she sees that you drank her nasty wine?"

"She drinks it with me." Stella takes a big gulp. I admire her boobs. "Does that bother you Mr. Unclean and Sober?"

Reflexively, I inspect my face in the pink mirror. She takes another drink. As she tilts it back, some of my joy dips toward her mug.

"You still have, um..." Proud of my achievement, but always courteous, I point at the wet dangling strand. "You have some in your hair."

With a side-glance, she grabs the globby tendril. Silently humming, she listlessly twists.

"Does that bother you too?" Casually, she licks her fingers.

"Not at all."

She's a good girl.

"Me neither." She smiles and chases me down with another sip.

Standing naked over her bed, I drink mineral water as Stella reads me tasty gossip from celebrity sites. I am about to direct her to CocoPerez.com when her Mom messages her. She's on her way home. *Barbara will immediately be able to tell that I've just spread joy all over her drunken daughter.*

Terribly disappointed to have neither a second scene nor a pink shower, I begin my rapid exit. With a moistened Hello Kitty towel, I wipe down before pulling up my Ksubi's and slipping on my Chucks. Britney sings *"Hold It Against Me."* Then I remember the theft.

"Hey..." buttoning the same black and white checkered short-sleeve that I saw on that Stroke who dates models, I ask, "Where's my shirt?"

"In the laundry basket. It got all smoky so I'm gonna wash it for ya Babe." She picks up her vibrating phone.

Her hamper is empty—surrounded only by a pile of unlaundered, pink delicates. But I'm in a great mood and a greater hurry. In her pink baroque vanity, I adjust the skinny tie that I left loosely knotted around my collar.

"What are you doing tomorrow?" I ask.

She doesn't look up from her text. "Oh, I'm kinda super busy."

"Oh okay, well I have tonight off." Her reflection ignores mine. "Do you wanna get YoGoGo or something? I'm feeling like some frozen low-cals."

Her phone vibrates. She giggles.

"Ohhhh, I can't Babe." Pouting, she types. "I really should be here when my Mom gets home. We've got a *Sex and the City* girl-night planned."

She's making up this previously unmentioned date with Babs. I know it. I wonder who's actually coming over. He's probably in a band.

"Oh okay cool. Yeah, that's cool. ... I actually need to get some stuff ready for The Premiere anyway."

She types.

"I can't wait! It's gonna be A-Mazing!"

"Yeah, okay."

Pausing in the hall, I silently watch her. She types.

Diving back into The Pink Room, I snatch the phone from its evil princess, text "I'm sorry, I have to go bang Michael Massi. We'll have to talk later DJ DiCaprio," hit send, and then do it to your pink highness all the way through the reveal of Bigs' real name. She makes me her prince. And together we rule.

Stella stops typing. Finally, she looks up.

With my board under my arm, I smile. "Okay, I'll see you Sunday."

"Bye Babe." She sings and looks back at her phone.

As The Pussy Cat Dolls show me the front door, Stella, in perfect unison, loudly joins in. *"When I grow up, I wanna be famous, I wanna be famous ... "*

....

At home, everything's fine. Frank and Gina are asleep, I'm only two nights away from throwing my dream party, and my relationship with Stella could rightly be considered 'sexually active.' In bed, I'm intimating to Eddie.

"Yep, as of right now I'm sexually active with one of the hottest girls in school." She winks, and I clarify, "Oh no, it's not like that, but it's still totally fabulous."

Were I Stella's boyfriend assuredly the relationship might be a bit trying (with my having to navigate around all the other guys she'd still be touching) but it could work. We look great together and since we both aspire to escape this town, we wouldn't have to worry about breaking up after graduation. She says that she's moving to LA, that she's going to be a star.

"Who knows? It's always something different." I feed my cats curiosity. "Acting, modeling, singing. ... Every time I ask she says, 'once I'm there, how I got there won't matter.' You can respect that, right?" Eddie pads from my chest and flops down onto the pillow next to my head. "I totally respect her ambition. She's a good girl. When I got there, when I walked in her room, she was totally naked, lying on her bed with this Hello Kitty vibrator..."

Chapter 12

It's Sunday. Finally. The Day of their Lord has come and given way to the warm summer night of our opening. I am attired in my black two-button Top Man suit, tie, and Chucks. I couldn't host my first party in anything less. Everything is ready. In our perfectly arranged theatre, my shuffling iPod is pumping secret music up toward my sock-less feet while I calmly await the arrival of our guests.

"Can you stop pacing?" Lynch, wearing his Dead Boys jacket, squints up at me from the WAMU curb. I make another pass in front of him.

"Can you go change into something less ventilated?" I point with distrust at the knee popping through the rip in his jeans.

"Maybe if you had some holes in your tux you wouldn't be so hot and bothered."

He's scrolling through photos of surfer girls.

"It's not a tuxedo." I plant myself next to him. "Where are they? Everyone's going to flake."

"Settle. They're coming." I press my moist brow to the shoulder of his coat. Without pulling away, he half-heartedly complains, "Aw, c'mon man."

"What? All my matching bandanas are in the wash. You want everyone to see me all sweaty?" I peer into his phone. "Thanks for those beach nudes by the way."

"They're killer right? Dustin took'm. None were as hot as this though." He holds up one of Stella's photos that I forwarded. Shaking his head, he smiles. "Man, she's a natural."

I haven't heard from her since The Pink Room. As I grab my phone to check my texts, someone calls out, "Ooooh, I see someone fancy."

"Here they come!" Standing, straining to find Stella in the group, I wave back to David. I feel like they're pacing up the street in slow motion.

"Mary Kate..." I kiss Michelle's cheek. "Ashley..." I kiss Drew's cheek. "Mia..." I kiss Jamie's cheek. Then open my arms to welcome Hector.

"Uh, uh! Where's mine?" He puckers.

"I apologize, Mr. Cruise..." *Smooch.* "Welcome!"

"I'm next Culito!" David plants one on me. He smells like the CK One cologne that my brother's circus friend wears.

"So, Volta..." I tug on his blue Nike tank top. "This is a new look for you."

"You like it Mr. Scorsese?" He twirls. "I wanted to be Bender but Hector already had the shirt."

The Boys are dressed as the characters from *The Breakfast Club.* Volta looks like The Sporto, Cruz has mussed hair, a red bandana around his ankle, and a short-sleeve flannel, partially buttoned over a thermal.

"I love the outfits, guys." I pantomime applause. "Fabulous." Then, to the stunning Jamie with her self-given Screename, I ask, "Mia, Where's your louder half?"

Her giant ass is curving violently out from her grey and baby blue striped jersey dress and her arms are curling around Lynch. She stares at me blankly before realizing that I'm speaking to her.

"Oh! Me! Don't worry cutie! Sarah's coming." She grins. "So, are we going to the 8-plex or something? This parking lot kinda sucks." Looking up over her shoulder, she begins to baby talk. "Zach what're we doing? Zaaaaach, tell me..."

Keeping our secret, my partner silently gravitates to the parking block on which The Twins are daintily balanced. As he looms, they listlessly lick melting ice cream cones—both double scoops of strawberry cheesecake.

"Why do you guys get two scoops of the same flavors?" I ask.

"Can't have too much of a good thing." In unison with her sister, MK licks her cone while my co-host practically drools onto their blonde heads. I covet their treats a bit myself.

Releasing Lynch, Mia turns her attention to a text. Lynch makes a hungry sound. Ash rolls her eyes, surrenders her cone and, as Lynch greedily bites through half of a scoop, Alvin trots into the parking lot with Stella on his back. Her arms are wrapped around his chest. Her thighs are around his waist. And her re-usable grocery bag is gripped in her fist. It's clinking.

"Hayyyy kids…" Giggling, the tardy equestrian bounces into our gathering. "Wooh!…" As she dismounts her heels *tik* and her boy-pony bails out onto the lot. "Am I late?" she asks.

"Fashionably, of course." I nod to her sack of supplies. "What'cha got in there?"

"Oh just a lil' something to celebrate your first party Babe!" Thrusting her hip like a swimsuit model in a liberty pose, Stella victoriously raises a large bottle of Cook's.

Her libations elicit praise from everyone but me, Lynch, and Alvin, who is silently hunting atop the warm black asphalt. Using his advantageous position to look up her dress, he stealthily captures ill-lit stills of Mia's vast wonders while she's yelling "Woooooo!" at the hoisted bubbly.

I knew Stella would bring booze. And if she didn't, someone else would have. This was inevitable, yet I still feel conflicted about permitting drinking at my party. If I don't put a stop to it immediately, everyone will be drunk, annoying, and potentially vomitous for all Premieres to come. Bagging her poison, Stella commandeers Lynch's ice cream and shares a simultaneous lick with Mia. *Though I wouldn't want to be seen as an ungrateful, oppressive host.* Their tongues circle the creamy pink—they almost touch. *Or discourage any loss of sexual inhibition.* I decide to overlook the thoughtful gift of champagne. A pink drop drips from the communal cone. Mia looks down to check her dress and, sadly, Alvin is caught.

"Little pervert!" Her furry boot kicks at his ribs. The baby pap screams like a kitten.

"C'mon! Don't Stifle!" Reaching out with his camera, unharmed and unashamed, he continues snapping. "Don't stifle. I'm a fucking artist, baby." *Flash, flash.* "I'll make you famous." *KICK.* "Owe! Cunt! " He laughs. "Don't be a bitch—"

Extending my hand, I pull him up. After wiping his black palms on his sleeveless *Too Fast for Love* shirt, Al takes off his shades to inspect his art. He shows Mia the shots of her own ass. She giggles. And I'm ready to go.

"Well, now that we're all here ... Shall we?" Grinning over his brother's camera, Lynch gives two thumbs up. I command, "Friends, if you would all be so kind as to follow us, we shall escort you into our new home!"

"You bought a house?" Mia throws up the horns. "Hell yeah! Michael Massi Cribs!"

Shaking his head, Lynch points across the street to the dark four stories. "We're going in there."

"No way, we're gonna watch fucking *Breakfast Club* in the fucking Palace?" Cramming his sentences into one breath, Alvin takes off toward the secret door. "I fucking love this place. I knew it. I knew you'd be into it Mike. It's totally fucked and creepy!"

In the center of a quavering streetlight halo, Alvin stalls, turns back, and waves. "Come on fuckers! I know how to get in!"

Chapter 13

We're gathered outside our secret entrance. Anticipation crawls back and forth between us, jumping to and from each aspiring Filmgreat. Alvin pries open the leafy mouth. I squeeze through the serpentine ivy, guiding Stella by the hand. The rest of my honored guests follow. The heavy mouth of the mystical portal snaps shut, and we all stand inside the cool lounge. Our new lifestyle begins now. We all sense the elevation.

"What the hell is this? I thought we were going to watch a movie? Are there spiders in here!? Or RATS?" Mia clings to Lynch. "OMFG. Are there fucking rats?"

"I think rats are cute." Seemingly speaking to herself, Stella curiously inspects the boarded front door. Alvin offers her his back.

"I like rats too. Rodents are fucking tits!" He crouches. "Hop on, let's go upstairs."

A filthy, powder-pink vermin, perched upon Stella's shoulder, gnaws on the gobstopper beads of her plastic necklace.

"No, no rats." I rush over to reign in the pony. "And we're not going upstairs. We're going down there." I point to the candle lit stairwell.

"You guys, this is great!" Cruz, already descending, sounds like a realtor checking off a list of innovative features. "I love the candles. The place is creepy … so I am a little afraid … and since we broke in I feel a little guilty too. … Oh my god, it's like church!"

"*Dios mio* it is!" Volta crosses himself. "Let us pray!"

The Boys bow their heads in mock piety. Weaving past them, I lead the procession down the Path of Prayers, across the ballroom, and up to the worn velvet wall. Lynch parts the curtains. Echo and the Bunnymen greet us.

"Alright kiddies, come on." Ushering our guests onto the stage, he steps on my lines. "Welcome to The Palace Theatre!"

I would have delivered a far better declaration. But it's fine. Finally, everyone is inside.

....

Running and launching from a couch's arm, Alvin flips into Heaven. I stifle a gasp. I can't have mattress diving. I can't have the kid killing himself. Death is the death of a party. Stella lands safely next to him. Her skirt bunches up and her pink panties remind me: a good host would join his guests in such revelry. Gently, I fold and drape my coat over inflated green plastic, take a running leap, and gracefully soar over her wrinkled jersey dress. Stella shrieks. I crash down on Al. A dog pile ensues.

Floating on air, we seven Filmgreats are a buoyant ball of laughter, grunts, faux-fur, and freedom. From beneath a Calvin-Klein-scented construction worker with an unidentifiable boob pressed to my throat, I see Lynch standing in front of the wall screen. Holding his remote control, he's grinning at our pile with pride.

"Come on man!" I creak. "Be the cherry!"

With a bounding dive, he tops off the sundae. A collective groan of compression heaves out of our flesh mound and we all squirm free. The pile-survivors wriggle up to admire the ambience of our theatre. I grab my coat and smooth my suit. Once I'm less wrinkled, I excuse myself. I've gotta lubricate my pipes before my opening speech.

"Mike, this place is amazing!" Slinking over to the mini-fridge, Stella moves in close to adjust my bangs. I smell cotton candy. "I never thought that it would be this cool. It's so street. Like Banksy or something... "

Finishing a long carbonated pull of Italy's finest, I choke. "Thanks!" I've already exceeded her expectations. Her first impressions shan't be hindering the sexually active status of our relationship. "I knew you'd appreciate our artistry."

"Let's celebrate!" With a bang, Stella turns all eyes on her. Raising her Cook's, she begins a great performance of popping the cork and filling red cups with the frothing champagne.

MK serves the drinks, my guests begin poisoning their minds and bodies, and I follow the hostess back upstage.

"Lynch and I thought it was time that we all had our own thing here. ... For once we'll have something cool to do. You know? We all deserve it."

"Well, I LOVVVVVE it!" Cradling her bottle like a little girl loving her favorite doll, Stella plops herself onto a pile of furry red pillows in Heaven.

"Me TOOO!" Mia falls next to her. The Twins concur, giving me identical sex smiles.

Secretly, Alvin captures the moment on digital. Fixing my hair, I throw my arm around MK and suck in my cheeks to make for better candid shots. When Stella puts on her modeling face, I know that she's noticed the baby pap too.

"Yeah, this place turned out to be pretty killer, right?" Lynch, hollering from the Play Station, spins the DVD on his finger and turns off Bat for Lashes. "Wait 'til you guys see it when I get the movie up there."

"I'm totally impressed already!" Mia says, skipping up to the soundboard. She hugs my partner from behind and marks her words with a kiss. As her mouth lingers on his neck, she absently looks at me. I find this both creepy and arousing.

"Hey fuckers, what the fuck?" Pulling me from the uncomfortable moment of discordance, Alvin emerges from the wings in search of the female attention that he's been digitally documenting. "Let us not forget who told you guys about this fucking goldmine!"

I take his camera. I review the shots of me. *I look good.* "It's true. ..." I turn to the girls. "If it wasn't for Alvin we'd had never known about this place."

Squeezing next to Ash, he drops his head onto her shoulder. "Aren't I killer?"

Immediately, The Twins ditch the cuddly longhair to join Stella on the mattresses. Al follows. I take my speech position.

Upstage center, in front of Heaven, I stand, facing the girls. Between The Twins, Stella lies, watching me attentively. She's grinning. Clicking my Zippo, I look down at three peering feline faces while The Boys bounce onto a purple love seat by the PA. The room falls silent. *Click, click. Click, click. I hope my hair's not* a mess.

"You're hot," Stella mouths, and I fall in love with the night, even before it puts out.

"Mr. Lynch, are you ready?"

Sitting downstage on green plastic, snuggled up next to Mia's huge stripped butt, he points to the catwalk with two thumbs, his hair, and flair. "Yes I am Mr. Score! Take it away!"

"My dear friends. ..." Channeling Leo Di. I spread my arms, splaying my palms like Titanic. "Lynch and I cordially welcome you to our very first Premiere party!"

"Woooo!" Mia toasts and the rest follow, raising their sloshy red cups.

"Now! ..." I hoist my Pellegrino. "We invite you to sit back, relax, have some popcorn and San P. ... or mind-numbing libations if you must ... and enjoy this very private, exclusive screening of ... *The Breakfast Club!*"

Lynch casts the movie across our screen. The room applauds and with the Universal Studios earth spinning behind me, I take my first bow.

....

Nestled into the host's position—between two girls—I watch our private screening glow as we all take ownership of The Palace, shouting out classic quotes in unison. "YES!" "NO!" "Eat my Shorts!" My guests gulp champagne and I keep an eye on them to make sure that no one pukes on my stage. When super-sized Principal Vernon begins to caution Bender against mouthing off, Stella pops up into the projection.

"Don't mess with the bull young man or you'll get the horns." She lip-syncs, perfectly imitating him, and throwing up the horns to her equally horny, intoxicated audience.

This first solo of hers receives applause, but her following enactment of Molly Ringwald's lipstick trick really wows us. With her cleavage and a splash of red, Stella becomes the star of the evening.

The theatre fills with cheers and whistles. I don't particularly care for being overshadowed on my big night, but putting on lipstick with those boobs is just too good to pan. I join in the uproar.

"Hot, hot, hot." I chant along with The Boys, and the acclaimed actress resumes her position next to me. Smooching my face, she leaves a classic lipstick mark on my defined cheekbone.

"Hey Al!" I strike a cheek-to-cheek pose with tonight's star. "Put this on the wire!"

Momentarily pausing his conversation at the back of the mat-tresses, Alvin flashes a few stills then proceeds to ask Ash about the secret needs of older women. She's two years his senior.

As the film flickers on, Stella and I remain pressed against each other until the 'stoned and dancing' scene of the Hughes classic hits. I'm up first to try the Anthony Michael Hall. The Twins rise with Mia to do the Molly Ringwald and Stella does the Ally Sheedy—the dance that ends with her on her knees. I pull her back up from the floor so she can join Al and I for the Bender shuffle. In a line, the three of us slide through the projection as I scan the stage for Cruz and Volta. I haven't heard a single obscenity from them since the lipstick trick.

Stuck to together in plain view, sucking each other's tongues, The Boys are silenced by a kiss. I've never before seen them make out in public, or anywhere else for that matter. For a fleeting moment, I'm jarred by my first real exposure to live boy-on-boy action, but the sight quickly becomes totally fabulous. *Those are the first activities ever to be performed on that couch: the first ever in this theatre*. I watch. Twisting across the stage, I witness the arousing revolution. I reel in the advent of unrestraint. Then Cruz and Volta jump up to start shakin' it.

Inspired, I tackle Stella back into Heaven and we start a full-length feature make-out session of our own. The Boys, Mia, and Lynch pair off to separate couches. The Twins and Alvin flop down next to us. Stella begins unbuckling my belt. I slowly work my hands up her dress then she drops me for Anthony Michael Hall. Casting my Producer into purgatory, The Premiere's It girl robs me of the boob I was so lovingly squeezing and leaves me empty handed. She grabs Cruz, drags him in front of the screen, and plants a Ringwald kiss on tonight's stand-in for Bender.

"Off my man *puta*! Off my man!" As we all applaud, Volta sends a friendly flurry of popcorn toward the touching ending.

Erection crawling, I snatch up kernels before Stella's feet can crush them into the blankets. On the edge of the bouncy mattress, I sit dumping the yellow bits into an almost empty Solo cup of flat champagne. When Bender walks away on Sherman field, we all join him in celebration, simultaneously thrusting our fists into the still basement air with a cheer. Though such theatrics would typically ruin a picture, down here it seems necessary.

Reclaiming upstage center, I bow through the scrolling projection as Lynch runs back to the PA. He unplugs plugs. He switches switches. He gives me two thumbs up.

I disco-point to the sandbags. "Let the after party begin! Let's dance!"

The movie goes silent and "Don't you Forget About Me" becomes Dead or Alive.

Chapter 14

"She ate your butt?"

"Yeah, man." Sitting in our sunny booth at The Grounds, Lynch grins. Last night after the dance party, while I walked Stella home, he and Mia stayed behind to enjoy some special features.

"Was it ... weird?"

"Totally!" He takes a satisfied gulp of his coffee.

"Wow." I'm fascinated. "Was your butt ... clean?"

"She didn't complain."

If anyone attempted to eat my butt and found it inedible, I'd have to kill myself. Or them, so they couldn't tell anyone. Sipping my iced Sencha, hoping to see Becca, I watch the front door as Lynch flips the brass locks of his guitar- case. His 1950s acoustic has 'FAIL!' sprayed across its black body in white.

"Man, Mike, that place is the best," he says. "We're gonna stay there again tomorrow night for a sequel. I'm hoping that she'll finally —"

"Wait. You spent the night?"

"*Her* idea." Looking up from his fretting fingers, he smiles proudly. "I didn't even have to suggest it."

"Man, I'm really glad that you're finally getting to touch it, but we can't be living in there or we're gonna get caught. And I cannot get caught..." I pop a scone crumble into my mouth. "For this or anything else."

The front door opens. The bearded guy in the Neurosis shirt is coming off of his smoke break to roast and disappoint me by not being Becca.

"C'monnnnn. Mike..." Putting a bluesy melody to intrepidness, Lynch sings, "You really need to settle. You're still seventeen. What's the worst that can happen?"

He won't rehearse, but he'll play his guitar in the fucking coffee shop. Grabbing the Gibson's neck, I mute his chording.

"You wanna be locked down in this town forever?" Panicking, I pull my Zippo from my jeans. "You know what they'll do if they catch us? We're talking Cal Trans levels of confinement. *Click, click. Click, click.* We're talking zero internet—"

"Dude, no one has even looked at that place in a thousand years." He leans the guitar against the bench. "But if you're gonna freak, I'll just bring Jamie back to my place." Slipping it from his breast pocket, Lynch whisks my iPod across the sheen of our table and smiles. "Thanks. We listened to Portishead the whole time.'

"Nice. Nineties sex."

"Yeah, that's what she's into.''

I turn away. Nobody has come in the back door. We're still two of four customers—none of whom are Becca.

"Hey..." Lynch reclaims my attention. "When are we gonna do the next party? Yesterday totally fixed The Sunday Problem don't ya think?"

The Sunday Problem: the metaphysical oppression and defeat embodied by Sundays. Somehow Sundays always feel weightier— like the gravity has been turned up, like the hand of the Christian God is firmly pushing down on our heads to prevent any fun from being had.

"Wow, totally. I guess capital H.E. can't find us down there. Sunday it is."

A flash of platinum disappears down the flier-covered hallway next to the pastry case. All my body hair does an impression of Lynch's head. And I too stand.

"You leaving?" He grabs the remainder of my scone. "You look rattled?"

Picking up his guitar, I strum the one chord I know until a soon-to-be freshman friend of Alvin's comes out of the bathroom. His hair is blonde but long—nothing like Becca's. And he's wearing flip-flops.

"Hey Sandles!..." The seasick strings resound as I throw my hands. "That's the ladies' room!"

"The men's is broken dude." Confused, the kid calmly defends himself to the rest of The Grounds and me. "What the fuck does it matter to you anyway, Mike? Is that where you keep your coffin?" Flipping me off, he walks out the front door.

Collectedly I un-strap the guitar, grab my skate, and then face Lynch's shocked expression.

"Excuse me. Slash. What the fuck was that bathroom drama?" He laughs. "You, like, *only* use the girls' room."

"I know. But, that kid didn't just throw the best party that this town's ever seen. And did you see his shoes? What gives him the right to my exclusive bathroom privileges? Fuck him. I'm gonna go work on the next invitations."

Chapter 15

It's too hot. Everything is dry. And still. If I didn't have the sense to favor wearing black, the subtle sweat marks in my pits would be completely visible; I'd have to go straight home for fear of embarrassing myself in front of Stella. Instead, I'm stopping for refreshments on the way to her house.

Stashing my deck behind the ice machines, I stroll into air-conditioned convenience. At the end of the aisles, I open the cold case. A frigid gust hits me, like a Dentyne Ice commercial and I bury my arms deep in the racks. Embracing soda, chilling, hoping the Pepsi in my pits will dry up their slightly discolored sweat circles, I can sense my judgment. I step back and check myself out in the security mirrors. My shirt looks the same. And my nemesis is vibing me. *Typical.*

Though I've never stolen anything from the 7-eleven, the guy at the counter always thinks I'm going to shoplift. I find his suspicion totally offensive so, knowing very well that he's Indian I make it a point to speak Spanish to him whenever I buy anything. Without fail, this causes him to pound the counter and insist, "I've told you I am NOT Mexican!" I reply, "That's racist!" And he totally falls apart. It's pretty cool.

Laughing at today's agitated defense to my standard accusation, I purchase my mini San P. bottle, bid the clerk *"hasta pronto"* and exit.

Cruising down the middle of the street, I call Stella. It goes straight to voicemail: *"I'm a free bitch, baby,"* the American female pop star informs me. Maybe she's still sleeping. I pocket my phone,

Pop Kids | 79

and skate through Fountain Square. *I hope Barbara is gone.* Last night in The Pink Room, when I found out that her Mom was home, Stella said she'd turn up some music; that Barbara wouldn't hear us, nor care if she did; that I had nothing to worry about. I disagreed, re-buttoned my Ksubis, went home, and comforted myself with new Vanessa Hudgens nudes.

Rounding the corner to Reisling, I avoid a sprinkler cascade, and a silver Prius slowly whirs by. It's blasting something that sounds like a video game. And the driver seems lost. Curiously, I tail the eco-friendly ride until it crawls to a stop directly in front of Stella's house. I can't believe she already has another guy over. I pound my push-foot to the pavement. Only hours ago I was feeling her up on that porch. I pop up my board. If I'd known that I was to be replaced so promptly, I would've just asked Katy Perry to join us last night.

It's fine.

I march up the sidewalk. The disco dies and the door of the import opens. What steps out is horrifying. He's at least six feet tall, wearing white jeans that are way too tight, a florescent yellow scoop-necked tank top that is way too baggy, about six necklaces that are way too long, puffy silver high-tops that are way too silver and, to perfectly complete his look, the man has put his hair in pigtails—the cheerleader kind, not the braided Willie Nelson kind. Pigtails, I swear to Moz. When he takes off his aviators to address my gaping mouth, I can tell that he's at least twenty-one. *Oh, and shockingly good looking too.*

"Hello hello!" With a ravishing smile, he slings a neon canvas bag over his shoulder. "You here to see Sarah too? " He's too poorly dressed to be this good looking.

"Who?" Flawlessly, I feign surprise as I notice the residency to my right. "Oh, Sarah *Johnson*. Oh no, no. I was just on my way home and stopped to check out your ride. I love the Prius man. They're so green."

The pigtailed one grins. A screen door creaks. And the sound of pattering Havaianas adds to my discomfort.

"Donnnnnnnny!" Running down the walkway, Stella throws her arms around him.

Donny. The DJ. Of course.

Barbara's daughter is wearing tiny yellow velour shorts, a white wife beater, a black bra, and yellow flip-flops. Her toenails are freshly painted pink. A small strip of her belly is showing and her shorts have the word 'pink' swooping across her captivating ass, in pink. Thinking invisible thoughts, standing here all young, unannounced, and car-less, right next to Big D, I hope, for the first time ever, that she doesn't notice me.

"Mike! What are you doing here?" she asks. "Did you guys meet? Donny's gonna teach me how to spin! Kickass right?"

The DJ wraps himself around her from behind. And smiles at me.

"Oh, yeah, that's cool. " Eyeing her, hoping to catch a look of concern, a sense of awkwardness, a tinge of guilt, I reach for my lighter. "I thought that most DJs did pool parties during the day, but that's cool that you've got so much free time Donny."

"It's Donovan, my brother."

"Oh, I though it was Donny. She calls you Donny. Can't I?"

"And who are you again?" Smiling benevolently, he releases her from his toned arms and extends his hand. "I still don't think that we've officially met."

He's too amiable. He must be stoned. *I bet you're stoned Donny. Fucking stoner*. Giving me a raised eyebrow, Stella introduces us.

"Donovan, this is my friend Mike." I shake hands as her *friend* Mike internally cringes at his belittling title. I would have expected 'my super-lover,' 'my reason-to-wax.' "He threw that amazing party that I was telling you about."

My grip freezes. I turn to her, aghast. I can't believe she told this random (albeit very good looking) guy about The Premieres. My stomach moths flutter at the breach of secrecy.

"Oh! You're Score Massi!" Donny grins, and I drop his hand. It's one thing for someone from our town to have heard preceding tale of me, but this guy doesn't even live here. He lives in the city. Where there's real life. He pats my shoulder. "The girls speak quite highly of you, my brother."

"That makes sense." *Not really.*

Popping his trunk with his keys, Donny walks back to the car. "I'm gonna load in some stuff okay Sarah Baby."

"Sure Babe." Looking into my aviators, she offers, "You know, you can call me *Stella* Baby if you want."

I share a smile with my sister Filmgreat.

"No worries." Burdened with metallic duffle bags, shiny backpacks, laptops, and little speakers, Donny lugs the gear in the house.

Stella and I are alone. I clack down my board, step onto it, and push once.

"So you wanna be a DJ now? I thought you wanted to be an actress ... or a model—"

"Yeah, why not? It will be fun." She catches me as I roll into her. "And anyway, DJ, actress, model ... it doesn't matter how you get there. It just matters that you get there. Right?" Still holding onto my waist, she smiles.

I glance at something that fell from the Prius before addressing my true concern. "That guy's not gonna tell anyone about the parties right?" Stepping off, I kick my board to her front lawn. "We can't have all of San Francisco showing up—"

"Mike..." She pulls me back into her hum. "You really think people are going to come here from SF for, like, anything?"

"Donny doesn't seem to mind traveling to be entertained."

Intertwined on the sidewalk, smirking, sharing breaths, we squint at each other until Stella breaks the stalemate. Slipping her arms up the back of my shirt and her tongue into my mouth, she wins the battle of will. Her sex buzz rattles the windows of the hybrid. Her neighbors hissing sprinklers skip. And I taste artificial watermelon. As my drop-neck tee bunches and her cool belly presses to mine, I slide my hand beneath the *in* in 'pink' to discover that Stella is panty-free. Delighted, ignoring the creak of the screen door, I continue to search her shorts while Donovan tromps by. When Stella eventually shuts down the show, she stares me down.

"Don't worry so much Mike. No one is going to ruin your party. And, anyway, no matter what happens, I know that you can handle it." Removing her arms from my waist, she adjusts my hair. "You've got what it takes, sexy."

"Yeah, Mike!" DJ Prius slams his trunk. With pigtails bouncing he plods toward us and takes Stella's hand. "No worries, my brother." He walks her into the house.

She doesn't wave, she doesn't say goodbye, and she doesn't look back.

Standing on the curb, I stare at the screen door. "I Kissed a Girl" comes bouncing out. I grab my board from the thirsty grass and squat to inspect the gutter by the passenger door of the Prius. I can't believe what I find: 'Murder King.' How disappointing. Donny's carnivorous conscious isn't as sparkling as his smile. Leaving a small breakfast-croissant-wrapper-fire behind me, I push toward the hills, humming something about cherry ChapStick.

Chapter 16

To further secure his place below me on the evolutionary scale, Frank has decided to grill tonight. And though he has prepared one of his exquisite vegan patties for me, it's hard to stomach when I'm sitting at table surrounded by flesh eaters.

"You're a murderer," I accuse my father. "I'm afraid to even sit here with you ... and to sleep at night. How do I know I'm not next on the Massi-man-grill?"

"Tell you what Mike..." Tearing mint leaves into his Ice Tea, he bargains. "I'll stop eating steak when you stop killing spiders."

Absurdity: comparing cows to spiders. Arachnids are pure evil. They're like a cigarette manufacturer or a terrorist. They're organized religion on eight legs.

"I hate spiders."

"And I hate cows." The ice in his glass clinks as he sips.

"It's not the same, Dad. You know it's not the same."

I spread fresh sun-dried tomato pesto onto my Cherie Cherie rosemary focaccia bun and bite into my homemade Shiraz marinated burger. Like a mime that's found his voice, Frank begins dramatizing his argument with gestures.

"I don't see how it isn't! Spiders have eyes! Eight of them! They're not plants! And that wood spider you killed the other night probably has children at home that are still waiting for their father to bring home the flies." Covering his mouth, he turns to Gina and gasps at the horrible thought. Gina shakes her head and forks a tomato from her salad.

"Okay Dad, it was self-defense. That spider was the size of your steak." I point at the massacre pooling on his plate.

"Well that raises another good point!" Conducting his speech with a bottle of A-1. Frank insists, "At least I eat what I kill! You don't even eat the spiders!" He snatches one of my baked thick-cut fries and bites it in two. "I think you should start eating spiders, Mike."

"You two are ridiculous," Gina intervenes. Confiscating his bottle, she tightens the cap, sets it on the far end of the table, and points at me. "You. Leave your father alone. You had sushi last week and eat calamari every Vigilia. *Marrone*..." She settles back in, and sips her Cabernet. "So, rehearsals should be starting soon. "

"They don't start until school's back in. Remember? I told you. Mr. Nalon is having the set built in Hess."

"Oh, I don't remember you telling me that."

Gina likes to forget when I tell her things that she doesn't want to hear, and insists that rehearsals keep me "busy and out of trouble."

"Yeah, I told you." I scoop up dripped pesto with my last fry. "You just said 'oh, okay'."

"Oh, okay." She offers me a bowl of greens. "Did Barbara John-son's daughter get the lead again this year?"

"Actually, Sarah didn't even audition. I asked her why and she said 'high school musicals are so high school.' She wants to spend more time making videos for her blog."

I steal Frank's last fry. He motions to stab me with his steak knife.

"I did meet the female lead though. She just moved here. She seems pretty cool."

At this small, accidental, complimentary description of Becca, Gina Massi's face lights up like a church dipped in Sterno. I rarely mention girls at home and make it a point never to do so in a posi-tive light. Though she regularly cautions me, "If you ever get some young girl pregnant, I'll put my head in the oven," she loves babies and wants grandchildren. But because both my parents are con-vinced that my brother is gay, Gina is counting on me to procreate. She is, thus, conflicted and whenever I mention a girl other than Stella, this conflict results in her matronly excitement.

"Really? What's her name? What is she like? Is she Italian?"

"Her name's Becca." Standing, I clear my place. "She's very blonde, and I think that her last name is Rose, so don't start making any wedding invitations."

Frank chuckles at my preemptive defense.

"Maybe it's short for Rosetti, Mike. Ya never know!"

Laughing, I pull his homemade sorbetto from the freezer. My fingertips stick to the frozen cardboard.

"Oh, that is NOT what I meant Michael. I was just thinking that it would be fun to have another family in town to share recipes with." After insisting that I don't eat straight out of the carton, she huffs, "It would be nice to have grandchildren someday, you know. But if you're not giving me any, I guess I'll just die never knowing what it's like. That could be any day now too … I'm no spring chicken."

She's forty.

"Mom, Joey is not gay. And could you please not hurl me into seventeen-year-old paternity?" I rinse our ice cream scoop and dig into the pint. "I've told you, I'm never getting married or having kids. The whole concept of marriage is obsolete … and this world has yet to prove itself deserving of my progeny."

"That reminds me!" In that mother-sing-song voice she says, "Someone has a birthday coming up! Eighteen!" Then points her spoon at me. "Should I still invite Pinky this year? Or is the concept of a birthday cake obsolete?"

Every year, Gina makes a red velvet cake shaped and decorated to look like a cat's face. Every year it comes out pink instead of red. Its name is Pinky. Frank likes to think of it as a mystical, Clausian feline that brings me my gifts through the cat door on the Eve of October 10. I like to think this as well.

"Of course, not." Kissing her cheek, I serve her a purple scoop in a frescoed arancio dish. "I'll always love Pinky."

Squishing my earbuds into my head, I clean the entire kitchen to the sound of my latest 'dishwashing playlist' before putting my own body through a similar rigorous ritual. In the shower with my new olive fruit oil Kiehl's conditioner stimulating my follicles and mind, I begin contemplating the first 'Premiere playlist.' The other night at The Palace, after a Marina and the Diamonds song ended, my iPod shuffled to some interview with two British guys. It killed the dance floor. I can't let that happen again. Especially if Becca is there.

I still want to invite her.

Thinking of her side-boob, I lather vigorously. I don't find shower masturbation sensually ideal, but it's the least messy place to spread my joy.

Bitter product drips down my face. I rinse my mouth, rub my eyes, and find myself high above downtown LA, stretched out in a cabana, atop a steaming, sudsy, spot-lit rooftop pool. Becca and Stella are naked and besides my McQueen skull tie, I am wearing nothing but their two scented bodies. World famous DJ Steve Aoki spins "Ghosts 'n' Stuff" by London's own Deadmau5, and Leo DiCaprio peeks his head in through the white, skull-printed, chiffon curtains to compliment my performance. Great work Score. *When he says my name, I spread glittering joy everywhere. Sparkling, it floats into the sky, filling it with stars.*

I turn off the faucet. Grabbing a towel, I wrap it around my waist and quickly pad to my room. Inspired and moist, I sit down at my Mac. I name a playlist 'Premiere Party Sunday, August 31.' I download and drag in "Ghosts 'n' Stuff," then research the artist. Deadmau5 isn't from England. He's from Canada. Wikipedia says so. *It's fine.* His beats sound British. I'm leaving the track in.

Chapter 17

I awake at 3:14 in the afternoon. I check my phone. Nothing from Stella. With a few hours to spare before work, I get up, grab a scone from the bakery bag that Gina wrote my name on, brew some Sencha, then take them both back to bed. Contemplating which movie to show next, I open my Mac and begin surfing celebrity sites. Overall, I find these online tabloids loathsome but I feel that I must study them. Daily. They're educational. They're helping me prepare for the day I'm a primary focus of Perez. Plus, they give me something to talk about with Stella. Forwarding her a new candid of Kate Moss, I type, *"Breeding might not be totally unacceptable if every mother could keep this figure. I still totally would."* I hit send then click through pics of a Nicki Minaj nip-slip.

As I make my way down the porn hole, Lynch messages me with a link to a video. In the short, Alvin, wearing nothing but a yellow bikini top, back flips off of a coastal deck railing, through the night, and into a pool. A stew of tattooed guys and girls receive him, cheering from the packed adjoining hot tub. The ocean is their backdrop. They're all topless. *I wonder if they're all bottomless.* I watch the video three times before leaving my kudos amidst a string of comments.

As his behind the scenes laughter foretold, Lynch is with his brother. In his message, he's attached a picture of himself standing in the hot tub with a topless girl posing on his shoulders. His stringy hair is plastered to his head. He's giving two thumbs up, grinning like a water-loving cat that swallowed the canary. The canary looks like an extremely young Cameron Diaz. Below the shot he's typed, 'I miss you.' Trying to suppress my feelings of being left out, I lament the terrible looking wreath of black flowers tattooed around the girl's navel, then type 'Something About Mary' into PornoTube's search engine.

After spending two minutes in web heaven with a homemade video featuring a buxom college girl named Mary, I shower off the joy, put together an outfit—black Ksubis, black short sleeve button up, black skinny tie and black Chucks—and take the long way to work. I wheelie through Fountain Square, wave at Gina through the window of Cherie Cherie, turn up Reisling, and see DJ Prius's Prius. It hasn't moved since yesterday. *I can't believe he spent the night.* I dial Stella. I hear *"I'm a free bitch, baby."* I bang on her front door. Donny answers. I am horrified. He's wearing Joey's shirt.

"Hey my brother! Glad you came back!" His snow-white smile gleams as his stupid, luxurious, unleashed hair crawls beautifully over my brother's vintage tee.

"Donny! Still here, huh?" I peer over his shoulder. The Pink Door is shut. "Stella must be a virtual Guetta by now with all this DJ training. Over twenty-four hours? Wow. You two gonna hit Ibiza soon? I see you've let your hair down."

Propping his arm above me on the door's frame, he tosses his mane. My shirt rides high on him. From it, an inch of a happy trail crawls under the low riding waistband of his distressed grey jeans. He's no longer wearing those awful necklaces.

"Yep, still here!" He looks better today, leaning in the setting sunlight, all rock n' roll. Still awful, but better. "We didn't actually work too much last night."

"Oh no, why's that?"

Prius squints.

"Too much sex." Putting on his aviators, he produces a cigarette from some nether region in his hair. He lights it, takes a drag, and then squeezes my shoulder. "But it's never too much with Stella, right?" Exhaling, he grins. "She's a good girl."

"That she is ... "

As he stands in my clothes, having a smoke after a full night of banging the girl whom I've spent years trying to establish a sexual relationship with, I try to keep my cool. But I just can't avoid the issue any longer.

"Hey, man." I point to his chest. "Great shirt. Where'd you get it?"

"Oh yeah. Weird. Weird." Shaking his head, looking down, he addresses the garment. "Actually, Jamie from The Kills left it at my place. It's his. Weird, right?"

I just saw a picture of that guy on WWTDD. He dates Kate Moss. If Donny's not lying, she may have touched that shirt. I want to smell it. He's gotta be lying.

"Yeah. Weird," I wave away the smoke.

Prius stares at the tee, pulling it taut away from his lean torso. The cherry of his cigarette is far too close to the sacred cotton.

"So, is Stella still asleep? I lent her something. I've gotta get it back."

"Oh, she's not here." He drops the endangered hem. "She got up early to get breakfast croissants with her mom. Now they're at a bake sale or something. They left a note... " He looks over his shoulder, as if expecting to see a Post-It fluttering around his hair. "You hungry? I'm about to make some pancakes with fresh huckleberries. Gluten-free, I make them with—"

"Wait, you're here alone?"

"Yeah," Taking another drag, he exhales. "You wanna come in?"

Kinda.

"Oh, no, no. Thanks man, no." I back-step, "I've gotta get to work. I'll text Stella and tell her that I came by."

"Don't bother. Her phone's in her room charging."

He follows me to the edge of the porch as I scurry down the steps, and hop on my board.

"If you wanna come by later we'll both be here!" He hollers. "I can make more pancakes! I've got tons of batter, my brother."

"Okay, thanks!" Escaping, flying off the curb, and bombing down the street, I yell back. "Maybe I'll get some syrup and come by."

Chapter 18

In the lobby, Shane is tearing tickets and wearing a nametag.

"Hey Mike, you here to see '*Attack of the Vampire Scarecrow*'?"

He giggles, tickled by his commentary on my aversion to skin cancer, my outstanding fashion sense, and my runway physique. Every time I see this animate action figure, he calls me a 'vampire scarecrow' and tells me to pump some iron and get some sun. We're friends. During our freshman year, Shane saved me from being beaten by one of his wrestling teammates. I'd made the mistake of trying to talk to a sweater girl that the smaller, yet still gigantic buffo had a crush on. Shane didn't know me at the time, but he's an unlikely sympathizer of fragile, sensitive, stylish, artistic-genius types such as myself. He wears self-tailored indie rock tees and power lifts to Antony and the Johnsons.

"Good variation Shane." His biceps strain to tear through the sleeves of his Death Cab For Cutie shirt as I ask, "You work here now?"

"Yeah, I heard that they were hiring. And I was bored."

"Oh. Well, welcome to the fun."

"Thanks! It will be great working together!" He directs some rich tourists to theatre number two.

"Yeah. So, I'll be in Booth Six." I walk down the matted red carpet then pause at the projection room door. "And you might want to get a tighter shirt."

"And you might want to do some pushups!" My new coworker's deep voice turns into his unsettling, falsetto laugh.

Shaking my head, I climb the stairs. Shane just doesn't under-stand. All the biggest celebrities are smaller in person.

....

Swollen huge, from having just accomplished eight pushups in the privacy of my dark shelter, I google the actor on the screen: Russell Brand is a vegetarian, a writer, and British. Katy Perry is his wife. Stella may have an uber-hip DJ but she'll be jealous when I'm hang-ing out with the Ameripop Star and her husband. Our friendship is inevitable. Russell and I have so much in common.

My phone buzzes.

"*Donny wants to know where his syrup is! Sorry I was gone! Let's hang out soon! <3*"

I stare at the words. The audience laughs. 22 minutes of delibera-tion pass and I write back, asking about Kate Moss and Joy Division.

Stella replies. "*I miss you!!!!*"

My stomach moths flurry. Impulsively, I type, "*Why don't you ditch the DJ, come to Booth Six, and get a new shirt?*"

She immediately responds, "*LOL! I love you. You're the best! XOXOXO*"

In this ragged chair, I sit staring at her text.

The clicks of the projector count the seconds. Then the minutes. Suddenly, two soft hands shield my eyes. "Guess who?"

It seems that having received no response to her written profes-sion of love was too much for Stella to handle. I turn around, with subdued sexy-cool. "Well I'm glad that you decided to come.*"*

"Hi! Shane let me in." Becca whispers and begins to pace the room. "It's cool in here. ... Moody." Turning back to me, she narrows her eyes. "I can't believe that you knew it was me."

Standing on the grey concrete in the flickering of the reel, she looks glorious. Her choppy asymmetrical A-line is bright white, lumi-nescent, defined by the contrasting shadows. Her green eyes cut as they question my sincerity. Their color is unearthly—they're like organic glow sticks formed in the crystalline waves of Hollywood Beach.

"When Shane surprises me he just kisses my neck," I whisper

back. "So I knew that you weren't him." Smiling, she suppresses what would have certainly been a huge laugh. I further whisper. "We don't have to whisper. They won't be able to hear us as long as we don't shout."

"Oh, okay." Padding over, Becca sits down and squeezes next to me. "As long as you're a gentleman, I promise that I won't scream." The corner of her mouth barely pulls into a subtle, lop-sided half-smile.

I can't tell if she's flirting.

"My dear, I'm always a gentleman." Trying to remain composed, I insist, "I'd never want to make you scream."

"That's good cuz I carry pepper spray." Looking around the room—at the film creeping from the trashcan, at the empty space beneath the steel shelves, at everything but me—Becca says, "But you're missing out." Her voice is rich. It sounds like vegan caramel. "I'm a great screamer."

She blinds me with her LED eyes. I want to act normally—to move in for some making out—but I can't. I just sit, staring, trying to interpret her vague signals.

"So, are you excited for the musical?" She slips out of her Vans. "It's gonna be my first lead."

"Oh, that's right! It's me and you this year." Perfectly feigning having forgotten our upcoming roles, I grin. "I hope you don't suck."

"Oh, don't you worry about me sucking, Mike. I've got a little experience."

She's got no makeup on, but Becca's thick dark lashes reach out sharply, enhancing her gemstone eyes. Her black Cheap Mondays are form fitting and her white, chewed-up zip hoodie is baggy. Leaning back in the velvet chair, she smashes down the mouths of her slip-ons with her feet, keeping them from telling secrets. Her toenails match her fingernails—unpainted.

"Did you do drama when you were down in ... where are you from again?" I ask, dying to know everything about the mysterious new beauty from tropical regions unknown.

"I'm from Newport, and I've been acting since I was seven." She crosses her legs toward me; her shoe flips, waffle-sole up. Listlessly, she begins fingering the tip of my tie. "Mom would take me out of school and drive me to the workshops and castings in Hollywood.

All the way up and back. Then a few weeks ago she drove me up to the middle of nowhere and stuck us here permanently. She needed to 'get away from everything'."

"I know *that* story," I huff. She drops her hand on my thigh. I straighten my back. Good posture is always attractive. "Is it just you and your mom?"

Quieting, Becca stands. She inspects the projector then pads further into the shadows. Her feet are bare, but her soles remain clean with each soft step.

"Yeah. It kinda sucks." The back of her long neck stands regally from her lowered hood as she runs her palms across the build-up table. "She got really weird after Dad was gone. First she got into plastic surgery, and then it was wine tasting ... which is really more like wine drinking. ... So..." She sighs, turns to me, and motions dejectedly at the clicking air. "Here I am."

"Fucking wine! That's why I'm here too!" I follow her to the table, hoping that she'll ask me to help her test its sturdiness. I boost myself up. "Did your dad stay in OC?"

She walks away. I follow her back to the seats.

"Well, sorta." Easing into the torn velvet, she casts her glowing greens up at me. "He got eaten by a shark."

"Fuck, no way." I sit.

"He was an ex-pro-surfer. ... One morning he left with a case of Corona and his board and never came back. So I guess if the shark is still in OC waters, then he is too." She shrugs. "I went vegan after the fish got him." She pulls a Red Vine from her sweatshirt pocket and snaps off a bite.

"So ... fuck." For the first time, I notice the small, round, black pin that is eternally stuck to her hoodie. On it is the silhouette of a great white. "He was eaten whole?"

"That's what Mom says." She waves the waxy whip. "But I've seen him a couple of times on the beach. He's always with this Hurley model that was three years ahead of me in school. We all act like we don't see each other." Chewing, she asks for a cigarette. "Do you smoke?"

"No, I don't. ... " *Moz. I hate kissing girls that smoke. But she's so runway. Maybe Shane has some gum I can give to her.* "You can't smoke up here anyway. It will wreck the film."

"I'd heard that you didn't drink or do anything. I only asked because you're always playing with that lighter... "

"Oh..." I hadn't realized that I was clicking. Dropping my Zippo, I pull my hand out of my pocket and set it on the armrest. "So you don't smoke either?"

"No. Just sometimes, when I drink. Which is, like, hardly ever. Or if I'm at a show or something—"

"Have you ever seen Morrissey? My brother has."

"No ... one of my friends back home has. I stole all my Smiths shirts from him."

"I steal all my shirts from my brother. It's pretty crazy how much we have in common. What other bands are you into?"

"You know, I pretty much like everything ... the usuals—"

"Joy Division? Depeche Mode?" *Why couldn't have you moved here sooner?*

"Totally, that kind of stuff. ... And Slayer."

"Wait, seriously?"

"You don't like Slayer?" She offers me a Red Vine. "I've never met a guy who doesn't like Slayer."

"Oh, they're cool. I'm just really only familiar with their radio hits." I slide the licorice into my chest pocket. "I pretty much exclusively listen to UK bands, like the rest of the stuff that you're into. I listen to Primal Scream every morning—"

"I know, Sarah told me. I love them too." She chews, "Do you like The Jesus and Mary chain?"

I wince. "Oh, no I'm not really a big fan of Jesus."

"They're not Christian, Mike." She grins. "They're great. The main Primal Scream guy was in JAMC first."

"Oh yeah? I'll check'm out! I just figured because of the name. ... But that's cool."

Click, click. Click, click.

"So, I think it's pretty cool that you don't do drugs." Curiously, Becca eyes my freshly reanimated Zippo. I immediately stop clicking and pocket it.

"Really? Thanks. Why? Do you? Not do drugs?"

"Not really. Rarely. Sometimes just for fun, but barely ever—"

The theatre below us erupts in laughter. It sounds canned. With a Red Vine trapped between her teeth, Becca stands and walks toward the window.

"I love these kinds of comedies." She peers down at the silenced crowd, sucking on the hollow tube. "Back home I'd see everything. And we'd go to midnight movies in Santa Monica and Hollywood. It was so fun. I really wish there was something like that here ... "

This is too perfect. I have to do it.

"Well, can you keep a secret?"

A black moth flies from my mouth. She turns. *It lands on her cheek. I rise to bat it away.* The reel scolds us, *tsk, tsk, tsk. It's fine.* Becca is trustworthy. She's vegan.

Tsk, tsk, tsk...

"Are you going to ask me if I want to see a dead body?"

"Um ... no." I cringe, creeped out by the weird suggestion. "I want to send you an invite to a party that I just started throwing ... promoting ... it's very exclusive. I think you're gonna love it ... but you really can't tell anyone about it, okay?"

"Well, I am honored that you'd like to include me Michael Massi." Speaking beautifully, she grabs both of my hands. "I promise. Your secret's safe with me." I return her grip. She pulls out her phone. "Give me your number. I'll text you my email."

This is going so very well. I save her name to my phonebook. She says, *"Guess it's over."* And, surprised, I look up from my tapping.

She's watching the credits of the film.

"Oh, shit. I thought ... excuse me." Dashing away, I quickly adjust the house lights.

"I should probably go anyway, Mike." As I scurry about the projection room, Becca slips on her shoes and glides toward the door. "Maybe I'll see you before the party..." She hovers at the top of the stairs. "At the Grounds or something..."

I shelve a reel and rush over to her.

"Okay, yeah. That would be fabulous." Lacking even half of my usual confidence, I stand with my hands shoved into my pockets. *Moz. I left my Zippo on the arm of the chair.* "I'm sorry. I've gotta set this up. But you can just walk into any of the movies downstairs—"

"Thanks, but I don't like to go to the movies alone."

Neither of us move. But somehow, suddenly, she's closer. She must have used her angelic powers to pull us together. Her lips are mere inches from my moth trap. She smells like cucumber ocean rain. We linger. I'm supposed to kiss her. I'm paralyzed with doubt.

Her signals are far less clear than what I'm used to with Stella. And her abrupt exit is throwing me.

Becca kisses her fingers. "Bye Mike." She presses them to my lips. "See ya soon." And disappears down the stairs.

I lick my tingling lips. They taste like candy. Quietly, I tell her echoing footsteps, "You can call me Score." Then my phone buzzes, calling me back to the booth.

After starting the film, I fall back into the chairs and think about my impressive party. Now that Becca is going to be there, the movie choice is even more important. I'm about to search IMDB for a Slayer documentary when I remember to check my new text. It's from Stella. It simply reads: ":)"

Chapter 19

I got up so early. I shouldn't have. I abbreviated my morning ritual, skipped the scone that Gina left me, pillaged a Jesus and Mary Chain shirt, put on my shades, and Somnambu-skated to The Grounds. Becca's not here. It sucks. Checking my messages, I wait outside for fifteen minutes before the Neurosis roaster finishes his morning cigarette and lets me in. After ordering a green tea from the beardy smoker, I stumble across the checkerboard tile and fall into my favorite booth. Next to me, on the warm bench, in a ray of light, lays a forgotten copy of US Weekly.

Sipping my eastern eye opener, I frequently glance up in hopes of seeing my vegan dream. I text Lynch, then begin searching for guidance from paparazzi'd panty-less pop stars and sharp dressed men. I flip through the mag. Its pages are totally marked-up. Certain socialites and leading men are circled in hearts, other actresses have blackened eyes—a few have had their heads smeared off with an eraser. I've just identified an Alexander McQueen suit on a Jonas, when a text buzzes in.

"I miss you!"

I respond. *"You're up!?"*

Three minutes later, Stella replies with a cell phone picture that she's taken of herself. She's topless in a pile of pink sheets. From out of my iPhone she stares up at me with a filthy smile. Her nipples barely make it into the frame. *"I'm not up. I'm still in bed."*

As I scan the neighboring tables to find someone with whom to share my nice surprise, Donny snubs his cigarette on the concrete sidewalk then strides in the front door. He's got on aviators, the same converse that I do, and a giant grin.

"*DJ Prius just walked into the Grounds.*" I type, "*He just littered outside.*"

Donny heads straight for my booth. He's dressed like someone who got eaten by the sixties and puked out by the late-seventies— but his bone structure is amazing. He sits down across from me.

"Morning Score! So good to see you my brother!" He smiles. His teeth are perfect.

"Morning, Donny." I force a yawn. "How are the DJ lessons? You up early to head home?" I glance back at the boobs in my lap.

"Lessons are good my brother, very good. Sarah's actually teaching me a few things." Removing his shades and raising both eyebrows he nods. "But we still haven't spent that much time on DJn'." Sighing, giving him a hidden-lipped smile, I shoot him an affirmative, one fingered point but he still finds it necessary to detail, again. "Too much sex."

"Gotcha."

"I just came to grab her drink. She's still in bed."

"Oh is she?" Blinded by the gleam of his teeth, I revert my eyes to my buzzing lap.

"*He's leaving Friday. I'll come visit you at work after he's gone. Mia and I think that the next Premiere should be Pulp Fiction XOXO.*" With this text, Stella has included a tight shot of her hand shoved into her pink panties—they match her nails.

"*That all sounds fabulous!*" I quickly type back, "*XOXO.*" Then look back up.

"Sorry man. Just working on the next party. It's a lot, you know?"

"No worries my brother." Prius nods then grins. I shift in my seat before trying to pull the truth out of Mr. Pigtails.

"Your teeth are really white Donny. You just brush a lot or are those veneers?"

"It's Donovan, my brother," he cordially corrects, "And, nah man, they're not veneers. They're mine. I use these." Fishing a chrome compact from his teeny smurf-blue shorts, he flips it open, pulls out a small white plastic cylinder, and tosses it to me.

Admittedly, I'm impressed. There's something right about a man who carries teeth whitener, even if his tie-dye tank top begs to differ. Wondering if green tea stains enamel, I roll the tube between my fingers. It says 'GO SMiLE.'

"I'm gonna go order." Donny stands. He doesn't push in his chair. "You want a scone Mike?"

I'm starving, but I'm holding out for banana bread.

"Oh, thanks my brother, but no. I've gotta watch my figure." I pocket the whitener then cordially correct, "Oh, and Donovan, it's Score."

"Okay my brother." Slyly, he agrees, as if we've just shared a secret. "I'll just get an extra one for myself then." He squeezes my shoulder before going to order from his fellow nicotine fiend at the bar.

I savor my Sencha and new nudes. Soon, Donovan returns with Stella's drink. I hope he doesn't plan on hanging out with me.

"Here you go Score!" He tosses one of two brown compostable bags onto my table. "I got you a vegan one. Sarah says you're trying to join the team."

I'm onto his game. Pastry surprises given, despite my expressed desire to diet, are obviously weapons of war. Prius wants me fat and unattractive to Starlets and is attacking me with carbs. I don't like his cunning. And I can't believe he's vegan.

"Hey, thanks a lot man!" Touched by the gift from the ethically handsome DJ, I exclaim, "I'll definitely want this tonight at work! That's really cool! Thanks so much."

"No worries. Can I get that US from you? It's Sarah's, yeah?"

The subscriber sticker has Barbara Johnson's name and address. I hand it over.

"Do you wanna stay a while Donovan?"

"Sorry my brother." He raises the icy, milky to-go cup. "But I gotta get this back to our girl. We should totally hang out before I leave though, yeah?" Sliding on his aviators, he insists, "You still owe me some syrup." And strolls to the door.

Outside, at the top of the front steps, Prius lights a magical hair cigarette then gets into his car. The muffled thump of dance music begins. The windows roll down. The American Spirit barely hangs from his beguiling lips. He looks almost, totally cool. He nods to me, then whizzes off—toward Reisling. I still hate his hair.

"*Que pasa*, party boy?" Cheerily yelling above a satanic cacophony, Volta leans out of the passenger window of the El Camino. Seeing me on the sidewalk in front of The Grounds, in the dry August heat, Cruz has pulled over the purple machine.

Between the well-groomed workers, Mia is checking herself out in the rearview. She ignores Cruz as he leans over her.

"The D-hole re-opened *Miguelito*! Come with."

Hogan's Donut Hole used to be our main hang. But one night we showed up and it was shut down. Supposedly, the owner was caught selling pot brownies.

"I'd love to but I'm watching my figure. And I'm on my way to work. You guys want me to sneak you into something?"

"Nooooo..." Throwing her head back, scrunching her face in an ecstatic tantrum, Mia pounds her fists against the broad shoulders at her side. "Boston Creaaaaaam!"

"Yeah *Guapo*," Cruz smiles, "We gotta get our sugar on. But maybe we'll come by later tonight. Get in, I'll drop you off."

I flip my skate. It clangs down next to the steel-toed boots in the bed, and I squeeze into the car. Even with one ass being as big as Mia's, the bench can seat four asses, which is perfect because I can't sit in the back. The wind would wreck my hair.

As we tear down Main, Mia squirms, my board rattles, and I strain to be heard.

"Hey, is this Slayer?" I yell.

The Boys laugh.

"That's cute *Culito*. This is Darkthrone." Sympathizing with my suffering, Volta reaches for the iPod. "You want me to put on some Morrissey?"

"Why don't you put on some Slayer? You got 'Raining Blood'?"

They laugh again.

"For real?" Cruz asks,

Mia desperately begs "*Gaga, Gaga, GA, GA,*" as her blonde locks flutter in my face.

"Yeah!" I insist, ducking back from the open window, "I kinda wanna check it out."

Informing me that the album is called *Reign in Blood*, Volta happily obliges.

"Ugggh, fuck you Mike!" Mia complains over the wind and death metal. "You were supposed to save me from this noise!" She socks Volta in the shoulder. "Why were you gonna change it for him but not for me?"

The Boys blissfully head bang. Cruz's slick hair stays perfectly in place.

"Come ON you guys!" She whines, "God, why can't you just listen to Britney like the rest of the gays in the world?"

"*Puta*..." Our driver happily fires back, "I taught Britney how to suck dick, just like I taught you, so just settle your big ass down and enjoy 'Angel of Death'."

We burn into the lot. Cruz screeches to a stop. I step onto the curb beneath the marquee. When I shut the door, as if her favorite fried food just took the stage at Wembley Arena, Mia throws up the horns. "Boston fucking cream!" She howls. The Boys join her in a "WOOOOOOOOH!" as they leave me standing in a fading harmonized guitar solo, waving away burnt rubber.

Chapter 20

My phone is buzzing like some tropical, bloodthirsty insect. I'd rather have malaria than be awake right now. Leaving a nest of brown fur on red sheets, Eddie flees from my bed as I grab the pestilent device. I recoil at its blinding screen. An illuminated picture of my choppy-haired partner gives me two thumbs up. It's too early to even breath.

"What the fuck is wrong with you? It's 8:00 am," I slur. I'm already re-deposited in the clutch of cameras, silk-screened onto my pillow. "Alvin didn't get eaten did he?"

"What? No. He's surfing. Sorry I didn't write back yesterday. My phone was dead. Thanks for the Stella nudes. Do you miss me? I miss you." There are squawks. I think he's calling from a seagull's nest. I rub my eyes. I might as well get up.

"There's all this shit happening." Dragging myself to my full-length mirror, I flex. *The pushups may be working.* "When are you coming back?" I do eyebrow raises.

"I'll be back by Sunday. What are we gonna show?"

"*Pulp Fiction.*" I smile, inspecting my teeth. They could be brighter.

"Killer! That should help me out. I'm gonna tell Mia that it was my idea. Hold on..."

A female voice woos him away from our conversation. I sit down at my pornography machine and open Becca's Model Mayhem page. There's a shot of her wearing a white bikini covered in black dorsal fins. She's in a sandy alley, leaning against a white wall that's been spray painted with ejaculating pink boobs. She's smoking. *Prop cigarette*. Lynch comes back to the phone.

"Hey, sorry."

"Becca came to visit me at work." I drag the photo into my Wish List folder, close my laptop, and begin wandering down the blurry hallway.

"Seriously!? Fucking Booth Six! Dude, did you touch it?"

"Hold on a sec..." I put him on speaker.

Rummaging through my brother's drawers, I recount my enthralling evening with the vegan wonder. When I finish, my partner is bewildered.

"Wait ... zero activities? Why? She's, like, beyond touchable."

"No. I know." I refold an old Britney Spears tour tee. "It was weird man. I just couldn't read her."

"What the fuck Mike?"

"It was still really cool though. ..." I drop a string of silicon beads, and pick up a soft black Smiths tee. "...She's really cool." The shirt is almost sheer from a million washes. *I've been looking for this!* "Wait 'til you see what I just found in Joey's—"

"Fuck you. I'm gonna pour Clorox on it if you don't invite Becca to the party. You can't worry about Sarah, man. If she sees that Becca is into you, it's only gonna raise the demand for quality Booth Six time with Score and then—"

"Lynch, Settle." I pull the shirt over my head and admire myself in the mirror. *Fabulous. I fit it perfectly*. "I'm gonna invite her."

....

I didn't think I could be more tired than I was this morning, but after a night of working behind the candy counter with a concessions creep who was 'fryin balls' I'm now both physically wrecked and emotionally drained. I feel like it is Sunday out. I need tea. I drag myself up my driveway. I can't wait for Lynch to get his car back.

With my steaming ceramic black-cat-head mug I sit down at my desk. I sip my Sencha. I plug my headphones into the Mac and start photoshopping to the sounds of The Jesus and Mary Chain.

After hours of reconstructing the original movie poster to contain the time and directions for maintaining the secrecy of the party, I flourish the invite with '*Score and Lynch Present Pulp Fiction*!' I critically stare at the screen. Something isn't right. Something is off. I juxtapose a picture of Lynch and myself under Uma's smoking cigarette: on the comforter, I'm crouching, and he's standing, giving two thumbs up. Contextually, we both resemble black-and white bed-elves, but I think our visages add the personality that the piece needed.

I save the file, and send out the invitation. I study WWTTD.com, Perezhilton.com, and TMZ.com. Then, knowing exactly where I should eat if I want the paps to catch me cheating on my celebrity girlfriends, I click down the porn hole to look for a nightcap. Forty-two seconds into a random fisting film featuring a green-eyed girl in a platinum wig, I release some joy. I clean my monitor, plug in my phone, and join Eddie in bed.

Chapter 21

Twelve hours of sleep can really do a boy right. It's Friday, DJ Prius is gone, and I'm in a great mood. Popping up my board, I compliment Shane on his Pains of Being Pure at Heart shirt then thank him for his scarecrow commentary before leaving him to tear the tickets for a pack of swooning twelve-year-old girls. He and I do make quite the handsome pair.

Upstairs, I struggle through nine pushups and set the movie rolling. Kicking back in the seats with my phone, I review the thrilled RSVPs. Everyone has replied except Stella. *It's fine.* She's probably planning to confirm in person, when she's here on top of me. She's probably on her way now. I start clearing the build-up table, happily humming something about watermelon ChapStick.

....

Miserably, I've almost finished closing up the booth when the picture of Stella, with her hand down her pink panties, pops up on my phone. *Finally.* Smoothly, I answer. "Why, hello…"

"*Haaaaaaay Babe!*" bursts through the still of the room.

Though she always sounds like a party, the sound of this particular soiree is giving me goose bumps. It's hard to say whether it's pure excitement or a survival instinct that's charging my skin, but my body's reaction to her is visceral.

"Are you downstairs?" In the background, a deep voice shouts, "Michael Massi." "Is that Shane? Tell him to let you in." I thought I was the only one left in the theatre. I lay a padded projector cover over the table.

"That was Donny. We're at his apartment. He's DJing this private party tomorrow in The Mission, so I decided to come with. Steve Aoki's spinning! And there's going to be an open bar! Amazing right?"

The booth grows darker as a pigtailed shadow eclipses my rising star.

"Yeah, that's pretty fabulous." *I can't believe she left.* Aimlessly, I pace the concrete. I put my phone on speaker and toss it to the chairs.

"Yeah, it's gonna be amazing!" Her voice beams into the especially deep solitude of my little booth, in this little theatre, in this little town. I can hear Donny's insistence in the background.

"Oh, okay, okay," she says, surrendering the phone. "Babe, someone wants to talk to you."

"Hello, my brother!"

"Hello, Donovan." I can hear his smile. Bending, I press my forehead to the window.

"Did you like that whitener?"

Yelling (probably from his bed), Stella demands burritos. Gum. Mochas. Weed.

"Yeah, thanks. It's great." Slowly, I bounce my head against the glass.

"It's very compact. Very whitening." The resounding thuds remind me of when I shoved Stella against the window. I stop. And sit down.

"Amazing, yeah? My friend at Sephora hooks me up. I'll get some more for you. But remember, you still owe me some syrup! Here's your girl." He passes the phone.

"Isn't he the sweetest?"

"So, you haven't responded to the invitation." I flick open my lighter and snap the flame to life. "Are you not going to be back for the *Pulp Fiction* party on Sunday?" I set fire to a red thread fraying from the chair next to me.

"Oh, I'll for sure be back! I can't wait, Babe." I smack out the flame. My phone bounces and I start clicking. "But I should go right now. I'll see you at the bank!"

Prius yells, *"Bye my brother!"* Just before she hangs up.

Click, click. Click, click. Click, click. Click, click. Click, click. Click, click. Click, click. Click, click. Click, click. Click, click. Click, click. Click, click. Click, click. Click, click. Click, click. Click, click. Click, click. Click...

I scroll through my phone, intent on deleting all of Stella's nudes. A few minutes later, after I've spread a not-insignificant amount of my joy into a recycling bin, they're still in my photo album. And I'm still on edge. I pull up my jeans, snap my flint, and light the inseminated renewable paper. *I've got to calm down.* The fire ignites the bin. The smell of melting plastic further turns my stomach. *It's fine.* I put out the flames with mineral water. Coughing, I un-button my fly and re-open my photo album. *Everything's fine.*

....

Downstairs in the theatre's girls' room, I turn on the hot water and brutally scrub the hands that have just nurtured me through three consecutively dwindling releases of joy. My fingers are now as raw as my abused Producer. And I don't feel any better. I stare into the partially steamed mirror—there's nothing to see. I find Becca's Vespa pic in my phone. *I wonder if she was in London when she shot this.* I want to call her. I can't. It would just be bizarre. Inappropriate. Unhealthy. Especially at 1:58 am. The hour is all wrong.

It's fine. Everything's fine.

With "Deep Hit of Morning Sun" blowing out my ear buds, I step into the back of the broom closet at the end of the stalls. I kneel down, push away jugs of industrial bleach, and pry up the corner floor tiles. Reaching my stinging hands into the dusty hollow, I grab my cleaning supplies. I stuff them in my Jansport. *This isn't enough.* I grab more fluid from the cache. *I'm sure it's filthy out there tonight.*

After setting the alarm, I lock up and step into the back parking lot. I'm met by the long awaited preface to fall: a cool night breeze kisses my neck. Welcoming it, I zip my black Obesity and Speed sweatshirt, gently pull my hood up over my hair, and disappear down the back alley.

On the south side of town, I start off small, eliminating a very unsightly church funded 'I am not a choice' bus-stop bench-ad that features a photo of an ugly baby. Then I move north, onto greater blights. Working my way toward the unholy mess on Rousette St., I illuminate the morning like a fashionable superhero in Ksubis. And as each little intermediate moment of warmth erupts from my touch, betrayal burns away with the filth. I feel better, lighter, like I'm floating, just inches above the ground. I tear through the valley, cutting like a cleansing angel, dancing like a tidying Timberlake, slipping through the littered alleyways, softly singing,

Shine on everyone.

Chapter 22

Through the bay window, I can see both elder Massis milling about the breakfast table. Frank's wearing overalls, eating sausage and peppers. Gina is reading her paper. The sun had crept up to catch me, and it sent me up my hill to a wakeful household. *It's fine.*

Stealthily, I slink up the driveway. Keeping low and close to the house, I creep underneath the kitchen window. I slip quietly around the garage and through the varnished wooden gate. The iron hinge creaks. I pause, then tiptoe through Frank's garden. The herbs are wet. *Thank Moz the sprinklers aren't still on.* Overcoming an urge to uproot a pot plant, I gently push open my window and crawl through to the safety of my room. *Gross.* The whole house smells like scrambled embryos. Plopping down in front of my mirror, I pull my head from the smoky tangle of my hoodie. I freeze in fear. But luckily, the smudge on my favorite black boat-necked sweater turns out to be a harmless patch of soot. I pat off my sleeve, finish undressing, and fall onto my bed. I badly want to shower but I'm down. I just can't get back up. I can't even get under the covers.

"Again? Are you fucking serious?" After what feels like two minutes of being asleep, I quietly inquire, "What time is it?"

"Hey man, sorry." Lynch laughs through the phone. "This was the only time I could get away from everyone."

Trying to focus, without lifting my head, I reach over to grab my hand mirror from the nightstand. "Why are you trying to get away from everyone? Where are you? Are you back?" I squint at my blurry reflection.

"No man, I'm still on the coast, but Leo and his sister are driving us back soon. They're gonna crash at my place so I was thinking that I'd bring them to the party tomorrow. I just wanted to make sure that you weren't gonna freak. ... They're cool, man."

"Oh wow. ... I don't know ... " I pick a speck of ash from my hair.

"Dude," Lynch sighs. "The Palace was theirs first. We wouldn't even know about it if it wasn't for them so it's not like they're gonna tell anyone. They get it." I inspect my teeth. They seem dull. "Oh, and Star has a present for you, I guess."

"She does?" I drop the mirror and roll over. "What is it?"

"I don't know. I showed her your profile and she said she had something that you'd be into. Some fancy shit or something."

"She's fabulous. She can come." I yawn, half asleep, with half of my face pressed into my pillow. "It's fine. Bring them both. It's a party."

I turn off my phone, plop it on the pillow in front of my face, and dream of McQueen.

Chapter 23

Skipping every nap opportunity and spending all day detailing our underground theatre has left me feeling drugged. Tonight, as I walk into work, I feel like I'm treading across the hazy, red-sanded floor of a popcorn-scented ocean. I bob up into the lobby for air. Shane meets me with a worried look and, upsetting me with their gestures of camaraderie, the Concession Creeps greet me with approving smiles. *Moz, don't let me resemble those steam punk stoners right now.* I reach for my shades as I pass my manager. Tying back his silver ponytail, he comments on the non-designer bags that I'm carrying under my eyes.

"You look tired Mike. What's with the dark circles, man?"

"Hey, better than red eyes, right Phil?" I slide on my aviators and swim further toward the stairs. My commentary on the hallucinogenic affinities of my coworkers is utterly lost.

"You should really get some rest man."

"I plan on it Phil. I plan on it."

....

Neglecting my semi-regular push-up regimen to preserve myself, I set up reels, drink San P., and slowly blink through the 5:20 pm and 7:50 pm showing. As the previews for the 10:30 pm screening start to roll, someone comes into Booth Six.

Becca's at the door.

My sleepy breathing hitches between the clicking frames. Though she's wearing the same outfit she wore when she last visited, to my amazement, it works. She's simultaneously overcoming fashion redundancy and achieving that "trying to be casual" beauty without even trying. I've seen Kate Moss do it, but it's not a feat that should be attempted by your average girl.

"Hey Mike." Her rich voice soothes. *I bet that she sings contralto.* "You busy?" She eases toward me through the shadows, like a girl from another world—like a Southern Californian.

"No, not at all." Standing, tossing my Jansport to the floor, I offer her the seat next to mine. "What's going on?" My shades rattle on the concrete. I wince and leave them.

"After our music talk I made you this." Sitting, she pulls a CD from the pocket of her hoodie and hands me the burnt disc.

I didn't think that girls ever made mix CDs for guys. I didn't think it was allowed, but there's nothing like breaking tradition, and I'm happy to be the guy to inspire change.

"What's on here?" I hold up what I'm hoping is my signed and stamped invitation to intercourse.

"I wrote down the tracks for you." Taking the translucent black sleeve, she slips out and unfolds a black piece of paper. "Here. There's no metal on it. I hope you like it."

Her silver writing is like calligraphy. I've never heard of some of this stuff, but all of my favorite bands are on here.

"I'm sure I will love it." Clearly enunciating each word of the song title as if answering a jeopardy question, I promise, "Even if there's no *Reign in Blood* on here." I punctuate the effort with an open mouthed, aren't-you-proud-of-me smile.

Laughing, she shakes her head, "No, no Slayer." And settles deeper into the chair. Covering her mouth, Becca coos out a yawn. "Ooh, I'm so sleepy." She shutters like a cat awakened from a nap. "I was up all night."

"Oh, really?" I fold up the intuitive track list and slip the disc into my backpack with my scattered aviators. "Wild date or something?" *Say no. Say no. Say—.*

"Oh no, nothing like that." *Thank you.* Overwriting the sexual DJ scene, into which I had already begun inserting her, she relieves me. "I spent the night at The Twins'."

"Oh, and you couldn't sleep because you were creeped out by all the crucified Nazarenes hanging on every inch of bare wall space?"

"God, I totally know what you mean. Their parents are twisted." She slips off her Vans. "Some of the stuff that they've gotten Drew and Michelle to believe is pretty crazy."

"Yeah, well, I know that The Twins call themselves Christians but they really just say that so their folks don't freak out. They're pretty level headed when it comes down to it. ... I mean, when they're not with Roxy—"

The Todds own Todd Pharmacy, and their daughters have a pet name for their favorite pilfered pill—Roxy. They can't go to church without her.

"I was talking about their thing with sex." An actor on the screen below screams. Becca sits up to glance down at the audience before turning back to me with a crooked smile. "Did you know that they think vaginal sex is a sin?"

"Like, *only* vaginal sex?" Intrigued, I lower my voice and lean in. "So, anything else is just another day at church?"

"You got it." Raising her sculpted brows, widening her glowing greens, she moves her face closer to mine. "Extra crazy, right?"

"Wow. Yeah." Reflexively, stupidly, I shy away to dig into my pocket. "Well, at least they haven't taken themselves completely out of the game."

"Good point. And they're certainly not totally repressed." She absently flips over her waffle soles with her bare toes. "We spent all night talking about vibrators. They know, like, everything about them but don't have any. They just research them online. Weird, right?" She smiles.

"Yeah. Weird." I let go of my Zippo. The simple broach of this topic shows my Producer to be, for Becca, at the very least, a consideration. Yet for some reason I still need to gather an inappropriate amount of courage to ask, "Do you?"

"Do I what?" She pulls her knees to the seat.

"Have any vibrators?"

"Oh. Yeah." Lifting her shark-pin-punctured sweatshirt, she digs into her tight pockets.

She must have misheard me. Perhaps she thinks that I asked, "Do you? Have any gum?"

She holds up a tiny golden vibe. "It's just a little guy. But it's got kick." She twists it to life. "See?" She passes me the buzzing bullet. "Touch it to the tip of your nose. That's how you test its power. Don't worry. It's clean."

Appreciating her concern for my skin care, I introduce the vibe to my nose. Soothingly I buzz, looking past the magical implement of our metaphysical connection, deep into the infinity of Becca's virtuous, sparkling eyes as she explains how this particular device can be charged at any computer. Bursting with new knowledge of the universe, and myself, I hand back the vibrator. And sneeze.

"So..." Very pleasantly, calmly, dying to know, I ask, "You carry that around with you all the time?"

"Yeah." She shrugs and pockets it. "It's good to have around. ... How long has the movie been running?"

I jump out of my seat, ready to flee to the lobby.

"It just started. Do you wanna watch it? Do you want me to get some popcorn? Or some red vines—"

"No thanks, Mike." Curling in her legs, she pulls up her billowy hood and nests into the velvet. She looks like a little girl ready for a nap.

"You sure? I have a stash of fruit pops. They're all natural."

"You're sweet. I'm fine." She pats the empty tattered seat. "Come here."

Taking a breath, I sit down. I shift toward her. Becca rests her head on my shoulder. *It's like we've been meeting here every night since we were twelve.* I put my arm around her. Sinking further into me, she nuzzles her face into my neck. We both exhale, and I smell cucumber clouds. My heartbeat booms, and the projector chides, *tsk, tsk, tsk.* Its judgment becoming distant, ghostly, as slowly, with ease, my dream girl and I turn into each other and give in to sleep.

Chapter 24

The sun is down, the valley sky is a mess of stars, and the bank lot is abuzz. The second Premiere is upon us. I haven't heard from Stella since our unfulfilling, three-way phone conversation, but this insignificant fact matters little to me as Lynch and I stare lasciviously at Becca and Mia. Sitting on the WAMU steps, the two Filmgreats dressed as Uma's character from *Pulp Fiction* are both stunning in black stretch pants, white dress shirts, and black bob wigs. Lynch's Mia has her shirt unbuttoned to give her showstoppers some midnight air while my OC snuggle buddy's nose trickles a subtle distinguished stream of fake blood.

"Fucking 'ell," Lynch sighs, popping a Mento. "Oy'd like to see that double feetchah." He offers me the roll.

"I can't say that I'd get bored." Supporting his bad innuendo, I accept two pink candies. "But I couldn't promise to last through the whole thing."

Noticing our stares, the girls stand and approach our post near the street corner across from the hotel.

"Fook. Y'really both just slept?" Lynch lightly shakes his head referring to my G-rated slumber party with Becca. "That's shite. Mike. That's shite." His British accent is awful.

"Yeah, but it was cool. It could have been worse. She wasn't annoying or anything." I chew and spit a mint into the dead bush behind us. "What's shite is that. ..." I point to the freshly inflicted and festering bejeweled wound in his face. The surfer who owns the beach house did it to him. "How could you let her mutilate you like that?"

"I thought you'd like it," he laughs. "It's a real diamond."

"Oh, that's pretty cool."

The girls arrive. Mia wraps herself around Lynch and I, fully in my element, greet our newest guest as the rest of The Greats gravitate toward their hosts.

"Becca, you look fantastic." She hugs me for four-and-a-half sensational seconds. "That wig really brings out your eyes." They're fascinating. They've shifted from green to an icy lupine blue.

"You look great too, Mike. Are you Vince Vega?"

Tonight, for *Pulp Fiction,* all my guests have dressed the part. Cruz has come as Bruce Willis's Butch, wearing a ball-gag around his neck and fake blood on his white tee shirt. Volta is Samuel L. Jackson's Jules. He found a perm wig and perm chops, and lost his Mexican accent. It's unnerving. The Twins are both covered in fake piercings. They look shockingly natural sitting on the curb next to us, eating berry ice cream, dressed as Rosanna Arquette's drugged out Jody. However, Lynch has performed tonight's most notable transformation. Having finally ditched the Dead Boys jacket to represent Ringo, the diner thief, he stands next to me sporting a Luau shirt, impressing Mia with his cultured cockney diction. He's lying about where he's been the past few days as I confirm, "Yep, Vincent Vega!" I adjust my tie, and Becca begins to lightly bat it. "So, I guess it looks like you and I have the leads tonight. Apropos wouldn't you say?" With the confidence of the man of the evening, I make a bold reach toward her mouth. "I like the blood. It's a nice touch." My skin tingles as she allows me to wipe a straying drop from her upper lip. *I wonder if she's got her toy in her pants.*

"I thought you would." Her slight, innocent smile is stained red.

Frantically, I search for a place to wipe off my fingers.

"Hey, wait. You're supposed to be Vince Vega?" Lynch butts in, sounding like the crocodile hunter. "Isn't that just the same suit you wore last week?"

"Oi, where'd you get that thing in your face?" Putting my arm around him, I massage my bloody fingers into a palm tree sprouting from his shoulder. "You can't get that done around here, right?"

"He did it himself! Isn't that amazing?" Impressed, Mia squeezes my arm then turns back to my pierced partner. "I totally want you to do me next."

Lynch victoriously smirks and a hot pink Sprinter pulls into the lot. Thumping, it stops a few yards in front of our congregation. When the back double doors fly open to reveal the spacious, black-lit, dub-stepping, lime-shag interior, Alvin bonelesses out from under a compact spinning disco ball. I'd expected him to show up as the drug dealer from *Pulp Fiction*, so I'm a bit surprised to see him clack down dressed in drag. Skating over, he takes pictures of the other two Mias and then smacks me on the back. It stings. I hiss.

"That salt air has done you some good, Al." I point at his chest. "Nice tits."

"Thanks baby" he coos. "You wanna touch'm?" I grope for a silicone cutlet. The tease jumps back. "That ain't free!" Laughing, he skates away. "I'll let you fuck me when you're famous."

Impressive in silver flats, Alvin nose manuals the entire parking lot as the scruffy driver of the mobile pink party flip-flops over to our planter. Offering a tattooed hand—the one that isn't occupied with the case of censored Lagunitas—he tells me that he's Leo and his sister's name is Star. With drab army surplus shorts, the shaggy chocolaty-haired surfer is wearing a fully unbuttoned black dress shirt that reveals his bare torso. Shockingly, his solid, dark geometric tattoos don't detract from his Abercrombie abs. I find his whole 'beach Adonis' thing overwhelming.

"It's so nice to finally meet you both." I shake Leo's hand before turning my attention to his sister. Her white laced spaghetti-strapped napkin-sized blouse showcases the metal rings in her perky boobs. The waist of her sky blue chords rides far below the opal dangling from her navel. Though she has a thick septum ring and cherry bomb red dreads, I think she looks like Catherine Zeta Jones. I offer her a handshake. Star embraces me.

"So nice to meet you too, Honey." She presses her soft cheek to mine and I inhale cinnamon. "I've been telling Dustin forever that he's gotta bring you over to our little bungalow."

According to Lynch, their place is nothing less than a seaside mansion. Apparently their dad made a killing on Kombucha.

"I'd love to, Star, thank you. I've seen some clips of your pool parties—"

"Star, watch this, Hey Star... " Clacking tricks on the pavement,

Alvin is yelling, and I'm becoming increasingly concerned about our scene's potential to attract attention. Sitting on the couch in the Sprinter with The Twins, Cruz and Volta are applauding, encouraging the skater.

"Yeah, you should come man!" Leo insists, "You can stay as long as you want." Discreetly, I ask Lynch to contain his brother as the surfer goes on. "We've got a killer au pair and a couple'a ... you seem a little stressed out dude."

Mid wall ride, Al gives Lynch the finger while reviewing his own prowess.

"Ooooh ... he's so handsome and dangerous."

"Oh, not really." Nervously I glance to the day glow pink beacon in the parking lot. Ash is playing Xbox while MK holds both of their cones. "I was just wondering if you could maybe park your van somewhere else. I just don't want to draw too much attention. Our party is very exclusive."

Nodding, Leo sets his bottles on the asphalt, pulls a swirly glass pipe from his shorts, lights up, and sucks in.

"We wouldn't want any uninvited guests to show up ... and arrest us..." I gesticulate wildly at the smoke, at the beer, at the heavens. "Right?"

"Ohhhhhh, man. No," With a relaxed exhale, shaking his main, he offers me the bowl. "You've got nothin' to worry about. We used to go in there alllllllll the time. We'd park out here..." He motions to the lot with the dreamy look of someone about to recount a timeless tale of heroic valor. "Once, our friend Riviera freaked out on some bad acid that we took in the hotel. He ran out here screaming and smashed up my '59 Abarth with a pair of stilts. ..." I look around to see if anyone else is catching this. Lynch has joined the gaming in the Sprinter. I'm alone with Leo and his sister as he solemnly confides, "The stilts were hand carved by an indigenous shaman. It was all fucked up."

"Yeah. Sounds fucked up." With my eyes tearing up, I wave away the filthy smoke. "So, did the cops come?"

"No, pretty." Star lays her hand on my chest, assuaging me with her tender touch, her observant descriptive, and her blue eyes. They glow like Becca's. But this girl's wearing contacts. "Relax. In all the years that we crashed here the cops didn't show up once. No one is watching us." *I believe you ocean goddess.* She reaches into her satchel, pulls out a pair of gold-framed aviators, and pushes them over my eyes. "There." She approves, smiling like an artist putting a final touch to a masterpiece. "They look great on you, Honey. ... Thank you for having us." She kisses my cheek.

I prance over to the van and bend over a mirrored cocktail table. "Star, these are fabulous!" They're Tom Fords. High fashion—high BRITISH fashion!

"Dude, you already have a pair just like those."

Ignoring Alvin's outrageous claim, I dash back to the generous, natty surf seraph, "Are you sure you don't want them?"

"Nah, Hon." Lightly, she musses her Raggedy Ann hair and smiles. "They make me look too much like a cop. ... And they look better on you."

Chapter 25

Through the crack in the curtain I can see The Path of Prayers flickering as I stand in my speech position. The Boys have filled their arms with pillows and blankets and are arranging a red nest in their purple love seat next to the soundboard. Lynch is at the controls. He's awaiting my cue. Downstage center, Mia is on a purple candy couch, drinking a Lagunita, awaiting him. The Twins and the surfers are lying in Heaven.

"Mike, this is great!" Becca, standing at the edge of the glowing corral, pulls on my tie. "The Christmas lights remind me of what my dad and I did to my bedroom back home." Raising her arms like a diver, she falls backward.

As she flops into the soft red sea of throws, Alvin yells, "Incoming!"

"NO!" I quip, but it's too late. He flips, his wig flies off, and the two mop-like mounds land, with a bounce, right next to her. Becca doesn't flinch. I'm about to scold the extreme drag queen for jeopardizing the wellbeing of our new, fragile, stunningly gorgeous guest, but Star beats me to it.

"Honey, you're going to hurt yourself." Leaving her brother with The Twins, she offers Alvin her hand. "Come sit with me."

In an act of obedience never before exhibited by our untamed friend, Al allows himself to be led to a couch. She sits. He drapes himself across her lap. She pets his long hair. Lynch and I exchange confounded looks then, shrugging, my co-host twirls his finger in the air. "Let's go!"

At my mark, I smooth my suit. I straighten my tie. With my black bandana-pocket square, I vigorously wipe my breath from my new shades then put them back on.

"Welcome Filmgreats and new friends—"

"Ooooh! Filmgreats, I like that *Culito*! It's hot!" I nod to the unsettling vaudevillian with the bloody boyfriend.

"My British co-host and I are thrilled that you could all join us for the very second Premiere party of all time!"

"Oi!" Lynch, pumps his fist amidst our applause. "Cheers! Oi!"

"Tonight…" I shake off the chill of his accent. "We will be showing the Tarantino Classic *Pulp Fiction*."

"Woooh!" Mia, now at the soundboard, wraps her arms around Lynch. "My man knows what I like!"

"Immediately following the film, the after party will begin, and shall feature a wonderfully danceable playlist, meticulously hand-picked by yours truly. I assure you, there will be no interruptions this time—"

"Wooooo, partyyyy!" Raising her bottle, Mia begins freaking my partner.

Awkwardly, yet eagerly, he returns the standing dry hump.

"Aw, c'mon you guys," I beg. "I'm almost done."

Ignoring me, Mia continues grinding to the eternal spring break in her head.

"But before I do finish… " I tug my cuffs, attempting to recompose myself. "I'd like to introduce our new guests, Becca and-"

"*Culito*!" I sigh and check my phone for texts from Stella as Volta motions to the Surfers. "We met them in the parking lot." Playfully, he throws popcorn at Becca. "And we all know Ms. Doll-faced Hollywood!" He sounds like Samuel L.

"I'm from Newport!" Retaliating with hurled Red Vines from Heaven, she rises up to her knees and waves her large box of treats. "I've got licorice if anyone wants some."

"Oh, whatever!" Catching a whip, Volta passes it to Cruz then claps for her to throw him another. "It's all Hollywood to me."

"Yeah Newport, Oldport…" Cruz swishes his Red Vine. "Hollywood, Holly Wouldn't. Either way, any day, I would if I could. Wouldn't you?"

"Yes." Becca confirms, "I most certainly would."

Her audience, Holly's audience, cheers.

"Well, Welcome Miss Wood. " Recalling my years of Improv training, I clap my hands together with a satisfied smile. "It seems that you already have many friends here, that is ... unless they all just want your candy."

All the cats call.

"Don't be jealous Mike. You can have some of my candy too."

She throws me a whip. It thwaps against my chest. Terribly attracted to the Filmgreat who has just further entered the esteem of our exclusive group, I clumsily catch the candy and put in my shirt pocket.

 "I brought goodies to share too!" Star stops petting her baby pap and raises an old-timey glass pill bottle filled with Flintstones. "If anyone hasn't taken their vitamin x tonight, I've brought enough for the whole class." She rattles it. "It goes great with Red Vines."

Her hair matches the faux fur throws that are draped over Al. Throwing them off, he springs up to take photos while Cruz, Volta, Mia, and The Twins line up to offer their tongues to a pastel dinosaur. With Leo, Becca stays in Heaven. Wrapped around a pile of pillows, she watches me.

"Well! Now that everyone is assured good health for the evening..." They all settle back into their seats. "And if you are ready Mr. Lynch?" My feral-haired partner sends two thumbs soaring upward. "We are pleased to bring you! ..." I point to Holly. "The private screening of..." I spread my arms wide, palms out. "...*Pulp Fiction*!"

....

Cuddled up in Heaven, having survived two popcorn fights, a wandering wrestling match between Leo and MK, and Volta's colorful rendition of Ezekiel 25:17, Holly is still nestled on top of me when we first hear the strange squeaks.

"What is that?" Without moving, my steadfast chest guest softly inquires, "Do you hear that noise?"

"Yeah, It's probably just mice." *I hope it's not mice.*

"Oh, mice are cute."

I think of Stella then Leo barks out another laugh, maintaining, yet again, that 'beer is not gross."

To our right, MK is cozied up to the shaggy surfer. The two have been debating this issue all night. After bark five, I finally join in on behalf of the flirtatious beer basher.

"Yeah Leo." I bean him with an unclaimed pillow. "Beer sucks."

Beyond the sea lion's betrayed expression, Ash sits on the stage, propped between Star's legs. On a purple candy chair, with her loving lap-dog-in-drag splayed across her chords, the surfer is braiding the sedate twin's hair. All three of them are staring at the wall screen. It's a strangely serene sight. Admiring the affectionate activities, I'm considering what permanent wardrobe modifications I'd have to make were I to grow out my hair when in falsetto unison everyone begins signing, *"WAS THE SON OF A PREACHER MAN!"* Holly and I join. She has a great voice. *She's a contralto. I can tell.*

As the giant Mia in the movie rails up some giant coke, I lightly drag my nails up and down Holly's inner arm.

"Thanks for inviting me Mike." Without rising from our cuddle lock, without looking at me, she tugs on the tip of my tie. "This is fun."

"Thanks Holly." This is the first time she's directly complimented me since way back in the parking lot. "I'm glad that you're enjoying yourself. " She loves my party. She must love my party's host! I gently run my fingers through her wig. "You know... you *can* call me Score ... and we can make out if you want."

Though my co-star clearly didn't hear either of my offers, after our song has ended and MK has pounded two Lagunitas and Alvin has received his second braid and Tarantino has brought us all to Jack Rabbit Slim's, I'm excited.

"Hey why don't you two show us how you twist!" I yell back toward Lynch's make-out couch.

Without relieving his relentless fingers from their job down the front of Mia's stretch-pants, my partner briefly unlocks lips. "I'm busy mate. Cheers." His accent is gone. And he's several scenes ahead of the rest of us.

With her black wig lying on the stage like a mound of unidentifiable road kill, Mia's blonde hair falls in pieces as her twisted hairpins scatter around the wooden floor. She lets out a series of sonorous squeaks as Lynch buries his face in cleavage and digs for joy with his right hand. *The Palace is a good place—things happen here.*

"Zach, shut your woman up!" Cruz takes off his ball gag, hurls it toward the shrill sounds, and then points to the girl on my chest. "Hollywood should dance." He flicks his wrist toward Mia's gaping blouse. "We've seen what she's got. We wanna see what you got girl! Get up there!"

"Come on." She jumps off me and, as if we've been practicing for this all week, offers me her hand. "Let's do it."

Ed Sullivan introduces us. *I guess I'm in.* We take off our shoes and as we rise into the flashing projection our audience cheers. Taunted by the impropriety of having paired them with a suit, I stare down at my orange monkey socks then look back up into Holly's ICEE blue eyes. Embarrassed, I smile. The sultry vegan swivels. I can taste my moths. They're thudding against the back of my teeth, desperately trying to escape to the projector to ruin everything. I swallow. I twist. They flutter back up with the fear of armpit sweat. I'm about to feign a sprained ankle. She grabs my hand. My skin leaps to life. Our eyes lock and without words she tells me that it's fine. *Everything's fine.* She's a natural.

"Ohhhh hellls YEESSS! You two go!" Cruz whistles to the rafters.

Star, Alvin, and Ash applaud. Mia squeaks. Holly gently smiles. I take her hand and a deep bow. Heaven is empty.

"You are hot, hot, HOT girl," Volta raves. "Where'd you learn to shake it like that? They got strip clubs in Newport? You even gave *them* some stiff competition."

One by one, he throws kernels toward the wings—where Cruz was pointing. Offstage right, in the shadows of Surfers' Paradise, Leo is making out with MK. Pressed to the wall she's digging her fingers into his ribs. The tattooed surfer's shirt is off and his back is covered in a black, bold-lined tribal lion.

Cruz grabs his man's throwing hand, shoves it into his crotch and like a bad blockbuster comedy insists, "The competition isn't the only thing that's stiff in here!" Pulled into Heaven by his nail-gun, he crawls on top of Volta and The Boys begin going for it. Hard. I'm concerned. Perez said that Orange County was a big 'yes on 8' supporter. I hope I don't have to ask them to cool it. I turn to Holly to gauge her reaction.

"That's so hot." Standing in the projection, she's smiling, staring down at the ravenous seventeen-year-old construction workers as they swap spit, fake-blood, and spray-on tan. "That's just so hot."

Chapter 26

Purring, Eddie pushes her nose into my ear and I awake to the warm sound. *I feel fabulous.* Last night, Holly danced with me from "Let's Dance" all the way through "How Soon is Now?" She took my hands, looked at me with her dazzling blue eyes, and said, "This is the perfect ending." I came home, showered, watched a porn clip of a girl who used go to our high school, and then slept like a cat on homework.

I reach for my nightstand and pick up my phone. There are no texts from Holly. Or Stella. I check the time. *Fuck.* I kiss my cat. She cringes. I'm going to be late for work.

With hopes of keeping my flawless record, I rush to make myself marginally presentable, abbreviating my morning ritual to only forty minutes. "Deep Hit of Morning Sun" plays sixteen times. I put on my jeans, Chucks, and an off-white oversized sweater, appropriate for today's refreshingly moderate weather. I grab my board and carefully bomb down the hill, stopping only briefly at my neighbor's driveway to pet Iman.

Seven and a half minutes late, I power-walk through the theatre doors, directly into my manager. With my nose just inches away from the prematurely white ponytail draping over his shoulder, I pick a black cat hair from my top and apologize. I've never been late before, so Philip is rightfully forgiving but throws in "don't let it happen again, man" as I dart upstairs. Luckily for all of us here at the 8-plex, our manager is very relaxed. He trusts me to lock up, lets us wear whatever we want, and doesn't bug us about our phones. I like him. Nevertheless, I still feel bad for being late. It's not my style.

Motivated by a touch of guilt, I quickly set the comedy rolling, build up reels, then settle into my seat to forgive myself with a grapefruit fruit pop from my private stash. Shortly before the 7:35 pm screening ends, Lynch calls asking if I want to meet to review last night's triumphs over some Americanos.

"I'm at work." He knows that I hate coffee. I chew on my soggy wooden stick.

"What the fuck? It's Labor Day."

"Movies, man. The stars never rest." I toss my soggy pacifier toward the green bin. It hits the wall and lands on the floor. I sigh and get up.

"Dude, you need to quit. School starts in eight days. We've gotta have at least sixteen more Premieres."

"Seriously." I pick up the splintered victim of my oral fixation. "Holly almost made out with me three times last night."

"Wow. ... Well I guess we should have seventeen more then. Maybe you'll almost touch her tits." He giggles. "Nice twist by the way. Did you watch Al's video? I forwarded it to you. It's pretty funny."

"What? Of me and Holly?" Frantically, I pace the room, clicking my lighter in double time with the projector. "We can't have footage of what goes on down there! What if someone sees it? What if The Twin's psychotic parents see it? What if the cops see it? It's funny?"

"Dude—"

"I'll call you right back." I hang up. I search for the clip—the evidence. I find it. I watch it, fearing for the worst, and then call back. "I think we look great. You think we look funny?"

"God. ... No. She looks better ... but you both look good." I can hear Ash and Star talking about hangovers in the background. I think that they're all in his room. "It's still funny though. What happened after you two left?"

I pocket my Zippo and curl back into the viewing chairs.

"I walked her to her car. That was it." I twist open a cold San P. It hisses.

"You just need to go for it harder." I hear Ash say 'Kombucha' before Lynch points out the obvious. "She's no Stella."

"Yeah, Holly wouldn't flake on me for some Friscy DJ's stupid pigtail party at a filthy dive bar in The Mission." I toss the cap. It pings into the blue bin full of green bottles.

"Damn. Little jealous?"

"Yeah." He knows me too well. "I suppose I am. Famous people always show up at Steve Aoki's parties. Y'know?"

"Totally. I bet it was killer."

....

In the lobby, I grab a large popcorn and a box of Red Vines from the Concession Creeps. I normally wouldn't touch the corn but another fruit pop isn't going to make up for my missed breakfast. The corn is for sustenance. And the Red Vines are for Holly, in case she makes another surprise visit. Turning from Karrie Creep's dilated grin, with my partially-hydrogenated-oil-enriched meal, I catch Shane hugging the big-butted blonde quarter of an intriguing foursome. At the front door, in his fitted floral Oh Land tee, he is tearing tickets for Mia, Stella, DJ Prius, and some guy I've never seen before. The stranger is wearing mouse grey MC Hammer pants, white splatter-painted TOMS slip-ons, a white oversized tank top, and a black beret over chin-length sandy blonde hair.

"Mike!" Stella squeals in perfect synch with Donny as they rush toward me. Her hair is in pigtails. She smooches my lips. I drop my candy. "I was hoping you'd be here sexy!" Hugging me, she mashes her boobs to my chest for 2.5 seconds. I outstretch my spilling popcorn tub.

"It's so good to see you my brother." Donovan hands me my fumbled treats, "You look great."

Yeah, I look great except for the black cat hair that's all over my white sweater.

"Thanks Donny," I utter. Setting down my corn, I debate whether or not I should risk drawing attention to the fur by attempting brush it off.

I fold my arms across my chest and Prius expands his radiant GO SMiLE.

"You missed a great party." Brazenly flaunting Stella's defection, he lovingly embraces me, pressing my treats and arms to my chest for six seconds. "You should have come."

I don't recall having been invited, nor do I really want to hear about it.

"Yeah, Mike, It was so amazing!" Stella titters, as I take comfort in noticing a few of Iman's hairs that have escaped from my shoulder to Prius's silver headband. "Aoki, Donny, and Soufflé spun till 3:00 am then we all went to this casting guy's suite at the W. Steve and his sister Devon are SO nice! She's a model and says that her agency would love me!"

"The casting agent loved me!" Mia glances up from her phone. "He's a hottie."

"I'm sorry..." Not really wanting to address the hottie agent or the party, or wanting to acknowledge Stella's certain future with Ford, or to further engage DJ Prius and his fabulous smile, I turn to him. "Who DJ'd with you?"

"Oh, sorry Mike." He sweeps his hand. "Meet my partner, DJ Soufflé."

It would seem that the guy with the beret is French and named after a fucking pastry. *I've got to get out of here.*

Keeping his hands shoved deep into his Hammer pants, while brandishing a blonde evil magician style mustache, Prius's partner gives me a cool chin nod. "*Cả va?*" His accent is bizarre.

"Hey."

In utter disbelief, I turn to Stella. She winks then kisses at me. For a few awful seconds the smooch hangs in the buttery lobby air.

Soufflé stares at me. And I stare at his hat.

"So..." I breakdown. "DJ Soufflé, huh?"

"Oui" he says, with emotionally trying austerity and, again, sounding very strange.

"I see." I further my attempt to disassemble the Eiffel Tower. "So you're French?"

"Naw kid." He huffs with an exasperated southern drawl. "I'm from Texas. Moved to SF about two years ago to team up with Donavan."

"Oh. Okay. But ... if you're from Texas," I innocently ask, "...why DJ Soufflé? Why not, like, DJ Oil Money? Or Cash Cow? Cash Cow could use the Chanel Cs for a logo if you still wanted to be French.

... But wait, why France again?"

"I spin French electro, kid." Playing with his facial hair, he scoffs as if I had just asked Johnny Depp what he does for a living. "It's my forte." He pronounces this last word like he just now managed to count past thirty-nine.

"Oh, right. Fabulous." *Okay, I've really got to get the fuck out of here.* "Well it's very nice to meet you ... man." I lie to the buckaroo then turn to Stella and smile. "Welcome back." I snatch my tub from the counter and begin retreating down the red-carpeted hall. "I gotta get to work guys. Enjoy the film!"

Leaving a trail of kernels behind me, I climb into flickering solitude.

....

Alone. In my fraying seat, recovering from having made the acquaintance of a pretentious pastry, chasing another mournful mouthful of corn with San P., I'm wondering if Devon Aoki's agency hires male models, when the dissenter struts into my booth.

"You ran away so fast, I didn't really get a chance to say 'hi' Babe." As if she's done no wrong, Stella clicks across the floor and straddles me. Swallowing, I offer her the tub. She pops a single kernel, sets my late lunch on the ground, and then props her hands over my shoulders and onto the backrest. "So..." Her long candy scented pigtails and fantastic boobs gravitate toward my face. "I hear that I missed a pretty amazing Premiere."

"Yeah it was great. Way better than the first, actually." Gently swinging, her hair tickles my jaw. I bat it away. "You know that we showed *Pulp Fiction*? Someone asked me to show it but I can't remember who..."

"Oh, don't be mad. You didn't even miss me." Deliberately stretching her arms above her head, she forces her breasts forward to threaten the permanence of any such accused apathy. "And you had Becca there to keep you on your toes ... or ... what is it now? Hollywood? I told you that she's adorable." Stella adjusts a stray lock of hair on my forehead and hums, "I totally would. Wouldn't you?"

She's staring at me the same way Eddie used to stare at Joey's poor bunny rabbit. *Moz rest his furry soul.*

"Um, Yeah." Looking up into her wild blue eyes, I hesitantly agree, "Totally. Holly's runway." Stella grabs the back of my hair, lunges in, and furiously has her way with my mouth.

With the image of disemboweled Freddy bunny terrorizing my mind, I run my hands beneath her dress, sliding them up her belly toward pink-scented bounty. I squeeze boob and black cotton bunches up to bare her mid drift. Abandoning her Bubble Yum flavored tongue, I dive toward her awful curved bellybutton barbell. I chew bejeweled steel. It clicks on my teeth. Stella undoes her bra. I lick upward. She forces her left nipple into my compliant mouth. Upon my first sweet suck, my co-star makes a pained sound that threatens my sanity. I'm forced to take a breath. Abating my intent to bite, I rest my forehead on her fragrant c-cups, panting, watching her black cotton panties grind against my crotch. Tonight, they're polka dotted with tiny pink hearts. And my skillful Ford prospect is commanding these speckled icons of affection so well that I may soon have to explain jean stains to Gina. My Producer stands to applaud. Stella moans. I'm about to christen my grey camo CK briefs. Then she stops. She pulls away, and stops.

"Ugggh," she chirps, stretching again before dismounting.

Panting, I watch her strap down my dessert, straighten her dress, and grab my licorice.

"I'd better go. I told them that I was just going to get some candy." She raises an eyebrow and the unopened box of Red Vines. "I should get back down there before Donny comes looking for me."

I feel that I may weep. Stella leans back down, shoves her tongue into my mouth for a few more vigorous seconds, and then backs away. "But they're leaving tonight. Mom's mushrooming." Her hand grasps the back of my neck. I swallow saccharine saliva. "You should come over tomorrow. ..." She hums, "If you forgive me."

Chapter 27

At dinner, I'm eating the remaining leftovers from Pasta Sunday while the folks feed on carcass. To protest their violent lifestyle, I've begun wearing my shades whenever they eat meat. With my eyes stylishly shielded from the horror, I twirl my spaghetti in cool opposition. Frank forks flesh filet under his brim. Gina sips Cabernet.

After the slaughter, I clear the table, scrub the dishes, then tell the elders that I'm staying at Lynch's. I skate into the valley with my iPod pumping Justice. Joey says we used to listen to them when he'd drive us to browse Barney's NYC in San Francisco in his baby blue T-bird convertible. I didn't know that they were French, but my brother assures me they are, and that the dissuading crucifix on their album cover is supposed to be viewed upside-down. It's no Britpop, but it's okay.

Wearing a grey scoop neck long-sleeve under a black military coat by OBEY—(the label is owned by some British street artist that never shows his face and is loved by Brangelina)—I climb Stella's porch, bandana the light moisture from my brow, and knock. She opens the door wearing the Joy Division shirt—only the Joy Division shirt.

"Hey kid." Grabbing the back of my freshly styled hair she pulls me in for a tonguing. I taste seconds of watermelon and wine before suddenly finding myself standing at the edge of her bed. In The Pink Room, I get straight down to business.

"Is that my shirt?"

"Yep!" Happily, she plops onto the fluffy comforter.

"Why aren't you wearing DJ Prius's?"

"Yours fits better." She pulls me down next to her.

"You have to give that back to me, you know."

"I know Babe." Humming, laying on her side, she traces my belt buckle with her finger. "But did you know that my mom won't be back 'til Friday?"

At sun up, lounging naked in the pink sheets, I'm awakened by Katy Perry and Stella. Wearing only Hello Kitty aprons, they serve me berry pancakes and a soy cocoa. Stella tries to add a kiss to her gesture of appreciation, but I stop her.

"Oh, fuck." I begin to roll off the bed. "I've gotta go back home real quick."

"What? No!" She throws herself on top of me. "Why?"

"I forgot my toothbrush. Morning breath."

"Oh settle, Babe. I've got a ton of new ones." Her bare thighs sandwich my ribs, trapping me. She motions toward her pink bathroom drawer. "I always have them around just in case I have surprise slumber parties."

"Oh, okay. Guess I'll use one that hasn't been claimed. So, what'd you do today?"

Releasing me, she grabs her pink coffee cup from the pink end table, takes a sip of red wine, and then offers me the acrid, stained mug. I decline with a look. She shrugs, takes another gulp, and then sets her drink atop the gum wrappers scattered about the nightstand.

"Becca and I hung out at The Grounds. She showed me some pictures from the party." Chewing her Bordeaux-soaked Bubble Yum, she stretches out inches in front of me. The bed creaks. My brother's old tee shirt crawls up her hips. *She's must be sponsored by pink Hello Kitty panties.* "It looks like I really missed out." She adjusts my bangs. "I think you should throw another one tomorrow!"

"Tomorrow?" I begin calculating the time needed to decide on the perfect film, detail the perfect invites, compile the perfect playlist—to make it all perfect. "I don't know ... I don't know what I'd show? And I'd have to go home to make the invitations—"

"C'mon, Babe." Derailing my train of excuses with her sex hum, she lightly scratches my chest as she tugs the relaxed collar of my shirt farther down. Every hair on my body stands at attention, and my Producer quickly catches up. "We've only got a few days before school starts and this could be our last summer together. You can just use my computer to make the invites in the morning..." She blows then implodes a bubble. "If you're not too exhausted. Annnnnd..." Her voice rises as she rolls over to grab her laptop. "I know exactly what you can show!"

Propped up on her elbows, next to me on her bed, Stella brings up download after download of celebrity sex tapes. I've only seen clips of a few of them but she's extremely familiar with them all. Naming each of the celebrated young ladies, she critiques their performance, explaining why some of them are more deserving of their fame than others. She tells me all about the girls' pre- and post-porn endorsements, reality shows, books, and makeup lines, while detailing how these rewards of fame and fortune are not only informed by sex skills but by social status and online presence. She schools me on Paris, Pam, Jenna, Kim Kardashian, a porn star named Faye who is now a model, and another named Sasha who 'stars in a straight film made by a totally respected director.' I recognize her. But not from the straight film.

"Ugh, I totally would. Isn't she a turn on?" My porn historian points to the screen. A dainty brunette demands to be choked by a massive tattooed boner while my smaller and ink-free, yet equally ambitious counterpart begs to be released from its denim prison.

"Totally." Uncontrollably breathing—deeply, like I just did nine push-ups—I turn from the monitor to watch Stella. She rises to her knees, takes off my shirt, and throws it to the floor. I make a mental note of where it landed with an addendum that reminds me to send a 'thank you' to each one of Stella's online teachers. "She's amazing," I agree. The topless Great tables her Hello Kitty Mac. Leaving the porn playing, she sets it next to the pink mug.

With her body naturally defying gravity, Stella barely bounces over to her pink dresser and presses play on a docked iPod. *Hello Katy Perry*. As a seeming afterthought, she picks up a giant, elaborately bobbled pink and black Tarina necklace and drapes it over her neck. In the pink baroque vanity, she approves of the way the kitty pendant lays on her boobs. *California girls are unforgettable*.

She stalks back, steps up, and stands on the end of the pink bed. *They'll melt your popsicle.* Her toenails match the bedspread. And her underwear. And the wall. And the pile of the socks by the hamper. And the hamper.

She points at me. "Take off your clothes." Then at the filth playing atop the pink nightstand. "And let's do that."

....

Katy Perry has a lot of singles. By the time I awaken to the sound of her latest, I know them all. Feeling haunted and heroic, I open the Kitty Mac and send out terribly boring invitations to the Flash Premiere. Stella's in the shower. Last night she was strongly endorsing the showing of a Jenna Jameson film. But I feel that tonight will be more of a *True Romance* sort of evening.

The confirmations come in. Reading the replies, I begin wondering if I'll be able to get everything ready in time. I'm not stressed out about it. Laying here in The Pink Room, on pink pillows, in the pink bed, with the pink computer on my lap, as Stella soaps my dried joy from her nakedness, I feel quite at ease. I put on my shades, roll off the bed, and walk to the bathroom.

"Stella!" I yell, through the open pink door. "Everyone's already responded. They're all gonna come. The surfers too."

"Oooooh, that's great Baby!"

"Yeah Babe." I force out the dulcet diminutive. "I'm gonna go help Lynch set up." Lingering in the steam, I wait for her to push aside the Hello Kitty curtains and insist that I not leave before marching over to give her a lick goodbye.

"Okay Baby!" She yells, as I begin gingerly padding over the shaggy pink bath mat. "I'll see you tonight!"

Chapter 28

As I ascend our hill, the sun descends. When I reach our driveway, it's dark.

Rushing into my room, I undress, slightly alter the playlist from the second Premiere then take my first shower of the day. It's only when I pull my dress shirt from a hanger that I remember my Joy Division tee. It's still on Stella's floor. *It's fine.* I suit up, style my hair, and grab my iPhone from its charger. *"You're coming tonight as Dick Ritchie?"* I smile at the text. By implying I'd show up as the pathetic, dorky, aspiring actor-character in *True Romance,* Holly is flaunting her knowledge of the cult classic, and, quite possibly, flirting. *I hope.* I'm really looking forward to seeing her tonight. I consider telling her this before I breast pocket the phone, triple check the mirror, grab my board, and bolt for the door.

"Well you look like a million bucks!" Franks stops me just before I step outside. "Big game tonight?"

"Thanks Dad, yeah." I straighten my tie. "Zach got a metal track pack and Hector and David are coming over. We're probably gonna be playing all night so I'm just gonna stay at his place again. See ya tomorrow." He tips his hat as I dart into the driveway.

....

For the first time, we have a full cast in my basement. But only two of the Greats have come in character. To match Alabama Worley, Holly and Stella are wearing teal bras: Miss Wood's shows through her sheer white shark-pinned-tee; Stella's peeks from her short red dress with purpose. I do miss Holly's bare supple side-boob, though I love the lace. And her hot pink leopard print tights are a lovely surprise. Mia has surprised us as well. Her once blonde hair is now a black bob with short bangs and she wearing an AC/DC hoodie. But she's not in costume. At least she doesn't think so.

Standing in my speech position, I watch the two Worley's slide next to each other in Heaven as Star invitingly rattles her bottle.

"These will be right here." She fills a large, hollowed Hello Kitty head that now lives atop our mini fridge. "The round ones with my name on them are MDMA." A magical rainbow scatters into the white plastic. "And don't be shy, there's plenty more where these came from!"

Having not been entirely upset with the influence that the Flint-stones had on my last party, I don't vocally object to the everlasting drug dispenser but do ask all hippies to "please keep weed smoking confined to the other side of the curtain" before giving an a eloquent unrehearsed speech.

"Good evening Greats. I wasn't prepared for this." I appeal to my room of already unruly guests. "But by the look of your outfits, I guess that you guys weren't either—" A flurry of popcorn and bottle caps rain down upon me. "So ... um, thanks for coming to the first Flash Premiere!" Batting away a Solo cup, I rattle off, "We bring you *True Romance*. Do it Lynch!" I flee as the unruly mob cheers at the opening credits.

With the movie and most of my guests rolling, I'm soberly lying in Heaven and hoping to casually reposition myself. Stella's to my left and Holly's pressed next to her. I'd very much like to be between the two of them, if not simply farther from Stella. Since the movie started, she hasn't stopped talking about how hot Patricia Arquette is, how hot Christian Slater is, and how hot I look. Unable to argue with any of these irrefutable, loudly stated facts I continuously agree, "Yeah he's ... she's ... I'm ... totally hot," as Mia's mating call adds to the bright white noise. Her squeaks are even more cutting than Stella's high pitched fawning, but everyone is so deeply involved in quoting, kissing, drinking, and pillow fighting that

Lynch's scene is no more than a blurry, x-rated backdrop.

As the rumpus escalates, Stella moves upstage to direct her chatter toward a captivated Cruz and Volta. Free from her physical proximity, and any misperceived obligation to pay attention to her, I scoot next to Holly.

"Finally," I sigh. "I've wanted to ask you something but didn't want to shout over Stella."

"Oh Yeah?" Holly shows me her crooked smile. "What would you like to know?"

"How could you possibly think that I'd host my own party dressed as character that wears boxers throughout the majority of the movie?"

"You're right. That was wrong." In an act of contrition, she offers me a Red Vine. "Forgive me?"

I accept the licorice branch. Cooled by her minty stare, I'm about to profess that I'd forgive her any transgression when Stella commands the room's attention.

"He's fucked everyone!"

She must be yelling about Prius.

Accidentally, I speak my mind. "Moz, just tweet it. It would be so much quieter."

Holly covers her delicate mouth to suppress an adorable laugh. "Do you even get any sleep when you stay over at her place?"

I'm not sure what she's asking me. I think this may be about sex.

"Yeah, well, sometimes she'll stop talking to text..." I pocket my licorice. "Or to watch videos—"

"Oh, right." Holly bites her lip. "That's what I've heard."

Discretely chewing moths, I'm struggling to decide exactly what it is that she has heard, who it is that told her, and how her eyes could possibly be so transformative when, from painfully close by, Stella squeals,

"Oh my God, my favorite scene is coming up!" Suddenly, she's looming over us in a stance very reminiscent of the private under-boob presentation that she gave last night in The Pink Room. "Hey kids!" She announces, "Hollywood and I are gonna do this one."

I swallow musty insect dust. Though it's restrained, I swear to Moz that I can see eagerness in Holly's viridian eyes as she gazes up at the brash brunette. Twisting her white locks, she's flushed, yet calm. I, however, am in a bit of a frenzy—as everyone here knows, the phone booth scene is THE sex scene. It's really one of the best PG moments to ever have graced cinema.

Sounding disappointed by her own words, Holly politely declines. "Oh, I don't really know this scene very well."

This causes me utter sorrow. But Stella, intent on creating what would surely be visual perfection, contends, "Oh, I think you do."

I look giddily back and forth between Alabamas.

This is wild. I really want this to happen. But it's so advanced. Stella's not asking for a Ringwald lipstick trick. She wants the two of them to get deeply physical onstage for everyone's enjoyment, and Holly knows this. We all do. Alvin's already got his camera out. And Leo has turned his back on Surfers' Paradise. Because this scene isn't about dance. Or dialogue. It's about doing it. It's about girls gone wild.

Feeling I should do something to either start or stop my fantasy from coming to life in front of me, I'm relieved when The Boys take the initiative.

"Come on Hollywood, you got it sexy!" Volta shouts.

Cruz joins in to encourage the ingénue. "Come on girl, you're a star!"

Blushing, Holly graciously maintains that she's not right for the part.

"Okay Babe." Rising from her knees, Stella grabs my hand and pulls me up into the projection. "Let's show'm how it's done."

Though I may have fumbled my speech, this impromptu performance doesn't seem like a terrible idea. We're proven to work well together. In affected protest, while folding my coat and fixing my hair, I reason, "It's not really that much of a scene. The dialogue is rather weak—"

Stella effortlessly drags me toward the life-sized pink Cadillac on the wall.

"What..." She raises her one offended eyebrow. "Just because it's not the Twist it's not good enough for you?" Brushing her lips up my neck, she secretly hums. "You know I twist better than her."

And I'm ready to steal the show.

With cinematic history flickering through my aviators, I channel the rebellious spirit of a nineties Christian Slater and reach up

Stella's dress. Digging my fingers deep into her naked thigh I spin her around, press my mouth to her, and press her to the wall. Perfectly, I mimic the action in the blanketing film. Her complete lack of inhibition decimates what's left of my own, while the cheers of the Filmgreats encourage our ravenous pursuits. I reach deeper into our performance, tasting watermelon, wine, sweat, and sweet adoration, until I become vaguely aware of Lynch's distant, deviant, goofy laughter. The dialogue of the film disappears and like a pop bomb dropped from the catwalk "I Kissed a Girl" booms onto the stage.

Internally, I smile at the surprise attack, though neither my messy haired partner, nor the Ameripop Princess is powerful enough to deter me from my mission in the phantom roadside phone booth. Maintaining audience approval, keeping both my ratings and my Producer up, I stare into Stella's wintry blues, Alabama Worley's mountainous cleavage, and finally, Holly's beguiling greens, before feverishly sucking down Stella's neck. I lick above teal-laced wire, across her overflowing cotton candy scented top-boob then, just as I have the bottom of her dress heading for her head, she whips me around and sends us crashing into Heaven.

....

Lynch has ended the pop terrorism. Over the silent film, Deadmau5 pounds as Stella and I play beneath the throws. An XX song begins. I come up from the fur to pocket square my brow and investigate. Aside from the music and the occasional squeak, everything has gone quiet. Craning my bed-head into the projection of a gun, I replace my fallen shades.

On the upstage right candy couch, Lynch has his hand between the thighs of his bottled brunette. Her acid-washed jeans are around her ankles, her AC is unzipped from her DC, and his mouth is clamped to a totally bare boob. Across from them, on their own love seat, Cruz and Volta are lazily kissing. Next to me, MK is drunkenly tracing Leo's geometric chest tattoo with her tongue and, on his side, he's pressed against Ash, who is passed out on Star, who to my delight is tenderly making out with Alvin. Stella and I are so good at what we do that we've inspired others to achieve.

Straddling my groundbreaking leading lady, I admire the surrounding activities as she rises, pushes away my unbuttoned shirt, and sucks my bare ribs.

"This Flash Premiere was a great idea, Babe." I further loosen my tie and nod to the surrounding savagery. "Check out the activities! Everyone's going for it." Ignoring me, she slides her hand down the front of my jeans and licks my neck. "We're totally doing this again tomorrow."

To get a better view, I ease Stella's head further down. Alone on a downstage couch, reclining amidst scattered Red Vines and corn kernels, Holly is a vision on green plastic. In snacky disarray, she looks serene. Her eyes are heavy but aware. They match the couch. *I wonder if her expression would be the same if she were beneath me, instead of Stella.* With such stimulating debauchery surrounding her, I at first think it odd that Holly is so captivated by the silent version of *True Romance*. But she's not. She isn't watching the movie at all. She's watching my performance, enjoying it as if I had already achieved my fated fame and come to grace this small-town party with my celebrity. I'd better make this look good.

With the confidence of DiCaprio, I pull Stella up and plunge my tongue into her open mouth. Like fresh escapees from a Christian cult, we go at each other and DJ Prius's protégé turns her sex hum up high enough to overload the PA system. I can feel it. I can hear it humming over Pulp as she flips me over, slides down my chest, unbuttons my Ksubis, springs my imprisoned Producer, and harbors him in her mouth. I look back to Holly. She's still staring. Sucking in my cheeks, I put on my pout and as Stella hums beneath the red veil, Holly and I watch each other until we reach the chorus: Jarvis Cocker begins to sing about hardcore, my whole body surrenders its joy, and my eyes flutter shut behind my Ford's to the roaring sound of golden buzzing.

....

I awake alone. The prayer candles are still burning. A few have fallen over. It was totally irresponsible of Lynch to leave them lit; they could have caught the curtains afire. But I'm glad that there's some light in the ballroom. I stand up from the blankets. My playlist has ended. The projector is off. And our giant screen has reverted back to an ominous bare wall. I'm surrounded by an eerie silence framed in the faint glow of Heaven's perimeter. I don't really like being here alone. I don't really like it at all. It's like being in an empty church. I check my phone. It's just past 4:00 am. I have a new text: "*Hey sexy,*" Stella writes, "*Donovan and Soufflé came into town. Holly and I went to meet them at Taco Bell. :)*"

All of this upsets my stomach. The sprint upstairs doesn't help.

Chapter 29

"No fucking way. ... No way. ... Fuck that!" Alvin, pissed off about something, is whipping a large bowl of chicken embryos when I shuffle into the sunny kitchen. Earlier, I crept through the dark into his room and found him in bed with Star. So I slept on Lynch's floor between Leo and scattered bottles of Kombucha. I'm glad I now have a stash of clean clothes here. The brothers are in their boxers. I'm dressed.

"I can't believe that you left me there." I put on my shades and head straight for their Sub Zero. "Do you know how creepy it was? What if God showed up? What if I'd gotten possessed by Jesus? Then what?" I grab the first San Pellegrino from a deep row of green mini bottles.

"You were all sandwiched between Holly and Stella!" Lynch, sitting, dangling his legs from the concrete island in the center of their kitchen, tosses me a lime. "I figured you wouldn't wanna be disturbed."

Holly slept next to me in Heaven. I can't believe I didn't notice. Stella must have put tranquilizers in her OJ. I must work on my tolerance.

"Oh, yeah, good call. Thanks."

"If you want something totally un-fucking-believable, try this one." Pouring his disgusting yellow goo into a frying pan, Al nods to his brother. "Tell'm fucker!" The eggs sizzle. They smell like poor Freddy bunny did when we found him, full of teeth marks, rotting in Frank's garden. *Moz rest his furry soul.*

"What's the deal?" I set my lime on a chopping board.

Alvin throws me a knife. I dodge it. It clatters onto the granite tiles. He laughs and answers for his brother.

"Dude. Mia won't put it in her mouth!"

"OJ strike?" I gasp. "That's pure evil." Safely, I slide clean cutlery from a wooden rack and slice. "Mia must store her evil in her ass."

Lime juice squirts on my chest. It barely misses my white v-neck.

"Yeah, man." Lynch shakes his head. "It totally sucks. It's weird. She'll do everything but that. I don't get it. I took her to YoGoGo like three times … told her 'get all the mochi that you want.' … I figured *Pulp Fiction* would help but—"

"That is total fucking bullshit." Alvin slices and slides fresh Cherie Cherie brown bread into a toaster oven before pouring himself a wine glass of Kombucha. "One host gets blown and the other just gets his fingers wet." He pushes his glass toward Lynch and grabs his wrist. "Clean'm off in here, it could use a twist of Mia—"

"You guys, did you not see what happened last night?" I back step away from the struggle as Al tries to baptize his brother in putrid mushroom potion.

"Other than you filling in for every fucking DJ in San Francisco?" Alvin laughs. "Nuh uh."

Rancid hippie tea is splashing all over the kitchen.

"Check this out" I pop my lime wedge into my bottle then set it on the far side of the island where I'm now safe from the spray. "The whole time that Stella was down there, Holly was watching me … and I think she was going for it with a vibrator!"

I smack my hands down on the concrete, thrilled with my own conclusion.

"Fuck off!" Alvin freezes. I've turned the frantic brothers to sticky statues.

"Yeah, swear to Moz. She keeps one in her pocket with her at all times." I take a pull from my bottle. "It's gold. … I think it's designer."

"I heard it!" Lynch jumps to the ground and Al, releasing his brother, hops up to surf the island in celebration.

"Yeahhhhh!" Shredding a flaming tube of elements, he almost kicks over his eggs.

"I knew that I heard buzzing!" Joyously, Lynch points at me. "I was getting a JO and just figured that the speakers were being weird!"

"Listen. We've gotta have another party tonight." Trying to quiet the raucous brothers, I save Al's toast from burning. "We're clearly on to something. I mean, Al even hooked up with Star! And she's, like, twenty-two." Alvin stops hanging ten to give me his full attention, and I go on. "We can show *Weird Science* or *Donnie Darko*. ... We'll show fucking *Twilight*. Who cares? We can go straighten up —"

"Fuck, man. We can't." Lynch apologetically admits. "We're going to Leo's. I promised Violet I'd come."

Dropping my hot toast on a seemingly never before used dinner plate, I give him a look that asks why I should care about a promise to a girl with terrible navel tattoos.

"She gives great OJ."

I turn to Al, hoping he'll tell me that his brother isn't truly about to forsake me for young coastal flesh.

"An OJ's an OJ dude." Still standing on the counter, he dumps a bowl of shredded orange cheese into and around his pan. It melts everywhere. *That smells better.* "*And* Violet wants to bang."

"Okay. Yeah. That's cool." I crunch into my dry breakfast. I understand. I can't begrudge my friend Oral Joy from pre-teen Cameron Diaz.

"You should come!" Lynch hands me a tub of freshly ground almond butter. "There's always chicks there!"

"I wish. I've gotta work." I stir the oil into the separated nuts.

"Fuck. Well, we'll have the party when we get back! It will be a killer last day of summer!"

"For fucking real!" Alvin stops shoveling mounds of yellow and orange goo into his mouth, reaches into a brown paper bag, and throws a pastry at me.

"Definitely! It'll be fabulous—blockbuster summer's end." I catch the berry scone. Then dust the crumbs from my shirt. "Hey, where the fuck did you guys get all this food? Did you finally get adopted or something?"

"No fucker," Alvin smiles proudly. "My girlfriend bought it for us."

Chapter 30

The Palace is ready for Sunday. The sun is down and I'm rolling uphill, sitting on a furry lime-green couch in a neon disco. Leo says the crunchy beats are Magnetic Man. Band FAIL! laughs at Lonely Island clips. Lynch shows me the Andy Samberg "Talks With Animals" sketch. I have an epiphany. Star paints my pinky nail purple. And they drop me off.

"You should go with them sometime, Mike. Getcha outdoors, in the ocean, put some salt in your lungs!" At our front door, waving to the passengers of the pink Sprinter, Frank fantasizes, "I bet they have some good smoke."

Warning him of the dangers of both marijuana and father-feeding sharks, I grab eight pieces of take-out Maki-Zushi from the kitchen and shut myself in my room.

At my Mac, with a belly full of imitation crab and my sinuses weeping from wasabi, I photoshop another masterpiece. Using the illustrated *Boogie Nights* movie poster as a template, I painstakingly alter the central image of Mark Wahlberg, substituting my face for his. This process ends up being so exhausting that when I attempt to put Lynch's face over Burt Reynolds's I have to give up after three tedious minutes. *It's fine.* The invitation already looks great. Below the heading, in a flourish of subtext, I add: '*Score and Lynch Present the 70s Sex and San P. Premiere Party! Appropriate attire is heavily encouraged.*' I show it to Eddie. She blinks with approval. I send it out to the Greats.

The alarm is awful but I'm glad that I didn't unconsciously shut it off. I don't want to be late to work again. When it assures me that it is 3:00 pm, I unplug my phone and check my messages. Stella wrote me at 4:32 am: "*Boogie Nights is close, but you should show the real thing Babe! Jennnnnnnna! Sashaaaaa! It would be a lot of fun! ;)* " In the attached picture, entitled 'Sweet Dreams!' Stella is pointing her phone at the baroque mirror on her pink vanity. She's topless, tugging her periwinkle lace Brazilian boy-shorts down over her left hip. A long string of oversized pink and white pearls drapes over her boobs and past her bellybutton barbell. I sigh. I shake my head. I forward the shot to Lynch. Then call him.

"Hey man, you still have that DVD, right?" Opening my computer, I pull the photo into Photoshop.

"*Boogie Nights*? Yeah, I'll bring it on Sunday."

"Fabulous." I darken the background of the shot. *Much better.* "Stella's bugging me to show a porno. Crazy, right?" Saving my changes, I trash the original then drag the edited pic into my Wish List folder. *I suppose I should start a Greatest Hits folder soon.*

"I think it could be killer. We should go for it."

"My dear partner, don't you think that's a little vulgar?" I open Photo Booth and slide on my Fords. "Think of our guests!" Thinking of Holly, I suck my cheeks, attempt to flex my pecs, and then click the camera. *Boop, boop. ... Stunning!*

"C'mon man." He pleads. "Mia says it would really turn her on. It could finally get me some OJ from her. Violet's cool but she doesn't even grab it. It's like 'look daddy, no hands.' Seriously, you've seen Mia's lips. Help me out Mike."

"I do appreciate your needs but I can't be held responsible for having to correct Mia's sadistic behavior disorder." I Tumblr my topless pic then walk into the bathroom. "The girl clearly has a problem. She needs professional counseling." I pull my black Tweezermans from their storage tube. They need sharpening. "*Boogie Nights* will be perfect. Think of what the girls will wear." I hear his phone vibrate. "That's probably from me. Check it." I pluck.

"Yeeeeah pearrrrrrls." Lynch admires Stella's photo then notices the flaw. "Woah dude! Yellow jeans AND pigtails!" Bringing the phone back to his face he asks, "The shirtless dude on the bed reading the US—that's that Friscy DJ right? Donovan?"

"Yeah, that's DJ Prius himself." Winning yet another battle against a uni-brow. I press play on my iPod. "He's a Dill. But he's got nice teeth."

"Yeah, I know. You've told me. He's in Stella's latest video. Have you seen it? You should see it. It's interesting."

Her video blog—I watched it once, freshman year. It made me so tired that I vowed to never look at it again. But it's got a ton of followers now. And Lynch is recommending it.

"Send me the direct link. If I go through the whole thing I might fall back asleep and I can't be late for work again."

Chapter 31

I'm five minutes early. I take off my aviators. Wiping them down with my bandanna, I stroll into the lobby. Philip, who hasn't bothered to deep condition his hair since the nineties, has the gall to tell me that I look like I need rest.

"I think you look good Mike." In his tight purple Frankmusik shirt, Shane comes to my defense. "Have you been working out?" Standing at the door, he's tapping a round tin of lip salve.

"What?" I await a comment about straw hair or neck biting.

"I like that shirt." He tugs and flattens my collar. "It reminds me of Johnny Marr."

My shirt is H&M. But Shane couldn't possibly know who designed it.

"Oh, thanks." Cautiously, I look down at my white polka dots and inform him, "It's actually Paul Smith. It's from the upcoming fall line."

In the girls' room, I dab freezing water on my non-designer bags, hide them behind my shades, and then lug them up to Booth Six. Pacing, I google Johnny Marr. .33 seconds later I'm mortified. Marr is not a high fashion label; he is not a designer. He was the guitarist of the Smiths. It's fine. My shirt is more Moz than it is Marr. Shane doesn't know what he's talking about. I slump against the window and click the link that Lynch sent, hoping that Stella's video will help me forget my Britpop *faux pas*. It helps a lot—and is indeed quite interesting.

The 1 minute 29 second long electro-underwear-dance-extravaganza takes place in The Pink Room. Under a strobe light, Prius and

Soufflé prance around in panties while Stella, looking filthy-fabulous in a teal bra and golden silk boxers, stripper dances between them. The cross-dressing DJs follow her into bed and begin poke-tickling her. Giggling, she demands, "Throw it to me beautiful!" Still filming, the camera flies through the air. Stella catches it. The lens turns back on the stunning camera girl. Standing against a bubblegum pink wall in hot pink leopard print tights, a white burn out tee, and teal lace bra, Holly tilts her head and pouts her lips. The frame freezes.

"Hey Mike, it's me." Before my fragile mind and raging libido can even begin to process this piece of recent history, Holly peeks her head into the booth. "Cool if I come in?"

"Miss Hollywood, you are welcome anytime."

I nervously pocket my phone like I'd just been caught watching something that's *not* meant for universal viewing. She sits in the ratty chairs. I join her.

"I like your shirt." She tugs on my sleeve. "It's very Marr."

"You think so too?" I tug at my cuffs, and channeling Prius give her a dashing smile. "Hey, you want some San P.? It's bottled in Terme."

She takes a long swig. I watch her welcoming lips through the translucent green glass. I want to bring up The Premiere—our moment—but I just can't.

"Great party the other night huh?" She wipes her mouth and hands back my drink.

"Oh," I stammer. "Yeah … it was … a lot of fun."

The bottle clinks as I set it next to my Jansport.

"Yeah." She lightly laughs. "I had a lot of fun." Her smile seems quizzical.

I have no answers. She's giving me nothing. On paper I know that I'm getting all green lights, but in here it's all flickering shadows.

Hoping it will conjure my recently deceased confidence, I imagine Stella, topless, smiling in front of me in an unzipped hoodie with a shark pin on it. My witchcraft fails.

"So, I heard you and Stella went for Mexican food? I woke up alone and confused. … It was quite awful…"

"Yeah, those DJ guys bought us burritos. They're cool." She flips up her hood and rests her head on my shoulder. "They know, like, everyone. Sarah and Jamie went to SF with them today to meet with some guy who loves Sarah's blog. He's thinking about putting her in a new reality show."

"Whoa. What's the premise?" I crawl my fingers toward hers.

"She doesn't know." Holly reaches into her pocket and pulls out a Red Vine. My hand awkwardly falls to the armrest. "The call was for 'fierce, fearless, and fucked-up females between the ages of eighteen and twenty-five.'"

"Oh. Well, three out of four ain't bad. She's been trying to get me to show a porno this weekend. Crazy right?"

"That could be hot." Pensively she chews her licorice then springs up. "But you know what could be hotter?" I marvel at her wild metamorphic eyes. She snatches my glasses. "*Jaws.* ..." Slipping them on, she asks. "Hey, have you ever been ice blocking? I haven't. Wanna take me?"

Ice blocking is miserable. It's cold and wet and the risk is not worth the reward. If you don't get arrested for trespassing and destruction of private property you can, at the very least, expect frozen buns and grass stains.

"Oh, yeah, for sure! I go all the time. I'd be happy to show you the ropes ... of ice."

"Fabulous." Standing, she hands over my Fords. They looked so right on her. I wasn't going to ask for them back. "I'll meetcha Saturday at midnight."

"Do you wanna stick around and watch the movie?" I follow her to the door, terribly disappointed that her visit had nothing to do with her pocket pal or the rumor that she's into me. "If you'd rather watch something else—"

"Thanks Mike, but I should go." Smiling a half smile, she hands me another mix CD. "See ya at hole one!"

On the disc she's sharpied a shark. Via word bubble, the fish is saying, "Mmm... Michael!" It's got more of my favorite bands on it. And Justice.

Holding the new track list, I watch her go down the stairs, then, still fascinated by her violet eyes, her violet jeans, her elusive golden toy, and her great taste in pretty much everything, make an emergency call to the coast.

The kid picks up his phone singing, *"I kissed a girl and I—"*

"Alvin, Alvin seriously," I demand. "You gotta tell me how to ice block."

Chapter 32

I promised Cruz a _Rambo_ Premiere. Now he's driving me. "Why are you dressed like an Eskimo?" Nordic nightmares shriek through speakers of the El Camino as we speed through the valley.

"Um, ice blocking." I scroll through his iPod and switch Burzum to _Bona Drag_.

"That dog fur hood ain't gonna help you get any ... even though I know she likes you." I reach over and lay on the horn as he runs a four way stop. "I told her that you were too much of a _maricon_ to go ice blocking." He grins. Morrissey begins to sing.

"Really, you think so?"

Cruz's insight is invaluable. The girls tell him everything both during and in between his 'how to please a penis' seminars. If he says that Holly likes me, it may be true.

"No," he admits. My stomach sinks as if he'd just told me that Stella is pregnant with the worlds next Ronald McDonald and I'm the father. "I know that your brother's man enough to handle a man but I'm not so sure about you."

He pulls into the 7-eleven lot and I step out of his rumbling ride.

"Come on. Do you really think that she likes me?"

"Don't be stupid. Bring me an ice cream."

Resolute to not validate the clerk's suspicions by participating in the tradition of stealing the ice, I drop a Pellegrino, a Dove bar, and a pack of Red Vines onto the counter then ask him to add in two of his finest blocks. Silently, he rings me up and takes my money.

"Wait." I look at my change. "You didn't charge me for the ice."

"Nope."

"So, you're not charging me for the ice?"

"Nope." His face looks like he's inhaled the men's room. "There's no ice."

I get it. He's being a good citizen by trying to subvert the town's great ice blocking menace, while I too am trying to be a good citizen by paying for his fucking frozen hose water.

"C'mon. ..." Without looking at my phone, I text "*STEAL THE ICE*." "Just sell me the ice."

"Nope."

I peripherally watch Cruz load his trunk. Fixed on me, my nemesis remains firm yet stoic. But when I finally plea, "*Por favor*, amigo!" to my joy, he loses it.

"Fuck you, you little shit, I'm not Mexican I'm a Sikh!" His thick Jersey accent gets thicker when he yells. "A Sikh fucking Indian, NOT a Mexican!"

I grab my snacks and declare in disgust, "YOU are racist."

They don't turn from their flashing Funhouse machine as the clerk screams, "I am not racist you skinny little creep vampire Eskimo shit!" But I'd swear to Moz that I hear one of the eternally silent Pin Kids softly comment "nice shades" before I march out the door.

Chapter 33

It's quiet and dark. A cool night breeze penetrates my hood. I can smell the grass. The greens are glowing beneath a blanket of full moonlight but I'm still having a hard time seeing. Sitting on an ice block atop hole one, I watch the shadowy form of the El Camino chase its headlights away from the clubhouse.

"Too bright for you out here Mike?" Holly's voice startles me.

"Hey!" Standing, I remove my shades. "Why are you in the forest?"

"It's so nice out that I figured I'd come explore before you got here." She Bjorks out from an unlikely patch of fog in the woods and eyes my parka. "What's with the snow outfit?"

"The blocks are usually a lot bigger. It really gets cold riding them." I take off the coat to reveal my black thermal. "But we should be okay with this smaller ice here. ... It's much warmer."

"Oh, well that's good. Cuz all I've got is what I've got on." She's wearing black jeans, a black faux leather jacket, and a baggy black tee.

"What's that shirt?" I fold my gloves into my jacket and stack them on my skateboard. "Did you make it when you were a kid?"

I think she's wearing a bra tonight. That can't be a good sign. Maybe it's a sports bra.

"Oh, no." She laughs, looking down at her chest. 'Flipper' is scratched above a dead shark that looks like it was drawn by a first grader. "This was my dad's. I think it's some old band shirt.

I just liked it."

"I know. I was just kidding. My dad used to listen to them too." Slightly tilting her head, Holly smiles. "Hey, who are The Presets?" I ask about the 'Mmm Michael Mix.' "I really like their accents. Brighton?"

"They're from Australia. They're SO nice. One of my friends knows them. He took me to see them at The Glasshouse. I can't remember most of the show, but it was fun. … So…" She points to the two beach-blanketed blocks. "Shall we get slippery and slidey?"

"Absolutely!" Wishing she were asking the same question while wearing nothing but underwear and hovering above me somewhere indoors, I bravely motion to the ice. "Lady's choice."

"I'll take the sharks." She begins to place her perfect, perky little Cheap Monday's skull on the cube.

"Those are actually dolphins."

"Oh." With disdain, Holly jumps up, as if ice burnt. "I'll take the sea horses then."

Saying a prayer to Moz, I plant my butt on the aquatic mammals, grab onto the freezing edges, and scoot myself into motion. About twenty feet later, in the midst of a totally out of control slide and minor panic attack, I bail out. Picking myself up, I check for grass stains, broken nails, and broken bones. The sound of applause draws my attention uphill. Next to my board, Holly stands with her arms circled above her head— it's a standing O.

I tromp back to her and immediately my Orange County snow princess proves herself to be a natural sledder. Despite the treachery and my stinging fingertips, I'm having a good time. In between our runs we sit on sea life, sharing banana bread and our excitement for the fall musical—a conversation that I hope to be an implicit expression of her desire to spend more time with me. We talk a about surf and skate modeling, her chance to pose for her favorite painter, Michael Hussar, Valley View High fries, Lady Gaga and Bat for Lashes. But we don't bring up the last Premiere. Or the fact that tonight is the eve of the Seventies Sex and San P. Party. Instead, smothering a fortunate sea horse, Holly asks me where I want to escape to next year, after graduation.

"I think Hollywood will be able to truly appreciate me." I chew on a bit of walnut. "So I might grace LA with my presence. Where do you wanna go?"

"I have to go back home. It's the best place to get my show made."

"What show?" I wiggle on the seeping ice. *Her eyes are malachite. Her tiny pupils are black pearls. It must be the moonlight.*

Holly finishes her third slice of bread then, with her teeth, rips open the Red Vines. *So Adorable.*

"I've been working on a script. It's like *True Blood* meets *Gilmore Girls* but with supernatural sharks. It's called *El Fin*."

"Wow, that sounds awesome."

I once tried to write lyrics for Band FAIL! but after staring at "Why won't you say that you'll stay? Why do you always run away?" for about 5 minutes, I gave up and watched porn. Wondering if there's a role for me, I ask, "Can I read it sometime?" Holly plants herself on my lap.

Facing me, she clings to my flannel like a sexy blonde koala, chewing licorice instead of eucalyptus.

"Let's go down together." She buries her head in my shoulder.

Her hair smells like unrefined sugar and herbs. I'm tingling everywhere but my numb buns. "Okay, hold on!"

Precariously sliding we make it almost all the way to the tee before falling off. Still locked together, she lands on my chest and I hit the grass with a thud that knocks the wind out of me. I groan. Holly rolls off. Giggling.

"Are you gonna survive Mike?" She hovers over me.

I catch my breath. I'm breathing hers. She half-smiles. She's so close. Her semi-precious eyes bewitch. *This is it. This is the time.* With Cruz and Lynch's assurance echoing in my mind, I move in for the kiss.

Holly jerks away and says, "Shit." I follow her gaze toward the clubhouse. A flashlight is rapidly approaching our romance. *Shit.*

Faster than we slid down, we bound up the hill. I grab my skate and my parka and snatch the towels from Holly.

We flee together. About twenty steps into our sprint, she turns to me.

"We should split up. They'll never catch us." Kissing her fingers, she presses them to my lips. "See ya in the seventies." And dashes down the moonlit green.

I've been here long enough. My ass is still moist but the risk of detainment has surely passed. Blocks away from the golf course, ending my Jiffy Luber impression, I roll myself and my board out from under the old Dodge van. I dust my hands and inspect my shades for scratches before losing a sizeable portion of my mind over a dime-sized oil spot on my parka. I check my phone. I have no messages and it's far too early to wrap such a trying, stained, un-kissed evening.

I'm going to clean.

Chapter 34

School starts tomorrow. I can't believe it. There's really no telling how the tribulations of senior life might get in the way of my party. Tonight could likely be the final Premiere. This may be my last chance to dress up before Winter Ball.

Standing in Joey's mirror, I adjust my suit. I refold my black bandana five times then arrange it perfectly in my breast pocket. I remove and replace my shades until I'm certain that I look good in all lighting. For forty-five minutes, I perfect my hair then, snapping open my tubular secret weapon, put the finishing GO SMiLE touches on my teeth. I smile at the handsome boy in my mirror.

"How do I look?"

Warmed by her nudging approval of my casual footwear, I kiss Eddie then rush down to summer's big ending.

....

Fashionably late and perfectly preened, I part the heavy curtains to find my own Studio 54 sizzling. Most of the trashed-out girls haven't searched beyond American Apparel for their retro costumes but they all look hot. There is no absence of bare flesh tonight. Stella, wearing heart shaped glasses and a leopard print raincoat, is tee-tering on spray painted roller skates, drinking from a Solo cup, and talking to Holly. The vegan is shifting her gold lamé bootie shorts on green plastic while deconstructing Charlie Sheen quotes. Her black tube socks should be embroidered with a parental advisory warning. As I walk to my speech position, I glance signature side-boob peeking through Holly's white tank top. *She is fabulous.*

Leaning against the wall screen, I assess the turnout. The Prozens have glued awful moustaches to their faces. Star's not here. Leo is smoking weed with MK in Surfers' Paradise and ... *oh no.*

"Hey my brother, glad you could finally make it!" Wearing a Bert-and-Ernie-striped tank top, Donny welcomes me to my own party. "We're about to start a new game over there." Tossing up a bloated, fist-sized baggy of white, he over-palms it with a slap and smiles. "You should come!"

After handing me what appears to be a cigarette case, Prius joins Soufflé, Stella, and Mia at the PlayStation.

I can't tell if they're in costume but the DJs' authentic seventies vibe is slightly compromised when they begin to chop and do lines off this decade's latest advancement in home gaming technology. It's a loathsome sight. But the coke is thematically appropriate and Donovan did just slip me a fully loaded, chrome GO SMiLE compact. I'm going to let their drug use and party-crashing slide. Stella leans over the console. Red satin and tight, deep cleavage makes it easy for me to ignore the pink straw. After powdering, she stands, wipes her nose, and waves at me. Donny's pigtail dips into a rail. They all laugh. I check my face in my new compact then clap my hands.

"Welcome, my esteemed Filmgreats and un-invited Extras, to the Seventies Sex and San P. Premiere!"

....

Heaven is almost full. Cruz and Volta, both wearing huge butterfly collars, are kissing on their Love Seat. The rest of us have cozied ourselves together on the mattresses where, with the DJs' encouragement, Stella is intent on telling me all about her reality show audition. She insists, "I know I'm perfect for the part!" Asks, "Isn't it exciting?" Then puts her tongue in my mouth before I can answer. This cycle repeats itself several times, and every time she kisses me it's both arousing and relieving. Finally, when Heather Graham starts stripping onscreen, she stops talking.

Wobbling up onto the stage, Stella peels off her spotted raincoat and throws it at me.

"Woooooh!" In red satin underwear, the revved up roller girl wildly laps the theatre twice, falls back next to me, and picks up where she left off. She tosses her feathered hair. "I know I'm perfect—"

I toss her coat and cut straight to the making out. This time our activities are escalating. Forgetting to stop and tell me yet again how much some guy named Blake loves her blog, Stella shoves her hand down my slacks. I begin gathering blankets in hopes of masking another OJ, and she breaks away to cheer on the antics of the fifteen-year-old with facial hair.

Upstage, in the projection, now wearing a gigantic white afro-wig, Alvin outdoes Dirk Diggler's karate moves for his greatly pre-occupied audience. He punches, spin kicks, then front flips back into Heaven. Ninety-eight pounds of boy thuds next to Ash. He begins braiding her hair, and with her face mashed into a mondo sequined-disco-ass, she remains unconscious while Mia continues tugging. Feet away from the tranquilized twin, Lynch's crusty eye diamond is hidden in the wrinkle of a tortured wince. In Mia's clutches, he looks like he's getting his Producer pierced. "Hang in there," I supportively whisper. "A JO's a JO!" He grimaces. Stella's record starts skipping again.

"Isn't it exciting?!" With my moths tickling my throat, I watch her, waiting, hoping that she will once again answer her own question with a tongue kiss. But I have no such luck. "Isn't it, like, SO exciting?"

"Totally!" The two girls squeeze hands, as Holly agrees. "So exciting ... so amazing ... so—"

Unwittingly saving the sober, cobalt-eyed beauty from the amphetamine fed monologue, Prius tackles the talker and begins poke-tickling Stella's words into squeals. The display is very reminiscent of a certain popular and troubling video-blog. *It's fine.* Donny has left a very desirable opening in Heaven.

Carefully, I crawl toward Holly. When I pause to count the hickeys that MK has put on Leo's ribs, Prius and Stella, giggling like kids on candy, bombard me. Using my pushup strength, I fend them off.

I twist out of the DJ's embrace. Heaven trembles. I grapple with Stella. Donny pins back my arms. I laugh. I squirm, inhaling the smoky pigtails whipping my face. I'm helpless. Stella unbuttons my un-tucked shirt. She pokes my ribs. She tortures me with tickles. She begins sucking my neck. And I stop laughing. With her amped hum electrifying me into charged submission, I pant, reaching out to test the structural integrity of her sleek bra. My hands have been freed. *I wonder where Donny went.* My co-star works her way under the fur.

Lying on my back, thanking Moz for answering my most recent prayers, I close my eyes and relax into my second Premiere OJ.

Small, satisfied sounds slurp beneath the blankets as I mouth the familiar *Boogie Nights* dialogue. "You know what?" Casually, I wag my finger at the sandbags, "I'm the biggest star here, man, that's the way it is. I wanna fuck. It's my big dick, so everybody get ready fucking now!"

Suddenly, the sounds of hardcore sex boom through the speakers. The Prozens giggle. I sit up to see what's going on.

"OMG fucking hot! Woooo!" Mia yells.

Band FAIL! guffaws. Cruz exclaims, "Oh hells yes!"

An oversized image of Jenna Jameson, getting it doggy style from a tan brunette in satin gloves and a strap-on, has mysteriously replaced my chosen *film de la nuit*. Emerging from the covers, Stella looks down at me like a proud mother.

"Oh my god! Good choice Baby!" She admires the screen. "Aren't Jenna's necklaces gorgeous?"

Clearly, the artful executive decision to show porn was a good one, though sadly, I cannot claim the bold move. It is my wise, carefree co-host who we all must credit for doctoring the *Boogie Nights* disc.

I squeeze Lynch's hand. He squeezes back, smiling with a slight nod of brotherhood. Not wanting to compromise our seemingly precarious position, we lay frozen, side-by-side, silently grinning as Mia shows him her appreciation and we enjoy our first simultaneous OJs.

Beneath the throws, my co-star giggles. His co-star giggles. And the skin flick sleazes on. Then everything changes. I can't say for certain if it's the magic of the porno, the power of us all being pressed together in Heaven, the red wine, the Colt 45, the

Cuervo, the cocaine, the vitamin x, or the perfect combination of all these elements that we have to thank for the following moment of Flimgreat history. But what happens next is this: Everybody starts fucking. And my leading lady is the first to make the big move.

Stripping off our cover, Stella pulls her shiny panties to one side and mounts my excited Producer. Right here. Next to everyone else. In the middle of Heaven. Only partially out of fear that she'll suddenly sober up and remove herself, I grab her hips. I trap her to me and as she contends for Best Leading Cowgirl she starts making sex sounds unlike any that I've ever heard IRL. It's really cool.

Although initially surreal, this end-of-blockbuster-summer-sex-explosion quickly begins to feel familiar. I've seen enough group sex online to take cues from. And if the rest of my guests have somehow not spent their childhood exploiting the benefits of their pornography machines, they must either be naturals themselves or intuitively looking to Ms. Jameson to guide them—because no one here is the least bit inhibited.

Ecstatically, I pat Lynch's shoulder and grin. Two thumbs up and a huge open-mouthed smile are shot my way as Mia slurps and Alvin hoists up to his knees to hobble next to his brother. His relatively sizeable Producer is jutting from a pair of orange boxers.

"Do me next!" Al's wig is still in place and he's now wearing Stella's red plastic rimmed shades.

"Eww. Gross. No." Mia pauses for a salacious breath. "You're brothers!"

"That's why it's NOT gross! It's, like, the exact same thing!"

Ignoring his persistent reasoning and the bowing saliva bridge from Mia's mouth to the head of Lynch's production, I return my hands and concentration to the girl on top of me. Continuing to agilely grind, Stella dexterously removes her roller skates. Their wheels rest against my shins. Her boobs bounce. Her mouth gapes. She touches herself. And I fully enjoy watching. Until like a wet-dream-gone-nightmare, our adult film turns into a spook show.

Arising over Stella's shoulder, all fifties movie-monstery, my only fully naked guest leans in, starts lapping at her neck, and squeezes her satiny c-cups. I'm devastated. *Now I can't see her boobs.* Keeping our rhythm, Stella turns, kisses Donny, and effortlessly spins into reverse cowgirl. During this smooth move, she neither breaks her lip-lock nor allows me to slip out of my reserved seating. *She is so talented.*

Prius stands. Our co-star takes him all the way into her wine-stained mouth, and I look away. I focus on her lower back tattoo then accidentally look back up. The DJ's expectedly huge hit-single is pistoning past her tongue. Smiling his dashing, ultra bright smile he's looking at me.

"Yeah my brother!"

I sigh. I wave. And Prius gazes off toward the candy couches.

It's fine. Everything's fine. I just hope he finishes in her mouth and not on me.

I look back down at the tattoo for seconds before a semi-familiar voice draws my attention from stage left. "Hey leave her the fuck alone you creep! She's passed out!"

Whoa, I've never heard a twin yell.

MK, having stopped sucking, is still holding onto Leo's long-board. "I'll kick you in the dick!"

Huffing, Soufflé rolls off of Ash and erection-skulks away. He's wearing a camelhair dinner jacket. And he's unshorn. *Gross. I wonder where his shirt and pants are.*

With the dour DJ out of sight, Lynch, Mia, Stella, Prius, Leo, MK, and I continue to weave a writhing, groaning, laughing mass of limbs in Heaven. Taking the squeakers lead we're all giving Jenna some stiff competition for the next AVNs while Cruz and Volta tear through their own private Idaho down on their couch. I reach over and grab Mia's boob. She giggles. Then I giggle. Keeping my left hand occupied with her, I work Stella's hips with my right and—"Yeah, my brother!" Donny smiles, nods, and gazes off.

I sigh, smile, wave, and close my eyes. Stella slightly gags, slaps her ass down on my Producer, then someone says, "So am I. Just don't get any on me." I tilt my head as far back as I can to get an inverted view of what Prius has been staring at between smiles.

Sitting on a candy couch, Holly has her shorts and panties piled next to her. With her feet propped up on plastic, her tube socks clinging to her calves, and her legs spread wide, she faces the screen. She faces me. Judged by the upside-down, clean-shaven deity between her legs, my breath is taken and my atheism is shaken. To avoid madness, I have no choice but to avert my gaze from the rapture and confront the two moustaches book-ending her in a high-noon standoff.

Stage left of Holly, with a double-handed grip, Soufflé is furiously brandishing his bread stick while Alvin, stage right, stands poised with one hand on his Dogtown lord and the other on his well-aimed Flip Cam. Their duel rages forth, as she feels herself up. Delicately, she moves her buzzing golden friend between her legs until, almost inaudibly, she breaths, "I'm gonna..." and causes a seminal chain reaction.

Soufflé blasts onto the arm of the couch. Alvin purposefully sprays all over Soufflé . Then, just before Holly rolls her azure eyes back into her head, right when the quivering Flimgreat in knee-highs looks at me and groans, "Ugggghoh FUCK," I release my joy deep inside of Stella.

SCH
NIG

OOL
HTS

Chapter 35

"Wake up! *Boop, boop, boop!*" My alarm is rudely screaming.
Regretting not having taken my GED, I force open my eyes.
"Boop, boop, boop. Get sexy for the new freshmen!"
Sick to my stomach with a case of the earlies, I unplug my phone, check my messages, fall out of bed, and turn on Primal Scream. I've barely slept. I had to clean The Palace. Mopping up after Soufflé the Saucier is not my favorite thing to do, but sometimes a lot of fun can be a little messy. Last night was a lot of fun.
Replaying the choppy footage of our first big sex scene in my sputtering mind, I shower, borrow Joey's Psychocandy shirt, then dash out the door as my beautiful long lost friend rolls into the driveway. The Cadillac has been released.
"Have a great first day boys!" Gina follows me from the house as I slip into the shiny black '59 CC. Alvin probably waxed it.
"Thanks Mrs. Massi." Zach yells over the music.
"Michael!" She hands me my metallic Union Jack thermos, "Have you thought anymore about what you'd like for your birthday?"
"Yeah." Slamming the heavy door I push my head from the open window and smile. "A McQueen skull tie."
Every year Frank tells me, "Despite what your brother may think, spending two hundred dollars on a tie is insane. Just insane." Gina shakes her head. Lynch backs out of the driveway, grinning.
"Last night was fucking awesome."
"It was." I turn down the tunes and sip my freshly brewed PG Tips.

"So fucking awesome."

"Yes it was." My tea burns my lips.

Holding the open thermos between my legs, feeling a touch anxious about my forthcoming clothed encounters with my friends, I ask, "Have you heard from anyone today?"

"No, have you?"

I shake my head. Lynch turns up the music. It's the Ramones.

"I can't believe that happened." He gulps his black coffee, sounding not like he was just granted invincibility but more like he just aced a pop quiz. "We've gotta throw another party. Immediately. Tomorrow."

"Yes but no. That's insane. Let's do it Saturday." Grabbing the Visine from his candy filled ashtray, I moan. "We can't do Sundays anymore. I feel like I'm gonna die. I don't know how I'm gonna make it through this week."

I pull the sunshade down and my eyelids up.

"Hey, did you hear?" He passes me his sixty-two ounce thermos. With my eyes dripping, I manage to choke down half of his black coffee. "Another church burned down."

He smirks.

"Yeah, I know..." I croak my caffeinated confession. "I did it."

"How black metal of you, Varg."

I don't know who Varg is but, presuming him to be a very handsome, creative young man, I thank my driver for the compliment then take a final gulp.

"Do they know how it happened?"

"They think it had something to do with candles and dried up flowers."

Lynch reclaims his bitter drink. Joey sings about glue. The CC climbs the hill. We just passed the police station. Now the jail. We're minutes away.

"That's cool." I stare out of the window. A black-booted grave cutter from our year is smoking in front of the cemetery. "I hope there weren't any church cats in there."

Lurching up, we park in the overflowing Valley View lot and my heart sinks. Now, again, begins the pointless homework, the exposure to cretinous classmates, and the overcrowded lunch breaks with filthy flesh eaters.

"Hey. Dustin." Glancing in his rearview, Lynch weakly insists. "Get up," then turns off the car. Cracking the window so his sleeping brother doesn't die, he gets out of the Deville. A dirge begins to play and together we walk toward our outdoor campus.

It's been months but I feel like I was just here.

As we step onto the school grounds infested with kids in their new poorly-put-together fall outfits, I lower my head, take a deep breath, and try to hold it in until the next party.

....

On this first day of senior year, when Filmgreats meet in the walk-ways, in class, or in the quad, almost nothing is explicitly spoken of The Seventies Premiere. We just smile like we've stolen the answers to the SAT and say things like "great movie" or "you look tired" or ... "That was so hot when you came in me last night."

"Oh, yeah, sorry about that." Startled by this whispered 7:00 am salutation, I put down my scotch tape and shelve my notebooks. "Are you going to be ... okay?"

"Don't be SORRY!" Stella, leaning against the locker next to mine, rubs her hand up the back of my head, messing up my hair. "I said it was hot. And I'll be fine. I know how to take care of myself. I'll see ya second period Babe." She kisses me on the neck then struts toward the arts building.

Her lower back flashes from between her white belt and a black shirt that says 'Dim Mak.' The last time I looked away from her cryptic tattoo I saw Donny's joy filing her mouth. I'm totally relieved that she didn't just kiss me on mine. I tape a new picture of Moz up between the tears of Agyness Deyn and Alexa Chung, sigh, then shut my locker.

....

Standing at the edge of the sunken quad, Holly and Mia are talking about some cute new guy at school and looking far less tired than I feel. Interrupting, I ask the handsome fellow's name.

"Mr. Snow." Mia points to a normal looking kid that's walking toward the language building. "He's our new Spanish teacher. He's a total hottie. We heard that he's hiding tons of tattoos and that he was in a band. But he won't tell anyone which one. Stella says she's gonna get it out of him."

"I imagine that she will."

"I bet he was in Nirvana." Ogling the Levis of the failed rocker, Mia follows them across campus.

I turn to Holly. "Wanna do the death march?"

We both have first period PE—a crimeless punishment that requires diving into a poorly heated pool before 8:00 am.

"I think you'll survive, Mike."

A group of wrestlers, clumped in front of the Science building, snicker as we walk by. I ignore them. *Please, not on the first day. Not in front of her.*

"All you *'The OC'* people took life guard training right?" I ask Holly. "I'm already having palpitations—"

"Nice fag-bag faggot!"

One of the animals has broken from its herd. In an Affliction shirt, it's complimenting my shiny white Ben Sherman PVC messenger bag—Joey got it for me as a beginning-of-senior-year present. I think the beast may have kept walking if Holly had refrained from deftly commenting, "Douchebag."

Whipping around, he glares at her, then me, in simian shock.

"What did you say faggot?" He shoves me. Hard.

I stumble backwards. I wish this wasn't happening in front of the brave and beautiful screenwriter. Shirking my fear of plastic surgery, I calmly explain, "I knew that you and your father had the same taste."

"What?"

"Well, he bought me the bag." I take off my Fords and hand them to Holly. I wouldn't want them scratched by an incoming fist. "He gives me presents, we suck each other off. You know. It's your typical sugar-daddy relationship..." I feign sudden astonishment. "I guess that kinda makes us brothers right?"

Holly laughs. The seething homophobe yells, "I'm going to fucking kill you!" I wince. Luckily this proclamation grabs the attention of a faggot-sympathizer who's on his way to class.

"Leave him alone, Bobby!" Shane bear hugs the daddy's boy. "He's my friend."

Bobby squirms, but is only released after promising to not fuck with me. Without saying another word, my red-faced would-be murderer storms off. And I blow him a kiss.

"Thanks, Shane."

The back of Bobbie's rippling tee says 'Throwdown.' My savior is wearing a baby blue cardigan over a white Smiths shirt.

"Richardson's got a temper." Shane puts his arm around me and giggles. "And what was a vampire scarecrow gonna do against a middleweight all-American grappler?" Pulling his round tin from his sweater, he dabs his finger into rosy balm and smears his lips. "I'll see ya in Lake Chlorine, Buddy!"

Chapter 36

Aside from the Wednesday trauma of seeing a freshman wearing my same outfit and the Thursday novelty of finding a note in my locker that reads 'You and your bag are gay,' the first week of school is typical. So far, I've found my classes even less stimulating than last year's, but this quarter isn't totally hopeless. Despite its wholesome and pedestrian nature, I know that the fall musical will be a good time.

Tonight in Hess Theatre, at our first rehearsal meeting, Rick explains how he plans on enacting the play's ultra-violent war scene without causing the school board to come down on us. He then claims, "I'd like to try to push the limits with the orgy scene." Cheers arise from our cast, and I shoot a saucy glance toward the Filmgreat in the aisle seat. Next to me, keeping her cool and surely not wanting to risk compromising our secrecy, Holly continues focusing on our director's lecture and ignores me entirely. I respect her caution. Smiling, Rick turns his back to grab a stack of photocopies.

Holly stands and begins undressing. She stacks her folded, yellow jeans on her seat. I admire the set. The kids who worked on it really outdid themselves, especially with the giant bed that the platinum blonde lifeguard/actress/sex-toy-expert has just slipped into with Stella. Both wearing golden underwear, the two are playing catch with buzzing vibes of various precious metals. Katie Perry is tossing the toys from stage left. Wearing black satin underwear, gloves, and Chanel pearls, the Ameripop pitcher calls a time-out and beckons me. I rise.

"All leads are welcome to run lines in here during lunch and free periods." Rick hands me a photocopied calendar. He's passing out the rehearsal schedules. "We'll start choreography with the players on Monday."

Holly and I flip through the time constraints of the upcoming weeks. *Fabulous.* Saturdays are free.

"I'm going to send out the new invites tonight." I whisper to the green-eyed Great. "Any requests?"

Rick is talking about costumes and haircuts.

"Oooh, that reminds me," she coos, then shouts across the seats, "Hey Mr. Nalon, when are we gonna rehearse the kissing scene?" Startled, I look down into my calendar as the cast titters.

"Not until the end of the month." Rick shoots a stern glance at my giggling, talent-less understudy before comforting Holly. "You'll be fine, Becca, don't be nervous."

"Oh, I'm not," she announces, then turns to me and whispers, "...You should show *Jaws*."

....

Leaning against a light post in front of our lockers, I'm discussing old Morrissey solo records with Holly while failing to re-introduce the topic of our musical-mandated lip-lock. I bring up *You Are the Quarry*, she mentions a b-side that I've never heard, and Lynch appears at the top of the campus stairs. He's come to pick me up. As he walks toward us, all the lights buzz to life, electrified by the passing of his kinetic hair. Kindly, my driver attempts to extend my time with the snowy blonde by offering her a ride. Holly turns it down. Stella is coming to pick her up. It's Friday night and they're going to meet the DJs at some live-in art space, somewhere between here and SF. How unbearable—dirty bathrooms, self-rolled cigarette smoke, a houseful of pigtailed men covered in paint. I cringe at the thought.

"Do you guys wanna come?" Holly flicks at my skinny black tie. "I could ride there with you."

"Yeah, totally! I love art." I hopefully turn to Lynch.

"Sure. You just gonna bail work man?"

"Oh, that's right, No. I forgot." Nervously, I check my phone. "We'd better go or I'll be late. Um, okay Miss Wood." Unsure whether or not I'm indeed demanding her attendance to a second private orgy, I hesitantly insist, "You better be there tomorrow."

"I wouldn't miss it for an open bar with Aoki."

I love her crooked smile.

....

"Look. It doesn't matter." Lynch is shouting. His 2012 system is blaring in his '59 Caddy as we speed toward the 8-plex. "Everyone thought it was killer. The Twins were definitely *not* freaked out. Mia thinks that they secretly want their parents to know about the party ... but that's insane ... whatever. The only reason people haven't been talking is because no one wants to get caught."

I turn from the sun visor mirror to face him. The purple and yellow bruises around his eye jewelry are almost gone.

"They'd better not tell Mr. and Mrs. Christ."

"Settle."

My co-host wants to show another porno tomorrow. I'm maintaining that we provide the comforting pretense of a straight film.

"How about *Jaws*?"

"What?"

"Okay. What about *Showgirls*?"

As I campaign, Lynch begins singing along with the glitzy vocals coming through the speakers: *'I don't care what the others say, when I've found a new game to play...'*

"It's not *actually* porn. The girls can tell themselves that they're going to a normal Premiere if they need to feel less weird about the whole thing—"

Claim to fame! Clamor for glamour!

"Lynch—" *Oh padeo.* "Hey—" *Oh pa padeo!*

I turn down the music. He shakes his head laughing.

"You're seriously way paranoid." Breaking into a poor falsetto impression of Holly's butterscotch voice he mimics, "'I wouldn't miss it for a Steve Aoki party.' Does that sound rattled? Doesn't sound rattled to me. But, okay. If you're rattled, we'll do *Showgirls*."

He pulls up to the curb in front of the glowing marquee and cranks his stereo.

"Fabulous. I know at least Holly will appreciate its B-movie mystique." Grabbing my Sherman, stepping out of the car, I lean in through the passenger window. "How cool is she? Did I ever tell you that we went ice blocking?"

Lynch eyes me like I just asked him to buy me a Big Mac.

"Are you serious?"

"Yeah. She's really cool."

"That's fucking weird man." His face diamond disappears into a solemn squint.

"Yeah. It was cool. She's cool. I'll see ya tomorrow." I shut the door.

Slinging my bag over my shoulder, I walk into work, thinking of gold.

....

Sequoia Creep is wearing a bowler with a brass clock in its brim. He's tearing tickets. Tonight, Shane has a new sweater and a new position. Reaching into my private stash of San P., I ask the wrestler why he's working concessions.

"It makes me happy being around so much candy." He hands a two hundred pound woman a 4.75-ounce box of box of Junior Mints. "And I like helping people in need."

"Oh, right, okay. Well, thanks again for saving me from Bobby last week, man." I pull a second chilled Limonata from the ice and hand it to him.

He reacts like I've just handed him backstage passes to see Tiga.

"For sure Buddy!" Bopping, the killer philanthropist cradles the little bottle to his two-toned barrel chest. "But you know, if you'd just hit the weight pile once in a while you'd be less of a *scorecrow* and no one would fuck with you."

"What did you just call me?" I'm hoping that my ears are deceiving me but to my horror, he whispers, "Can I come to the party

Mike?"

Shane's eyes look like Eddie's do when something that only she can see runs through our house.

"What party?" *Turning, I spit a swarm of moths into the popcorn machine and shut them in. They bounce against the glass.*

"The movie party. C'mon—"

I drag him down below the lower level of Sour Patch Kids.

"How and what do you know?"

"In Tailoring I heard Sarah talking with Jamie about 'Score's Party,' —something about Caligula I think." He rapidly confesses, as I curse the girls. "I asked them what they were talking about but they wouldn't tell me so when I saw Hector in Physics I told him that Score said for me to ask him when the next party is. He was surprised and said '*Miguelito* told you to ask me?' But then he wouldn't tell me anything else."

I'm impressed by both his cunning and his Cruz imitation. *Thank Moz that he doesn't know everything.*

"So can I come Mike?" he pleads. "Is it at Zach's?"

"Um, sure." Reeling from his use of our old names, I brace myself against the glowing glass and stammer, "I'll send you the invite once I have it made, but Shane … " I cup his Brad Pitt jaw-line. "You have to promise to not talk about the party to anyone."

"Like *Fight Club*! I promise man." He's ecstatic. Even his stubble feels happy.

I can't believe he has stubble. So Colin Farrell.

"I don't really talk to anybody but Jamie and you anyway … *Score.*"

He smiles his gentle, yet rugged all-American smile, and we arise from our concession case conspiracy. After pounding my sweet-citrusy Pellegrino, I drop it into the recycling, shove my hands in my Ksubis, and step out from the lair of the creeps.

"That's a nice sweater, man." I admit in passing as I click my way down the stained carpet.

"Thanks Buddy!" Looking like a bouncing bee in his yellow and black striped top, he raises his bottle of San P. and booms. "It's Paul Smith!"

In my black Paul Frank devil-monkey robe, I'm stretched across my red comforter. My Mac is open on my lap and my iPod is shuffling in my ears. Fresh from an after-work shower, shampoo, and conditioning, I google up a black-and-white still of Gina Gershon. She has her hand on Elizabeth Berkley's chest. Both lingeried ladies are lying on a strip club stage. Behind them, sitting in a bar chair, is a leering lascivious man. After a moment or two of consideration, I substitute my face for his, paste on my standard rules and regulations paragraph, call it 'The NC-17 Premiere!' and send out the invite.

Chapter 37

I probably could have spent more time on the *Showgirls* piece this morning, but its imperfections deterred no one from coming. Tonight, we have our second full cast. Yet, as my guests socialize, partaking in popcorn and Pellegrino or pills and Patrón, I'm standing rigid in my speech position, becoming more and more unsettled. The school week has crawled by and, still, no one has mentioned our first big sex scene—only Stella, barely. A tension is building behind the curtain. It feels like we've all spent hours in line and are finally about to step onto X2 at Magic Mountain. Our rollercoaster is just clicks away from its zenith.

"Welcome Filmgreats to the NC-17 Premiere!" I'm now unsure about my adamant decision to un-invite Jenna Jameson. If the porn splice really was the essential catalyst needed to propel us into public debauchery, I'm fucked. Well, not fucked. "... A brand new playlist made especially with tonight's after party in mind..." I look out at my audience, full of high school girls dressed as hairdress-ers, fearing that last week's love-in was a once-in-a-lifetime cosmic moment, like the passing of a concupiscent comet, or sexy solar eclipse. "We bring you *Showgirls!*"

I kill the lights, join the talent on the floor, and realize I've indeed made a big mistake. I should have just yelled, "Premiere Sex Scene. Take two. ACTION!"

It all explodes so quickly this time that I don't even know who starts going for it first. With the Xmas lights low and Gershon high on the wall, everyone in Heaven immediately gets down to the dirty work. Though it's not all business. Our grade school make-out sessions quickly graduate to adult activities, but we all take occasional pause to enjoy refreshments and shout out *Showgirls* quotes. This relaxed atmosphere should have forewarned me of the impermanence of my position but, right now, I'm feeling totally confident lying next to Lynch. He has Mia on top of him; I have Stella on top of me. The girls are doing it to us like they're being filmed. It's fabulous, until the brunettes start focusing on each other. Dismounting, Stella pulls her BFF in front of the screen to showcase their performance and suddenly our scenic ride is over.

"Woah!" Lynch motions to the living movie magic. "That's pretty cool,"

Unable to ignore its rudeness, I point back at his accusatory Producer. "That's pretty cool, too."

We laugh, and I erection-prance over to the soundboard.

Standing socked and pant-less, I turn knobs and flick switches. "Lynch, C'mere!" I'm frantically trying to start my Sex Scene playlist but my slacking sound tech is too busy manually making up for Mia's abandonment to help me. Hovering over Holly's couch, he, Soufflé, and Prius are fully respecting the buzz bomb's 'both hands on yourself' rule. Touched by her elegance, I'm transfixed. I can't imagine why the DJs aren't. As if in the midst of a gentlemanly competition they keep turning from her solo to sternly gaze into each other's eyes.

"LYNCH come on man!" Having just tied a triple knot into an unruly bunch of chords, I pause my fidgeting. Confronting me from about two feet away, Volta's ass is hoisted in the air as he and Cruz quietly 69 on the purple love seat. Their chinos are barely hanging onto their thighs. "*Culo* suave!" I compliment,

One of them makes a slurpy sound that I take to mean 'thank you.' Wondering if our own red headed siren is enjoying our party's new triple-x-rating, I cue up La Roux.

Patting my brow with my pocket square, I check Surfers' Paradise, then turn away from MK's oral work on Leo to find that his sister, Star, sitting cross-legged on a pile of furry pillows in Heaven, has her head turned toward Ash. Propped up on her haunches, dressed like a stripper, the semi-conscious twin is feeling up the sea goddess as they kiss. I'm shocked. I was expecting to find Alvin victoriously exploring Star's universe, but this is not happening. It's not happening at all. He's lying with his head in her lap and she's petting him while sucking Ash's tongue.

I don't feel too bad for Al. Laid out with his jeans and eyes at half-mast, he is slowly massaging his Dogtown lord and staring emotionlessly at the buzzing gold between Holly's legs. He looks serene.

As Alvin films his right hand, "Bulletproof ... I Wish I Was" begins miraculously bouncing off the walls and I prepare for my glorious return to group activities. I pocket square my Producer, fold my coat, and confidently step out from behind the soundboard—only to find that Prius has beaten me to the next level. With the exception of the girls' black thigh-highs, he, Mia, and Stella are completely naked, leaning in a row against the wall screen, heavily petting. The movie flashes across their flesh. The site is fabulous, even with Mr. Pigtails in the center of the Great sandwich. I can see his teeth glimmering from here. But his radiant presence shan't discourage me.

Donny has made it very clear that he's not selfish.

Driven, yet unsure how to insert myself, I erection-prance over to the playful threesome, and arrive just in time to see Mia reach around the DJ and guide him into Stella.

Now I don't know what to do.

Lurking behind Mia, my Producer stands at awkward attention. She leans into Donny. I graze her gargantuan ass, but she doesn't notice. She's kissing the back of Prius's neck and, I believe, doing something with his production house. Stella is jolting with his thrusts. Catching me watching, she rolls open her melting blues and turns back.

"Hey Baby!"

Her mouth gapes. She gasps, surprised, as if she's just been stabbed. She clenches her teeth, bites her lip, then in an act of unparalleled humanitarianism, commands Mia, "Go for it girl. I know you want to."

With vitamin-wild eyes and an almost malevolent sneer, Mia looks over her shoulder, snatches my Producer, and slips it inside herself. *Fabulous*. I cross my arms around her, grab boobs, pull her to me, and start feverishly kitty humping.

Gripping double D's, bopping away, I'm admiring the giant buns mashing into my crotch when a hand slides atop mine. Donny, having spun my former co-star, is playing handsies with me. While still doing it to her, he caresses my fingers. "Hello my brother!" He smiles a huge GO SMiLE and I get freaked out. I can't understand how his teeth are so perfect. *Moz, I forgot to use my whitener.*

Looking down, I suck in my cheeks and we all hump on. I compare and contrast Mia's internal physiology with her BFFs. She squeaks, and as I've begun considering where to release the impending joy, a fourth Filmgreat delays my happy ending.

"Excuse me sir." He taps my shoulder. "May I cut in?"

"Hayyy Rock Star," Mia boozily gushes. I immediately pull out.

I turn to gauge Lynch's demeanor. His two thumbs up, erection, and open-mouthed smile reminds me of a Mastercard commercial: priceless.

"Certainly my good man!" Relieved that my co-host didn't suddenly get weird and go all Alpha upon seeing his best friend banging his regular, I remove myself. "The scene is yours!"

Now a free agent, wavering like a half-stripped fifth wheel, I consider joining Stella and Prius. With his pigtails flying everywhere, he's dripping sweat and grunting. She's screaming to the catwalks about the diminutive size and reliable seal of her vagina.

I'm going to go freshen up and check in on Holly.

At the mini fridge, I douse and wipe myself down. I polish my teeth, fix my hair, and then cautiously approach the couch of the green-eyed enchantress. Having left behind some French dressing on the floor, Soufflé has gone to dress in Surfers' Paradise. When I creep up, with my Pellegrino-primed Producer peeking out from the last button of my sweat soaked shirt, Holly is alone. Her head is thrown over the back of the candy couch. Her eyes are closed and her mouth is open—barely. Her left hand is squeezing her right boob. She's left on her black lace bra but her black jeans, remixed Smiths shirt, and black panties are balled up next to her on the couch. With her legs spread and her sock-less feet propped up on the plastic, she reclines while giving it her all.

Standing a few feet upstage, a lone voyeur, I watch her—dizzied by her magnificence until she senses my presence.

"Hey Mike." Raising her head and showing me her chameleonic

lavender eyes, she pauses her play. "Mind if I watch?"

"Oh..." Slightly embarrassed for having not known that it's been working independently of my brain, I look down at my frantic hand. Like I'd just been caught trying to steal a VMA, I drop my hot Producer and politely return the question. "Do you mind if *I* watch?"

"Just don't get any on me." Raising the bullet, she presses a hidden golden button. Her vibe kicks harder. "And take off your shades."

My eyes don't leave her face. The beats of Crystal Castles throb. And she watches me. She raises her gaze from my hand, to my eyes, and back again. The sound in the room shifts. All I can hear is her buzzing toy and her rich groans. All else disappears into a homogenous euphony of indistinguishable ambient sex, until Holly shutters.

She finishes. It sounds like the Smiths. And her expression takes me with her.

Carefully I catch my warm joy in my clammy left hand then look down at my Union Jack socks. I'm considering using them to wipe off when the echoes of Britpop angels are suffocated.

"Hey Babe!" Stella is on all fours in Heaven, yelling over Deamau5. "Oh fuck, Donny, fuck yeah. ... Come get in Score, I can handle it ... shit, fuck fuck fuuuuck."

From behind her, Prius seconds.

"Yeah, my brother!" He waves me over. "There's room for one more."

What I mistook for a white beret in Surfers' Paradise was, in fact, my dear friend's bleached hair. Lynch was dressing offstage. Now, he and his disheveled co-star are standing at the mini-fridge, re-hydrating. They left the scene that I left them in. And I wish they hadn't: I wish it *were* my co-host's Producer gagging Stella between her attempts to coerce me into being number four of four. But it's not. It's the pastry's bread stick.

The man does not shave.

"Come ON sexy. Fuck m—!"

Soufflé silences her. I shudder at the sight of it.

It's fine.

"Come tag in my brother!"

Everything's fine. I have a good excuse.

"Thanks guys, I'd love to!" Waving at the welcoming two-out-of-three, I present the joyful evidence dripping from my fingers. "But I'm done."

Chapter 38

I need to shower again. I feel slimy. But The Palace is clean. It looks fabulous. Today I brought my arsenal: Lysol, Oxiclean, Comet, bleach, and apple cider vinegar. I vigorously scrubbed away all the sticky, gooey, musty remains, put a pair of plaid boxers in the new lost-and-found milk crate, and then arranged a hygiene station: stain sticks, sugar-free Altoids, Kleenex, baby wipes, paper towels, hand sanitizer, and Tom's of Maine mouthwash. I've stacked the overstock behind the mini fridge, where I now stand grinning with pride for what I've achieved.

Contentedly, I sigh, redeposit a few rogue rainbow pills back into the Kitty head, and inhale the smell of overnight success. It's caustic. My stage smells like a science project. *It's fine.* I have an idea.

"Hay Babe!" Stella actually picks up the phone. "I can't talk long. I'm waiting for a call from my casting agent friend."

"Hey, okay." *I'd sure like to meet this guy.* "Can you bring a bunch of your mom's scented candles to the next party? I just cleaned up in here but I think the smell of the bleach is already giving me cancer." I check the recycled Amazon recycling box to make sure we have enough empty bottles to use as vases. "I'm gonna ask everyone to bring fresh flowers too."

"Oooh, Sexy! I like it!" Stella exclaims before playfully adding, "Maybe they'll get you in the mood and you'll actually give me what I want next time."

Holding up an empty Patrón bottle, picturing it full of gladiola,

I tense. She is calling me out on my hesitant gloppy hand-wave.

"Yeah, well you know, it's hard for me to get turned-on when I'm looking at berets and pigtails."

"Hey, at least they know what tits are for." She jabs back, crudely referring to my risky business of improper fluid disposal at the Sex and San P. party.

"I thought you said that it was hotter that I did it ... not on your tits." Nervously, I defend my accidental internal joy release. My voice rises in pitch as my moths make for the Xmas lights. "You said it was hot! You said that you could take care of yourself—"

"Settle sexy. I'm just playing." Stella laughs then purrs. "I like playing with you."

"Hey. I'm done here, why don't I skate over—"

"Oh, I think this is him."

Her incoming call is inaudible.

"I've gotta go Baby. I'll see you tomorrow." She hangs up.

As I begin to text her to tell her to bring my Joy Division shirt to school tomorrow, a message from Shane buzzes in.

"*Where are you buddy? Are you okay?*"

....

"You look fuckin' terrible man." Sitting in his office with the door open, my manager is eating out of a wooden bowl.

"Sorry I'm late Phil." I put on my shades, fearing that he's right.

My Ksubis are dusty, my black v-neck is sweaty, and my ankles are showing. Having resorted to using them to wipe up after Holly's Smith's song, I sent my socks out with Al's laundry this morning.

"Mike, this is the second time in two weeks. Are you okay man? You look terrible. Here." He offers me Kombucha.

"Oh. No. Thanks. I'm great." *I'd be much better if you'd stop telling me how terrible I look.* "Sorry, I just lost track of time."

"Well man, just don't let it happen again."

When Holly walks into the booth with her Gloomy Bear lunchbox, I stop reading my dry text. Being far more interested in my own glowing future than the played out past, I'm happy to have her surprise visit excuse me from my attempted History studies.

Greeting her, I cloister my books on the build-up table and as I return to our seats, she hands me a cellophane wrapped rectangle of banana bread. Slipping off her shoes, she crosses her legs and unwraps her own slice. Only after pulling off a tiny piece, chewing it, and swallowing does she finally speak.

"We haven't really had a chance to hang out since our fun got ruined by the groundskeeper."

Beneath her white hood her eyes are glowing lavender, just as they were last night. Everything about her is elegant: her hair, her poise, her toe ring. They're usually so tacky.

"How are you Mike?"

"How am I?" I cringe. *She thinks I look terrible. Great. I wish I hadn't taken off my shades to read.* "I'm … I'm good." Clicking my lighter with one hand, I run the other through my hair and squirm. "I just didn't have much time to get ready for work today. The party and all … you know?" *Click, click.*

"Oh yeah, I know. I stayed pretty late too." She laughs mysteriously, "I thought that you might have noticed me."

I turn toward my History book, thinking it may have just sat up to offer some wisdom. As usual, it offers me nothing.

Tsk, tsk, tsk. Click, click.

Discussing scenes with other Greats isn't a big deal, but when Holly brings them up, I get weird. I don't know why.

"Oh, that WAS you wasn't it?" *I turn back, as Morrissey and Katy walk up the stairs behind her. I ignore his demand that I sing Ask.* "Did you … have a good time?"

"I thought that was kinda obvious." Swallowing a bite of bread, she reaches for my San P.

Then horrifying me with its libertine behavior, my mouth opens up and this absurdity falls out "Oh good. I'm glad. I thought that maybe you weren't into it."

She shakes off her carbonated swig. "Why would you think that?"

"Well, I was just worried that it might bother you..." I stammer—stumbling over my thoughts, my words—speaking like English is my seventeenth language. "Watching other people ... I mean ... Stella can get so loud—"

"Mike." She raises her black, arched brows. "Did I look like I was uncomfortable?"

I turn back toward my mute textbook. *Katy, topless, sitting on the table, is reading it to Moz.*

"Well..." I light upon the quandary of Holly's chic abstinence. "It's just that you've never joined a scene. You can you know? You have my personal invitation."

I GO SMiLE as brightly as I can.

"You're so sweet." She dryly flatters, half smiling. "If I ever feel like it, I'll take you up on that. But really, Mike..." Her hand absently slides over the cylindrical lump in her pocket. "It's been pretty cool just watching." After popping a crummy crumble, she elucidates, "It's not something that you see everyday, you know?" As if it is, in fact, something she has seen everyday since she was ten.

And maybe she has. Maybe her dad used to take her to similar surfer soirees on the OC beaches. Or maybe The Premieres are tame compared to her nights out with her friends in Hollywood. Or maybe she's totally untouched and has implemented her 'hands off' rule because she wants to save herself for a private scene with me. I don't know, but I do know that somehow all she's just said, or the way that she said it, or the way that she's sitting there eating banana bread bit by tiny little bit, has turned me on in such a way that you'd think she'd just strutted in, thrown off her clothes, pointed at a porn clip and said, "Let's do that. And film it."

Feeling my Producer outrageously stirring, I can't say anything. I erection-stare at her, speechless.

Tsk, tsk, tsk, tsk, tsk.

"Oh God!" Worried by having unwittingly pressed my well hidden, hard-to-reach mute button, she places her hand on mine. "I didn't hurt your feelings did I?"

"No! No, not at all!" I recoil, shocked that she's confused horny with hurt.

"It's not personal. It's not about you."

"Oh, I know. I didn't think it was. My feelings aren't hurt!"

Trying to shoo her upsetting 'it's not about you' comment from my mind, I spring from the seat to search for her lunchbox. "I just like to make sure that all my guests are happy. Can I have some more banana bread? There's not honey in it right?"

As I reach toward the bloody-bear guardian of her treats, Holly grabs my hand and stands between us.

"Good, because I like you … and I'm exhausted and plan on spending tonight cuddled up with you watching this movie." She nods to the window, turns back to me, and smiles. "We just finished the last of the bread. Can I have some popcorn?"

I flee to the lobby to regain composure. I rub concession ice around my eyes, polish my teeth in my compact, grab a tub of corn from Shane, and then race my heart back up the stairs.

In the seats, I relax and we reposition. Holly snuggles up to me, munches about twenty kernels, laughs once at the big-haired Brit on the screen, and then falls asleep.

When I saw her walk through the door tonight, I was very much looking forward to, almost expecting, some real activities. But I'm okay. The corn in the air smells like it was popped in cucumber oil. I can feel her angel breath on my neck. This is nice.

Chapter 39

Monday morning, Lynch and I are talking business over The Dead Boys. As usual, the music in the Caddy is too loud and I'm straining to compete with the abrasive voice coming through the speakers. But at least the sonic attack is helping me wake up.

Swallowing an almost tasty swig of coffee from his mug, with a revolutionary plan in mind, I politely ask my partner for his film suggestions. By way of a long, satisfied 'I told you so' he begins pointing out that our guests no longer care what movie we show, what songs we play, or about anything that doesn't eventually end in a joyous mess. Having already admitted this to myself, I suggest that this Saturday we show another porno.

"We can call it the 'Let's Not Pretend Premiere'," I yell over the feedback. Lynch immediately begins suggesting whom we should invite to our upcoming exercise in honesty.

"Her. Her. Her…" He points out the window, hand picking potential Extras as we drive by girls, walking up the hill on their way to first period. "No. Wait. She's a bitch. DEFINITELY her. Oh, ALL the Sweater Girls." An auburn-haired grave-cutter in a black lace tutu and white combat boots leans against a vacant cop car and lights a cigarette. "Man, have you seen that new freshman yet? Look. Look. Look!"

Though I'm not yet comfortable inviting complete strangers to The Premieres, I like the prospect of adding variety to the cast and enjoy our window-shopping as it delights us all the way to the top of the campus stairs.

Vocally fantasizing about the girls tennis team, we walk past a threatening circle of school colors. An irregularly large freshman in a varsity jacket throws a French fry.

"Faggots." He and his friends laugh.

Slowing our stroll, I begin to verbally pontificate on how the buffo's deep-fried diet has affected his cognition and ability to dress properly. Lynch just flips him off. A flurry of fries rain down upon us and we press ahead. As we make our way through the starchy storm, I notice Mia hanging out by the cafeteria with Shane. *I wish we could have finished our scene.* I nod toward her.

"That was cool with you right?" I check my jeans for salt and grease.

"You mean, you two the other night?" Lynch snatches a fry from the air, and bites into it. "C'mon. It was totally disco. We were all going for it..." Chewing, he vulnerably sighs. "Though, I might get my feelings hurt if I don't get a scene with Stella next time." He grins. "That's cool with you right?"

"Totally cool." I laugh, then confess, "You know who I totally want to do a real scene with? Holly."

"*Phh*. No shit. But who doesn't?" A final fry bounces from his GI Jacket as we saunter out of the waning junk food hail and into the locker stalls. "That French guy was strugglin' to get her to go for it the other night but she denies. She just denies, denies."

"Yeah, I know." I spin Morrissey's birth date. My lock clicks open. I stack my books. "I don't think it's gonna happen for him."

"I don't know, it could. He is le big deal DJ." Lynch leans on the locker next to mine. "You know how much chicks are into that."

"No, it's not gonna happen!"

My good friend meets my unexpected burst of defiance with a sobering, curious look.

"I mean, she's just ... not like Stella or anything." Regaining composure, I search for the scotch tape in my Sherman. "I asked why she doesn't do scenes and she said that she's just not into it."

"Huh." Pondering, he eyes me with suspicion then scoffs. "What a weirdo. Whatever. She'll go for it with someone soon."

"Yeah. Maybe. Probably." I tape a tear of Katy Perry up near the mirror that's hanging above the signed glossy of DiCaprio on my locker door. "At least I hope so."

By the time the bell for fifth period rings, my virtually sleep-free weekend has chased me down and unjustly punished me. I'm exhausted, and though I have sixth period Lunch, I'm using the camouflage of the fifth period feeders to stealthily slip into Hess Theatre. The modern stage is empty. No one ever skips lunch to run lines.

Sliding my bag under the exceptionally tall frame, I climb onto the prop bed and slide under the covers. While breathing in the comforting aroma of flammable fresh paint and lumber, I sleep for what seems to be about ten minutes before Holly scolds, "Shouldn't you be in class young man?"

I awake to her opulent gaze. In here, her eyes have wildly waxed to an almost golden hue.

"Ohhhh, it's only the second week of school." Still sleep con-fused, I prop myself up on my elbow. "I'm not missing anything. And the bed wanted to practice." Opening the comforter I pat on the mattress with hazy bravery. "Come on, help it learn its part."

"Okay." Hopping in, she opens her bag and pulls out a script. "Let's run some lines."

Leaning against the headboard and squinting at the dialogue, I feel like an old married couple. Struggling to suppress thoughts of activities, I ask Holly to repeat her character's line a third time when a deep voice explodes from the front of the house.

"Son! What are you doing in here with that girl?"

We're scared into silence until Cruz emerges from the darkness. He strolls down the center aisle.

"Did I get you guys?" he asks in his regular lilt. "I think that's a pretty good voice, don't you?"

"Yeah. You got us man. Good job." In our musical, the versatile construction worker is playing the part of my dad, King Char-lemagne. "What are you doing in here?"

"I just came to practice my booming royal voice," he explains, in his booming royal voice (which is totally unnerving). Once he's hovering over us, he thankfully returns to talking like himself. "I like to practice it where I can really project." Cruz inspects our coupling beneath the sheets. "What are you guys doing in here? Having a little private Premiere?"

I turn to Holly, hoping that she'll confess her plan to soon turn on her golden toy and get naked.

"Wait, Hector, are you at lunch?" she asks. "Is it sixth period already?"

"I got out a little early. ... But yeah, it's about to start."

"I gotta go." Jumping out of bed, she bags her script and jogs across the stage. "I told Sarah that I'd meet her before class. I'll see you guys later." Before leaving through the side exit, she stops to yell through a ray of warming natural light. "We'll have to practice our kissing scene later Mike!"

The heavy door latches shut behind her.

"I'd like to be around for that." Playfully, Cruz turns to meet my wide, excited eyes.

I shut my gaping mouth. He sours his expression.

"I'm mad at you."

"Really?"

Though I can't imagine how or when I could have wronged him, I immediately feel guilty. You can wash your hands of the church but its stains take years to get off.

"Why, because I never found your ball gag?" I'm wildly guessing. "Oh, wait, not because I said that thing about Volta's ass the other night—"

"*Phhh*, NO! His ass is *pan dulce*." Lightheartedly, he laughs. "You promised me you'd show *Rambo*! Remember? You'd better keep your promise *Miguelito*!"

"Oh, man, I forgot, I'm sorry. I'll play it soon."

"You'd better!" Appeased, Cruz relents and sits down on the edge of the bed. But his momentary disappointment in me has brought up a concern I've been having lately.

"Hey Hector, I have been meaning to ask you ... about The Premieres. You and David don't feel weird about doing scenes in Heaven, do you?"

"What do you mean?"

"I just noticed that you guys have been keeping to yourself and I'd hate to think it's because you feel uncomfortable, or unwelcome—."

"*Phhh.*" Smiling, he rubs my leg through the comforter. "*Miguelito,* you're so sweet." He sounds much more dulcet than Holly did when she said the same thing to me last night. "We like it on the couch. We can't get that kinda comfortable-lovin' shit at our houses. Any second my dad or his grandfather could walk in and they'd fuckin' shoot us if they caught us holding hands let alone sucking each others' cocks. For real."

"Wow, well…" I slide next to him and like a used car salesman or a minister throw my arm over his shoulder. "You're always gonna be safe at The Palace my friend. Seriously. You guys can do whatever you want, wherever you want. And even if I have become a bit lax by letting in strangers like that French nast, I promise that I'll remain strict on the anti padres policy." I pat on the mattress. "C'mon. Let's talk about *Rambo* more after our nap."

"Thanks, but I'm gonna practice my lines playboy, so you might as well go eat lunch." Standing, switching to his loud, weird, booming voice he points down at my repose, "You look very pale my son! Go get a cheeseburger inside of you."

Chapter 40

By Tuesday I've managed to shake off the sleepiness left over from **Showgirls.** Last night I was in bed before nine. Today I had the fortitude to remain conscious through all of my classes and now, at my desk, in my room, I still have enough clarity to ignore my Biology homework and do research while making the Let's Not Pretend invite. It is an unapologetic and orgiastic photoshopped flesh menagerie featuring some great Alvin shots and the caption 'Dress To Undress!' I'm pretty pleased with the tagline, but as a whole the work is admittedly unimpressive. *It's fine.* I save and send the invitation. It's already past midnight. Eddie purrs on the pillowcase paps behind me. *I should go to bed.* I click on my Firefox window. *Right after I memorize at least two new techniques from bestsexpositions.com.*

....

Since the last Premiere we've all become more relaxed about discussing our extra-curricular activities and though I am slightly concerned by any public discussion of our controversial affairs, I'm finding our graphic conversations comforting. I feel that the vocalization of our aspirations will further ensure another great party this weekend. Plus, I was starting to think it was really weird that no one was talking about the good stuff.

On my way to Wednesday's last period, I step out from the shady overhangs to quietly ask Alvin about his special guest. For the first time since the sex scenes began, I've agreed to allow Extras. I've already seen Al's photos of Violet. I now only need to make sure that he can vouch for pre-teen Cameron Diaz's character.

"Stella's friends are gonna bring flowers. She'll bring flowers, right?"

"Violet is a flower." Standing above me on concrete planter, Al moonwalks away.

I follow him. "Oh, and do you have any idea how old she is? She looks twelve—"

"Hey Mike." One of the Sweater Girls—the cream one, the hottest one on the tennis team—has just walked up to mute us with her cream, low cut, short sleeve angora sweater dress. She's speaking to me for the first time in our four years of sharing the same English period. "You coming to class?"

"Um, tennis anyone?" Alvin, completely losing control, jumps on my back, leans into my ear, and stage whispers, "Fucking invite HER! She's not twelve!"

I shake the longhaired devil from my shoulder. He lands on his feet and pulls out his phone to take pictures of us as I, suppressing my urge to follow his advice, walk Cream to class.

I explain to her that he and I had just been discussing the fall musical.

"I'm playing the lead." I GO SMiLE. "Would you like to be my guest for opening night?"

Happily she accepts my offer, and our animated shoulder-rubbing stroll catches the eye of her overgrown freshman friend—the moron who threw the fries at Lynch and me. Literally slack-jawed, he stops to stare. I brush away Cream's long chestnut hair, whisper in her ear, and flash him my polished teeth. Snapping his mouth shut, Fry Guy turns his head and walks past. Having successfully blinded the potential attacker with my radiance, I safely escort the sweater into the English building.

Confined to my desk, I'm finding it impossible to pay attention to my teacher. As he drones on about some dead existentialist named Albert, I practice my autograph on my book cover. I make hearts out of the *o* in Score and the *a* in *Massi*.

The girl behind me passes me a note written on a tennis ball. Following its fuzzy instructions, I slip out the back of class to meet Cream in my Hess dressing room. Propped against my vanity, warmed by the heat of its bare bulbs, surrounded by hundreds of fragrant white roses, I pet her discarded dress as she congratulates me with celebratory opening night OJ. The cheers of curtain call echo. Cream pauses, unhooks the top of her angora Lacoste lingerie. Holly, wearing the shark embroidered version of same bra and panty set, struts into my private dressing room.

Class is dismissed. My good sport pulls out her cell in synch with the rest of the exiting honors students. Checking my messages, I follow her to the senior lockers. Cream meets Canary, and the two sweaters continue on past my stall. After fixing my hair, I tape a small print out of Holly's Model Mayhem graffiti pic next to the photo of Alexa Chung and then invite Leo Di to sit in on tonight's rehearsals.

....

While Mia was whining to Rick about the October deadline for script memorization, I was in a massage train. Eventually she came backstage, linked up, and calmed down. Now we're both relaxed, hanging beneath the campus lights, awaiting our rides. She compliments me on the Let's Not Pretend invitation. "It's hella horny." I agree. Stella appears at the top of the campus steps. In black patent pumps, white high-waist hot shorts, and a matching pair of suspenders, pressing my Joy Division shirt to her boobs, she intimidates the sun. It ducks all the way behind the hills as her heels *tik* toward us.

"Hey kids!" She kisses me.

"Hey, Babe." With France's oral occupation fresh in my mind, I furtively wipe my mouth. "How're things going with the casting? Has that guy called again?"

I take off my shades. Mia looks up from her texting.

"You spoke to Blake?"

"Yeah! He wants to meet again!" Stella types into her phone.

"Wait. You mean on Monday? At the callbacks?"

"He wants to do a one-on-one first! I guess there are only, like, five girls doing them!" With a hair toss and a smile, she looks up. "I'm so gonna get the part!"

"Oh..." Mia quietly forces out, "That's cool." Then returns to dourly, yet rapidly, texting.

Un-sanitarily, Stella presses a spent wad of gum against the light post before digging her last piece from her pocket. She peels open the paper, balls it up, flicks it away, and I begin flattering the soon to be TV queen.

"You're gonna be perfect for the show, Babe." I kneel to retrieve the litter. "Do they need any male roles?"

"I don't know, but I'll ask!"

The dainty freshman dancer who was giving me a dry shampoo minutes ago ghosts me as she walks toward the parking lot. She is holding hands with her senior boyfriend.

I trash the wrapper and walk back to Stella. "Hey, do you want to do something Friday night? We can celebrate the one-on-ones, one on one."

"Yeah!" As if I'd forgotten that I'd agreed to accompany her to her first Teen's Choice Award, she insists, "I wanna go to one of Score's infamous Premiere parties."

Mia takes a fake sounding phone call to the top of the campus stairs.

"But that's Saturday. ... I was thinking that maybe we could do something Friday, like, just the two of us. ... We could go to the D-hole ... or watch stuff at your place ... or go to the golf course or something—"

Stella's sex hum pressurizes the thinning air between us as she moves closer.

"I know Let's Not Pretend is on Saturday. I'm on the invitation Babe." Grinning, she throws her arms around my neck. "But I think you should have a pre-party on Friday. Another Flash. The last one was *amazing* ..."

Her hips sway ever so slightly to the Katy Perry song looping through my head.

"Have two in a row?"

Hosting just one Premiere a week has already made it really tough to manage work, homework, script memorizing, and seven full periods of wakefulness.

Her sugary watermelon breath hits my face and tightens my jeans. I salivate.

"Yeah, sure. It's fine, why not? I'll make it happen."

"Rockin'!" She raises one sculpted brow, grins, grabs the back of my hair, and kisses me. Deeply. My heart beats on fast forward.

She pulls back and, with her lips grazing mine, breaths, "It's a date."

Chapter 41

Thursday after school, I'm pleading with Lynch as he's driving me to work. The quick invitation that I made last night for The Friday Night Pre-Premiere Party hasn't received the response I'd hoped for. Serendipitously, Soufflé isn't coming (he has a solo gig at some SF club called Rickshaw). Neither are the surfers. They're throwing a pool party on the coast that, despite my current begging, the Prozens will be cutting school to attend.

"But we'll all be back for Let's Not Pretend." Nodding, Lynch lasciviously grins, "Violet's really looking forward to it."

"You're abandoning me." Frantically, I polish the fear from my shades. "How am I going to work everything? Is MK going too? To see Leo? I haven't heard from either of The Twins."

"I think she's staying here. But Ash is coming with us."

"Ash?" I turn down a song about someone named Richie Dagger.

"Yeah." The neon of the marquee hums to life, as he pulls up to the curb. "Star's gonna show her how to make psychedelic Kombucha."

"Jesus fucking Christ." I grab my Sherman, slam the door, and lean through the passenger window. "Just make sure that she comes back with her brain in place. I don't think I could handle seeing her in tie-dye. Or sandals. And don't put any more holes in your face."

He begins pulling away.

"And you better show me how to work the soundboard before

you go!"

With one thumb up and the other texting, Lynch rolls onto the main street, steering with his knees.

....

I'm actually early this evening. In my dark booth, I ditch my bag on the seats and call Vegas on speaker. When I ask for Joey, the stranger that answers says, "*He's not here. Who's this?*"

"Oh, okay." *This guy sounds just like Cruz.* "Who's this?" My brother lives alone.

"This is Marcus." The voice curtly lilts, as if questioning the validity of my inquiry.

"Are you Mexican, Marcus?"

"What?"

"My friend is Mexican and you sound a lot like him."

Innocently, I remove my compact and polish my teeth in projection light.

"NO." He gasps. "No I'm not, and you should know that the politically correct term is 'Latino,' not 'Mexican'."

"My friend's family is from Mexico City and they call themselves Mexicans."

"Who is this?"

"This is Joey's brother." Proudly, I toss the empty tube toward the recycling. It plinks against empty Pellegrinos.

"Well..." The uptight version of Cruz spits, "then I imagine that you have Joe's cell number. I suggest you use it."

I dial Joseph's cell. When he picks up, I ask who the bitchy guy in his house is.

"Oh God, I told him that he had to leave this morning. Why? What'd he say to you?"

"Just some weird racist stuff. He hung up on me."

Exasperated, my brother apologizes for his rude friend's behavior and I ask for a favor. I want to borrow one of his old outfits for the next party.

"Wait," He asks. "*Which* suit? For what?"

Excitedly, I relate all the miracles I've worked thus far in my career as host and when I've caught him up to tomorrow night's Flash Premiere, Joey is perfectly impressed. Praising my efforts, he tells me exactly where to look for his clothes then with older-brotherly love, imparts, "Hey Mike, you should really bring by some condoms to this thing of yours."

"C'mon man." Laughing, I scoff. "What, is it the nineties?"

"Just do it for me. And you still gotta tell me what you want for your birthday. You name it. The tables have been as hot as your fabulous basement ballroom, baby brother."

"Okay, thanks Joey." When the door opens and someone steps into the booth, I'm startled. I take my brother off speaker. "I'll email you a list. Break a leg tonight."

"Thanks Mike. Kiss kiss. Love love."

"Kiss kiss. Love love."

I set down the phone and stare back at my company. A few seconds of silent, mutually questioning, proximate eye contact pass.

"Was that Joey? I miss him." Shane is bopping, wearing the yellow and black stripy Paul Smith sweater. Again. He's had it on since last Friday. "Tell him I say hi."

"Will do. What's going on man?"

"Score..." Looking like he's about to take flight, he whispers, "I know all about the party. Can I please come this time? I won't even fuck. I just want to watch."

Gripping the edges of the build-up table, to prevent myself from falling to the cold grey floor in a swoon, I pray for Moz's strength. "Who told you?"

"Jamie... a while ago." He meekly admits. "I never actually asked Hector anything. I made that up cuz I didn't want you to get pissed at her. I really want to come, Mike. Just to watch. Can I come?"

"Why did she tell you all of this Shane?" I don't get it. I could see Mia maybe telling some guys at a club in San Francisco, or perhaps some of the freshmen that constantly follow her around school.

"Don't worry Buddy." He shakes his sandy blonde head. "We tell each other things that we'd never tell anybody else..." Abruptly, he inhales. A concerned look cuts through the shadows cast by his eighties James Bond bone structure as he holds his breath. "Shit no one else can ever know, and will never know ... so, I swear, the secret is safe. Can I come? I just want to watch."

Tsk, tsk, tsk, tsk, tsk, tsk, tsk, tsk, tsk, tsk, tsk, tsk.

Unnerved, I stare at his hopeful, bristly smile. The oddity of he and Mia being secret besties is somewhat upsetting, but I still trust him. *It's fine.* I know Shane. *Kind of.* He's saved me on numerous occasions. And apparently he knows my brother.*Everything's fine.*

"Okay man." I hop off the table and grab one of the destroyed *Taxi Driver* reels. "It would actually be cool if you kept an eye on everything for me. There's this French Texan that I've never been totally sure about, and there's gonna be a few more new people coming on Saturday, so maybe you could kinda act like security."

Shane hugs me. Loving the idea of playing bouncer, he reassures me that he won't say a word, thanks me profusely, and leaves me splicing off bad ends. But before he goes back to slinging sodas, he pauses at the door.

"Hey Score, ... do I get a Screename?"

"Um ... sure." I search for a new roll of tape. "What do you want it to be?"

"You give it to me."

The names of several different cinema badasses run through my mind before I realize that the best one is right in front of me.

"How about Bickle?"

"*Taxi Driver*?! Kickass!" Bouncing down the stairs he yells, "You'd better do some push-ups before Saturday buddy! No one wants to fuck a *scorecrow*!"

When the door shuts, it blocks the sound of his exit. But I know that he's still giggling.

Chapter 42

Friday night is unusual. As it begins, I graciously accept flowers and arrange them in empty bottles about the stage. While elevating the décor, the assorted bouquets only partially mask the chemical scent in the air; however, the fragrance of Barbara Johnson's candles slowly turns everything rosy. When Stella lights the last scented soy pillar, the smell of vinegar and bleach is barely noticeable. It's lovely.

Inhaling, I smile and thank her as she hands me a Hello Kitty punch bowl. I set it next to the vitamins on the mini-fridge and begin filling it with bootie from my Planned Parenthood brown bag.

"Condoms?" Stella laughs. "What, is it the nineties?"

"Condoms and lube." I pour the rainbow assortment into the hollowed-out cat's head. "Joey insisted that I provide some."

"Oh, really? I thought we weren't supposed to *provide* anyone with information about the party."

"My brother?" Aghast, I wave a ribbed Trojan. "You're bringing kids who I've only seen online and you're worried about Joey?"

"C'mon Babe, I'm just playing." She blows then implodes a bubble before tapping my cheek with an old-timey pink and white straw. "I'm gonna go warm up."

Standing at the soundboard, skipping my formal speech, I alert my guests to the optional prophylactics, and begin to stiltedly start and stop *'Fourth Blood.'* I'm trying to get the sound of automatic weapons to fire through the PA but Lynch left without showing me how to work it. Instead of John Rambo, we're hearing Kylie Minogue.

And the distracting sounds of snorting.

Mia, Stella, and Prius have formed a powder triangle over the PlayStation. They giggle. I struggle to interpret the directions that just buzzed into my phone and Volta accuses me of summer blockbuster sabotage.

"I'm really trying!" Cuing up Slayer to appease The Boys, I continue losing my battle with electronics until a hot young secretary enlists herself in the war.

Taking my phone, Holly reads Lynch's notes aloud while I plug, unplug, and push useless buttons. Then, just as Cruz lets me off the hook—"It's okay *Miguelito*. Don't worry about it. I'm just gonna be sucking cock anyway"—Mia unfolds. Jerking up, she jumps back from the console, and starts screaming.

Oh fuck! Oh my fucking god!

From her center stage candy couch, MK begins to repeat, "*Ew ew, ew...*"

And I mute the music.

Blood is pouring out of Mia's nose, gushing all over her face. Her scene has just gone from coke party to Carrie. It's dripping from her chin, through her fingers, and onto her long white belted-off tee shirt. *That's a lot of blood.*

Stella and Prius flee from their friend as if she were a geyser at Hep C National Park.

"Oh my god, oh my fucking god!"

The hysterical girl is a horror show, and I'm completely unhappy about the whole thing. As host, I feel that I must deal with this unfortunate situation.

"*Shh, shh* Mia. Its fine, everything's fine." Backing against the curtains, I soothe the screeching blood fountain from a safe distance. "You're going to be fine."

It seems like she can't hear me. And the way that she's squealing, "Fuck! I'm bleeding! I'm bleeding! Oh my god I'm gonna fucking die!" is making me question my own calming claims. I'm not entirely sure that she won't die.

"It's fine, everything's fine," I softly mother.

"Fuck, Fuck, Oh my god!" Ignoring my compassion, Mia runs off-stage then reappears with a filthy chemical-tainted rag pressed to her face. "Sarah take me home! Take me home!" She scream-sobs,

"You've gotta take me home!"

"Um..." Pressed to the wall screen, her BFF hides behind the DJ. "I walked here."

Donny plugs his ears.

"I have the jeep! Oh my god, I can't drive!" Mia does a bloody jog. "I'm gonna fucking die! I can't drive!"

Holly hands me back my iPhone and walks upstage to put her arm around the shrieking Filmgreat's bloody waist.

I gasp. I can't believe she's touching her.

"Just breathe, Jamie. You're gonna be okay, it's just a nosebleed. You probably just nicked yourself with the straw. I'll take you to get cleaned up and then I'll take you home." The sober vegan comforts her as she walks the mess past me. "You're gonna be fine, just calm down, take deep breaths..."

Their exit sounds like crushed kittens.

"Thanks, Holly!" While shouting through the swaying curtains, I compose a text asking her, "*Please burn her shirt*! It's too much of a conversation piece.

"Mia, it's fine!" I holler and hit send.

Amidst a heavy silence, we remaining Greats look back and forth at each other.

Prius taps an American Spirit soft pack.

"Well that was a drag."

"Yeah. What the fuck was that Donny? Is she overdosing? Was that shit bad or something? Was it heroin? Is she gonna die?"

"Nah." He lights up and takes a drag. "It happens my brother."

"Huh. What a drag."

On purple plastic, dressed in designer forest camo and gazing at the movie, MK rattles Roxy from her purse. She dry-swallows. And the silence returns. It presses upon us like a forty-eight hour Sunday until Stella saves the evening.

"Yeah. That was a drag. Okay..." Stepping into Heaven, she pulls off her lemon yellow shirt, throws it at me, and asks, " Who wants to fuck me?"

What a relief.

After catching the pink heart dotted souvenir and admiring her especially large boobs, I quickly scroll through my iPod. While I'm replacing Slayer with Stella's favorite Flo Rida song, Cruz walks over to inform me that he and Volta are leaving.

"I dunno, *Miguelito*." He runs his comb through his slick hair. "The blood just grossed us out. We're not in the mood."

Like MK, The Boys are both wearing war paint.

"The Blood? C'mon guys, I'm finally playing your movie." I motion to the silent massacre on the wall. "...*Rambo*."

"I know *Guapo*. Thank you. I'm not mad at you anymore." Cruz kisses my cheek. "We're just gonna go park in the vineyards and watch videos on my laptop. We'll see you tomorrow night, though. F'real."

Left behind the PA, with my Producer giving a Standing O, I admire Stella. On her back, she's moaning in Heaven. I'm considering going in alone to try to negotiate some OJ for myself—before Donny pulls his pigtails out from between her splayed legs. He wipes his mouth on the sleeve of his De La Barracuda jacket, takes a drag from the smoldering cigarette hoisted in his left hand, and flashes me his GO SMiLE.

I'm going to need back up.

I steal a breath mint from Sponge Bob, check my compact, then creep over to court the camouflaged wallflower.

Alone on purple plastic, watching the Oral Joy, the sedated twin ignores me as I ease myself next to her.

"Hey MK. I'm really sorry that Leo's not here."

Without expression or words she turns to face me. So I go on.

"I can't believe that none of those guys came, can you? Jerks."

Nothing. No response. She's simply attacking my Premiere confidence with a heavy, glassy-eyed stare. Yet I press forward.

"But I'm really glad that you're here..."

Wondering if I've offended her by unwittingly sitting down on Roxy's lap, I'm almost ready to give up and join the American Spirit as it enters Stella. I shove my hand in my pocket.

"So..." *Click, click*, "Ash went to hang out with Star?"

A semester goes by before her expression slightly shifts and through a faint, almost imperceptible, understanding smile, she finally says,

"You can fuck me if you want, just not in my cunt."

I'd thought that the 'C word' was a sin, but I do not question her expression of faith. I dart to the kitty, sift through the condoms, grab as much lube as I can carry, and return to MK with my pockets bulging. Taking my lady's hand, I guide her holiness to the mattresses. With my teeth, I tear open a little red plastic pillow. Flavored goo spurts out. I taste strawberry. I see lime. The green couch where Holly should be playing is empty. I miss her, but as I commit several uncontestable crimes below Stallone and next to Stella, in Heaven, I'm elevated.

This is fabulous. MK is asking me to do things I've never even done to wild-reality-girl. I slide my slippery Producer out of her divine loophole and deep into sin.

"Owe, owe, owe ... mm ... ugh..." Sounding almost pained, the grease-painted, half conscious twin shutters. "Jesus fucking Christ Leo."

And I flow with the scene. *It's fine.* I'm having a good time. MK's having a good time. Prius and Stella are having a good time. Everyone's having a good time. Mia's probably not dead. *And it's fine. Everything's fine.*

Chapter 43

I'd forgotten this tracksuit was powder-pink. I remembered it being black. Having spent most of the day sleeping, cleaning, and showering off last night's blood and sodomy, I hesitantly pull two pastel pieces of polyester from a box in my brother's closet and put them on. My suit has proven to be a real pain to get off. I need something that better facilitates quick undressing. I turn in front of the mirror. I'd always thought Joey's Y3 jogger was really cool. *This might be a bit too informal for a host to wear to such a grand affair.* I stare at myself—inspecting and adjusting—then realize exactly what I need. Adding a skinny black tie to my shallow white v-neck and polishing my teeth up to the reflective shine of my Fords gives the outfit a whole new look. I've got a new-wave, soccer-hooligan, rock-n'-roll-runner-type thing happening here. *I can totally pull it off.*

....

Though there are strangers and small aggravating sanguine stains on my stage, I can already tell that this is going to be perfect. All the Extras brought flowers. The basement is packed with flora, Filmgreats, four art-house kids, and Violet Diaz. Sitting on a stage-left couch, she's impressing The Twins with the big yellow buttons on her belted grey trench.

Tonight, all the girls have conspired. Like myself, they've taken the invitation's 'dress to undress' command to heart and are wearing long coats over little else. Even the two pixie-haired, art-house Extras are taking part in the flasher fashion trend, which, I'm sure, was started by Stella. She and Mia have on identical fuchsia raincoats—Mia's covers teal underwear. Stella's hides only a Hello Kitty tattoo. At my speech position, I learn this as she stands and flashes me. The outline is perfectly centered over her own hairless anatomical feline.

"Is that permanent?"

"Nah." She re-belts her coat. "I was thinking about getting it done but I only want stuff that's unique. Stuff that means something."

"What's the kanji on your lower back stand for again?" I ask, having never known.

"Love." Plopping back into Heaven, she takes a pull from a bottle of wine, passes it to an Extra, and attacks Holly. "You're overdressed, beautiful, let's get those jeans off."

As they giggle, Stella strips the blonde of her raspberry pants. Standing and posing, flaying wide her polka dot lined raincoat while spreading her black silken wings, Holly reveals a red cotton bra.

"Well how 'bout now?" Across her matching hot shorts, a silk-screened shark swims between her dairy-free thighs, "Still too much?"

Alvin takes a picture.

"Welcome everyone! Welcome!" I raucously clear my throat and clap. "Ladies, I must say that your complimenting coats look wonderful..." I motion to the trenches. "But you should have left them at the door, because this, my esteemed guests, is the Let's Not Pretend Premiere!"

Throwing out my arms, I wave Jenna Jameson to the wall and in near choreographed unison, unveiling bras, panties, and fully naked female forms, the girls toss their constricting coats to toward the sandbags. *Perfect!*

....

I'm on my back, unzipped in a pile of faux fur. I was making my way to Holly's couch when two Extras pulled me down. Stella is next to me. She's moaning, and Prius is enjoying her Reverse Asian Cowgirl. Having used my feet to ball my sweats around my toes, I stare down past my mauled necktie. The Extras are giving me OJ. I'm trying to recall their names, but Stella is distracting me.

"Oh fuck I love it!" She announces, "It's so fucking huge!"

A mustached Extra has positioned himself in front of the bare-backed rider and unbuttoned his APC fly. He looks like a cross between the dark-haired girl below my waist and Mr. Pringles. He's even better hung than Donny, though I imagine that Stella's big love profession is more a testament to the abnormally large size of our audience—for whose attention she has newfound competition. One of The Twins has been challenging her.

"ChristfuckLeoFUCKMEJesusfuckingchristGOD! FUCK FUUUUUUCK!" As MK repeats this prayer, the god of surf snickers.

"Ahee hee hee"

"OHgodLeooooGod,fuckingchristfuckFUCK!"

"Ahee hee..."

Leo clearly finds The Twin's uncharacteristic oration funny. I find it transcendent to hear her proselytizing so freely, especially while a strange blue-haired girl with genital jewels is mounting me.

The Blue Extra pushes her palms down on my chest. She rolls back her aqua contacts and begins grinding in brutally slow, syncopated thrusts. It feels like a succession of ever growing waves pounding upon my Producer. The raven haired Extra swoops in and bites her shoulder. *This is pretty fabulous.* The Blue Extra cringes as I try to decipher the scrolling script tattooed across her collarbone. The last word is 'destroy.' I first met this girl online. When Stella introduced us, IRL, she simply smiled. I've heard her voice once—she was talking to her black-haired, biting friend about a white ring. The Raven Extra twists a nipple ring, and blue nails dig through my black tie. Silently she is taking her pain with pleasure. Unlike Mia.

"*Cállete* hooker!" Understandably disturbed by the force of the eerie, piercing noises coming from the mattresses, Cruz pauses his downstage OJ. "You're creeping me out!"

Past my feet, arcing her little butt into Lynch's face, Violet is probing away between Mia's trembling legs. If the perennial, ostensibly fourteen-year-old surf flower is indeed young, her oral work proves that she is certainly not green. She's licking out some of the loudest squeaks that any of us have ever heard.

"Yeah, Lynch. Shut your woman up." Volta pushes his BF's head back down below his Burzum shirt. "I'm turning straight listening to that shit."

"I'm on it guys!" As the Blue Extra is repositioning herself over my face, I slip out from my scene. I erection skitter to the PA and scrolling through my iPod promise, "I'll have Ke$ha up loud in a second."

Bickle, a few feet downstage, is looming over the purple love seat. I'd forgotten that he was here. Fully clothed with his giant arms folded across his bumblebee chest, he stands statuesque, hawking over Cruz and Volta, just watching. He's not even brandishing his stinger. Some sort of philanthropy, I suppose. *He's fine.* I'm glad I invited him. I start the playlist made in honor of Stella's one-on-one callbacks, then erection-walk back through Heaven.

Between the Xmas lights and the mattresses, Star is giving a twin OJ. Ash's new collarbone implants sparkle beside her crucifix as I pass. Upstage, The Pringles Extra is playing with my pixie-haired Extras. Covered in Jenna, they're all leaning against the wall screen as a shirtless bearded Extra Bjorks out from a cloud in Surfers' Paradise. Shambling into their scene, he snubs his joint on a projected dildo then sucks a pierced nipple.

Tik tok on the clock and the party don't stop.

Cautiously, I step over Prius's crumpled grass green baby briefs, lie down, and spoon my way into the pigtail-free side of a 69. I creep my arms around Stella and reach for her boobs. When my nails accidentally scratch Donovan's downy belly, she turns over her shoulder and licks at my mouth. Artfully dodging the sloppy DJ-flavored kiss, I strike a stunning pose. Stella's mouth moistens my neck and Mia's eyes meet mine. Hers are red with tears. And a thin string of thick drool is dripping down from her chin. Lynch found the missing ball gag from the *Pulp Fiction* Premiere, took Cruz's advice, and silenced his co-star.

"Look Score!" Catching me, as I watch him hump the spit out of her from behind, my co-host raises his arms to the catwalks. "No hands!"

Al, running by, wearing nothing but Violet's silver bra across his chest, a camera around his wrist, and a sizeable erection, slaps his brother a high five.

After slathering my jaw, Stella re-arranges our threesome. On her hands and knees, in kitty-style, she's giving the standing DJ some OJ. I'm behind her, on my knees. Sexily I thrust through our scene, singing along to Amerigirlpop while watching the baby pap pet red dreads. When Al grabs his camera, I pucker my cheeks and wait for him to take my picture. Holly moans from the green couch behind him. *Her performance is so heartfelt. So moving. So genuine.* Keeping the beat, I admire the classy blonde through one Nicki Minaj song and half a Gaga mega-hit before my co-star stops sucking Donny. Turning back to me, she drunkenly criticizes, *"What the fuck Score?"*

"What?" Ravishing Stella with my perfect timing, I look from Holly to Prius for some insight on this uncalled for and sour attitude.

Still in her hands, he smiles and shrugs. Then, abruptly, she detaches herself from our trio.

"Okay!" Standing the middle of Heaven, Stella declares, "All guys on me!" And drops to her knees.

Happy to do my part to help her live out her dream scene, I form a circle with Prius, Soufflé, Alvin, Lynch, and the well-hung Extra. At our center, Stella is taking on the role of the sole participant in a lurid horizontal tasting event. It's obvious that she's completely wasted. Even on her knees she's stumbling. She's barely able to hold herself up.

It's fine. This is the first time I've participated in a scene like this, IRL. I'm not going to be the one to call cut just because she's blackout-drunk. I'm the one who tells her not to drink anyway.

Stella starts with Alvin but before the longhair finishes, she turns to test Lynch's mouth-feel and bouquet. Flipping off his brother, Al proceeds to handle himself, while my co-host gets his moment of OJ, and Mia quietly lies bound and gagged behind him. Lynch left her to join our circle just as Leo left a sleeping and satisfied MK to get prime placement in front of Holly.

Patronizing my own Producer while the surfer waxes his longboard, I focus intently on the OC soloist. Opening her phosphorescent green eyes, she adjusts the speed of her bullet. Even if I can't get any on her, I bet that she'd let me come close or maybe hold her toy while I'm trying. With my eye on the gold, I'm about to exit our scene when Stella tears me out of my buzzing trance.

"Come on Mike," she slurs. "It's been so long since I've tasted you. Give it to me."

I look back down into the circle and confirm that all my genital attention is self-applied, just as the Extra begins to violently fuck-punish Stella's grape-stained mouth. What a relief. I thought she just called me by my old name in front of everyone, but it seems that Kid Pringles is named Mike too.

Frantically, Mike spears for wine soaked Bubble Yum. The noises that start coming out of Stella begin shifting the light-hearted mood of our mingler. Horrible, inhuman choking sounds burst between coughs, as thick, streaming, viscous spit drips down from her chin and over her breasts. I've never heard anything like this before. It's beyond animalistic: it's preternatural. Her muffled gagging pulsates. She sounds like she's about to puke. *Moz, don't let her puke.* Her teary eyes roll back in her head and Mike, grabbing a tangle of her sweat-dampened hair, forcefully relieves her of his art instillation.

With her head lolled back, Stella gasps one thick, wet breath of bleached-rose air and demands, "Give it to me."

Weakly, she forces out her tongue, giving all that she has left. Being naturally talented with his hands, the artist instantly bursts all over her. His joy drips between her swollen lips and spills from her mouth. "Yeah..." she groans, grinning with Bordeaux eyes. "That's what I wanted."

I look down.

Smiling, satisfied, covered in joy, haunched onto her patent heels, Stella tenderly holds her gum between the thumb and fore-finger of her limp left hand.

"Wow," I say to no one in particular, "That was kinda cool." And not wanting to compromise the power of our circle, keeping my stance, I speed up my wrist work.

Somehow, seemingly suddenly, I'm the last man standing. Everyone else is crashed out at my feet, dressing in the wings, or beautifully buzzing on green plastic. Britney Spears is singing and Stella is unconscious. Presuming she was still on her knees, I just overshot. Like the rest of the guys, I was watching Holly. So now my success is icing one of our fur pillows.

For a full chorus of "Toxic," I stare at the comatose Filmgreat, still barely hanging onto her bubblegum, then call it a wrap. Flaccid-walking, I go to freshen up with Lynch.

"Man, am I glad I wasn't paying attention at the end there." Dousing my raw Producer with cold Pellegrino, I gently wipe down with baby wipes. "I don't think I would have been able to make it happen if I'd have seen her like that. Did you see her eyes? They are all rolled back and, like, half open."

"Gross." Lynch swallows a swig of mouthwash and then pours me a shot. "She said she was gonna do some more coke to sober up. Guess they ran out."

I swish mint, spit into a vase, pull on my sweats, and then snatch more towelettes. With my bottle of cleansing San P. in hand, I navigate my way through Heaven, stepping over Star, Violet, and Mia's legs to get to the broken centerpiece of our disseminated circle. I soak the sticky pillow that caught my misfire then, wondering which joy came from which boy, begin cleaning Stella. She doesn't move or make a sound. I wipe off her face, her hair, her shoulders, her boobs, and her belly. I dry her with a clean, fuzzy throw. Her fake tattoo is cracked and peeling. I take her gum.

Slipping into the musty, smoky, passed-out pile of guests, I lay down next to Stella. She smells like bleach-flavored cotton candy. Beyond her, the blue-haired Extra is facing Holly and mirroring her play. A fallen bottle of Patrón is spilling its poisonous magical potion on the couch between them. Katy Perry is singing "Teenage Dream."

Before I fall asleep, I think I hear the Blue Extra speak. Then Holly's voice cuts through the pop.

"I am too..." *bzzzzzz.*

Someday, I will be golden.

"...Just don't get any on me." *Bzzzzzz.*

She's such a good girl. She really is such a good girl.

Chapter 44

On Monday morning, I drift into the Cadillac with a horrible case of the earlies.

"I don't give a fucking fuck, I'll tell Score!" Alvin crawls into the backseat. "Hey Score, I'm in love. Wanna throw the wedding?"

I wince. He's loud. I don't understand how he can be so alive at this hour.

"You're insane." Lynch backs out of my driveway. "She's like, twenty-two."

"Twenty-three, Fucker!"

They're talking about Star.

"Whatever. She's old." Our driver tilts his rear view. "If you're so in love, why do you barely touch her?"

"We kinda made out a little when she stayed over that one night—"

"What?" I stare at him through the mirror of my compact. "You guys only made out?"

"She said it felt weird so we stopped. She said we could try again later, but when we got to her house and I asked her if it was 'later' yet, she didn't know what I was talking about. I don't think she remembered. " Al points at me and yells at the passing sweater girl. "He thinks you've got sick tits!"

Lynch yells, "So do I!"

The sweater girl ignores us. Al takes her picture then drops back through the window of the Caddy.

"Seriously? The only part of her that you've touched is her hair?" I turn around to check the kid's pupils. "What the fuck Al? Are you on drugs?" I reach for his shades. "You'd better not be dipping into the little kitty."

"Fuck you, fuckers." He slaps away my hand, raises two forward middle fingers and smiles. "*We're* in love. *You're* just jealous."

I sigh, take Lynch's thermos and gulp hot bitter blackness as "Bicycle Race" rings us into the parking lot. The Deville eases next to a fat-bottomed Filmgreat getting out of her dad's black Cherokee. Lynch honks. He waves and Mia flips him off.

Alvin laughs. "What's that bitch's fucking problem?"

"She's still mad about me leaving her tied up in the basement." He shrugs and turns off the car. "I guess she wasn't passed out the whole time."

"*Phhh,* whatever."

"She'll get over it."

....

I'm exhausted. After sanitizing the stage last night I made a futile attempt at early morning studies and now blurry ghosts and sparkles haunt the corners of my eyes. I think that the amorphous, droning specters may be my teachers and classmates. I can't account for the sparkles. Throughout Biology I'm vacant, but halfway into third period, I can sense a curly-haired, orange-corduroyed haze hovering over my desk. I've been starring at the same Calculus problem for over twenty minutes. All that I've accomplished is filling some grid paper with my autograph.

"You look like hell Massi." Chris looks down at me through his forced Buddy Holly frames. "Are you okay?"

"I had a really long weekend." This is my fourth year having Mr. Pope. He knows me for the exceptionally bright student that I am.

"If you took off your shades it might allow you to read the equation a little better, cool guy." He scribbles out a hall pass. "Go get some fresh air."

Despite his pants, Chris is pretty cool.

Thanking my charitable teacher, I pack my Sherman then float across campus, and into Hess. I sink into bed. I pull up the sheets, breathing in the ethereal smells of the set. The paint still smells new. I close my eyes. *I wish Holly were here.*

My prop comforter shifts. Bare, dairy-free thighs graze my balled hands. Wearing only her sweatshirt and white monochromatic Union Jack underwear, Holly slides in next to me. She feeds me a bite of banana bread, tilts a cup of The Ground's finest Columbian into my mouth, and whispers, "Just don't drool on me." Entwined with her, I sleep. Our bed catches fire. Everything is good, so warm-

"GET UP!"

Startled, I reflexively pull my hall pass from beneath the pillow and hold it over my head to protect me.

"You know Massi..." Ignoring the yellow slip, the blur that sounds like Rick Nalon pokes me with its very tangible man finger. "I'd think that having missed rehearsal last Friday, you'd be spending your lunch memorizing lines rather than taking a damn nap."

I've been asleep far longer than I'd thought. *I wonder which period it is. I wonder how I'm going to handle this.*

"Hey Mr. Nalon..." A sparkle alights the theatre. "Sorry I'm late." It descends onto the edge of the bed. My vision clears. Holly hands me a script. I smile. Rick looks pissed.

"Why are you here Becca?" he asks.

"We came to run lines. That's still okay to do in here right?"

"Be at every rehearsal from now on." Shaking his head, our director pokes me again. "Get it together Massi! This BS doesn't suit you."

He power walks out of the theatre. The door slams.

"Boy." I croak my first words since the rude awakening. "How dramatic. Thanks for saving me, Holly." I run my hands through my hair then find my shades beneath the sheets. "What are you really doing here?"

"Looking for you."

"Fabulous." Still mostly asleep, I scooch over, "Hop in. We still have time before sixth period." I snuggle up to the pillow. "Or is it sixth period now? Which lunch is it? Are you cutting?"

"Come on Mike." She grabs my shoulders and pulls me back up. "We should practice. You know that we don't have much more time to get our lines down right?"

"Noooo, it's fine." I insist. "Deadline is two weeks away."

"It's nine days away. Next Wednesday." Ever so sensually, Holly grabs my Fords from my face, gently tosses them to the comforter, and shoves her unwrinkled script into my chest.

"Okay..." I flip through the pages. "Let's start here." I tap my favorite stage directions—the kiss'n ones.

"Hey, have you seen Sarah today?"

"Yeah." *Have you seen this part, where you and I are supposed to kiss?*

"Oh, cool. I figured that she might have skipped. She was still pretty fucked up yesterday. I hope she's okay."

"She looked fine in class." I put my aviators back on and grin. "How 'bout we practice this scene now?" I tap the page.

"You don't even know your lines." Her sculpted brows arch. Almost smiling, she snatches back her script and flips to the front. "Let's start at the beginning."

Chapter 45

Before first period on Tuesday, with a Cherie Cherie scone jutting from my mouth, I'm putting away my Union Jack lunchbox when Stella appears.

"Hey Babe, did you miss me?" She leans against the lockers. Her white dress shirt is buttoned low enough to show off the lace of a hot pink bra. The shirt is far too big for her. She still looks great.

"Miss you?" I mumble then catch my falling breakfast.

"You didn't even notice I was gone yesterday?" Pouting, she peers toward the photos taped above my notebooks.

"Biology was torture." I shut the door, locking away Moz, Leo, and my favorite ladies. "I could barely focus on my lab without you. Luckily I still have your pics in my phone so —"

"I was in SF for the callbacks!" She hops once. The chains on her new purse jingle.

"Rockin'."

"That's exactly what Blake says!" She walks toward the cafeteria and I follow. "He's always, like, "This sushi is rockin', that shirt look's rockin' on you Babe—'"

"Who's Blake again?"

"He's my casting agent friend."

"Oh. Right." I chew on a dried cranberry and brush a crumb from my tie.

"He's really hot for an old guy. He's thirty-three but totally doesn't act it at all!" Her pink and black Betsey bag vibrates. She reaches in. "Oh my god, this is him..." Stopping a few yards from the donut line at the snack bar, she holds up one finger to me. In her honey-dipped sex-buzzed phone voice, reserved for conversations with males, she oozes, "Hey Babe, what's up?

"Thirty-three?" I ask, over the incoming murmur. "I thought he was, like, Donny's age—"

"Oh, that was just my boyfriend. ... Yeah, Donovan loves him. ... Yeah! The party kid—"

Most of my senses shut down. After so many years of hoping to up my status with her, I'm now Stella's boyfriend. I guess. The smell of fried dough disappears. Although I can't imagine what this title could possibly mean. We're Filmgreats. None of us practice anything close to monogamy. I brace myself on a nearby light post and watch Stella's mouth move. Except for Holly. In her auto-monogamy she is well beyond faithful. She's practically chaste—like a nun. I bet she's a virgin. I hope my new BF status isn't going to compromise my chances of being her first.

Absently twisting the last buttoned button on her shirt, Stella ends the call.

"He just wanted to make sure that I'll be able to get down there again on a weekday." Pursing her phone, she joins the queue for coffee and crullers. "He never can do weekends for some reason. He always has to fly back to LA for something. But he keeps his suite at the W and says that I can stay whenever I want—"

"Is he casting any guys?" She needs to ask Blake to audition her boyfriend.

Two kids wearing pot-leaf beanies step behind us. They smell like their hats. "Oh ... " Stella digs through her bag. The chains rattle. "Maybe. Yeah. I'll have to ask again." She pulls out a pack of Hubba Bubba.

"You know what could be huge? He could make a show about..." I look around then mouth the name of our secret party.

Stella pops a pink cube into her mouth, rolls the wrapper in a ball and flicks it onto the pavement.

"Babe..." Getting very serious and soft-spoken, she chews. "Can I ask you something?"

"Yeah, sure." Looking up to her face, I try to pay close attention while imagining what I'm going to wear to the Emmy's. "What is it?"

"Do I look fat?" A varsity jacket cuts in front of us, and I step out of line.

"*Phhh*, no!" Kneeling, I pick up her litter, stopping it before it blows into the quad. "You've got nothing to worry about. You look great." I toss the wrapper in the trash then walk back to her. "Have you seen your boobs lately? They're unstoppable."

She looks upset. It's odd. I know Stella appreciates a nice set of all-access passes, whether they're hers or not. Perhaps Mr. Thirty-three-year-old-casting-agent doesn't like big boobs. Being a sensitive boyfriend, I take her hands.

"Seriously. I should know. I spent an extra long time on them when I was cleaning you off the other night. They're great..."

She looks worried. I've never seen her like this. I embrace her.

"Come on Babe." I whisper sweet everythings in here ear, "You look like a star. The camera will love you. That 'adds ten pounds' BS is a myth."

Stella gives me a fragile smile.

I bet that casting guy only likes waifs. I can understand wanting a girl to be able to wear designer, but nice boobs are nice boobs. Blake must be a real dick.

"You're sweet Babe." She kisses my cheek. "I'm over coffee."

As she struts to class, shoving her hands into her tight black denim pockets, I notice that her ass may be starting to give Mia's some competition.

"Hey Babe!" Walking back to the trash, I call out, "You can link Blake to my profile!" Then I toss the remainder of my scone.

I hope that dick doesn't think I'm fat too.

Chapter 46

I failed my third pop quiz of the week today. My first D+ has put me in a worse mood than Thursday's Fs, and Rick is doing nothing to help make me feel better. The memorization deadline is days away yet, despite my showing up early to his inconvenient Friday night rehearsal, he's picking on me for reading from the script. I star in far better roles than this every weekend. Commanding the stage as he continues to taunt me, I consider quitting, until I notice Holly waiting in the wings for her cue. I will persevere. *For now.*

After faking my way through three dance numbers, I totally nail a duet then leave Hess with the impressed cast. On the concrete benches above the front parking lot, encircled by doting freshman chorus girls, Mia is talking tanning, techno, and six-packs, while Holly and I discuss literature. She's remixed the vintage Smiths shirt that I gave her yesterday—it's now sleeveless. Her side-boob is her gift to me. Standing beneath a campus light, hoping to make her giggle like a Pillsbury Dough Boy, I poke her ribs through a moth hole in Moz's knee and she asks if I've read Camus.

"Oh yeah, he's great." I pull back, as she swings her lunchbox at my probing finger. "I love 'Killing An Arab'."

Clicks of ascending unseen heels resound from the overhangs as Holly explains, "That's just The Cure song. Have you read the novel? *The Stranger*?"

"Totally. I'm real a sucker for murder mysteries." I pull another poke and Stella marches between us.

"Hey Beautiful." She smooches Holly then leans in toward me. "Hey Babe."

"Oh, you don't wanna do that." Instantly recalling cleaning Kid Pringle's ranch dip from her lips, I recoil. "My breath must be terrible." I cover my mouth. "From singing so much."

"Ew!" Stella kisses my cheekbone then rummages through her purse.

Breast pocketing the gum that she hands me, I ask, "Have you heard from Blake lately?" She turns to Holly. "Becca, do you think I look fat?"

"Seriously Sarah? You always look gorgeous. You're perfect."

I remove my shades to see if the staunch vegan is indeed blushing. She is. And Stella is so uplifted by the fertile flattery that when her BFF comes to stands next to her she appears to have grown a few inches in height

"Let's party ladies!" Throwing up the horns, Mia joins our trio. "Let's go!"

I turn to Holly, "Where are you fabulous girls headed this evening?"

"Sarah's, for *True Blood*. We're having girls' night."

I think that I hear the faint rumble of the '59's engine as Stella moves toward me. "Unless you want to do a pre-party."

Humming, she adjusts my hair. I peer over her shoulder, waiting to see my driver.

"Sorry, what?"

"Another Flash Premiere! It could be amazing. We'll move girls' night to The Palace." Her smile looks like Eddie's does when reflected in the water of Frank's fish tank.

"Well, yeah, that would be cool..." *Wincing, I plug my ears as Mia shrieks and sprays us all with nose blood.* "But I've gotta work."

"We should have regular girls' night anyway, Sarah." Holly taps the pink bear head on her metallic box. "I brought some really good tea."

Mia joins the campaign.

"Yeah, and The Palace isn't as fun without Zach! I don't think he and Dustin get back 'til tomorrow."

"Oh fuck. They're on the coast!" *I sleeve the blood from my Fords.* "Mia, can you give me a ride to work?"

"Sorry Mike. Daddy dropped me off. We're walking,"

"Shit. I've gotta go! See you guys at the bank!" Sprinting away, wishing I had my skate, I head for the steps.

With my Sherman bouncing painfully at my side, I'm three minutes off campus when I remember a few things: sprinting sucks, I need to make a new playlist for tomorrow, and my manager is always cool. Philip is a nice, mellow hippie. They're nothing if not tolerant and understanding. Stopping in front of the cemetery, I wave at a disinterested grave-cutter, text Phil to tell him that I'm sick and then call Cruz.

Sitting on a marble bench, inhaling secondary clove-smoke, I'm playing Words With Friends when my driver swings open the sparkling passenger door of his ride. Blasphemy blasts toward the dead. I hop in, grab the iPod, and scroll to the *M*s.

Chapter 47

Fall has finally found our town and brought its transformative potential. In honor of 'The Dark Grey Premiere'—a hybrid of *Donnie Darko* and Stella's favorite porno—today was considerately sunless. Now, a cool breeze is lighting upon the WAMU lot, waving its autumnal wand and accenting outfits. With my tie tucked into my waistband and my track jacket freshly washed and ironed by Gina, I stand by our planter, greeting guests and admiring the cold nipples of my huge turnout. Tonight, Extras have brought Extras and all of them have come carrying bouquets and wearing either tightly tied raincoats or baggy sweats. Welcoming so many uninvited unknowns concerns me at first, but after one of them gifts me a pair of Varvatos Chucks, I recognize how well mannered and attractive they all are.

With Lynch at my side, and my new shoes hanging in a velvet bag strapped around my wrist, I shake hands and kiss cheeks, while discreetly pointing out which Extras I hope to work with. I overhear one of these mysterious ladies asking about me.

"Yeah it's his party," Stella confirms, "He's my boyfriend. You've gotta try him."

She's a good girlfriend.

The intrigued UC Berkeley Extra glances over. Beyond her, on the bank steps, two Grave-cutters open their riding-hood cloaks to gratuitously kiss for Alvin's camera. MK hands Lynch her ice cream cone. I clap for attention.

"Everyone. It's time!" I raise my hands, and shoes, to the failing streetlights. "Grab your goodies, and let me show you to your new home!"

....

The basement is higher than usual. Stella is playing hostess in her Sanrio raincoat. The mini-fridge is obscured by a swarm of DJs, Marc by Marc shop girls, and MAC counter kids. They're drinking, eating vitamins, smoking—someone brought a gurgling pink Louis Vuitton bong. Mia is overcoming her fear of cocaine. Jake Gyllenhaal has yet to hit the wall. And almost everyone is fucked up. *It's fine.*

"I'm pleased to bring you, for the first time anywhere..." The wild eyes of my rolling audience barely focus. "Score and Lynch's mash-up masterpiece *Dark Grey!*" I wave to the screen. The projection casts over a THC tainted smoke scrim. Trench coats fall open, strangers start licking each other, and I begin with what I know.

"Come here Babe!" As Mia stumbles over a string of lights, Stella grabs her furry boot. "I wanna see my BF fuck my BFF."

The bottled brunette drops to her knees.

Giving me unfocused OJ in Heaven, the two Greats sloppily make out with each other, giggling: "Oh my god I'm so wasted," "Oh my god, this is so hot," "Oh, my god I wanna fuck you," "You're sooo hot," "Oh fuck, I think I'm gonna throw up—"

I gasp and tense. Standing, Stella outstretches her arms.

"C'mere, girl." She, giggles, summoning her with both hands, "Let's go sober up."

As The BFFs sniff the PlayStation, their two massive butts protrude proudly toward Bickle. They glow in the Xmas lights. But my unsuspecting muscle doesn't notice. With his arms folded, he's looming over Cruz and Volta, completely fixated on their homoerotica. Again. When the Blue Extra turns up the fury on the already upsettingly violent JO that she's been giving me, my toes curl, and I distract myself with his broad stripes. *If I had a Paul Smith sweater I'd wear it all the time too.* My nails dig into my palms, and the raven-haired Extra begins torturing my co-star's nipples. Cringing, The blue girl momentarily releases my abused Producer, and I notice that my security has strayed.

"You need to take your hands off her." With one hand, Bickle forcefully grabs Soufflé's shoulder. "She says she doesn't want a massage."

Dejected, the mousey Frenchman cowers out from behind Holly's couch. Bickle bounds back to the The Boys. The Boys continue to ignore everything but their deep, deep interest in each other. I instinctively try to applaud my security's diligence. But the Raven girl stops me.

"Oh no Daddy!" She squeezes my wrists, cinching them tighter behind my back. "Not until you give her what she deserves."

Until now, I'd never wanted to be a father but, as the blue-haired Extra silently turns her head away and I spread my joy on her neck, I understand how fulfilling parenthood is. With her blue nail she scrapes a goopy taste from her black tattoo and feeds it to the baby bird behind me. Then they flutter away.

Good girls. I've gotta remember to ask Stella for their names.

At Bob, I gently wipe off my still totally-connected, yet red and chaffed Producer. I hand sanitize and crack open a San P. In the movie, a pretty brunette wearing a pig nose is getting OJ from a guy in an industrial shirt. I pop a curiously strong mint. The splice cuts back to *Donnie Darko*. Two voices loudly quote, "What's the point of living if you don't have a dick?" With his knees on pillows on the stage, in front of the wall, Lynch has Stella in an anvil.

"Cheers!" I raise my bottle.

Laughing, my co-host throws up a wobbly thumb, re-props his right hand and without looking over, Stella responds to my voice.

"Scoooooore. Come fuck my ass Baby!" Her bouncing calves scissor my friend's pink neck.

I glance toward Holly. I can hear her toy, but in front of her couch a cluster of ab-tastic Extras are giving each other OJ, obscuring my view.

"Baby, there's room for one more. Your boyfriend won't mind."

On her back, with her toes above Lynch's ears, Stella is drunkenly slurring. "Score fuck my ass!" It's unappealing. "...Score!" Her tone is wilting my Producer. Her words are making me want to rinse my own mouth. I twist open the Tom's. Then coming to my rescue, one of my guests fills in for me. Bridging over her face, Prius pushes my name back through Stella's lips. I swish, spit, and return to the obscene mess in Heaven.

Roughly, I am delivered. Rising from the mats, the Raven Extra pulls me down into a sweaty, groaning, writhing cast. It's moist. The smell of sweat, weed, wine, and joy oozes between slick flesh and crusty matted fur. It's filthy. *It's fine.* Calling action, I slide between the wet bodies to mingle with my guests. *This is going to be unforgettable.* This scene is going to be a timeless classic and the foreign fluids will come off in post with some orange cream body wash. I suck in my cheeks. Maintaining the expression of a leading man for Alvin's omnipresent lens, I begin a captivating struggle with the Blue Extra, but soon can't tell who is who, what's on what, or who's on me. Some vaguely familiar pierced parts asphyxiate me. I grab Mia's ass. My hand falls asleep. I see bright red dreads out of the corner of my eye. I roll toward the beacon. And end up on Donny. "Hello my brother!" I face 3-D teeth and pigtails but what I feel dueling with my Producer is even bigger than his grin.

"HellllO my brother!" I cheerily return then roll on, into another teenaged knot.

Some girl pins me down on top of someone else's leg. Holding me captive between her fishnets, she clamps my face with her thighs. Instinctively, I begin licking upward, peering breathlessly past under-boob, toward razor-cut indigo bangs. Proudly I watch the Blue Extra's expression change. Someone whispers. "Finger her Daddy!" I follow the order. I presume it came from the Raven Extra, before she slipped down to give me this OJ. "Harder! Hook it! She'll give you a bath." She's still in my ear. I glance down at the brunette that's sucking my Producer. Her technique is unique—toothy. Brushing her hair from her face, she pulls a strand from her mouth and looks up. I lift my head from between garters, press my chin to my chest and in a constricted creak ask, "What the fuck—"

"Don't worry about it fucker." Alvin keeps his grip. "It's for Star. She's way fucking into it." Grimacing, he wipes his lips with the back of his hand. "Just let me know if you're gonna blow. Don't fucking cum in my mouth."

It's fine. He's in love. Everything's fine.

"Come backkkk! I'm so close!"

The Blue girl speaks! Driven, I return my tongue, and when she showers my face in whatever it was that Holly didn't want on her last weekend, I have no choice but to follow.

"Fuck! Dick! You're a DICK!" Al spits my joy back onto me. "What the fuck man?"

"Sorry Al, I forgot. Really, I swear, I'm sorry." The Blue Extra and I can't stop laughing as I wipe her rain from my eyes. "Go get some mouthwash, you'll be fine."

"Fuck you man!" Shaking his head, he skulks away.

"The poor boy doesn't know what he's missing!" Still giggling, the Blue Extra finishes what Alvin left behind.

With my torso tongued clean, I leave the big scene to towel off my soaked hair. I pass Bickle. We high five, and he points toward my soggy tie.

"Looks like those push-ups are paying off Scorecrow!" He giggles.

He's right. Proudly I grab a cold bottle from the fridge and douse my chest with Pellegrino. I've already completed two fantastic scenes, my left pec is pulsing, and my Producer is still relevant. With my confidence soaring, I down the remains of my fuzzy water, zip up my jacket, and pocket some lube. I'm ready for the grand finale.

Erection-creeping behind her couch, I stealthily lean over Holly to deliver a French-Texan accent that's down right *magnifique*. "*Ce va*, lil lady? Want a back rub?"

"Fuck! Mike!" Laughing, she whips back her hand and smacks my chest. An empty wine bottle bounces off her couch. It rolls against a Mac counter Extra's heel. "I was almost there ... but yes..." She slides her golden vibe back between her legs. Her smile twinges. "I'd love one."

Biting open a tiny plastic green pillow, I spit out the tab and squirt water-based goo all over her soy-milky skin. Tasting artificial apple, I rub her neck, while my right hand attends my sensitive, overworked Producer.

The view from up here is exquisite. With her head thrown back, Holly breathes through slightly parted lips. Under the pornographic score, I can hear her toy buzzing. I can smell her cucumber though the thick musk in the air. I run my hand across her shoulders, over her collarbone, and down to her boob. When I squeeze a hallowed handful of red cotton, the autoerotic OC-angel finishes me with a super-sexual quickness that only the divine could achieve.

"You're... " I joy all over the back of the couch, "...fabulous." And as the sublimity of her trembling climax surges into me through our once forbidden physical connection, I fall.

Lips first, I dive into oblivion and kiss her, upside down. *In the ether, an un-released Smiths song begins to play.* With my mouth open to hers, ignoring a faint familiar taste that reminds me of Stella, I savor our delicate union and softly Holly responds. Driving her tongue down my throat, she grabs a fistful of my hair and pulls. I barely save myself from toppling onto her fragility and gently free my head from her hand. Looking into her soul, I slowly pull away. And we are consummate. *Our scene is pure romance.*

I rise. She speaks. And our spirits interweave, exploring each other for the eons within each fleeting second that passes before I reply,

"I'm leaving."

Fleeing to the wings, I pull on my track pants, grab all my shoes and, scurry barefoot off the stage. *I know why she has been so hesitant with me.* I run down The Path of prayers. *It's because I mean so much to her. I can feel it.* I knock over a candle on the way out of the ballroom. The wax spills into the stairwell. *I could turn back. I could gently push, succumb to my desires, and convince her to further our activities. But I don't want to cheapen our moment.* I take off my shades after tripping up the final step to the lounge. *I have to keep running because it was beautiful, because it was perfect. ... Even if she did whisper something that sounded like, "I want you to fuck me like that pig on the wall."* The leafy mouth of The Palace creaks. I breathe in the fresh middle-of-nowhere night. In a few hours, Gina's making gluten-free huckleberry pancakes—with tempeh bacon. *I've got to get home.*

....

I'm on the top of the WAMU steps lacing up my new shoes when I first see them.

All four of are drinking Sparks and have fat joints stuffed behind their ears. I stand to make a disappearance and the blonde-haired, blue-eyed mohawked one notices me.

"Sup bro?" Holding his belt to prevent his sagging shants from falling completely off, he limps toward me. "You heard of some party happening around here?"

"I wish." Laughing, I remain planted above them. "No man. You guys aren't from here are you?"

Their dumb hazy pink eyes all blink at me.

"Nah." Grumbling in unison, they crane their tattooed necks, searching for a mailbox decorated in streamers and balloons.

"Yeah, there aren't parties in this town." I grip the laces of both pairs of Chucks. A light breeze swings them at my side. "It sucks. Nothing ever happens here."

"Fuckin' toldya dog." The cranky kid in the black flat-brimmed Rockstar energy drink hat spits onto the sidewalk. "Let's get the fuck outta this bullshit town."

Suspiciously, they eye my Union Jack socks. I stand, frozen, hoping they didn't see me leave the hotel. The mohawk spits. The wind blows. A Solo cup scrapes across the lot. The kid with the awful, colorful throat tattoo lights a joint, takes a drag, passes it to the guy with a matching soul patch and, holding their belts, they all limp away tossing crushed Sparks cans into my lot.

Chapter 48

"Mike! Pancakes!"

Springing out of bed to Frank's call I check my phone, tie on my devil-monkey robe, and speed down the hall to join the Massi breakfast table. Waiting for me at my place across from Gina is a tall glass of citrusy San P., a side of bacon, and a steaming stack of my favorite mini Mickey Mouse cakes. Sitting down, slicing through the silence, I stuff my mouth with three of the all-natural maple syrup soaked rodent ears before Frank gravely says, "Mike, your mother and I want to talk to you about something." They haven't touched their food. I stop chewing. *This is it. I'm caught.* Twisting beneath their suspicious, critical stares my brain scrambles to figure out exactly which details of my secret life they've discovered until Frank sighs, "Are you doing drugs?"

I chirp a laugh that shoots gooey crumbs into my palm. Rain or shine, every weekend, when Gina's at work, Frank gets naked, lights a joint, and paints surrealist still life in his garden. If she knew about the weed, he'd be sleeping at Uncle Cosmo's. Vigorously shaking my head, I swallow. "No. I'm not on drugs, Dad."

"It's just that..." He agonizes, "you've seemed ... run down lately—"

Wiping my hand on a napkin, I fix him with a guilt-rendering gaze.

"And you carry around that lighter." Gina flails her hands in a tizzy. "And your clothes smell like smoke!"

"You guys." I place a comforting, slightly syrupy hand upon hers. "Despite the lack of stimulation in this joke of a town that you moved me to, I don't do drugs. I promise. Some of Alvin's friends get stoned while we game. But I do not. Swear to Moz."

"Oh, okay. Well, that makes sense." Frank appeals to his wife while squirming in the sticky stinky resin of his own hypocrisy. "But don't be smoking any of that crap yourself. It will get you hooked and rot your brain."

"Yeah, and pot impairs your fashion sense." I eye his hat. "Obviously you don't need to worry about me. I'm the best dressed kid at school."

Gina and I share a hand held smile of relief. Frank claps his hands. "Great then!" Rubbing his palms together he wipes them clean of the drug interrogation. "There is something else that I'd like to talk to you about. Pinky! You still haven't told him what you'd like for your birthday!" He gives me a conspiratorial look. "How about an easel and some canvases? I could give you a few lessons out back?"

....

In my unwashed Top Man button-up, I'm napping on my bed, dreaming of skinny ties, when my phone buzzes.

"Where are you?" Lynch asks. "I'm in the driveway."

Running my hand through my hair, I shade my eyes and jog out to the Deville. A monotone voice sings about Russian roulette, as I swing open the door and drop onto the bench seat. Before I can even reach for the volume, Lynch mutes the song.

"Man." I sigh, as he speeds down our hill. "Last night was legendary, but things have just been going downhill ever since." I open my compact. "This morning I sit down at breakfast and Frank says, "Your mother and I want to talk to you about something.'"

"Oh shit—" Lynch sounds more concerned than I'd expected.

"Yeah, right?" I bare my teeth. *Eh, good enough for my co-workers.* I replace the unopened tube of whitener. "So I of course think that he's about to ask me if I've been throwing wild drugged-out sex parties in abandoned hotels, but instead he just asks "are you on drugs?" Can you believe that shit? Frank. But man—"

"Mike. I've kinda got some bad news." Stopping for a thrash kid who's shucking his flipped bill through the crosswalk, Lynch turns to me.

He just used my old name. Unnerved, I snap shut my mirror.

"Don't freak out." Driving on, he keeps his eyes on the road. "But one of my brother's videos went up on Stella's blog this morning."

I freak out.

"Fuck you. Are you serious? How the fuck did that happen? Is it still up?" He stutters half answers as I continue to explicitly agonize. "Fucking Alvin and his fucking camera. Fucking Stella. Why would she do that? We're fucked man. We're so fucked..."

Spent, I throw my head back over the seat. Envisioning a future of eternal shopping at Walmart, I stare through mirrored lenses at the peeling sticker blighting the perfectly restored ceiling of his ride. It says 'The Damned.'

"It's down, Mike."

Stop calling me Mike.

"And I don't think a lot of people saw it." Lynch swings right, parking next to a red Mini Cooper in the theatre's lot. "Stella said someone hacked her private video section. But after I saw it, it totally disappeared. I can't find it anywhere. Alvin swears he never sent anything to her—"

"Was it one of my scenes?" Rubbing my right temple, I picture myself with sweaty red cheeks, crusty pink pants around my ankles and a purple Producer choking in my clenched fist. "Was it the one where I *joyed* in my own face?"

"The clip only goes like seventeen seconds before it cuts off. And the shot is so tight that you can't really tell that you're the one that's doing it to her."

"Who?"

"Stella. Well really..." Laughing, he corrects himself. "She was doing it to you. She was on top and totally going for it for the camera. She actually winks and blows it a kiss."

"If that gets out we're all so fucked man." The weight of fear and Sunday crushes my voice "You know that right?"

Paralyzed, I stare.

The Damned

"We're okay." I can hear him opening his Mentos. I think he just offered me one. "No one's talking about it. And *I* couldn't even figure out how to pull it down before it was gone. Sucks really ... "

Silently, we both sink into the re-upholstery. The motor churns. Lynch stares at me. I peel the sticker from the roof, and try to make sense of everything: potential party crashers, the pancake incident, McQueen denial, and now, video blog terror. Balling the torn vinyl, I shove it in my shirt pocket. *It's fine.* The Dark Grey Premiere was an unparalleled success. It was huge. *Everything's fine.*

"Oh." I scrape goop from under my nail. "I've gotta tell you something too. About Al—"

"Yeah?"

I face him. "Or did he already tell you?"

"Is he on drugs?"

"Oh, no, it's nothing like that. It's not that big of a deal." I grab my Sherman from the backseat. "It's just that, he gave me an OJ."

"Oh yeah. I saw. Star, right?"

"Yeah." I push open the heavy passenger door with my foot. " I'd better get in there. I'm a little late —."

"Mike, don't freak about the video." He leans over the armrest. "It's whatever."

"It's fine. I'm over it. Everything's fine." I smooth my wrinkled shirt. "I'll see you tomorrow."

He drives away texting and I head toward the ticket booth. *Honk honk.* "Hey Mike." Stopping, I turn back toward the lot. Rolling toward the street, steering with his knees, Lynch has both of his arms pushed out his window. He's giving me two thumbs up.

....

Sulking behind the hot pretzels, Bickle is wearing his immutable black and yellow stripes with an exaggerated frown. He looks like a sad-face emoticon. *Moz, I pray that this has nothing to do with Stella's stupid fucking blog.* From the door, I head straight for the concessions. Mia probably told him something.

"Mike, man..." Intercepting me, shaking his ratty pony, Philip is wildly waving his hands in a 'no-no-no' sort of way. "Don't even bother coming in. I'm sorry man but you're fired."

"Are you serious?" I take off my shades.

Bickle looks like he's going to cry.

"Man, this is the sixth time that you've been late. And you pulled that crap of not showing up on Friday?" My oppressor throws up his hands in fascist hippie disbelief, "What happened to you Mike? I'm sorry, but you've left me no choice."

"Whatever." Turning to leave, I pull out my phone, and dial, muttering. "A year from now you'll be bragging about knowing me. I don't have time for this place anyway."

Lynch's phone begins to ring and Bickle bounces up.

"I'm sorry buddy." Blocking my exit he sympathetically hands me a small grey, animal printed paper bag. "I tried to talk him out of it." His eyes are glistening like his lips.

"It's okay man, really. ... I've just gotta try and catch Lynch."

Ending an unanswered call, I dig through tissue paper.

"What's this?" In a daze, I pull out a skinny, black skull tie. *How the—?*

"I got you something else too but wanted to give this to you early so you could wear it at ... well, you know, your birthday party." He enfolds me in his massive arms. "And I figured that you might need some cheering up today too."

"You bought me a McQueen tie?" His muscular sweater muffles my voice. "They're, like, two hundred dollars. That's too much man."

"Oh, no, no." He nervously laughs. "Yeah, no. I made it. In tailoring. Cost me like ten bucks."

"That's really impressive." Suspiciously I look up at him. "Thanks."

Feeling the vibration between us, Bickle releases me and smiles a sad, chiseled smile. "You're welcome buddy."

I answer my phone.

"Come back and get me." Freeing myself from the uncomfortable lobby, I pace out of employment. "I'll tell you when you get here."

I hang up. Phillip affectionately calls after me. "Hey Mike, try and get it together man. Take it easy."

Turning, I shoot him a backward peace sign.

In the night breeze, leaning against the humming neon tower, I put on my Fords and inspect my first eighteenth birthday present. *He even made a McQueen tag for it.* When The Caddy rolls up to the curb, I slip the tie into my Sherman, swing open the door, and fall back in.

"You two are not in love," Lynch demands, before hanging up his phone. As he guns it out of the lot, my co-host turns to me. "What's going on?"

"I got fired."

"Whoa, weak."

"It's fine. I still know how to sneak in there."

"Phh, why would we do that?" He grins. "They're not gonna let us fuck in there are they?"

"Good point."

We pass the last of the weekenders crowded outside of the new wine bar.

"Why'd you get fired?"

"It's fine. Don't tell anyone though. I don't want my parents to find out."

"Yeah man, okay." Stopping at the stop sign in front of the closed record store, he unpeels and slaps a new sticker above me.

The Damned.

He shakes his head. "What a bummer. Lame day."

"It's fine."

"Totally. We'll be out of here in a few months anyway."

Aimlessly he drives me further from my last day at the quaint old theatre. After all these years— I can't believe it. I'll never have another scene in Booth Six.

"What do you want to do?" Turning past Cherie Cherie, he heads toward the freeway. "I'll make you a fake ID. We can go get matching 'Fuck Philip' tattoos in The Sco."

Click, click. "Let's go clean The Palace." *Click, click.*

Chapter 49

It has remained grey since Saturday. The clouds have kept the sun back, though they've not been able to keep school from breaking through the weekend. And what's happening on this chilly Monday is making me think that Stella's supposedly obscure blog indiscretion was actually more pervasive than the first period warning bell.

On my way to PE, two swim team guys pat my back and cryptically congratulate me. When I pass the benches in front of the science building, the grey and the crimson Sweater Girls cease texting to end their four-year denial of my existence. Indiscreetly they whisper about me in a 'oooh, he's so sexy and stylish, I wish I were in that video' sort of way. I begin putting it together. *I've gone viral!*

Strutting past the quad, I bask in the glow of my long-deserved universal admiration. Then I see someone grinning at me through the gym's windows. Ceasing my swagger, I scan the campus. My protector bee is nowhere to be seen. Bobby steps out into the cold. I begin deeply fearing for the safety of my perfect facial features, and he holds open the door.

"Those shades are hella sick Mike." High fiving him as I pass, I duck into the locker room and he generously bellows, "I never really thought you were a fag bro!"

By the end of second period, I've gathered that no one is certain of the identity of the guy who appears in the fabled seventeen-second masterpiece. *Thankfully*. They just know that they've seen or, more likely, simply heard of a sex tape that I am suspected to be starring in under Stella. *It's a shame she's not here to enjoy all of this.* Presuming that she purposefully leaked the video, I was planning to ignore her all day but she's absent. *I'll have to text her the good news.* The bell rings, our class pulls out our cells, and I type: "*Where are you Babe!? Our video is a hit!!!!!;) <3*"

At break, with my hood up, leaning against my spot against the cafeteria wall, I am the man of intrigue. In the girls' bathroom, the aloof grave cutter asks me to light her clove. On my way to Pope's class, Cream introduces me to the crimson sweater girl. This morning is so entirely invigorating that I make it all the way to sixth period without even considering cutting for a nap. Swinging my Union Jack lunchbox, I sway across campus.

"Hello my dear partner!" I sit down next to Lynch on the cold oversized concrete steps of the gloomy quad. "Great fucking day isn't it?"

"Sorry Mike, I really didn't think anyone saw it." Popping a Mento, he chaws encouragement, "But don't freak. I think everyone just assumes it's you because Stella's told the world that she's your girlfriend. Some people think it was Jason Milmo, and that longhair-electro Dill's not doing anything to discourage the rumor, which is good for you, but—"

"Lynch." I pull out a quarter of Gina's PB&J special. "It's pretty awesome."

"What?" He looks at me like I just turned down a part in the UK version of *Skins*. "I figured you'd be super stressed out."

"No man, this is great," In an energized sotto voce, I explain. "The video is already urban legend and it only happened yesterday."

He continues to squint at me. I offer him my backup gas station shades. He declines, so I slip them back in my Sherman.

"Listen, anyone who's seen the clip is dying over it and the kids who haven't are dying to see it. Either way, right now, every guy at school wishes that he were me and the girls all wish that they were Stella. The spotlights on *us*." I bite into my peanutty oat bread. "Who knows? We could end up being bigger than Rebecca Black."

"Okay cool man." Lynch shrugs. "I'm glad you're not bummed."

I smile back at three waif-ish, rich winery girls. Drinking Coke Zero, wearing keys around their necks and striped Chanel tights on their long legs, they parade through the no man's land at the bottom of the quad.

"What do you think about having two parties this weekend?" I tap him with my Pompelmo Pellegrino. "Friday AND Saturday?"

Shaking his head, Lynch smiles his huge wondrous smile. "Fuck it."

"Brilliant!" I grab my sage by the shoulder of his ragged GI jacket. "That's what we'll call it! Friday we'll have 'The Fuck-it Premiere' and then on Saturday ... 'Fuck-it Again'!" Satisfied, I ask, "What do ya think? Seems apropos no?"

"You know, a lot of people do think that it was Milmo in the video..."

"I'm not gonna make invitations." Frantically I tap my touch-screen. "I'm just gonna send out messages right now."

Chapter 50

The whispers of Stella's blog have turned to shouts, but my leading lady is still missing the exhilarating clamor. On Tuesday at break, Bickle approaches my confident, cool, two-piece suited stance against the cafeteria.

"How are you buddy? Are you doing okay?"

"I'm fabulous. How are you man? Where've you been?" I chew up my last bite of scone, dust my hands, and check my tie. "Are you sick?" I'll have to ask him to take this weekend off. I can't have my security spreading germs.

"Oh, uh, no." Stuttering, he shoves his hands in his new waxed-canvas trench. He looks a bit melancholy and terribly anxious. "I drove Sarah yesterday. She didn't want to go alone—"

"Oh! Did she go to see Blake again?" He must just be exhausted from having heard about her one-on-one both to and from San Francisco. I begin texting her. "Is she back? Do you know if she told him about me?"

"Um, I don't know." He pulls his salve from his breast pocket. His coat has yellow plaid lining that matches his sweater. *Maybe Blake bought it for him in SF.*

"Don't worry about it man, it's fine." I wave at the grey sweater girl as she walks into the band building. "I'm sure that I'll get some sort of part."

My loyal supporter deflates, dips his middle finger into his tin, and despairingly glazes his lips.

"Hey, I meant to thank you." I pat his shoulder. "Great job regulating Soufflé the other night. That French nast should know better than to try to get all handsy with Holly. She's not into that."

"Sure thing," he whispers. "But we really shouldn't be talking about that in public."

"You're right." Lowering my shades, I wink at a pair of pale sophomores, combat booting off campus on their way to grave cut and smoke in the cemetery. "But really, it's awesome having you there. With all the Extras that are showing up these days, I sometimes get nervous that things might get weird, you know? But then I look over and see this big killer bumblebee and I know that everything's fine."

"Thanks, buddy!" With his high-pitched titter, he throws his arm over my shoulder. "But if you just keep getting big on those pushups, you'll be a bee someday too."

....

Twenty-three hours and fifty-seven minutes later, I still haven't heard from Stella. I can't stop thinking about her, nor can I bring myself to send another text that will surely be ignored. Looking outstanding in my new polka dotted suit that came in the mail from Grandmama Massi yesterday, I lean against the wall again, staring at my phone, deliberating as my schoolmates swarm into the ever pervasive, deep-fried odor wafting from the cafeteria. Swallowing the last crumble of cranberry pastry, I dust the crumbs from my lapels and give in. I hit her speed dial. I don't want to seem desperate but I've got to know if she got the part and if she's finally mentioned me to Blake. "*I'm a free bitch, baby … boop.*"

This is ridiculous. I hit call. It's 10:03 am in the middle of the week, my girlfriend is off partying in San Francisco with a thirty-three-year-old casting agent, and I haven't heard from her since she was yelling about her ass last Saturday. I redial. Our film is still big news. The mysterious scandal is the hottest thing at Valley View right now. "*I'm a free bitch.*" Stella and I should be enjoying an esprit de corps for our new status. She should be here with me, by my side, going over the contract of our new reality show, practicing our autographs, and discussing our future. As I dial for a fifth time,

Mia and Bickle walk toward me, adding bafflement to my agitation.

"Why are you two holding hands?" I end the call. "Have you guys heard from Stella?"

Dropping her like a flaming bible, Bickle looks desperate as he turns to Mia.

"No," she answers. "I haven't."

"I left message at the W. Do you know Blake's last name? What the hell is she doing? She's been there for days."

Mia looks away. Bickle looks at his feet. Both look guilty. They're acting like they've been caught wearing Christian Audigier Crocs.

"Hey. Look you guys. You don't have to get all rattled." I gently acknowledge their weird PDA. "I don't care if you two are secretly dating or something." I turn to Mia. "Lynch won't care. No one's gonna care. What's the big deal?" Comically hooking my thumb at Bickle, I stage whisper, "At least you won't have to worry about this guy screwing around with twelve-year-old surfers. He just likes to watch."

"Yeah, I think she's in SF." Un-amused, she sighs. "And we're not dating, we're just friends."

"Yeah." Bickle pulls a little round metal thing out of his pocket and hands it to me. "Just like me and you buddy."

I stare into my palm at the second gift from my buddy. It's a black pin—like Holly's button but instead of a shark, there's a golden bumblebee on it.

"That's for when I'm not around to look out for ya. I made it."

It doesn't look like he made it. I turn to Mia to for an explanation, but she's not paying attention. She's fully distracted by the white stucco behind me.

"Thanks man." Pinning the badge onto my bag, I dryly declare, "Now you'll always BEE around."

He smiles. Mia doesn't. She just shakes her head and leaves us both leaning against the wall, simultaneously dialing Stella.

I'm a free Bitch, baby ... boop.

Chapter 51

This evening at rehearsal there are only three of us. Rick relieved the rest of the cast so that Holly and I wouldn't have to rehearse kissing for the first time in front of everyone. Though I'm a professional, I do appreciate the unnecessary courtesy. I don't much care for public displays of affection.

In our prop bed, running through the scene, I'm finding it very difficult to get into character. Rick is in another one of his foul moods. Every time I call for a line, he tirelessly reminds me that today was the deadline for having them all memorized. I improvise with Holly. He harasses me. I shoot him weary looks. Sprightly eyes peer through the black, mood-killing aura of his irritation.

In hopes of glimpsing the impending lip-lock, cast members are sneaking into Hess. Dancers whisper from the back row. Rick kicks them out. A techie snickers from backstage. Rick kicks him out. After the first three disruptions, if anyone so much as cracks open the side door he threatens to drop them from the play. When I again effortlessly improve upon a few of the bland words of my dialogue, Rick imparts this same threat upon me.

"Mr. Nalon." Knowing that the show would surely stop without its leading man, I patronize him. "I'll have my lines down by Monday. I just need one more weekend to brush up."

He accepts my oath and, to his dismay, I continue to artistically liberate the rest of my lines until, finally, we arrive at the moment of truth. Between the sheets of my nap shelter, with only two agitated rose-bespectacled eyes watching, my lips are about to make their second impression on Holly's. I touch her hand. I move in. And we both giggle.

"Come on you two, this is a serious moment." With regard for our uncomfortable position, Rick puts down his coffee, stands, and fluidly conducts with his chewed-up pencil. "This isn't Michael and Becca remember? Be your characters."

"Okay, sorry." Centering herself, Holly takes a deep breath. "I've got it this time."

Picturing Alvin filming from offstage right, I put on a drop-dead-sexy kissin' face and move in again. This time, Holly relaxes. She opens her mouth and softly we melt into each other. I taste citrus-sweetness. Rick is wrong. I breathe cucumber. This is not acting. I gently caress her face. This is the furthering of a deep connection that was established between a flawless girl with great taste and a fabulous guy with flawless style last summer at The Grounds over Britpop and tea. Under the sheets Holly presses her palm down on my polka dots. My Producer pushes back.

"Slow it down kids." Our director taps his coffee mug with his pencil as I reel at my first full taste of my untouched Filmgreat.

How could a vegan be so creamy and delicious? She's exquisite. I want her to meet Gina.

I begin sliding my hand up her hoodie.

"Hey you two, that's enough!" Frantically, Rick dings his java-stained time-out bell, until a familiar voice overpowers his ineffectual frustration. My driver is early.

"Wooooah! Can I get in on this scene?"

Holly unzips my fly and I look up just in time to catch Nalon pushing Lynch out of Hess.

"Student battery!" he cries. The stage door slams, shutting out his laughter.

"That's it!" Rick throws his notes into the cheap seats. "You both be gone when I get back. And you Massi! ..." He points, as if trying to summon lightning upon my head. "Monday! Lines! Get it together or you're out!"

The door slams again. And we're alone.

"Please. ..." I slide on my shades. "Draaamatic."

"Well..." Holly sighs, adorably sticks a wad of gum behind the headboard, and turns to me. "That was nice."

"Yeah. He's really tiring lately." I shake my head. "He needs to settle."

"No." She flicks the tip of my tie. "That was nice."

She's not being sarcastic. She's reviewing our spiritual frenching.

"OH! Yeah. Yes. Yes it was." Overheating, I anxiously pull off my blazer. "I think we work quite well together."

"I agree." I pause my folding, and face her warm hazel eyes. In the following silence, I'm hoping that she'll follow my lead, and take off her shirt. "Have you heard from Sarah lately?"

I put my coat back on. "Not since the party." *I don't feel like talking about Stella right now. Not here, alone in bed with you. It feels too temporal, too mundane.* I tug on my London Underground cufflinks. I used my eyebrow tweezers to poke holes for them in my shirt. "Why? Did she get the part?"

"I'm just wondering if she's okay. I figured that you might know. … You guys are official now right? She changed her profile status."

"Oh, yeah." As if for Rick, I improvise my lines with natural eloquence. "Well … I don't know. Not really?" I search for my lighter. "We're Filmgreats…"

Click, click. Holly tilts her head like Iman does when she hears that sound. *Click, click.*

I don't want her to think Stella stands between us. Nor do I want the world's next reality celebrity to hear that I take our relationship lightly. I drop my Zippo and begin waving my hands like a Massi.

"And what kind of girlfriend disappears to the W for days and doesn't return her boyfriend's calls? Right? I think we're more like BFFs … Best Filmgreat Friends."

I nod with the satisfaction of having perfectly illustrated our relationship.

"Oh, Okay."

"Yeah," I smile. "So, do you want to do something on Friday night?"

Holly looks confused. "You mean, before the party?"

"Well … no." *Moz, I forgot. It's Fuck-it Weekend.* "I was thinking you and I could just hang out … maybe go to a movie?" Fearing their own intention, my words start sprinting away from me. "… Or ice blocking or something. I'll cancel Friday so we can have all night to ourselves."

"Really?" Holly's eyes go *hentai*.

I'm as surprised as she is.

"Totally..." My rebellious tongue riots. "It would..." *—be my plea-sure, be an honor, be rockin'—* "...make me happy.*"

"I'd love that."

She smiles. And we kiss until my driver barges again.

....

As Lynch drives, I send my guests an apologetic message calling off tomorrow's Premiere on account of work.

"Wait, so you're canceling just to hang out with her?" He turns down the song about Ghost Rider. Lynch doesn't understand the magnitude of the cataclysm he has just witnessed.

"Holly's never let anyone touch her. No one. She's like, totally pure. But I've now kissed her thrice." I hold up three fingers. "She's a model who loves Moz, Lynch. Her spit tastes like a creamsicle. I've gotta hang out with her alone."

"I get it. Yeah, that makes total sense." We skip the turn to my house. Cruising past The Grounds, he wryly translates, "You'd rather maybe get to touch Holly's other boob than definitely bang twenty girls in one night. You gonna cancel Saturday too?"

"*Phhh,* Come on." *My suit smells like cucumbers.* "I'm not insane."

"Well, if you don't, I hope Stella shows up." Passing The D-hole, Lynch parks in front of our towns latest frozen yogurt boutique. "I liked fucking her a lot."

"Yeah ... me too..." I slide my iPhone from my breast pocket and check my messages. "She still hasn't responded to any of my texts."

"Maybe she's already too famous for us."

Maybe she is.

The analogue synths drone through the speakers, rolling like the soundtrack of some twisted old-school video game as Lynch's headlights pop the pink and green pastels from the YoGoGo logo.

"I think she's still in San Francisco."

"Wait! Whoa!" He kills the engine and perks up like a cat chauf-feur who's just seen a bird land on the other side of his windshield.

"Is that her?"

"Where?!" I peer through the windows. I see the XIV decal on Volta's cousin's Impala, a well dressed vineyard couple ordering dessert from Mr. Chang, a cowboy on an outside bench eating yogurty blue berries with his fingers. "Dude, what—?"

"*Shh, Shh.* No. Listen!" Throwing out his hands he cocks his head, hushing like a psychic communing with the dead. "I can hear her. She *is* still in The Sco. Can you hear her?" His big blue bejeweled eyes question mine. I cup my ear and gravely he reveals, "She's shouting 'Blake. Fuck my ass'."

"You're right!" Mournfully, I shake my head. "I can't believe it. She should be shouting my name." I perfectly affect her sex voice. "Oh Yeah, Score, Score ... Score needs a part in your show. There's room for one more Baby!"

Laughing with raucous approval, Lynch swings open his door. While somewhere in SF, Stella is getting her 'love' tattoo covered in Blake joy we'll be here eating YoGoGo.

"Seriously though, I do hope she's back on Saturday." I admit, "It wouldn't be the same without her."

"Totally," he steps out then leans back into the Caddy. "What flavor do you want?"

"Whatever you have. Just put gummy bears on mine."

He slams the door. I hit speed dial. Her phone doesn't ring. I hear "*I'm a free bitch*, baby." My eyes begin to sting.

Chapter 52

By Friday night, everyone but Stella has courteously responded with disappointment to the cancellation. But any thought of her having married Blake, gotten cast alongside DiCaprio in a Scorsese film, and skipped town to live in Hollywood without me, is far from my mind. All that I can think of is Holly and how good I'm going to look when she gets here.

With my teeth sponged in GO SMiLE and my body misted with a tester that Prius gave me, I throw back my shoulders, adjust my maybe-McQueen tie, then grab Eddie. I moosh her face to my neck.

"It's called Angel. How do I smell? Heavenly?"

She meeps, wriggles, thuds to the hardwood, and my phone buzzes. *She's here*!

Grabbing a nearby lint roller, I frantically remove all traces of my feline affair, flounce out the front door, and confidently plop into Holly's mint Bug.

"Hey, Mike." She tosses her lunchbox to the backseat. In her orange jeans and white hoodie, she looks orange-cream delish. "Sorry I'm late."

"Oh no problem." I unbutton my coat to assure that my designer tie is totally visible.

"You look great." Looking over her shoulder, backing out of my driveway, she tells me, "I thought that maybe you were gonna wear the pink track suit." I realize I've forgotten both my lighter and my shades.

Though the D-hole has historically offered little for those with refined diets such as ours, it does provide privacy. Holly slides her little butt into a booth at the back of the empty shop and I head for the counter.

"Hogan?" I yell toward the back, peering into the glowing treat cases. *Mmm, French Crullers.* I miss donuts. I haven't eaten one since I realized there were eggs in them. *Woah, he has vegan brownies now.*

"Be there in a hot one!" The scraggly haired owner pops his head into the kitchen window. "Ayyyy Mike!" Recognizing me, he throws open the swinging counter doors. The dusty back roads growl in the old biker's voice as he embraces me. "It's been a long time brother. Good to see ya man!" Firmly, he shakes me by the shoulders then hollers toward our booth. "Hey gorgeous. Good to see you again too!"

Dropping a baggie of loose-leaf tea back into her lunchbox, Holly waves and I smile at my warm welcome. Hogan's making me look great.

"Great to see you too man. I'm glad that you're back."

"They can't keep me down brother."

There's flour on his hands. The pot-leaf tattooed behind the skull on his forearm has faded. But the green lettering is still bold.

"That's Holly." Dusting my suit, I nod back at my date. "She's a screenwriter. And an actress. And a model. And a vegan. Can we get a couple of those brownies?" I point to the top row of the case. "And some hot water? She brought her own tea. She only drinks organic herbals.

"Hell yeah you can!" Hogan laughs and marches back through the swinging doors.

I've only just folded my jacket when he returns to our booth with two brown mugs, two bags of English breakfast, and a pink cardboard box.

"Here you go kids!" Setting down the treats, Hogan lifts the lid. An assorted dozen is layered below two brownies—one is twice the other's size. "Compliments of the house!" I read 'FUCK YOU' below the skull tattoo as he points to the un-frosted brown brick. "That one's for you Honey. It's fresh from the oven. Make sure you don't get'm confused now, I know your boyfriend here hates walnuts!' Laughing like a conspirator, Hogan slaps my back.

"I don't hate walnuts..." Puzzled, I watch him chuckle back to the kitchen. Lynch is allergic to nuts. Maybe Hogan has us confused.

"That's good." Snatching both brownies, Holly shoves them in her lunchbox and pulls out a loaf of banana nut bread. "...'Cause I made this especially for tonight."

In the fluorescence of my old hangout, delicately sipping the black tea that she chose over her private stash, Holly tears through three huge slices as we discuss music, cinema, scripts, and sharks. I'm amazed by her extensive knowledge of sea life.

"You'd make a really good host for a beach party reality show. Maybe you could start it online if *El Fin* doesn't get picked up right away." I finish off a cruller for old time's sake. "I bet you could do it a Leo's place. And Alvin could shoot it ... and I could be—"

"Hey. Wanna go see that 3-D horror movie?"

"Um ... I don't really feel like being at work tonight." Sucking my sticky sweet fingers, hoping for 3-D activities within a room from which I wasn't fired, I haphazardly suggest, "How 'bout we go watch a movie at my house?"

"Okay, sounds good." Holly latches her lunchbox and stands. "We could stop by my place and get my *Planet Earth* DVDs. Or maybe we could watch *Donnie Darko*. I missed most of it last week-end. I'd be into seeing the director's cut again."

"Fabulous." Thoroughly napkining the saliva and remaining glaze from my hands, I rise to button my coat. "Lynch's version did have its merits. ..." I offer Holly her hoodie. "But I prefer the original too."

....

On the way home, just to make sure that some lost Extra (or Stella) isn't disappointedly waiting in the WAMU lot, I have Holly drive by The Palace. As we pass Crystal Eyes, I see four tall tees creeping the cracked sidewalks. *Fuck.* I think these may be the same nasts from last weekend. But I can't tell. These people all look the same to me.

"Can I help you guys find something?" Turning down "Killing an Arab," I lean from the passenger window.

Holly picks at her brownie as we slowly roll up to the curb.

"Yeah..." Holding up his pants with one hand, the kid with a blunt behind each ear spits on the concrete then glares. "Are there more fags in this town or just you?"

"Oh yeah, tons." I swish my wrist. "But all of us are only into straight guys so you boys should just go back home."

As we speed away Holly laughs. Sparks cans hurl toward us and four middle fingers rise up into her review mirror.

Chapter 53

We made it. Having just barely escaped being force-fed candy corns, fun-sized Butterfingers, and Gina's freshest Cherie Cherie selections, I shut my tear-sheet-covered door to lock us in with Moz, various models, and Leo Di. Apologizing for the motherly onslaught, I crawl onto my red comforter, grab my laptop, and lay down next to Holly. We enjoy about twenty-two minutes of a straight film. Then start making out.

I'd almost entirely lost interest in this delightful PG activity but with Holly kissing is anew—it feels taboo. I haven't done this with anyone since the early days of The Premieres, since The Pink Room. It feels fabulous.

Slowly, I slide my hand up her worn grey, remixed D.A.R.E tee, struggling with my hesitancy. My parents are rooms away. *It's fine.* Holly thrusts her tongue in my mouth. I squish unexplored boob in my hand. *Everything's fine.* My co-star unbuckles my belt. Pulling her to her knees, I liberate her shirt and toss it to the ground. She falls back onto the bed. Her jagged, icy, asymmetrical a-line shatters across my black and white paparazzi pillows. She stares up at me in anticipation. Her black lace bra pleads to be set free. I straddle her, admiring her perfect face, her perfect body, and all her perfection. Then, envious of the pillowcase paps, I grab my phone from its charger. *"May I?"*

Holly poses lusciously for the camera. *She's a professional.*

After presenting the stunning stills for her approval, I begin undressing. I loosen my tie, unbutton my shirt, and close myself over the surrendering angel. I brush back her luminous locks.

"Holly?" Kissing the delicate cucumber-scented spot behind her un-pierced lobe.

I romantically whisper, "Can you be quiet while we do it?"

"I want to make you happy Mike." With meekness usually reserved for only Stella, she sighs. "But I don't know if I can."

"What?" I sit up, shocked to hear her question her natural ability. "Of course you can. I have no doubt. You can make me very happy." I recklessly toss my shirt on the floor then realize I've been right about her all along.

"It's just that I—" Looking away like an actress in an enhanced reality TV drama, Holly pauses. Beyond our heavy breaths, the only sound to be heard comes from plates clinking in the kitchen.

I relieve her from having to make the awkward confession.

"Wait." I hopefully ask, "Have you never ... Have you only had sex with ... toys?"

Clearly shocked by my insight, she laughs. "Um ... well ... basically. Yeah." Struggling to choose her words, she's looking at me like I have the answers.

She shouldn't be embarrassed. She's like a perfect ten amateur posing for nudes in a sea of silicon.

"I mean, I've fooled around with people ... I guess..."

"Not even OJ?"

I knew it. She is pure: A virgin. She's like a saint. She's like Morrissey.

"Nope." Looking up at me, she deliberately shakes her head. "Never gotten it ... but I'm willing to give." Sliding out from between my legs, she kneels up, throws her arms around my neck, and professes something that will haunt me for the rest of my sexual career. "Mike, I really like you. I wouldn't want it to be anyone but you."

For the first time, that old-timey song "It 'Has' to Be 'Me'" starts playing. Sinatra is insisting that my acclaimed Producer be the first to go where no boy or girl or DJ or thirty-three year old casting agent has ever gone before.

"Fabulous." I push her back down to the paps and passionately recommence our improvisation.

For all the Greats and Extras that I've worked with, I've never been as inspired as I am right now. I unhook Holly's overflowing a-cups. *This was always meant to be.* I toss her bra into the surreal intimacy of my bedroom. *It feels like we've been typecast.* I cup bare side-boob and suck. *She must soak her nips in agave.* Reaching down, cautiously, as if trying to pet a strange cat, I delicately begin unbuttoning her fly.

"That's it! Fucking killer!" In a director's chair, backlight by studio cans, wearing silver lamé lingerie, Alvin films from the shadowy corner of my room. I suck in my cheeks. "Keep it slow, rom-com. Ease it in there."

Shifting her hips, Holly assists, and together we slip her loaded pockets down past her knees. We kiss for an eternity. Almost one full minute of pure make-out seduction burns away before she places her hand on the top of my head and gently pushes. *The camera boy chants, "OJ, OJ, OJ..."*

Like a cat cleaning traces of spilt soymilk, I descend. I lick her neck. Her collarbone. I explore the sweet succulence of her soft, neglected left nipple. She pushes me further. I taste my way down her smooth, un-trodden trail of happiness. Firmly pressing her immaculate skin, I slide my fingers over her soft belly, her waist, under the thin black strip of lace hugging her right hip, *Everything is coming up cucumbers.* I graze my lips a few r-rated inches below her belly button. She pushes me further. My heavy breath beats against the cotton barrier to her unplumbed sanctum. She trembles, hooks her panties, and tears them down.

I see Moz. And the sound of my old name cuts through the rhapsody.

"Michael!"

"Yeah Mom," I yell back, totally annoyed.

"It's awfully quiet in there! No babies please!"

Sinatra has silenced.

"I thought you wanted grandkids!" I protest, and Holly's blissful expression changes to horror. Gesticulating wildly for her to stay put, I whisper, "It's fine."

Bucking me, she springs up to find her bra.

"Don't be smart!" Gina Scolds from the kitchen.

"Mom, we're watching a movie!" I stand to yell through the

locked door. "...And I just had to pause the best part!"

My Producer, still fully prepared to start the scene, grazes the wood between Morrissey and Moss.

"Oh! Sorrrrry ... do you kids want some fresh pumpkin pie? We've got cider..."

By the time I convince Gina that we have no interest in seasonal snacks, Holly's standing next to me, completely dressed and ready to leave.

"Mike, I'm sorry." My overdressed paramour whispers, "I thought I could, but I just can't with your parents here. It's weird."

"Yeah, totally. I get it," I take both of her hands. "We can finish this tomorrow. I promise my folks won't be at The Palace." I smile.

My Producer stares up at us, frowning.

"Actually, I don't think I'm going to go tomorrow."

"Why not?" I recoil. *My tummy hurts. I feel like Jesus kicked me in the nuts.*

"I think I'm just gonna stay in, and lounge." Her expectant, unearthly, dilated green eyes are disabling. She gently shrugs. "Maybe you can come over?"

She's wants me to cancel another party. I'm bound by the female Morrissey's gaze. I suppose I could. We could sneak into The Palace alone. Fulfill our destiny in Heaven. Maybe Al could shoot it. She half-smiles. *But what about my guests? My reputation?*

"I wish I could." Dropping her hands, I run mine through my hair. "But tomorrow ... It's gonna be huge. Bigger than *Dark Grey*," I stammer. "And I mean ... I'm the host. I just—."

"I understand." Holly wraps her arms around my waist and kisses me. "I really should go."

....

Alone in my room after walking Holly to her car, I take off my pants, open my Mac, and pull up a dorm room solo. I fast forward through a strip tease. The small-boobed bleached-blonde spreads her thighs and suck-slickens a red silicone rod. *The soft voice of Old Blue Eyes is interrupted. Threats are being whispered. "We're gonna out you and your party, fag."* The college girl shoves the toy inside her and I immediately release my pent up joy. It flies wildly from my relieved Producer. *The hateful vows subside.* I wipe my misfire from the monitor, clear my history, plug in my phone, pocket square my production house, and then crawl into bed.

It has to be me.

Chapter 54

The Fuck-it Premiere starts off well. In freshly washed Y-3 sweats, a Bickle-for-McQueen tie, a black Top Man suit coat, and a fantastic Massi mood, I greet our overwhelming turn out. Hot unfamiliar girls looking like flashers with flowers are coming to the corner planters and introducing themselves in between the whispered details of my almost perfect date. Lynch accepts a Germs sticker from an Extra wearing a black shoelace choker. She pins a *Bona Drag* button on my lapel. I light her cigarette. She licks me then vanishes in the smoke screen.

"Man, that's crazy." Peeling the waxy paper back, Lynch pats a white vinyl square onto the breast of his black hoodie. "It sucks that she didn't come tonight. I would love to see you DV Holly. And I could have been her equally unforgettable number two. ... I mean, if she really is a virgin and not just totally lying."

"Yeah..." I glance over the drunken, raging lot to make sure that no one is listening. "I'm actually kinda glad that she stayed home. I'm really into checking out some of these new Extras." I nod toward the hippie girls, twirling on the bank's steps with Star. "And there's only so much joy to spread around, you know?"

I can feel Lynch's mutilated eyes staring holes through my flaw-less reasoning. I turn to face him.

"Dude." He knowingly grins. "You want Holly to yourself. You're dying over her and that's why you don't even care that she *still* hasn't gone off with any real activities! Fuck, you and Dustin should start a club." He laughs,

"I just want to be first, man." Calmly, I reposition my new Morrissey pin. On the other lapel, it will draw eyes to my good side.

"Did you propose yet?"

"C'mon man, someone's gonna hear you!" I beg, fearing and hoping that Stella might still show up. It's been a week since I've heard from her.

"Okay. But you do like her right?" He pops a Mento and smiles.

"Yeah." Grabbing my phone, I hide my eyes in my overfull inbox. "I guess I do."

I'm about to open a PM from someone named Moore when Lynch says, "Holy Fuck." I look up. Chewing, he's pointing to a hot blonde in a Hello Kitty raincoat. I take off my shades.

As if summoned back to the valley by my confession, Stella weaves through the late-night parking lot social and sputters to a wavering standstill in front of me.

"Hey kids! Miss me?"

She has on too much eyeliner. Her hair is chopped, straightened, and white.

"Where ya been Babe?" I ask, tempted to bring up my twenty-seven ignored texts and forty-three unanswered calls. "I mean, other than the salon. Did Blake make you do that?"

"*Phhh*, I make Blake." With a medicated toss of her hair, she hums, "It was all for you Babe," and raises a single brown brow. "I knew you'd like it."

She looks bizarre. She's lost those few extra pounds on the Frisco diet, but her new look is unnerving and she's being weird. I feel like she's either going to fall down or start doing back flips off the planters.

"Rockin'." I put on my Fords as she fingers a particularly interest-ing corner of the sticker on Lynch's chest. "So how did it go?" Did you get the part? Did you ask about me?" Her unfocused eyes roll toward the far end of the lot.

"I'll know next week…" Giggling at some unknown joke she falls into me with a sloppy hug. "I'm gonna get it Baby. And when I do, you're next!"

"Fabulous." She needs to go home and sleep off her weird. I'm going to insist upon it … in a second. Holding her up with one arm,

I poise my phone. "What's Blake's email again?"

"Donnnnnnnavon!"

Her squeal rings in my ear as she wanders toward the Frisky DJ's and their harem of San Francisco socialites.

"I think she's on that Salvia shit that Leo does." Lynch watches her weave away. "Where do you think she's been?"

"I don't know—" Smiling, I shake the hand of a bearded Extra in an Upper Playground sweatshirt. He slips me a ten-dollar bill. "One-on-ones." I shrug, pocket the money, then realize that I've been selfish.

Pulling out my phone, I tap my photo album and hold out the screen.

"Check it out. Pretty cool right?"

Lynch grins at the first shot from last night's session with Holly and Stella begins wandering back through the overfull lot.

"I'll show you the rest later." I hide the evidence.

My long lost co-star wraps herself around Lynch. He squeezes her butt and I motion to the raucous crowd of Extras.

"We'd better get this downstairs."

"No, no wait, Babe." Obliviously escaping my partner's paws, Stella hooks my elastic waistband and pulls me into her. *At least she still smells pink.* "My friend is on his way. He'll be here in like ten minutes."

"Babe." I look down into her unfocused blue eyes. "I've gotta get everyone out of here. We're far too visible." Pointing to Mia's distant areolas I insist, "And your BFF and her fans need to close their coats."

"Thannnnks Babe." Stella connects with a sloppy kiss. "Just ten minutes." Sprinting away she hops into the Sprinter's thumping lounge to dance in the strobe light.

Shaking my head, I pocket square my mouth and pull up more underwear pics. Lynch asks about Holly's nipples. I tell him about Hawaiians who believe that their dead friends can turn into shark gods, and a pigtail brushes my shoulder.

"Hey my brother!" Putting a consolatory arm around me, Prius empathizes, "That Sarah shit is pretty crazy man."

"It is right?" I stash the private photos in my breast pocket. "Did you know she was going to do it?"

"Yeah." Taking a drag of his American Spirit, he blows smoke over his shoulder then opens and offers me his compact. "I got her the best guy in San Francisco. You freaked out over it?"

It's nice to have someone who can understand the emotional impact that aesthetic disasters can have on a guy.

"Well, it's weird," I bravely admit. "But I'll get over it." Snapping the comforting GO SMiLE tube, I sponge my teeth. "And it will probably help her get the part. Everyone loves a wild blonde and—"

My heart stutters like a broken projector.

Timidly, I gasp. "Oh fuck."

Through the storm-ready sea of young Greats and Extras, Stella is walking toward us again, this time holding hands with her featured guest.

"Hey kids. This is Ryan."

Her friend extends his hand to Donny "Hey my Brother!" Then to Lynch.

Giggling, "Fuck," my co-host shakes Ryan's hand before the fully tattooed arm reaches out to me.

I have no words. Silently gripping Mr. Snow in a paralyzed handshake, I stare at Stella, wondering if the high volume hair bleach also stripped the sanity from her head.

"Hey Score." Recognizing my arresting terror, Ryan assures me, "Don't worry man. None of the other teachers really know what's going on. They haven't even seen the video." He smiles. "Thanks for having me."

Chapter 55

Everyone is in. I take my speech position. I'm still a bit dazed. A bit concerned. But we're all in this together: Filmgreats, Extras, and teachers who party together, go down together. I'm not going down. Except on that blue-haired water ride. And I'm not going to think about the video. Looking out over my fabulous full house, I begin to settle. I see schoolmates and surfers amidst sexy strangers. This is my biggest Premiere by far. *This will be fabulous.*

"HAYYYYYY! Hay everyone!" My unruly masses begin disrobing. "Welcome to an evening of opulence, eminence, and posterity!" I open my arms. "Tonight Lynch and I bring you..." Two awestruck Sparks boys wander through the curtain. "Fuck It!" With my grand gesture, pornography hits the wall.

....

Don't think about the Sparks kid with the mohawk. A fully tattooed arm grazes mine. *Don't think about Mr. Snow. Concentrate on the OJ.* The blue-haired Extra squeezes me. Hard. Embarrassed, I reach down and hopelessly tug a nipple ring. Switching up her technique, she licks lightly. Maybe a Katy Perry song will come on and save me. Lying limp in Heaven, I glance back to the soundboard. There, standing a few feet from the purple love seat, The Mohawk mixes his Sparks into his Jim Beam. Teetering in his puffy sneakers, he chugs from his swirling swill, raising and lowering his bottle, glaring at Bickle's back.

"C'mon. I wanna save some in here to pet my kitty with." The frustrated Extra has pulled a vial from her raincoat. "Do you want me to play with your butt or something?"

My Producer won't wake up.

Apologizing to the Blue girl for leaving her very high and totally dry, I pull Lynch from his tag-team scene with Mr. Snow.

"What man? What? C'mon." He resists, tying his hoodie around his waist as I drag him to Surfers' Paradise. "You so need to settle. Ryan's totally cool. He was in a band—"

"No man, I'm over that right now." Pulling on my sweats, I nod toward the PA. "Who's the X Games reject?"

Sparky, in his tall tee, stands out like a storm cloud amidst my rain-coated guests.

"Oh. Yeah, I thought those guys were weird too. They were creeping around before I started the movie." Lynch slumps against the dusty wall. "They said that Stella invited them. But she doesn't recognize them."

"I'm not sure that she'd recognize her own face in a mirror right now."

On the mats, Mr. Snow is wearing my GF like a reverse Hello Kitty backpack.

"True, but they're definitely not her friends. When the first scenes started, the dude with the throat tattoos freaked. They started arguing about staying. Then he went, 'You're on your own faggot,' and bailed on that guy." Lynch points to Sparky then wipes his slick hands on his naked hips. My partner smells like cherry lube. "Can I please go fuck Stella now? Or Someone? Please?"

"That guy's a nast," I insist. "He's one of those kids that have been creeping around outside. He called me a fag."

"I mean, yeah. He's for sure a nast, but he's not really doing anything, and he's so wasted that he can barely stand up. Fuck him."

As if on cue, the saggy pants miscreant stumbles like he had just been pushed by one of the hotel's spectral ex-residents.

"See, don't worry about it man." Revealing his mid-level Producer, Lynch re-ties his hoodie around his shoulders like a cape and gives me two thumbs up. "I'm gonna go fuck something."

He's right. I take off my pants. Sparky looks like he won't even remember what town he's in, come morning. I suck in my cheeks. *I hope he doesn't puke.* Bounding after my heroic partner, I begin acting like a Great host.

My tie is in knots. It's binding the blue-haired Extra's wrists behind her back as we do it upright kitty style. After tying up my co-star, the raven-haired Extra wriggled between our spread legs. Below us, she's guiding my pulsing Producer, helping me make up for my earlier outtake.

"You'd both better fucking give it to me!" Opening her mouth, the dark haired dominator begins to suckle my production house.

To prevent getting accidentally bitten, I slow my pace. The blue-haired Extra thrusts her hips faster and asks me to bite. I do. She makes a fabulous anguished sound. It almost finishes me, but Mr. Snow's voice cuts through Ke$ha's. Threatening 'detention' and 'the principal's office,' his tired role-play reminds me of my unwanted guests and impedes my rising joy. I turn toward the soundboard. Sparky still hasn't puked. But his expression has changed. His face is twisted into sweaty pink disgust— pure, seething, drunken hatred.

Raven begs for a shower and I hump harder, wondering what the wasted mohawk has against Bickle. Maybe it's some rival wrestling team grudge. Maybe he's jealous of the Paul Smith sweater. A small blue voice tells me 'I'm about to go' as I realize that the drunken piece of trash hasn't even noticed my dapper security. He's looking through him, gripping his knuckles white around the neck of his whiskey bottle. *I know what he's about to do.* My whole body tenses. I pull out of the Blue Extra and joy into her friends open mouth just as Sparky takes his final swig.

"Fucking faggots!" He yells and hurls the bottle at the two boys in love.

The glass shatters next to their couch.

Startled, Cruz and Volta sit up and freeze their scene.

The Blue Extra soaks the girl below us. I reclaim my wet Producer from the Raven Extra's mouth and frantically search for my pants.

As I stand, pulling up my Y-3s, I'm terrified to meet my guest's reactions but— they're all still in scenes. No one is paying attention. Except for The Boys. And my killer bee.

I start running.

Bickle wraps his hand around the throat of the unwelcome guest and pins him against the stage right wall. Suspended from the ground by his throat, Sparky wretches and pukes as Bickle connects a solid right to his guts. Nowhere near as dismayed as I am by the vomit, my security somehow keeps his grip through the spew.

Erection sprinting over limbs, pillows, underwear, rainwear, bottles, and boots, I watch the kid's ugly veiny red face cave in. The wet, snapping sound of skull mingles with the sonorous sex-slaps rising from the rest of the theatre; I, too, feel like I may throw up. Because this is bad.

This is really bad. This could end everything.

In seconds, I'm at the scene, but by the time I call cut, Sparky is completely unconscious, dangling like a used condom from the big bee's bloody, pukey fist.

"Fuck, sh...it..." Almost letting an old name slip out—*with a moth*—I place a calming hand on his flexed bicep. "Bickle. Stop. You gotta stop."

Turning, recognizing me, he discards the mess. The phobe's head hits the floor, resounding like a dumbbell dropped in the school gym. I stare down at the mangled kid in the stinking puddle of blood and regurgitated booze. His face is a grindhouse still. His clumpy hairline is pink. His blonde mohawk is spattered with blood.

Moz, gross.

"He threw a bottle at The Boys."

The love seat is empty. Cruz and Volta have gone to dress in Surfers' Paradise.

"I know man."

My fear for the safety of myself and the secrecy of my party rises with the unnerving reappearance of Sinatra's song.

It has to be me.

"It's fine. We just have to get him out of here. Is he dead?"

"I don't think so."

"Can you kill him?"

Sparky sucks. I hope he dies.

After turning down my plan to gather all the drugs at the party, force them down the craggy hole of Sparky's swollen face, and then sink the hate criminal in the infinitely deep lake on the outskirts of town, Bickle agrees to carry him out of The Palace. Begging Cruz to go get his car, I get dressed and, with my arms full of cleaning rags, follow the ghastly procession upstairs.

It seems like hours have passed when I finally hear the El Camino screech up the side street. I hold open the mouth of The Palace. Bickle brings out our dead, and I begin lining the bed. While he bungee chords the body, I notice its unicorn all-ages show hand-stamp. I take Sparky's wallet, cover him with Sponge Bob bed sheets, and then get in the car.

....

It's 2:36 am when we reach the bovine scented North Bay town. Before we became the Gods of The Greats, Lynch and I used to come here to see bands play at an old theatre on Washington. Tonight, there was a hardcore show there. I think this is where our envoy got his hand stamped.

As we speed into Petaluma, Bickle suggests that we either drop Sparky off at the hospital or at the address that's on his ID. I insist that we leave him behind the Phoenix. If he comes to, he'll hopefully presume he'd been beaten up at the show for being a drunken prick. If he dies, I at least won't have to worry about him remembering anything.

Standing guard at the gravely mouth of the deep, dark alley, I'm infinitely grateful to be texting while my muscle handles all the manual labor involved in our totally fucking annoying task.

Bickle carries Sparky to the end of the dusty path. Next to the dumpsters, he unwraps and deposits the body onto a splintered box spring. I tell him to save the sheets. He balls them up, brings them back, and stuffs them under the boots in the El Camino's bed.

On the freeway, I cue up Morrissey. He sings, "*I want to start from before the beginning,*" over the voice of Ol' Blue Eyes. The three of us sit, silently pressed together as Cruz drives the speed limit.

When our driver pulls over to pee behind the abandoned gas station, Bickle confesses.

When we arrive at the littered WAMU lot all is quiet. But Bickle's words are looping through my mind.

I need to clean. With an armful of soaked sheets, I step into the desolate street. *It's too late.* I look toward the hills where my parents are soon to be making breakfast. The sun is almost up.

I drift into The Palace. I pace across the empty ballroom. Springs eerily creak beneath my steps. In an unlit offstage bathroom, I douse bloody rags with thoughts of Stella, her TV show, Blake, Mr. Snow, The Premieres, Sparky, and Gina's pancakes. I burn the sheets in the sink. I watch them smolder until they're completely clean.

Saving my tie from the lost-and-found, I follow the still flickering Path of Prayers up to the purring Camino. I fall in and we peel away from the curb.

With my eyes still stingy from the smoky incineration, I thank the guys for all their help. Bickle hugs me. Cruz says, "Love you *Miguelito*." They leave me at the end of a driveway in the nicest part of town.

I creep through Lynch's door. I step over Star and Alvin then tiptoe down the hall. Morning light seeps through the blinds onto the California king. I undress, tie my wrinkled tie over my eyes, and crawl into Al's disheveled sheets.

This is too tight. I loosen my blindfold. A virgin, draped in diaphanous, white shark-screened silks, encircled by a ring of fire, descends through the ceiling. Slipping between the purple satin, she swaddles me like the Christ child for McQueen.

"I missed you tonight." I look up into her beaming greens. "Did you get my text? We shoulda hung out. Even if Gina was ruining my chances with pie, I know I woulda had a better time. Sharks are cool. I have a picture of you in my locker now. I don't know if I can handle this." As my eyes well, Holly joins Frankie in song.

It has to be me.

Chapter 56

In her kitchen, Gina is packing my PB&J while I, scanning for any mention of a body found behind the live music venue of a nearby town, flip through her Monday paper: pumpkin growing competition; drunk cyclist arrested on 'Bike to Work' day; Interview with the baker at Cherie Cherie. *Good.* Still nothing. I grab my lunchbox and kiss the chef. She asks why I need my shades in this type of weather. "Just because it's cloudy doesn't mean that I can't be seen, Mom." I dash to the Deville.

Rolling into the flats, I ask Lynch if he's heard anything regarding Bickle's correctional service. He hasn't.

"You. Need. To settle." He turns up his voice with The Stooges. "Nasts like that get beaten up all the time. It was probably just another night out for him. Focus on your future man. You've got a huge party, a hot girlfriend, and a virgin with a vibrator who's begging you to be the one. You'd better start dealing with that cuz if you don't make it happen soon, someone else will." He points to himself.

"Fucking yeah, dumbass!" Alvin springs up from the backseat.

I didn't even know that he was here. Checking my hair in the sun visor, I sigh.

"I know. If I'd just hung out with Holly on Saturday, I'd have nothing to worry about now." I pull open my eyelid and drop in Visine. *I'm getting better at this.* "I called her last night to see if she wanted to come over to touch or just hang and talk or whatever, but she had too much homework." I palm the saline tears from my face. "We were on the phone for an hour. She didn't say anything about our date or The Premiere." I sniffle. "...Did you know that there are invisible sharks?"

"What the fuck is wrong with you?" Lynch stops one-handedly texting and points his phone at me.

"It's just the eye drops—"

"I'm talking about fucking a virgin and you're talking about marine fucking biology. You called her to see if she wanted to come over to 'hang and talk?' What are you? In love?"

"C'mon man." Blinking in the mirror, I see Alvin filming the Sweater Girls, walking up the hill in their rain boots. "I just want to be first. With a girl like her you can't just—"

"Oh can't you? Or are you just in fucking love? You are, aren't you Mike!" Throwing himself over our seat, Al turns his camera on me. "What's it like being in fucking love? It's like Black fucking Sabbath ALL the fucking time, right? Right. I know. Do you wanna have babies? Little bleached blonde babies with green contacts? You're getting old fucker, time to breed!"

I snatch The Flip cam, turn it off, and toss it in the backseat. Silencing, Al fetches it and resumes filming. The Grave-cutters at the cemetery gates strike tragic poses.

"Woah! Wait! He's right! Your birthday's this week, Hugh Grant! Eighteen!"

I'd almost forgotten. It's this Friday. *I wonder if Holly knows.*

Lynch shakes me by the shoulder.

"We're doing it big this weekend Mike! Three in a row! Sunday matinee!" He pounds the steering wheel detailing our duty. "For your birthday! It must BE!"

"I'm totally in!" Alvin turns the camera back on me. "Fucker?"

I was planning to spend the entire upcoming weekend with Holly. But I mustn't be short sighted. If we can pull off three Premieres in a row, it would be like the Oscars, VMAs, and AVAs all rolled into one. And if Blake heard about it, he'd for sure want to do a show about me.

I put on my shades and smile to the camera.

"I'm in!"

"Fuck yeah." The brothers rejoice in unison.

It begins to rain as we cruise into Valley View.

Chapter 57

The buzz about my video has died down. I only miss it a little. With the way things have been going, I'm thankful that a 'Live From the Fuck-it Premiere: It's Teen Orgies and Murder' video clip didn't mysteriously appear on Stella's blog this morning. When the break bell rings and the phones come out, I toss my D+ into the lab's recycling bin and try to catch up to her. "Hey Babe, wait up." She doesn't stop. *I wonder what her problem is.*

"Babe!" I call out again then watch her curvy pink pea coat disappear toward the art buildings.

It's fine. I'll tell her about my birthday aspirations later.

Beneath my old Sponge Bob umbrella, I pull my Cherie Cherie bag from my Sherman and stroll toward the cafeteria. Someone is sitting at my spot against the wall. She's slouched over. Oh, and she's sobbing. *Great.*

"Hey Ash." Hovering over The Twin looking down and chewing dried cranberry, I hold my scone out as an offering. "What's going on?"

"Michelle's gone, Mike." She looks up. There's a clarity in her puffy blue eyes that hasn't been there in months. Her hair is soaked. She's shaking. "Mom and Dad sent her away."

"Why?" Fearfully, I wave my pastry like a crumby magic wand. "They didn't find out about the party did they?"

"No." She bristles. I exhale.

Terribly relieved that my scone spell worked retroactively, I take another bite as she turns away to stare through the drizzle and into the gloom of the empty campus.

"They found out that she's pregnant. Michelle is pregnant and they found our pills. They took away our fucking pills."

"Oh, good."

"Good?" As if I'd ratted out Roxy, Ash turns back to me with a terribly hateful glare. "How is that *good*?"

"Oh, um..." Covering my mouth, I chew and clarify. "I just meant that it's good that your parents don't know about the party ... and that you guys are off the pills. It's sucks about MK, though, for sure. ... You're not thinking about telling them how it happened are you?"

"Of course not." She seethes.

I wonder when she stopped wearing her crucifix.

"And stop calling her MK you fucking freak. Her name's Michelle." She palms her red cheeks. "They sent her to live with my crazy fucking aunt in Florida. They want us separated and they're talking about rehab and exorcisms. ..." She looks away. "But I'm not sticking around for that bullshit."

"No, no of course not," I say, because I don't know what else to say.

I dodge her sober glare, checking to see if the straggling snackers are alarmed.

The rain has driven most of school indoors. The few students braving the elements are running beneath umbrellas to find shelter. Ash sobs again. Crying, the mascara-smeared twin in four-hundred-dollar jeans melts in a rain puddle. The storm is building. *This is bad.* Moving in, clicking my lighter, I shield her from public view.

"I'm gonna get her out of there." Over my metallic cry for salvation, with muted impunity, she defiantly insists, "Star is gonna help me. I'm leaving tomorrow. And I'm not coming back."

"That's good. That's fabulous." I soothe, supporting the runaway. "You two shouldn't be apart ... and Star's cool. She's like full on adult. And she's loaded. It's f—"

Sinatra's voice crackles through the school's PA. My skin shrinks.

"Do you hear that?" I pan the campus in horror.

"Yeah, so what?"

"Um..."

The song disappears beneath the warning bell.

"I mean ... we should probably go to class."

Ignoring me, the leftover twin digs a little box from her purse and pops a pill.

"Okay, well, I can't be late for Pope. He's such a hard-ass." I back-step. "So ... message me. Tell your sister to message me too."

As I flee, I begin to recall all the good times I've had with the excommunicated.

"Um ... hey..." Pausing, I turn back to her and hesitantly ask, "Is MK having the baby?"

"They say she has to." Ash stares down, through the rain, tapping out a text.

"Do you know whose it is?"

"No Mike." Snapping her head up, she threatens a life sentence. "We don't know. How the fuck could we? Maybe it's yours."

Okay. Solemnly, I nod in acquiescence. Then retreat.

It's fine. I've survived last weekend. This is nothing.

"Hey, Mr. Pope." Happy to be the first to show up for Calculus, I shake out the thick layer of black moths trapped under my yellow umbrella.

"Mike!" My teacher turns from his sprawling chalky equation. His face drops. "Are you okay? Are you crying?"

"Oh, no." I dab my cheeks with my bandana. "It's just really coming down out there. Everything's fine."

Chapter 58

"Maybe I should start using the condoms..."

"It could be anyone's man." Lynch dips a cluster of fries into a chocolate shake. "You've seen Michelle's scenes."

A pink-haired girl from the Christian Club squeaks by in plaid rain boots. A flyer for a harvest party lands on our table. I light it and drop it into my lunchbox. Transfixed on its writhing deterioration, I consider some desperate actions of termination. It could be rather ceremonious if I were to close The Palace on my birthday.

"...Or maybe we should say fuck it all and shut down. Some Interscope guy named Sammy just messaged me. We could just use The Palace for Band FAIL! practice. Or maybe we could do study groups down there—"

I can't believe that my ever-licentious co-host is advocating ending our party. I don't like it. I was just thinking the same thing. But I don't like it. Hearing Lynch's doubt doubles my own.

"Fuck that." Wounded, I snap shut my lunchbox. "It's my birthday."

"Dude, like I'd seriously suggest canceling your birthday? Like we practice. Settle." He pours the remainder of his coffee into his shake and takes a steamy gulp. "This weekend is gonna be legendary." He points across the packed cafeteria. "And you'd better bring me her as a party favor."

Cream, sitting with a table of monochromatic girls, keeps talking to Periwinkle.

"Sorry man." Smelling fetid, burnt propaganda, I pick at my PB&J. "I'm just all rattled." I wave away a trace of escaping smoke. "I promise to bring you at least one of the sweaters."

"Killer. I'll getcha something good, too."

"Hey, have you talked to Stella?" I ask, as he twists the orange frosting from a halloweeny Hostess cupcake. "I think that she gave me the wrong email for Blake. I tried to ask her about it but she's being a real bitch today."

"She's pissed about you canceling the first Fuck It." He obscenely licks lard.

"What? Why?" In disbelief I scan the moist, fluorescent-lit tiles for Hello Kitty. She's standing in the pizza line with Mia. "So, Stella disappears for a week, doesn't return my texts or calls, doesn't ask Blake about me, doesn't even respond to the Fuck-it invite, and now she's all pissed off about last Friday? That's TBS."

"Yeah, but I think it was more about you canceling the party to try to bang your soon to be wife." Shaking his head, sucking in, he hisses through a tickled grin. "I think that's why she's burned."

"Wait. How did she know? She wasn't even in town."

"I don't know man, ever heard of the Internet? Chicks talk." He offers me his second Hostess. "Maybe Holly told her."

This isn't good. She can get vindictive when she's pissed off. Freshman year, after Mia copied her hairstyle, Stella got her wasted then shaved her BFF's head.

"We're fucking Filmgreats." I proclaim, eschewing the snack cake. "How could she possibly care what I do with Holly?"

With a sneer, Lynch shrugs. "I guess cuz she's your girlfriend."

"Oh, yeah. Right. The status." I rise to take action. "I guess I'd better go clear up this BF thing."

....

I avoid Stella for the rest of the day. After final period, I text Holly to ask her for a ride home and meet her at the less congested hillside end of the parking lot.

Fully reclined in her passenger seat, I watch my platinum

chauffeur pull into exit traffic. She waves at someone who I can't see and as "How Soon Is Now" eases through the speakers so begins the best twenty-four minutes that I've spent since last Friday.

Holly lightly sings along to Moz, soothing me with her contralto. Heat from the VW vents warms my feet. Rain batters the windshield.

I'd tell her everything about Saturday—Mr. Snow, the blood, the pit-stop confession. I'd worry over MK's procreation and Ash's imminent defection, but I don't have the strength. I'd rather just listen to her.

"So..." Sighing, I reach up to touch her hair. "What do you know about cat sharks?"

"A lot, they're ground sharks, dogfish..." Keeping her perfect posture, she glances down at me, and smiles. "What do you know about Spanish teachers having sex with high school girls?"

"You heard about that huh?" I drop my hand and fall back into my seat.

Waffle-sole footprints are pressed against the roof's lining. I turn to watch the rain.

"Sarah filled me in on most of it. It sounds like Saturday was pretty sketchy." Holly pokes my side. "Looks like you should have just hung out with me."

"Yeah, seriously." Jolting, I face her smirk.

Outside her window, pacing us and biting a soggy joint, Sparky's stretching his bloody smile behind an orange and silver Flip cam.

"I absolutely should have." I turn away and stare up at the girl-sized footprints.

"It's really too bad. Mom was out all night. No parents anywhere ... no teachers—"

The mohawked mess jumps onto the hood, flipping me off while he films.

"Hey, c'mon you don't need to be evil." Popping up, I point toward the muddy clearing alongside Iman's winding driveway. "Pull over here, I'll make it up to you."

"Sounds romantic." Caressing my cheek with the back of her ravishing right index finger, Holly speeds past the shoulder. "But damn—"

Sparky tumbles off the hood.

"We're already at your house."

"Okay." I GO SMiLE. "But can I at least have a kiss goodbye? Just so I can remember what I missed out on?"

Parking in front of the garage, Holly accepts my bargain. She cranks the e-brake and climbs on top of me. We kiss. I taste orange cream. I begin sliding my hand up her sweatshirt.

"Mike." She giggles, grabbing my wrist. "I think I can see your dad in the backyard ... and I think he's ... painting?"

Silently, I curse Gina's new work schedule as my Southern California shelter rolls off, sending me into the storm.

"So Stella told you about Saturday?" Raising my seat, I step out of the car, open my umbrella, and obscure Frank from her sight. "She was acting kinda weird today. She hasn't been a bitch to you has she?"

"No, not at all. She even brought me some of my favorite cocoa. It's Mexican. I think she got it at a chocolate bar in the Mission."

"Oh. Cool. She probably went there to try and get drunk after she realized what she did to her hair."

"Ugh, I love it! Don't you?"

"Really?" My laugh mists through the cold. "It looks like a failed attempt at yours."

"You think so?" Holly twists her a-line. "Thanks!"

As she plays with her snowy locks, her aqua eyes alight with virginal glow. She's beaming. She is adorable.

I don't want her to go. I want her to come in and tell me about the second season of *El Fin*. I want her to lie down on my red sheets and hand over her golden bullet while Frank paints naked beneath a golf umbrella. I want her to assure me that The Twin's parents are as much in the dark about The Premieres as they are about the advent of man. I want her to tell me that Sparky is dead or forgetful. I want her to insist that I run lines with her. I want her to eat her banana bread.

"Hey, you still haven't met my cat. Do you wanna come in for a minute?" I smile, as big as my yellow umbrella.

"Oh...I'd better get home. I'm gonna make some of Mom's wine disappear before she gets back from the derm." Rain blows through door onto her red Naked & Famous denim. She doesn't care. "I can get away with it if the bottle's already open."

With admiration for her genius plan to subvert her mother's drinking, I thank Holly for the ride, watch her roll down the hill, and then I slosh up our front steps.

"Well, Eddie ... "

Tapping on my window, I wave. With a start, Frank drops his joint.

"It may not be tonight, but you'll meet her soon. And you're gonna love her."

Following me to my bed and padding onto my chest, my furry confidant reminds me that I still need to make the birthday invitations.

"I know, I know." I scratch behind her ear. "Let's take a quick nap first. Eddie, my pet, I am exhausted."

Chapter 59

Along with my lunch and freshly drained thermos, I stuff my umbrella into my locker. This cloudy Tuesday morning snuck up and attacked me during my nap. I've yet to make the 'Birthday Blow-off' invites. But my procrastination is paying off. As Bickle escorts me to first period, Holly detaches herself from a female Filmgreat trifecta and trots up.

"I hear it's your birthday soon!" Wearing a faded Cats shirt under her hoodie, she squeezes my arm.

Stella, whispering to Mia, watches us from the quad. I still haven't discussed the specific terms of our BF/GF agreement with the moody Great, nor have I gotten Blake's real info from her. I need to do both. But in reverse order.

"Yep! Friday." With a glance, I relieve Bickle from his guard. "I'll be eighteen!"

"You know what *else* happens on Friday?" She flicks my tie.

"I reach my sexual peak?"

Stella glances over. Bickle is holding hands with Mia.

"Maybe." Half smiling, Holly gives her lively anime hair a quick, rigid, heart-melting toss. "But I was talking about wine tasting in Marin."

I'm sure I look perplexed.

"Mike, my mom will be gone all night. You should come over."

"Yes I should!" I mentally edit Friday out of the unmade invitations for the three-in-row. "What time?"

"Seven. She should be long gone by then. Can you get a ride?"

"Totally, I'll be there." As I text the date into my calendar, Bobby, with some old time crooner blaring through his Dre Beats, pats my back on his way to the gym.

"Yeah? You sure?" Twisting her shark pin, Holly considerately asks, "You're not going to have a birthday Premiere? Won't your fans be disappointed?"

The sinister yellow eyes on her shirt peer out at me.

"Oh well, yeah." *I flit a moth away from her hair.* "I was thinking about throwing one but, you know, I'd really rather just stay in with you. That sounds way more fun."

"It does, doesn't it?" Kissing my cheek, she leaves me and glides toward the History building.

Rather than admiring the curvature of her new pink jeans, I watch more black informants fly from my mouth into the grey morning sky. They settle over Stella, wreathing her blonde hair, and she blows me a kiss.

On this side of campus, there's no cell reception indoors. As I stand in front of the gym, the rain mists under the overhang. It blurs my touch screen and compromises my blow dry. After accepting twenty-seven new friends, I am about to make the dash to the Science building when I hear heel clicks. They sound pink. Exposed, I await unchecked verbal punishment, but when Stella *tiks* around the corner, she gives me shelter. Squeezing me beneath her Hello Kitty umbrella, she takes my arm and strolls me to Biology.

Notably sober and magnanimously refraining from bringing up my D-hole Date, Stella seems to be back in a good mood. And she's looking fabulous. Her cleavage is spilling out of her pea coat. Her upsetting hair is starting to become her and though she won't shut up about being the next extreme teen reality queen, her sex hum is turned up high enough to sweeten her incessant bragging. Sharing the thick, moist air of our vinyl dome, I'm finding myself as attracted to her as I was before we started touching.

"So, Babe..." After reconfirming Blake's email and her promise to put in a good word for me, she purses her phone. "You gonna have a totally insane birthday Premiere or what?"

Her Betsy bag jangles as she shakes out her umbrella in the breezeway outside the lab room.

"Obviously! But it's gonna be on Saturday ... " I mouth 'hey' at Grey and Crimson as they pass. Their umbrellas match their sweaters. "I still need to make the invitations..."

"Perfect." Nuzzling me, Stella purrs in my ear. "That means you're coming over on Friday. I've got a surprise for you, and you won't have to get all cute and nervous because Mom's gonna be mushrooming all weekend."

On 452 Reisling, Katy Perry frosts herself in The Pink Room.

Inhaling October rain and watermelon with my back against a stucco wall, I struggle to find a way to make this double-booking work. *There's no way I'm canceling on Holly.*

"Rockin!'" I agree.

Stella presses me against the Science building and licks me. I can feel her cool satisfaction glistening on my cheek as she hums, "Tell your folks that you're gaming at Lynch's. You're not gonna want to leave."

"I can totally do that ... but I'll have to come pretty late. If I don't celebrate with them that night they'll be really bummed," I appeal.

Stella's mood palpably drops.

"You know, it's a whole big thing." Attempting to reason away the unexpected tension, I further detail, "Mom makes homemade pasta, Dad makes fresh pesto with his basil ... we watch the Godfather Trilogy. ... Pinky's gonna be there—"

"Oh yeah. I know..." With a touch of resentment, she snaps her gum. "Pinky."

The red headed grave cutter mutters 'pink sucks' before ducking through the door next to us.

"That's actually perfect, Babe." Shaking off her fleeting sour, Stella reactivates her sugary hum and adjusts my bangs. "Later is better. It may take me a while to get your present ready anyway."

....

Standing in front of a very underwhelming chalkboard illustration of the Prefrontal Cortex, my teacher is droning on about Post-traumatic Stress Disorder. Ignoring him, practicing my autograph on a Safeway-bag-book-cover, I'm feeling like things are getting back to normal. This weekend is going to be the best. *I'll see Holly. Then Stella. Then, on Saturday, along with a huge cast of Extras, I'll have a late birthday celebration with them both. I wonder if I should invite Blake.*

"*Aren't you going to invite us, love?*" *Each holding a puffy kitten, three Sweater Girls wearing angora union jack bra-and-panty sets to accompany their new British accents have walked in the back door.*

"*Oh, yeah, thanks for reminding me*" *I whisper back.* "*You ladies are definitely invited. I still haven't made the invi—*"

"*You know,*" *The crimson Himalayan advises,* "*You should really have your bee bring some of his wrestling teammates in case any vengeful Sparks boys show up … or at least this time make sure that none of the Extras are violent homophobes.*"

"*Or teachers,*" *the canary yellow cat demands before Cream's creamy feline finalizes,* "*Or fertile Christians. The Christians are so frightening.*"

"*That's a good idea.*" *As a torch bearing, mohawked mob in bloody tall-tees crusades across The Palace stage to detain my guests and try them for heresy, I shove my hand in my pocket.* "*I'll do that.*"

Stepping in time with the muffled meter of my clicking Zippo, the cats walk their sweaters out of the classroom.

Chapter 60

The video is back, buzzing around like the ruinous demonic twin of Holly's angelic golden toy. It's troubling Wednesday resurgence is due to 'the fifth hand,' which someone has recently discovered reaches into the frame and grabs Stella's ass. For, like, half a second.

"Is that another chick with you guys?" Bickle and I blow-dry in the locker room as Bobby stomps up and lecherously grins in the mirror. "It looks like a chick's hand to me."

It could have been anyone. This is not a good time for this kind of attention.

Over the screaming hot air, I insist, "I don't know what you're talking about."

"In your sex video bro." The shirtless man-boy jostles me. "The one with your girlfriend? What? Did you make, like, a million different ones or something?"

"He doesn't know what you're talking about Bobby." My protector unplugs our appliances. "Leave him alone."

Throughout the rest of the day, as I'm met with equally upsetting inquiries from random classmates, Bickle repeats the same command. "He doesn't know what you're talking about. Leave him alone," "He doesn't know what you're talking about. Leave him alone," "He doesn't know what you're talking about—"

By the time Alvin intercepts me on my way into the cafeteria, I'm somewhat, rather, totally, freaked out.

"Fuck, c'mere, c'mere." He pushes me out of the slippery,

rubber-boot-dotted dining hall.

Desperately, I struggle to re-open my umbrella as Al drags me back into the rain and shoves me into a band room alcove.

"Fucker. Six people have already asked me—today—if I was the one who shot the video of you and Stella. Six fucking people!"

"What did you tell them?"

"I told'm 'fuck yeah it was me'!"

The rain turns to hail. I wander back through the unforgiving ice. Alvin is laughing. "Wait, Mike, Dude, Fuck, I didn't..." I tread away from his trailing words. The ground shifts, capsizing the entire campus. I stable myself with my broken Bob umbrella. It's icy, it's wet, the pavement is swaying, and I need shelter. I need to go inside. And I need to shut it all down. *But it's my birthday. My eighteenth birthday.*

Dripping on the cafeteria tile, I excuse Stella from her lunchtime celebrity gossip to speak with her privately.

"Babe, are you okay?" She asks, as I corner her at an emergency exit. "You look terrible."

"No, I look fine." I reach into my coat for my aviators. "Everything's fine. There are a lot of people talking about that thing again. I think it might be a good idea if you took down your blog. I think it would be safer for us all if it didn't exist—at all. And if anyone ever asks, say that it never did. And that you're celibate."

"Oh Babe, don't worry." Surging my body's voltage, she combs back my sopping hair with her electric fingers. "I took it down days ago."

"Really? That's great. That's perfect."

"Yeah. I figured that once I have the show, I'm gonna need to own my own website, so I started one: bubblegumandbordeaux. com. I just put all of my stuff up there now. It's *so* amazing. Really high-end and sexy. You should check it out. There's a totally hot pic of me and Holly on the front page."

....

Back in the gym—in the locker room, alone—I blow-dry my entire body. I manage to stay dry through the final bell. But no matter how tight I cinch my plain black hoodie, I can't shake the cold that surged into me during the lunchquake.

When I show up in Hess, weak and shivering, Rick senses my vulnerability and pounces.

"Michael Massi!" Before I can seat my Sherman, he starts firing lines at me from the stage. Holding a script, he cues, "Well he's not that nervous."

"Can I have—?"

"NO! Well he's not that nervous!" His rose-tinted glare stares me down. *MK and I sift through the Florida sand abrading my brain, failing to find even the first word.* "Do you still not know your line, Mike?"

"No, Nalon." Incensed for being ridiculed in front of the whole cast, in front of Holly, I insist, "I don't."

"Do you know any of your damned lines?" Removing his glasses, he rubs his face.

Insolently, I stand in the aisle, trembling amidst the chilly stares of my classmates—many of whom are now Extras, *my guests.*

"The next line is your second line in the play." Shaking his head with a sudden calm, Rick laments, "You don't even know your second line Mike. You're out. Jason is taking your place."

As if I've already been forgotten, he turns his back on me. "All right people. Places for the top of the second act."

He's dropping me. I can't believe it. He's replacing me with that poorly dressed dilettante, Jason Milmo. My less talented, longhaired understudy takes my rightful mark. *Upstaging Milmo, Frank Sinatra marches across the set, carrying a torch and the baby Jesus. The Christ child is wearing a Walmart onesy.*

I feel strange. This is way worse than when Philip fired me.

"Jason?" I point at the lanky hack in the RUN DMC tank top. "He's a sophomore. What about his hair? You can't be serious."

"He knows his part Mike." Rick doesn't even turn around to face me. "Now get out. You're wasting our time. You've held us all back long enough."

It's a pointless high school musical, with no potential. Fleeing the grey campus, I jog through puddles and past the few remaining cars in the lot. *I have so much more going for me.* It starts to drizzle. *It's nothing.* I fall apart.

I can't remember the last time I cried, and no matter how much I try to reason with them, the tears keep coming. If someone saw me right now they'd think my cat had just died. *I must look terrible.* I've got to get off the street.

In a cascade of silent weeping, I wander unseen through the woods of the park, down the empty suburban roads, and into The Grounds. In the girls' room, rinsing the mud from my boots, I try to pull myself together. I wash my face, shine my teeth, dry my hair with the hand blower, tug my hood further down, and then drift to the counter to order black coffee. Gleaming in the pastry case, there's an ornate silver tray of bread. Stuck in the top slice, there's a little sign. On it is a hand-drawn hungry-shark about to eat a happy banana that's perched atop a frowning vegan loaf.

I feel worse. I wish Holly were with me. *Sort of.*

Strewn over my table, I text Lynch. "Can you come get me?"

Three minutes later, the Caddy lurches to the curb out front. I put down Stella's copy of US Weekly, leave my drink, buy all of the banana bread, and go to my partner.

"Hey man, I was just on my way to get gas. What's up?"

"Nalon said he didn't need me." I shut the door. I watch the windshield wipers, listening to their rhythmic cleansing. "Ever. He kicked me out."

"Whoa. Lame."

Turning down the music, he eyes me, and the bursting compostable on my lap.

"Are you okay? You don't look good."

"I look fine. Everything's fine. I'm just really tired. Rick has no vision."

"Fuck him and fuck the play..." He flips off the 8-Plex as we drive by. "Fuck you too, Phil. ... Mike ... your birthday weekend is gonna rule." Helping himself to the bread I've just unwrapped, he chaws.

"But, am I not invited or something?"

"I'm gonna make the invitations tonight." I duly promise us both then hesitantly explain the necessity of Friday's cancellation.

"Man, that's awesome." Parked beneath a 76 carport, Lynch opens his door, and I roll down the window.

The smell of high-octane rain soothes me.

"You're gonna DV Holly, and Stella is for sure gonna have some filthy twisted birthday sex carnival set up for you. Then on Saturday, it's you and me against the sweaters. Tag-team! Two against six!" In awe, as if it were a winning lottery ticket, he holds his treat up to the dome light then bites it in half. Smacking, stepping toward the pumps, he settles. "I was actually starting to worry about you man, but you've obviously got your priorities back in line."

"Please..." Bolstered by my best friend's admiration, I snatch my bread back from his hand. Crumbs fly everywhere. I take a bite and smile. "I've never once lost sight of what's important."

Chapter 61

With a quart of chocolate Silk and a decimated bag of baked goods on my desk, I'm adding the subtext 'Get eaten at the *JAWS* Premieres' to the glowing heading 'Score's Birthday Blow-off' when Holly calls. Rehearsal must have just ended. Mortified, I pick up the phone.

"Are you okay Mike?"

"Oh yeah. I'm fine." *Everything's fine.*

"Listen, I spoke with Mr. Nalon. He agreed to let you audition again."

"What? What do you mean?"

"He says that he'll audition you on Monday and if you have your part down, he'll take you back."

This depresses me.

"Are you kidding? I'm not auditioning. It's my part. And anyway, that's way too soon. There's no way. I've got my birthday and—"

"There's time," she, insists. "I ... well ... Mom's thing got cancelled. I've gotta flake on our plans. I'm sorry ... but I'll make it up to you. I promise."

This depresses me even more. Since I fled Hess, Holly is all I've been thinking about. I was hoping she was calling to convince me to hang with her all weekend—to not send this invitation. I want her to sing The Smiths to me. I want her to watch me eat donuts. I want to try her loose-leaf tea and her Mexican cocoa. I want to do another shoot with her. I want to be her first.

"Oh, okay." Completely defeated, I stare at the shark on my Mac and knowing that she will demand that I cancel everything to run lines with her, bargain, "Well, then I guess that maybe I will throw a party. Promise to come?"

"Okay. But you have to promise me that you'll kill the audition. I kissed Jason, Mike. He tastes like milk."

I swoon.

After picking myself up from the keyboard, I finish the invitation. Clearly stating that no cameras, Christians, or uninvited Extras will be allowed at *Jaws 1* or *2*, I send it off to my 102 closest friends in the greater NorCal area. And Blake.

Eddie nudges my leg. I pick her up. I scratch under her chin. She purrs. Starting with the fated Sparky Premiere, I begin to tell her everything. We haven't spoken in a while.

As I'm about to admit, Stella doesn't really do blonde very well, Eddie meeps. She jumps off my lap, runs out of the room, and I start crying.

Chapter 62

The fourth period bell rings over this strange Thursday. The rain is gone. The shocking heat hasn't been like this since August and once again, I feel like a ghost floating through the halls, waiting for someone to catch a chill and call for an exorcism. I spent all night cleaning. I haven't slept. My hair is a mess. And I need respite.

Pocketing a hall pass from Pope, I drift into Hess's air-conditioned shadows and crawl into my bed where Jason Milmo shall soon lay in sin with Holly. Wrapped in my black McQueen skull scarf, I fall into deep, dark unconsciousness. My bed begins swaying. And I awake to a man gently shaking me. I don't know why my father is whispering my Screename.

"What?" I grumble. "Don't call me that. Give me twenty-nine more minutes." Prying open my eyes, I push away chiffon and peer through the dark haze toward the voice. "Mr. Snow?"

"They're not sure it's you Mike." Whispering, beside my bed, Ryan tips me off. "Don't tell them anything." Then, like some spy in a noir, he vanishes.

Addled and depressed, I pull my birthday scarf back over my head and go to sleep.

Chapter 63

Until recently, I'd been an exemplary student. I had a 4.0 average GPA, a great attendance record, and a good relationship with Mr. McCarry. So I am able to keep some composure when I find myself sitting in front of his brown oak desk after school. Back before there was Madden for XBOX, Jerry, too, was a student at Valley View. He was the star wrestler and the leading quarterback. Now he's the football coach and the principal.

"Massi." Pacing behind me, he insists for the third time, "We know that it's you."

"It's not me." I stare at one of hundreds of framed photos of Kibble, his boxer terrier. "Why don't you just show it to me? Maybe I could tell you who it is."

"Massi, I can't do that. It would be inappropriate. And I know that you've seen it already, you're in the damn thing, you lived it."

"I really haven't." Fantasizing about smacking Alvin around like he's a blue-haired masochist, I speak to the empty leather desk chair. "And, like I said before, I don't think it even exists."

"You know champ." Behind me, he's chewing peanuts. He keeps a big bowl of them by the door. "This kinda thing is illegal. This kinda thing can really come back to haunt you."

Sinatra croons, "I hope you know that this will go down on your permanent record," pins a Walmart badge to my pea coat, then steps back out of the window.

"Okay, this is all that I've heard." In the reflection of his sporty plaques, I watch my tormentor dust husks from his Polo-shirted beer gut. "There's an Asian chick in it who is like, twenty one. Supposedly she lives in LA. If I'm really the guy, shouldn't you be talking to her? I'm still a minor. That would make me a victim of terrible abuse."

Had this all had happened back when he was still teen-jock supreme, Jerry would have been begging to come to my party. I'm sure he's curious about the clip, but I swear to Moz this interrogation is mainly out of obligation. However, if the truth got out, he'd come down on me. Hard. He'd have to. *I've got to get out of this.*

"Nice play Massi, but you're not gonna score any points with that one." I jump at the sound of my Screename, as he squeezes my shoulders. "Champ, your teachers have been telling me that you're fumbling this quarter but I must admit, this kind of foul ... this video smut, it just doesn't seem like you—"

"It's not me Mr. McCarry," I insist, holding my breath.

"But your name keeps coming up. Why? Do you know who filmed it? Where was it hosted? Who's the Chinese girl?" He sighs and beseeches, "Give me something Massi."

"I'm sorry." I crane back my neck to make sincere, upside-down eye contact. "I really don't know anything else."

"You're a good kid."

His inverted image relents. The nut bowl rattles.

"You're off the hook. But I don't want to see you back in this office unless it's to tell me that you wanna try out for the team. And I don't know what's going on with you but let's get those grades and attendance back up, Champ."

"Yeah, no problem. I've just been really tired." I grab my Sherman and dash to the door. "Shane has been helping me work out after school, and it's been brutal."

"Well, that's good, that's good." He laughs. "But you gotta make time for the books too, kiddo. Shane will be the first to tell you that. He's looking like an early favorite for valedictorian."

....

The sun is still out. But it feels like winter. Freezing, tightening my scarf, I power down the campus stairs and dial Stella to tell her what happened, to tell her that I didn't rat her out, to see if she'd been called into Jerry's office too—"*I'm a free bitch, baby.*"

I pace in front of the cemetery. Inhaling the spicy smoke of the unseen Grave-cutters' cigarettes, I redial. "*I'm a free bitch ... I'm a free ... I'm a...*"

"Hayyyy *Miguelito*!" Cruz stops the rumbling El Camino at the curb. "You need a ride?"

I drag open the flecked door. It feels like it weighs 1000 lbs. Mumbling something about my house, I crumble into the passenger seat. He's staring.

"Are you okay?"

"Yeah. Everything's fine," I say.

"Okay, *Guapo* ... it just looks like you're crying."

Chapter 64

Tomorrow marks my eighteenth year. I'm not going to clean. I'm going to sleep tonight. Having just covered up my fragile temperament with a chipper birthday-eve face for my folks, I scrub a marinara encrusted casserole dish. Rinsing, I ruminate.

Everything was fabulous. Now it's all out of control—melting, flipping, freezing-over. I squirt a stream of lavender soap on a wooden spoon and sponge it with vengeance. I want to shut it all down. But things can't to go back to the way they were before The Premieres. That would be worse than dealing with any of this. I throw my scarf over my shoulder, away from the suds. And Moz only knows what I would do then. I wouldn't even have the musical to go back to. Though, if I ended it all right now, I could spend all weekend learning my lines and get back in with Nalon. Suds splash on my arm. I roll my sleeves up further. Blake might not make a reality show about me right away. Stella and the rest of The Greats and Extras might never speak to me again. But Holly would be proud of me. As I begin to dry, Eddie hops up onto the counter. I ask her opinion and she agrees. The stunning sober virgin would love it if I stepped down from my attractive position as host. If there were no Premieres, there would be more time for her and I to spend alone. I could finally DV her. She would love that. Pausing my dishrag, I peer out of the kitchen window into the dry night. I should ask her what she thinks about me shutting down The Palace. I should ask her to be my girlfriend. An evening of hiding out in Hogan's with her sounds perfect—it sounds so quiet against the screaming. I push my earbuds deeper in. I turn up the Smiths and Moz drowns out the distorted nightmarish version of "It Has to Be Me."

....

"Happy birthday to you..." At midnight, when I reach over my pillows and pick up my phone, Joseph sings to me. *"Happy birthday dear. What is it now? Snatch?"*

"Score."

"Oh, yeah. Fabulous. *Dear Score, happy birthday to you!"*

I immediately start feeling better.

"Joey, I love the Scarf man, thanks, I haven't taken it off since yesterday." I proudly boast before unloading.

Quietly, I review all that has been amiss, and my brother's uplifting, encouraging words of wisdom put me in a good mood that will carry me through the rest of the day.

This day. My birthday. It has arrived.

"Kiss kiss. Love love."

"Kiss kiss. Love love."

Chapter 65

In the Caddy, singing along with Joey Ramone, we park between two empty spots. Responding to an R-rated birthday text from an Extra, I step out of the cretin hop to dignify the quickly filling Valley View lot. This is my runway, and I am pre-maternal Kate Moss. My smile is a Go, my dotted suit is Tops, my shades are Fords, my scarf is unquestionably McQueen, and my new Chucks complement everything. I look great. I'm wide-awake and resolved in my plans for The Premiere.

Birthday, here I come.

Beneath the bright morning, as we lean against the Deville I play the brothers my 2:17 am suggestive video message from Mia. Thirty-two seconds of escalating squeaks build to a very cute, "Happy birthday Score!" We all giggle, hit replay, and then Bickle pulls up.

Throwing open the door of his red Mini Cooper, my muscle runs over to hand me a black and yellow striped Zippo. "Happy birthday Buddy!" Darting back, he pulls four cases of Sterno green and four cases of lighter fluid out from the car.

"Wow. I love it, Thank you." I admire the 'Score' engraving on the lighter as my generous protector loads the inflammable boxes into Lynch's trunk.

"Hey! Hey Brooke Hogan!" Squeezing next to him, Alvin hero-ically rescues a Hustler store bag. "Don't fuckin' crush those!" He tosses me a liquid-filled, yellow plastic ball. "Try it!"

"I know you asked for that jacket you saw on Kate Moss's

296 | Davey Havok

boyfriend." Lynch grins. "But I didn't wanna ruin your chances with Holly. I don't think it's vegan to fuck someone who wears a leather."

"Woah!" Pumping a drop onto my finger, I taste the sweet slime.

"Yeah, random right?" As Al snatches the sex lube, tosses back his hair, and squirts a gooey stream into his gaping mouth, Lynch explains, "I couldn't find banana bread but figured banana cream pie flavored would be close enough."

....

Throughout PE, the birthday messages continue to buzz in, and by the end of Biology I've heard from almost everyone except Stella. Standing in the small strip of shade, leaning against the cafeteria, I text her, worried. She wasn't in class.

"*We still on for tonight Babe? I've got a big Xbox party that I won't be attending.*"

"*I'm playing hookie and getting ready for you Babe ;) <3 XXXOOOXXX*"

I send back a smiley emoticon as Holly appears with The Boys. Volta is carrying a delicacy that he had overnighted from New York. Singing, "*Feliz cumplianos a ti,*" Cruz lights the candle, then slips me an envelope containing three burned Slayer CDs and two personalized gift certificates—each good for one OJ lesson. On the detailed, professional business cards, a childlike, hand-drawn portrait of Cruz smiles, gripping an anonymous Producer. I fan my gold-leafed gifts, offering for Holly to join me for a course in oral craft. She declines.

"It's not that I'd think you'd need them. I'd offer you cannoli." I motion to the Magnolia bakery box. "But I'm pretty sure it's not vegan."

"It's okay Mike, you're right." Her pure indigo eyes shame the candle into melting. "I don't need them." She smooches my mouth. "You'll get your present from me later."

"C'mon Blow *Culito*," Volta insists, "Blow!"

I inhale, as the rest join in. "*Blow, blow, blow ...*"

Through lunch the tangible excitement for my birthday follows, bringing with it the rebirth of my anticipation for The Blow-off—my final Premiere. Last night, after confessing my feelings for Holly, my brother avidly alluded that I put The Palace behind me. I'm taking his advice. Tonight I'm going to tell Stella that we can no longer be anything but excessively attractive friends and tomorrow I'll exclusively do scenes with Holly. On green plastic, my Producer shall know the ingénue. *I've only ever wanted you Score. You're so fabulous. Of course I'll be your girlfriend.* Simultaneously we will explode with joy, then as Moz sings his last song, I will tear myself from Holly, take my speech position, and announce the closing of The Palace. I've yet to fill Lynch in on any of this but together, we are working to ensure that the final Premiere will be the pinnacle of magnificence.

My co-host and I stroll through the no man's land at the center of the quad to recruit the three key necks, who we've been admiring since we first heard the rumors—during class, beneath the veil, and through the scissor-holed pouches of oversized hoodies, these winery sisters give exceptional JOs.

"It's a very classy and *completely* exclusive. It's a good time." I lurk over their spot on the rich-kid corner of the steps. "There's going to be a legitimate Hollywood casting agent there too..."

Each of them has a Coke Zero in her hand and a small blue heart drawn on her index finger.

The skinniest one sighs. "Will there be coke?"

I assure the innovative young ladies of the availability of a variety of refreshments. They agree to attend and on the way back to my locker, I text Prius to make sure that he'll be bringing his usual amenities: hot new Extras, and more GO SMiLE.

All day I've been coming up with special ways to make the last Premiere unforgettable. I've been taking notes: Cherie Cherie cupcakes; party-poppers; a retrospective slide-show montage of Alvin's photos. Leaning against the Caddy, waiting for my driver, I add *piñata* to the list before responding to Prius. He's linked me to the profile of a twenty-year-old yoga teacher from Marin. *Yes, she can come.* Typing, I'm wondering if I'll hear back from Blake when I see Lynch and Mia at the top of the stairs. They step aside. Al board-slides the infamous Valley View handrail. His hair blusters like an eighties metal video. He clacks down onto the sidewalk, ollies a flowerbed, and nose-manuals through the lot.

"Hey Grampa, can I borrow some of your banana cream pie?" Popping up his deck, he pulls out his camera. "I miss Star really fucking bad. Fuck Florida."

"Al, I've got a favor to ask you. Do you think that you could shoot this weekend without letting the pics leak?" Sucking in my cheeks, I strike a smashing pose. "I think it's gonna be legendary."

"Fuck yeah!" He gets low to snap another shot. "I've been filming most of them anyway."

"Oh ... okay, great." I turn to profile. "Also, could I borrow your Flip?"

"Sure." He pulls the mini-cam from his jeans and tosses it to me. "You gonna film yourself jerking off and send it to Dracula?"

"I'm going to Stella's later, She's got some big thing planned."

Al shoves his digital still into my face.

Taking off my shades, I review the photos—I'm a hidden TMZ treasure, waiting to be discovered in a high school parking lot.

Chapter 66

Through the dining room window, the night's potential sparkles up from the valley, as I share my birthday dinner with the Massis. Devouring Gina's beautiful homemade gnocchi and soy balls, Frank and I expand then unbuckle our belts to welcome the main event. "Ooooh!"

Pinky pounces upon the table, aflame and delicious. Sacrificing himself once again in my name, this year my kitty confection has come offering up his cakey goodness along with *Guitar Hero: Warriors of Rock*. I dislike video games. I really do. But it's fine. I know that the best gifts are still to come so, when my cake tells me that he knows how much I enjoy this particular gaming franchise, I feign delight. "Thanks Pinky! Lynch will be stoked! We're seriously gonna be up all night."

After the ceremonial feast, sucking my frosted fingertips, tasting traces of artificial banana flavoring, I grab my game, wrap up a frosted ear, shove my plunder into my Sherman, and conquer the dishes. Once the plates are shelved and the elders are in bed, I dim the dining room. I relight the candle stubs and sit back down at the table.

Katy Perry, Russell Brand, Kate Moss, Leonardo DiCaprio, Morrissey, Steve Aoki, Deadmau5, Perez Hilton, Paris Hilton, Jenna Jameson, Sasha Grey, and I share a single slice of cake. I pass it around. Silently, we dab the corners of our mouths with chiffon napkins. The Caddy rolls into the driveway. They each ask "Is it I?" and I leave them chewing on a black licorice whiskers.

....

Lynch tears into the pink-smeared cellophane. Stuffing his mouth, crumbing pink cake onto his jeans, he careens downhill as I type. I send out my text thirteen minutes before our headlights shine across the four-way stop by the post office. This is her cross street. Planning to have my driver change course, I've asked Holly if I should come over—if with her mom there she'd help me run lines. My phone remains still. We drive on. And park in front of Stella's.

"Hey man!" Shouting over an inquisitive lyric about having 'fallen in love with someone' I attempt to resign myself to another evening without like-minded virgins. "Do you have any condoms?"

"Yeah, totally, they're in the trunk with my bibles and Jonas Brother's CDs," Laughing, Lynch turns down the music. "Wait..." Facing me, he looks terribly crestfallen. "Are you serious?"

"*Phhh* no..." I sneer.

He leers. So I admit, "It's just that the MK thing still has me a little rattled ... and if I'm going to be Holly's first tomorrow I don't wanna—"

"Come *on* Mike! Settle. Please settle. It's your birthday. Stella has some major shit planned for you." He points toward the shadowy porch. "So go in there and have a fucking good fucking time!"

Chapter 67

It's 11:03 pm and it's dark. Holly hasn't written back. Standing in the porch light with my phone dangling from the tips of my fingers, I begin a staring contest with Stella's front door. *She's waiting.*

Last night, Joey insisted that I have a good time. "Fall in love with your birthday weekend and then see how you feel on Monday before locking anyone or anything down. Okay? You're eighteen, Baby Brother! Kiss kiss..." His dramatic advice seemed great. But now I'm filled with doubt.

I can't go through with this. I feel like Holly is already my GF. We're connected. *Click, click.* I'm connected to an amazing girl. *Click, click.* She's vegan. She loves the Smiths. She doesn't do drugs. *Click, click.* She looks like a runway model and carries herself like a lady who carries a vibrator around twenty-four/seven. *Click, click.* She's even writing a hit TV series that offers a wide array of male leads. I should cancel the final parties. Both of them. Maybe. *Click, click. Click, click. Click, click. Click, click.*

Releasing my Zippo, I pull up Holly's underwear pics and stare. I scroll through my phone book. I reach the *H*s. I'm going to call her.

A swift palm smacks my face. My phone hits the porch. And, with my hands pinned behind my back, I watch the door.

"*Daddy, don't you fucking stop.*" *Two pixie-haired voices sternly whisper over my shoulders.* "*You can't stop. It's too good.*"

"*And what about Blake? He'll love it as much as we do.*"

"*You, me, and Miss Faux Platinum Purity would be lost without it.*" *Something cold, metallic, and buzzy, brushes my cheek.* "*You know it's true Score."*

I re-open my photo album. I scroll through some Extras' birthday nudes. I scroll to Stella's fruit pop pics. If I almost exclusively limit my performance to scenes with Holly, we'd enjoy intimacy amidst the brilliance of The Premieres. I would maintain the status of the world's youngest renowned promoter and The Filmgreats would live on. I like this plan. *A lot.* I scroll to the photo that Hogan took of Holly and I at the D-hole.

I don't know what to do.

"FAGGOT!" A whiskey bottle whizzes past my face and shatters against the door's frame. Next to my Chucks, the shards of orange glass melt into the wooden planks.

I scroll through my phone book. I hit dial. "Hey, I'm outside."

Chapter 68

The front door was open. She said to let myself in.

Hesitantly, I pace between the rows of rose scented candles, holding my breath, swallowing my moths to protect them from the low laying flames. When I reach her bedroom, I stop and inhale The Palace.

The Pink Door is closed. But as I stand here, frozen in a scatter of pink rose petals, listening to the familiar sounds—the giggling, the groaning, the Amerigirlpop—I know what's inside. Stella's going to make my closing speech much harder. But it must be made—even if it means having to forsake an offstage, aboveground private threesome.

I can do this. I'm going to go in there and tell her that we'll forever be the greatest of Filmgreats, but that I have deep, meaningful feelings for Holly, which must be observed, explored, and reciprocated.

Pressing the red button on the Flip, extending the camera in front of me like a VIP laminate, I twist the pink ceramic knob and step onto the set of a pink-and-white adult film. In front of me, on The Pink Bed, surrounded by soy candles, balloons, streamers, and McQueen skulls cut from pink construction paper, two Greats writhe, lost in their intimate scene.

Crouching atop her comforter like Eddie at a saucer of milk, Stella licks fastidiously as she slowly works three fingers in and out of Holly. Above them a six-foot glittery banner reads 'HAPPY

BIRTHDAY SCORE.'

As my eyes begin to accept this invasion, my ears deny everything. Mindlessly, I aim my lens through the surreal silence.

Stella, wearing my Unknown Pleasures tee, slinks upward. She folds over Holly. The blondes kiss. Stella removes her slick fingers to feed them to her co-star and, suckling away her own orange cream glaze, Holly lazily replaces her soft touch with solid gold.

Standing rigid, like an overlooked Extra, I play the mannequin in the doorway. Completely ignored, encased within my soundproof phantom display, the silence suffocates me until I gasp over the noise of the golden vibe. The low hum rises to the buzz of a biblical plague. And Holly senses a ghost. Tilting her head with curiosity, she stops the bullet and waves at me. She smiles then squeezes her eyes shut at the return of her leading lady's tongue.

As if her lips were pressed against my ear, I hear Holly groan. Then everything starts to scream.

"Happy birthday Babe!" Lifting her glistening mouth, Stella turns to me with a smile. My insides contract, my lips part and my beautiful black moths swarm the room. I remain still. "Come join us!" Her voice is amplified—inhuman.

The volume of it all makes me wince. She's even louder than Sinatra is right now. If god weren't a lie, this would be her voice.

"Come on Babe." She demands, "Come—"

Holly forces Stella's mouth back between her thighs.

In this deafening coupling, the blue-eyed blondes begin to look identical. When one of them flops her hand against a spilt bottle of pills, I turn my camera to the cluttered pink end table. There, in front of a pink bong, amidst rose petals, baggies, Holly's lunchbox, Tarantino hairclips, bubblegum wrappers, and coffee cups, The Pink Laptop sits open. It's playing a sex tape.

On the moth-infested monitor, I watch a tight shot of brunette Stella. She's riding someone here in The Pink Room. *Riding. Riding. Riding.* She blows a kiss to the camera. She dismounts and exits the frame. The shot pulls back. Wearing only a teal lace bra, Holly enters the strobing scene. She crawls onto The Pink Bed. She takes Prius's huge single into her mouth. She comments favorably on Stella's flavor, then switches positions. With her back arched, Holly grabs the headboard. She offers her ass to the DJ. When Donny erection kneels behind her to rocket his hit to my number one, the clip ends. Then it repeats. And I catch 'the fifth hand' reaching into the looping full-screen, un-edited, full-length version of *my* video.

"Come ON Babe! I found out that I got the show!" Stella stops licking and turns back to me. "I'm gonna get you a part to go along with this hot fucking bitch." She rises to her knees. She's wearing panties, but her shirt—my shirt—is gone.

Oozing upward, Holly sucks a nipple then falls back into the pink cloud.

"For your birthday. It's a double celebration!" She puts on her model face, as Holly reaches for the kitty in Stella's crotch. "Put that shit down and come play, Babe. Come on."

I try, but can't plug my ears. I can't move. A distant, gravely Newport accent echoes, "Come on Babe," as I watch Stella's fingers fervently work through the moaning, drug addict liar/amateur-porn actress.

I don't know what to do. I feel like I'm back on the porch, staring at the door. Yet this is far more interesting. Far louder. Far brighter. And this door has a lower back tattoo that stands for 'love.'

Stella glances at me one last time, "Come on," then turns to watch her pistoning hand.

"*Come on.*"

Her insistence is soft yet piercing. Her sex hum is separating itself from the buzz of the toy. I can hear it distinctly, just as Holly must.

"*Come on!*"

"Fuck ... Sarah." Twisting, the blonde in my Smith's shirt helplessly gasps, "I'm gonna ... "

Unable to lower my camera, I stand. I film. I watch. In pink panties, diligently eclipsing her pink nails, Stella breathlessly repeats, "Oh yeah. Do it, Come on Babe, Come on..."

"Oh fuck, Sarah ... fuck!"

"Yeah Babe. Come on, fucking come—"

Holly finishes like a car crash.

Stella lustfully laughs, "That's fucking right, Beautiful!"

The former angel lets out a final, tremulous groan then opens her eyes. She waves at me from the wreckage. "Hi Score."

Her driveled salutation sucks out the sound. The Pink Room is silent again. No unreleased Smith's song. No Katy Perry. *No Sinatra.*

I drop the camera to my side. Accidentally, I record my Chucks as they retrace their steps through the flaming path. Then I stop. I turn. And wave.

I think. I think I just waved back to her, but I can't be sure. *It's fine. Everything's fine.*

Chapter 69

In the dark, wandering down the center of Reisling, I type: ***"ATTENTION: MK and Ash's parents have somehow started to suspect that something 'ungodly' has been happening at The Palace.*** *They've alerted the Police. The parties are off. Keep away from the hotel until further notice."*

I send the warning. A pick-up truck swerves around me. I feel the warm gush of its near miss. The driver has his window down. He looks like he's yelling.

I flip through my photo album. I delete corrupted images as I drift. I'm at the golf course at the top of hole one. I'm leaving the 8-plex. I'm weighted down—sweating. I'm on the ground, sobbing, propped against the Crystal Eyes dumpsters like an abandoned twin. Something soft and wet is tickling my hand. *Hello Manx.* My vocal chords vibrate. And the grey cat disappears.

I pull myself up. I pat the dust from my suit, the tiny bits of gravel pressed into my palms. I pocket square my stinging eyes. I sling my heavy bag over my shoulder. The air is warm. I take a deep breath.

Click, click.

Chapter 70

The weekend was exhausting. I'm wiped out.

Last night, I cleaned out my Wish List folder, called my brother, used Uncle Cosmo's birthday money to replace my burnt Obesity and Speed hoodie, perused Perez, abused PornoTube, then shared everything with Eddie over a cup of Sencha. When my alarm screamed, it sent me to school exhausted. But everything's fine. Lynch made me a hall pass.

I'm napping now. And when Holly interrupts, her voice is neither distant nor bombastic. "Mike, I'm so sorry." She sits down, shaking my Hess bed,

Yawning, I squint. Her brown eyes are bloodshot. *She looks tired.*

"Sarah told me that you wanted us both ... for your birthday. I didn't know if I could do it..." Her roots are a shade darker than the rest of her hair. She needs a touch-up. "I was nervous so I smoked to relax. ... She had some weird shit. I actually barely remember any of it ... but I know you're upset. I'm sorry." She sniffles. "I care about you a lot Mike." She wipes a tear and touches my hand. "I'm so sorry."

Slipping my arm around her waist, I run my fingers underneath the back of Joey's Smith's shirt and pull the actress into me. We kiss, lightly at first. Then with shared intensity, as I strip her to begin our first real scene.

With her grey jeans bunched around her ankles and my Producer inside her, Holly desperately thrusts, countering my slow rhythm. I consider unhooking her teal bra, but I don't bother. I don't care. *Holly is a lie and I am a liar.* I squash the deck chair. She digs her toes into my chest. *It's fine.* Her nails scratch my back. She's no Stella, but I've had worse scenes.

Folded up, bouncing on her back, Holly starts talking dirty. "Oh my god I love you Mike. I love you..." Her eyes are still wet. "Mike, I'm gonna—"

She finishes and I force myself to follow. As I spread my joy in the general direction of her lying lips, we're spot lit—a beam of natural light hits the bed. The stage door is open.

Covering herself, Holly pulls up the sheets. And I snatch my brother's shirt.

"What, you two didn't even think to invite me? And after I set up that amazing surprise that you bailed from like a vampire zombie weirdo, who can't return texts and ignores me in class." Stella strides to the end of the bed. Folding her arms across my Joy Division shirt, she mildly scolds, "What the fuck Score?"

Erection standing, I mop myself with the soft vintage tee then begin to dress. Holly uses her hoodie to wipe the embarrassment from her face. "Sarah, what are you doing here?"

"Babe!" Ignoring her, Stella incredulously re-addresses me. "It's over."

I belt, kneel, and pull up a Union Jack sock.

"What do you mean?" Holly's voice compresses. "What's over?"

"The Palace. It burnt down."

Moz. I pick one of Eddie's hairs from the hem of my jeans. *I really hope there weren't any cat's inside.*

"What?" Holly bursts, "How?"

Briefly, I look up into her wide dull eyes and puffy flushed face. She's still gaping at Stella. Stella's still fixed on me. I grab my Chucks and sit on the edge of the stage.

"They don't know. They think it had something to do with dried flowers and candles. The fucking candles! I can't believe it's over." Stella sounds pretty pissed. She's starting to get loud. "Score, it's over! Can you fucking believe it?"

Lacing, serene, I finish tying my shoes. I sling on my Sherman, slide on my Fords, and stride across the stage. As I pass Stella, I pause. Lightly, I kiss her luscious, livid lips then exit into the dull glare of the lunchtime campus.

Before the theatre door latches them away, I can hear both blondes yelling. They yell names. And things: "Mike!" "Score!" "What the fuck?" "Where are you going?" "Don't pull this weird shit again!" "Say something."

....

Through the bustle of a bleak fifth period, I stroll to my locker to grab my lunchbox. My fatigue was overwhelming, but now that I've power napped and spread some joy, I've worked up bit of an appetite.

On dry concrete, with a desire for solitary contemplation and some cold San P., I sit my Ksubis chewing over creamy peanut butter and the sticky current events.

The Palace is gone. The Premieres are forever over. But it was time to wrap. Things were getting weird. And when I consider all that I have achieved, I find little room for regret. Something finally happened—a big something that will never be forgotten. And I made it happen.

Now I must move on. I twist the cap, and take a nip of my Limonata. *It's fine.* As Joey said last night, "Promoting a great party is like dating a great fuck—it's better to end it before it gets boring." When that old hotel burnt to the ground, the chaos went up in the same flames that solidified the legendary status of The Palace and its Host. In this calm I will focus on my transcendence into the next plane of fame.

Sipping my San P., I watch Stella strut out of Hess. Without hesitation she heads directly for my wall. She knew right where I'd be. She didn't even have to look. *We have a true connection.* Her heels tap on the concrete as her storm approaches. *Tik tik tik.* I pull off a jam-stained chunk of brown bread, chew, swallow, sigh, and smile.

Friday's Pink Room surprise may have had touches of nefarious intent, but I completely respect her ambition. Even before Bickle confessed that she had disappeared for a week to recover from having surgically opted out of maternity, I knew that she had her priorities straight. *Tik tik tik.* To this day, my considerate heroine has never troubled me with the terrifying news of my brush with being a daddy and, after all that she suffered through has kept her head, her figure, her focus, and landed the lead in a hot new reality show. *Tik tik tik.* I don't know how she did it, but how she did it doesn't matter. She did it. *She's a true inspiration.* Her patent pink pumps kiss the rounded rubber tips of my Chucks. I look up. *She's like a muse.*

With her regal boobs stretching my shirt out past her unbuttoned pea coat and her hands on her highborn hips, Stella is about to ask me a million questions. "What the fuck—"

"Stella, wait, I'm sorry." Holding my sandwich, I rise to face her. "I should have said this the other night, but I've just had a lot going on lately and was, just … surprised." Motioning with my crust, I gush, "Congratulations on the show. I knew you'd get it Babe. You're truly amazing."

"Thanks Score." Smiling like an angel, she flips her luminary hair. "I'm so stoked. … But? The Palace—"

"It's fine. We'll discuss later. I want to hear about the show!"

"Okay, well, check this out. I was going to tell you before … on Friday…" She raises a single brow. "But, whatever. Blake wants me to move to Hollywood—"

"That's Fabulous! Babe, you're gonna be—"

"Wait, that's not it." Her purse buzzes. Without looking at it, she sends the call to voicemail and drops her phone back into her jangly bag. "He wants me to move there, like, now. They want to start filming as soon as possible and they've got a place for all us girls to live. … I think I'm gonna go this weekend. Donny's gonna help me move."

Holding down my moths, I struggle to say something supportive, but before I can find the words to set them free, Stella adjusts my bangs, and asks, "Wanna come?"

She wants me to escape with her. The potential of this romantic deliverance is infinite. We could be a power couple. Reaching into my pocket, I silence an interjecting call.

"Blake says that there will probably be a part for you in the second season. And we have, like, everything paid for." She offers me a piece of bubblegum. "Pretty rockin' huh? So are you ready to pack or what?"

I chew the pink sugar. And Stella reads my reaction like it's posted on Perez. Knowing that I am silently planning our mornings at the pools with Katy P, our days on the lots with Leo Di, our nights at the clubs with Ms. Moss, and our amiable relationships with the paparazzi, she doubtlessly declares, "Babe, they're gonna love you."

"Of course they are." I grin. "They're gonna love us."

Overwhelmed by a deluge of emotions, I take off my shades and kiss her. Deeply. It's rapturous. *This is sacred.* I can feel the grip of our mystical bond tightening as we mingle our geminating souls with artificially flavored saliva.

Campus security tears us apart. He leaves us with a warning, and a mess that resembles Holly emerges from Hess.

I take Stella's hands. I stare into the complexity of my GF's profound essence, bathing in her satisfied smile, enraptured by her sacrosanct sex hum. I'm tempted to tell her. *But I won't.* I'm tempted to say it out loud. *But I don't need to.* She already knows. *We both do.*

Soundtrack

Download at http://www.popkidsbook.com/soundtrack

Katy Perry — "I Kissed A Girl"
New York Dolls — "Personality Crisis"
Portishead — "Sour Times"
Massive Attack — "Angel"
Guns N Roses — "Welcome to the Jungle"
Primal Scream — "Deep Hit of Morning Sun"
Adele — "Rolling in the Deep"
Joy Division — "Day of the Lords"
New Order — "Blue Monday"
Depeche Mode — "Shake the Disease"
The Smiths — "Shoplifters of the World Unite"
The Beach Boys — "Woudn't it Be Nice?"
Immortal — "Wrath From Above"
Morrissey — "Alsatian Cousin"
The Ramones — "Pinhead"
The Damned — "Jet Boy Jet Girl"
T. Rex — "Get It On"
The Cult — "Love Removal Machine"
Morrissey — "The Last of the Famous International Playboys"
Simple Minds — "Don't You (Forget About Me)"
Lady Gaga — "Poker Face"
Britney Spears — "Hold it Against Me?"
The Pussycat Dolls — "When I Grow Up"
Echo and The Bunnymen — "Heaven Up Here"
Bat For Lashes — "Daniel"
Dead or Alive — "You Spin Me Right Round (Like a Record)"
Darkthrone — "Transilvanian Hunger"

Slayer — "Angel of Death"
The Jesus and Mary Chain — "You Trip Me Up"
Dusty Springfield — "Son of a Preacher Man"
Justice — "Genesis"
Katy Perry — "California Gurls"
Katy Perry — "Last Friday Night (T.G.I.F.)"
Deadmau5 — "Sofi Needs a Ladder"
The xx — "Crystalised"
Pulp — "This is Hardcore"
Magnetic Man — "I Need Air"
Burzum — "Lost Wisdom"
Morrissey — "Piccadilly Palare"
Ramones — "Now I Wanna Sniff Some Glue"
The Ark — "Clamour for Glamour"
La Roux — "Bulletproof"
Crystal Castles — "Birds"
Deadmau5 — "Ghosts N Stuff"
Dead Boys — "All This And More"
The Germs — "Richie Dagger's Crime"
Kylie Minouge — "Can't Get You Out of My Head"
Slayer — "Raining Blood"
Flo Rida — "Low"
Ke$ha — "Tik Tok"
Nicki Minaj — "Super Bass"
Lady Gaga — "Just Dance"
Britney Spears — "Toxic"
Katy Perry — "Teenage Dream"
Queen — "Bicycle Race"
Lords of the New Church — "Russian Roulette"
Suicide — "Ghost Rider"
The Cure — "Killing an Arab"
Frank Sinatra — "It Had to Be You"
Ke$ha — "Blow"
Morrissey — "Maladjusted"
The Stooges — "Search and Destroy"
The Smiths — "How Soon is Now?"
The Smiths — "Unhappy Birthday"
The Ramones — "The Cretin Hop"
The Buzzcocks — "Ever Fallen In Love (With Someone You Shouldn't've?"

About the Author

Davey Havok was born in 1975. He dropped out of UC Berkeley for Rock N' Roll. He is vegan straight edge and lives in Oakland, California with his modest art collection. He enjoys the beautiful things while achieving new levels of self-deprivation. This is his first novel.

When not writing, Davey can be found:

Singing in AFI and Blaqk Audio
  (http://www.afireinside.net and http://www.blaqkaudio.com)
Designing for Eat Your Own Tail
  (http://www.eatyourowntail.com)
Hanging out at Timeless
  (http://www.timelesscoffeeroasters.com)
Acting on stages and screens everywhere
  (not as frequently as he would like)

Photo by LOUIE AGUILA

CPSIA information can be obtained at www.ICGtesting.com
Printed in the USA
BVOW08s2333201213

339781BV00002B/45/P